SAINT

LILAH LANCE

To anyone who ever lost their way
and just needed a chance to find the light again

CONTENT WARNING

This book contains:

- A morally gray Alpha—male
- Mature themes
- Explicit content
- Graphic Language
- Mentions of human trafficking/kidnapping
- Violence

AUTHOR'S NOTE

Liam's book is the third installment of the Underworld Kings.

Informally, I've always considered Lara an extended member of the O'Hara family—even though she is not a direct relative.

If you are walking into this story as a standalone and have never read any of the previous Titan books or Underworld Kings books—**there are spoilers in this book for all the others.**

Liam's story does happen alongside Gabriel's so you'll be getting spoilers.

It is recommended to avoid spoilers to check out the Titan Security Series or the previous Underworld Kings books—but it's not mandatory since each and every single story has a standalone HEA (Happily Ever After).

However, all of my books are inter—connected along similar timelines in the series.

All of the books intersect with all the other characters in the series.

PART I | THE LOST BOY

LIAM

I was thirteen when I met her.

She was in jean overalls. Mahogany hair long down to her back and these bright caramel eyes that stared at the class with a smile in them.

"Class, this is Isobel Santos," the teacher Miss. Barnes smiled at her politely and I heard the tell—tale snickers of people in the classroom. Something about her clothes looking old.

Where'd she get those shoes from?

Heard she's got an accent.

They'll let anyone into this country.

Fuck these kids.

I got shit on all the time.

And my clothes had holes in them. Even my shoes.

My clothing was always dirty and too big for me but that was the point. It hid where it hurt. The bruises along my body.

Dad put his boot through my ribs and I still had the imprint there.

But Isobel Santos didn't shrink from them. She just acted like they weren't there as she sat down two seats from me.

Nobody sat next to me. Not Smelly Sullivan.

But I knew at some point someone would try something with her.

~

It was during lunch. They tried tripping her.

She was carrying her tray back and navigating the rows and rows of

1

people like a minefield. Isobel didn't understand the hierarchy that existed in school in America. The teacher said she came from Mexico. And already, I heard the things people said about her.

Tommy Miller was the one who stuck his foot out. His friends giggling and I know she saw it. But she stepped over like it wasn't there, frowning down at him like he was an insect.

I didn't understand her. Most American kids just kind of ignored their bullies. She just shot him a dirty look like she didn't even care.

We were heading to fifth period after lunch when I heard them cornering her by her lockers as she was taking out her books. My lockers were on the opposite side of hers. And maybe I was watching her. I was a little curious.

And she was pretty.

Madison Elliot was an absolute bitch.

Her father invented something stupid like a *paperclip* and so she thought she owned the world.

Her two back—up dancers Jenny Williams and Renee Curtis were no better.

I knew because they had picked on me for years.

Until they realize there was zero amount of bullying that was gonna change my current situation.

"We heard your father came here illegally," Madison said to Isobel. Everyone heard her. "We can just deport your ass back to Mexico."

Isobel didn't look angry or upset, just annoyed saying something to her in Spanish. I didn't understand her.

I didn't think anyone spoke Spanish in this county.

"Hey!" I didn't even feel myself moving. I don't know why I did it. I just felt drawn to her. Maybe because she was pretty. Maybe because when I saw her, I saw an opportunity for something different.

Technically, she was brand new, but she was also the one person who didn't really shit on me. She didn't even look at me. I don't think she knew existed.

But she did now.

"Madison, I saw that pregnancy test in your fucking bag," I said out loud and I saw the way Madison turned red.

"Oh, look it's Smelly Sullivan."

I rolled my eyes. "What are you like eight? That joke wasn't funny years ago it isn't now." I ignored Isobel because

I didn't wanna see the disgusting in her eyes when she realized I *did*

2

smell bad. And my clothes were fucked up. And I was not the ideal person to be defending her.

Madison being an absolute cunt flipped her bleach blonde hair back. "Nevermind, it makes sense trash would defend scum. My parents told me about people like you—"

"Help!" I screamed like a lunatic. "Help! Miss Burns! Madison said she's going to—"

I saw the girls scramble back as I laughed it off. Miss Burns did have a soft spot for me.

When she looked at me it was like she knew I was in a shit situation. She saved me snacks and she was good to me.

She also told me if anyone ever hurt me to let her know.

Small mercies. I'd take them.

"Jeez, freakshow." Madison and her girls scurried off and I sighed not missing a look at Isobel who stared with wonder and amazement. Not disgust. Thank fuck.

"Ready for class? We gotta go or we're gonna be late."

She shook her head at me and then I realized something.

"Do you...understand me?"

"Un poquito," she held up her fingers together a small distance apart. She did have an accent when she spoke. "I try. Learning slow."

I felt a small smile light up my lips. "You have no fucking clue what I'm saying."

Her eyes widened as she tried to understand it. But she didn't.

Small mercies.

I motioned for her and pulled out my schedule I folded into a square in my bag.

"Ah," she said. "Si." And then she took her stuff and walked with me. I tried not to freak out. I did.

I walked in quickly with her going straight to the back where I sat quietly.

To my surprise she followed.

It was there I realized where everyone avoided me, she didn't. She sat next to me. Me. In my ratty old jeans for a year that hadn't been washed. And my oversized hoodie that smelled awful.

It was halfway through class she bent down into her backpack and pulled out a package of snacks.

Without looking she set down a candy bar at my desk and water bottle. Before opening up some grapes and offering them to me.

I didn't want to touch her.

3

I was dirty. She wasn't.

If she sensed my hesitation?

She reached in and plucked up some and handed me a few. I took those making sure not to brush her hands.

I didn't want her to be grossed out by me.

And so the rest of the class I sat with Isobel Santos while she fed me snacks.

~

THAT ENTIRE WEEK SHE CAME TO SCHOOL WITH EXTRA SNACKS AND FOOD. Extra water. She began sitting next to me in all the classes.

Even lunch.

One day she brought wet wipes and passed them to me without saying a word and motioned to my hands and she showed me how to tidy up a bit more.

I felt ashamed of myself, but she simply shook her head and helped me.

It lasted about a week.

Only a week.

I shouldn't have been surprised. I was walking out with her when I saw her eyes widen at someone. "Papi!"

She waved with a bright smile and she motioned for me to follow her. I don't know why I did.

A man with darker blonde hair and honey eyes stood there, strapping and tall as he took her in with a smile.

She motioned to me saying something in Spanish and I was instantly threatened. People didn't like me. Adults especially. Most of them besides Miss Burns shot me nasty looks.

I lived with my father after my mother walked out on us. He hated me. Said my eyes were hers and he didn't wanna see me coming.

Most of the time he drank himself into an oblivion. In the moments he remembered me he didn't talk with his mouth just his fists.

"My Papa," Isobel said with a smile like she was proud of him.

"Hola, Liam," he held out his hand. "My daughter tells me about you." Did she?

Isobel father, William was big, not fat but strong. Like he could kill me strong.

For a moment I wondered if he would hit me too. Was that normal? Did all parents do this?

4

I had to go home. Or did I? Would my father notice? Did he ever?

We didn't have much food at home and when I ate with Isobel it was the only time I didn't have to eat out of the trash cans or search for food.

Or clean anything.

"Isobel wants you to come for dinner tonight?" He asked me. He motioned to his car and Isobel beamed at me taking my hand in hers. Her father noticed.

Shit.

I was nervous.

Wasn't there something about not going to a stranger's house?

But Isobel…she had been nothing but nice to me.

Nothing but.

Instead her father eyed me carefully, his eyes were kind and his smile even softer as Isobel glanced between us. She said something to him quietly.

He looked like he was struggling with himself.

"Just one night, I will return you to your home, after."

I nodded before I could think better of it because I was going to get something warm and be fed for a few hours. I wouldn't have to go home and Dad wouldn't even know I was gone.

He barely knew I was home.

I agreed.

WILLIAM SANTOS LIVED IN A DECENT APARTMENT.

Better than the trailer park I existed in. I walked in and Isobel took off her shoes motioning to mine.

I didn't want to. Shame crept up on me with the holes in my soles and the back. I shook my head standing there feeling out of place and lost.

He motioned to his daughter and she shrugged a little and walked in after putting on a pair of slippers.

I followed them already feeling like my grime was contaminating their soft space. Some boxes lingered since they'd moved, apparently, but for the most part it was clean.

Warm. Ordered in a way I liked.

I smelled food on the counter and my stomach rumbled.

"Liam, come let's eat after we wash our hands." I obeyed as he showed me where his bathroom was.

I was trying to be good but I felt out of place.

5

Did he know about me? Did he know I was Smelly Sullivan? Did I fit in? I liked it here and hated it at the same time.

I didn't understand how that was possible. I felt like an oil stain. Nasty. Disgusting. A waste.

I saw packets of soap on his counter and as much as I hated it? He had plenty. I didn't have one.

I took the a packet smuggling it into my hoodie feeling guilty the moment I did it.

But I didn't have any and the Santos's wouldn't miss it.

When I opened the door though William stood outside.

I froze. Did he know? Did he know he let a rabid dog into his house? A thief? A dirty child?

"Liam, do you have family?"

I nodded. "I have a dad."

William nodded and he looked around the hallway. I wonder if he knew I stole from him. I wonder if he knew what I'd done at all. Or that his daughter fed me all the time.

And I was the reason why she brought so much snacks to school.

He seemed uneasy for a second and then he said. "Come with me."

I followed him feeling the fear creeping up my spine. Just because he looked like a nice man didn't mean he was. My father had friends who looked nice at first. Promising soap and hot food.

They touched me when they did and it made me feel sick and uncomfortable with they did, and I tolerated it because I got what I needed out of it.

They'd pet my skin until it felt like I wanted to crawl out of it.

Now, William Santos scared me.

He led me into a room and he had me stand outside as he walked in rooting through his closet.

"This is my old shirt but if you want you can have it, from when I was younger." He smiled at me and passed me something. "If you want you can go and try it." He motioned to his shirt.

What?

I was confused. What did he mean?

"I can't take that." I motioned against it. In my experience anything nice always came at a cost. Except Isobel. She didn't come at a cost. She would give it for free.

I knew that much.

He looked nervous and I stumbled back out the room. Right into Isobel. Who blinked at me confused. She handed me some more clothes.

6

"For you." I looked down. These were sweats. We were the same height. And then I realized they were both trying to give me clean clothes.

I blinked. Confused and unsure of how to react.

She then motioned to the bathroom. "Change."

William Santos stepped out of his room and he did the same. "I can show you how the bath works and if you want to clean up, here? You can."

I blinked up at him as my heart raced. Faster and faster.

What?

Isobel smiled as she gently pushed me to the bathroom. I followed dumbly as she showed me the bathroom and then she passed me a towel and she motioned to the bath.

"Good for you."

And then she took the shirt from her father's hands as I looked down at the tub where the shower turned on and steam rose up. She smiled at me as she set all my things down on a rack and then—Isobel left me in her bathroom.

To clean up.

With *new* clothes for me.

My hands didn't stop shaking as I looked down at them.

LIAM

THIRTEEN YEARS OLD

I don't know how long I spent there, but Isobel did come back with a towel and her eyes averted. She was checking up on me. Asking me if I was good.

In Spanish.

"I'm great." I was. The hot water felt like heaven and I scrubbed until I couldn't scrub anymore.

She passed me another towel and I emerged feeling like a new person.

Only when I was covered in many towels did she peek and she grinned wide.

"You look good," she was practicing her English with me at school. I was teaching her how to curse first and everything else later.

Priorities.

"Thanks," I smiled. I had put back the bar of soap I stole.

I used up some of it in the shower but it had been my first shower in forever with soap. So I was grateful.

She led me to her room and I knew because of all the butterflies.

Isobel smiled as handed me beauty products. Deodorant. Some lotion that smelled like flowers. And then she left again.

I got the feeling she was waiting outside the door until finally I put on her black sweats, and his oversized shirt but it felt so much better than mine. I didn't know what to do with my clothes. Or my shoes.

She knocked and I said. "Come in."

She poked her head in and held out two slippers. "Yours."

Isobel came in smiling at me as she passed them for my feet and her father poked his head in. "Liam, dinner is ready when you are ready. I am going to throw your old clothes out, if that is okay."

I blinked almost hurt by that. "But it's all I have."

He looked...lost as he blinked several times and nodded. "I understand. Tomorrow I am going shopping. I will bring you something nice. Better."

I didn't know what to say. It was the weekend. He came to get me on a Friday. So I suppose I had time.

I went out to dinner and sat with them as he plated it up and I sat there quietly as Isobel chattered with him.

The two of them were close and he often rubbed her hair and passed her food, I noticed he put more on my plate and poured something for me to drink.

"It's electrolytes," he explained. "It's good for you."

I nodded. "Okay."

I don't remember time passing with them.

I just sat there and ate and ate even after Isobel was done eating. And William refilled my plate.

Over and over again. Until I felt stuffed to my throat.

Even then I chugged the water until I felt like I was going to explode.

William Santos smiled over at me. "You have a father."

"I do."

"And where do you live?"

I told him. His frown was polite too. He knew it was a shit part of town. "You don't have a phone?"

No. Isobel said something to him. And William glanced over at her. And then back at me.

"Isobel says if you want you can stay here, sleep tonight here, tomorrow I will get you new clothes and you can go home then. You want I can call you father?"

I shook my head. "It's okay. I can go home..." but even as I said it? I felt uneasy coming home after this.

I was warm and I was clean for the first time and I had a full stomach.

I don't wanna go anywhere.

Isobel looked at me chewing her lip as her father stood up to clear their plates finally.

She motioned to my arms. And then she surprised me by rolling up my sleeve. One of them. She pointed at the bruises and I saw the concern in her eyes.

"Stay."

And just like that I realized two things.

One, they both knew. They knew everything.

Two, they were offering me a break. Without conditions.

Without…touching me. Isobel let me go and smiled reassuringly. She motioned to their couch. Warm. Soft. Inviting. Something I knew would be cozy curling up into.

It was the stuff you saw on television. Which they had too.

"Stay."

And I did.

The next morning William Santos made me pancakes.

He gave me a toothbrush and Isobel and I brushed our teeth side by side like we were siblings. And then we ate again. I felt like I was dreaming.

Maybe Dad had beaten me up so bad—I had died.

But it was real. She was real. They were real. At one point William Santos did leave and when he came back, he did have sneakers with him. Another pair of clothes.

Isobel kept me company and she forced me to sit down so she could trim my hair.

The two of them tackled me like a school project until I felt a world better already.

My stomach ached a little from all the normal amounts of food I was eating and I couldn't stop going to the bathroom purging it out of my gut because I wasn't used to this.

I never had two square meals like this.

Clean ones too.

If Isobel understood she was with me until her father came back and he passed me medication too.

"That's for your stomach," he said. "And this for pain."

I was in pain? I took them both and suddenly my bruises didn't hurt anymore.

I had lived so long with them…it was the first time in my life I didn't feel them. I felt my eyes well for ninetieth time.

Over and over until I swiped at them.

But I noticed William Santos didn't try and touch me.

It was time for me to go home soon.

Eventually. I couldn't play house forever.

He drove me back without Isobel who stayed home doing her homework. She had wanted to come but he motioned for her not to.

She had glanced at me with nervousness in her eyes.

Did she know where I was going back to? Did she know my life?

When William Santos pulled up to the neighborhood in his decent car I saw stares. People were looking at him as he stopped near my father's trailer.

I could hear the television blasting from here which meant he was watching it and drinking. With friends.

I heard their laughter and flinched as I slowly got out the car.

Thankfully nobody was out here. My hands practically shook struggling with the door.

I was going back.

I didn't want to.

I didn't know when it would be my final day there.

I knew that I was studying really hard and working in school to get myself into a better high school and into a better college to get out.

It was my only way out of here.

I looked back at William Santos who was watching me and I knew— he knew. He knew. And I slowly took one step after another finding myself standing at the foot of the steps.

My hands froze on the door handle as it wrenched open. One of my father's friends—Skip—looked down at me.

There were several of them inside.

I felt my stomach sour as he yanked me inside.

"Where have you been, boy?" My father stood drunkenly from his recliner as his friends all made noise ratcheting him up.

They always did this.

Always fanned the flames of it as he came to me.

I saw the hit coming before it did. They loved this part and they got excited about it.

And then the doorbell rang as it landed.

I bit back a noise at the sting of the blow, as he reached for William Santos's shirt. "What the fuck is your problem?" He slurred.

Someone got the door and I fucking prayed it was Mr. Santos.

I did.

And I looked behind me.

"Well, well, it's a fucking wetback." Skip smirked at Mr. Santos who stiffened.

"Liam," Mr. Santos focused on me ignoring everyone else. Like his daughter did. *"Liam, ven paca."*

I didn't know a lick of Spanish the same way Isobel barely understood English but I knew what that meant.

Come here. I fucking knew it.

"Who the fuck is this?" My father said sneering at him. "We ain't got no work in this country for folks like you."

"Liam," Mr. Santos said over him his gaze once warm now lethal. "Now."

I moved before I could think better of it.

Before someone could grab me again I practically tore out of there.

"Get in the car!" Mr. Santos said to me.

"You ain't taking nothing fucking scumbag—" Skip said. My father was too slow and I turned over my shoulder to watch how clumsy alcohol made him. Skip tried to hit Mr. Santos.

"No!" I couldn't live with it if he did get hit, but he shoved me back ducking from it.

Skip went stumbling as Mr. Santos shoved the door and I heard them hit it scrambling. He ran for the drivers seat as I bolted into the passenger side.

For a bigger man he could move.

Mr. Santos was already turning the car on as the doors slammed open again and I saw my father's friends and him come running out and I ducked, my heart hammering in my ears as Mr. Santos tore off.

I saw them trying to run and block him but he was too quick.

I thought I was in a nightmare.

I couldn't breathe as I heard something hit the car. Mr. Santos didn't stop.

He didn't stop. He just kept driving faster and faster.

"You stay with us. With me and Isobel." He said panting. He looked stunned too. He didn't stop until we made it back to his apartment complex.

And then he sat there in the car panting. Looking at me with a stunned expression.

And then his lips lifted in a smile. "You have a new home now."

I didn't remember what happened after that, just that his arms wrapped me and I felt my hot tears sliding down my face.

~

That night I slept on the Santos's couch again. Only this time, the reality no longer having to go back to where I was didn't occur to me. It still felt like I was having a weird dream.

That I would wake up in my father's trailer.

The shadows at night in the room seemed to morph into demons taunting me. Making fun of me the way Skip did.

The way my father did.

They seemed to crawl over my skin and laugh at me.

I didn't think twice as I panted away and tugged at my shirt trying to get in air into my lungs. My feet moved of their own accord sliding into my house slippers in the Santos's home and finding Isobel's room.

He had just put us both to bed but I knocked.

"Isa," I whispered into the darkness. "You sleeping?"

A moment later I poked my head into the door and found her blearily opening her eyes. I felt guilty for waking her up.

"Can I come in?"

She nodded turning on her lady bug lamp as she did.

Her favorite color was red. I knew that much.

"I can't sleep," I whispered. "I'm scared. I'm scared my dad is gonna find me and kill me. I..." I trailed off realizing she didn't understand. I motioned to her bed. "Can I sleep with you?"

She blinked and then scooted over on her bigger bed. Just like that. I slowly got in with her laying down on her pillows and she put the blanket over me.

For a moment I laid there with her honey eyes on me soft and warm and cozy.

"Your blanket is hot." I frowned feeling how warm it was. She shook her head a little and put more of it over me. Like I was cold. It was cozy in here. Like a nest. She smiled at me then.

"You stay."

I nodded. "I stay."

With her. For good. Forever.

She smiled and then my stomach did that thing where it rumbled. Loudly. And Isobel giggled slowly getting up and reaching down under bed.

She pulled out a bin of snacks saying something in Spanish about her father.

I got up with her and under her heated blanket Isobel passed me soft chocolate chip cookies and she snuck into the kitchen to get milk.

Mr. Santos found us the next morning with crumbs on our faces and the carton of milk there.

If I thought he'd be mad at me in his daughter's bed he just shook his head at us and rubbed both of our heads. Isobel hugged him easily, but I kept my distance feeling guilty.

"Breakfast?" He asked me.

As though the night prior didn't happen.

I dipped my head unsure of how to act. How to be.

This was new to me.

All of it.

A family. A chance. A new life.

By some stroke of luck, the girl I had befriended less than two weeks ago...was now the most important thing in my life.

Just like that.

Isobel smiled at me as she motioned for us to go to the *banyo*. The bathroom.

I was picking it up.

I followed and we brushed our teeth side by side again before I headed into breakfast.

With my new family.

1

LIAM

Isobel became my...I didn't know.

Mr. Santos called her my sister and I played along.

No fucking way she was actually my fucking sister.

Not with how I felt about her.

Isobel was pretty in a way that always took my breath away.

Isobel was beautiful like the sun. I orbited around her. Long mahogany hair that shimmered in the sunlight, her grin wide on me with sharp canines that were prominent when she did. She always looked like she was ready to get into trouble.

And she did.

I didn't understand how pretty she was growing up. Sometimes she had untamed waves, sometimes she straightened it in frustration. She was slender for the most part and every so often she wanted to watch her figure. Even if she didn't need to.

And her eyes—Isobel's eyes were the part that got me suckered in. They were the warmest part of her. Kind. Playful. Intelligent.

And her attitude rounded her off.

Isobel always laughed like she didn't care what anyone thought about her.

Because she didn't.

Not when she was raised by William Santos who really didn't give a fuck about people.

His mother and father had been Brazilian's who'd come to America, he was an only child and he had his citizenship in the States when he went back to Brazil and had met Adrianna Santos visiting from Mexico.

He'd chosen to raise his daughter in Mexico despite having a right to come back to the States because it had been important to Adrianna—to keep her around her culture.

Isobel had a spine of steel being raised by her parents.

Adrianna and Mr. Santos had divorced for some reason.

He didn't talk about it.

We went to school again and to my surprise—my father never showed face. But I was expecting it. I was all the time.

I sat next to Isobel as people whispered about me being cleaner.

Miss Burns looked surprised to see me and I started doing better in school

Isobel and I acclimated together.

I learned Spanish and she learned English and together we went to high school.

We shared a room and I eventually got my own bed as I was shooting up in height. Isobel was about five—four maybe five. *Max.* I shot up taller than Mr. Santos to six—four as a freshman.

Which didn't work in my favor.

I ducked my head embarrassed at the way I shot up and felt out of place in my new body.

That was around the time I started getting into fights at school and in general? I did get into trouble.

With neighborhood boys. With people. Seniors in high school.

Seniors in the local college.

Mr. Santos dropped me off at a karate class. *Kyokushin.*

I got my ass kicked there at fourteen. And I just kept going back.

Mr. Santos didn't make a lot of money but he made enough. He worked construction and sometimes he worked at a gas station for extra money.

When I turned fifteen I realized he was supporting me. A second child he hadn't intended to have. And I ate more than Isobel did.

I got a job at sixteen mowing lawns or washing cars sometimes so I could help out, but Mr. Santos quickly shut that down. He said I needed to study and focus on doing better for myself.

I felt guilty. I did.

"If you help Isobel, you are paying me back," he said slyly. I did then. But I would've helped Isobel regardless. She saved my life.

I practiced English with her and she taught me Spanish.

18

She blossomed in front of my eyes. Time made her the fucking prettiest girl I had ever seen. She was *beautiful.* Long mahogany hair. Softer caramel eyes with a hint of mischief in them.

She never changed.

She was always my light.

I noticed how I felt about her when I was sixteen and when I realized little things about her. I slept in the same room with her.

And I fucking loved Isobel.

When we were in school and she was in PE and I had to physically restrain myself from kissing her.

I didn't know how to tell her I liked her.

Not when she called me her brother or I shared a room with her and saw her in all states of dress. Her pajamas. Her walking around in a towel.

Mr. Santos thought it was all platonic.

I didn't have the heart to tell him I was in love with his daughter.

Isa and I went away to college together.

It was my first time living without her. I fucking despised it.

I spent every waking moment with her.

When I turned eighteen I legally changed my name to Santos on everything. Finally feeling like I belonged in their family after years and years of being Santos.

I was doing karate a majority of the time, ice—skating with some hockey players in college, and Isobel and I were both focused on working in IT.

It was good money.

It was in my senior year I saw the application posted on the billboard in the halls of our dorm.

One of my buddies mentioned he was doing it.

The CIA was hiring…for their cyber—intelligence program out of all things.

I don't know why I picked it up. I don't know why I talked to Isobel about it.

"I think we should," I explained. "It's good money, good reputation, security clearance which is a pathway to more money—"

"No," Isobel frowned. "I don't want to this." Her English had gotten so good over the years even with her accent still thick. "I don't like this, I don't know what we will do."

I told her. "It's a desk job. You sit all day at a fucking computer. Isa, it's great for money, it's even better for us because we can support our father." I had to say it like that.

Isobel didn't know how much I cared about her.

She could never know. She never looked at me like that.

Not even in junior year when I almost killed that douchebag for trying to sleep with her and bragging about it?

Even then I had been 'her brother' and not *Liam*.

A man.

A person. Who could want her beyond wanting air. Over the years my love for her transcended into something beyond what I thought was possible.

I would do anything for her. I would lay on glass if she wanted me too and let her walk on me.

I moved mountains for her. I did everything for her.

She was the love of my life.

And she had no idea.

I talked to Isobel about joining the CIA. Not wanting to be a part from her. Not for a second.

"Please, just do some research and think about it. It would get us where we need to go. We would only do it for a short time, and then when we got out, you could afford your dance studio and I could afford my martial art studio. It would get us what we need, and it would get us in a way where we wouldn't have to suffer like everybody else. Government jobs are solid and stable. You might even like it."

I pleaded with her.

Isobel's eyes were soft and worried as she took me in.

"Liam..." she trailed off. "I am scared now."

I didn't even hesitate to take her in my arms. Because I had comforted her for years. I knew her inside and out. I knew everything about this girl. I knew everything she liked and everything she didn't like.

I knew her.

"You're afraid something will happen?"

She nodded. "I do not want to lose you or Papi."

I rubbed her back as she sat on one of my thighs. She curled into the crook of my neck like she always did.

I inhaled the scent of her in my lung.

"You won't," I pressed my lips to her forehead. "I'm not going anywhere. I promise. Just think about it. People don't really consider going into government work, but I did some research and it would give us security. And I know that something that our father would want."

She nodded. "Very secure."

I smiled a little.

"Think it over."

She didn't have to.

She agreed.

I don't know why I felt guilty.

∽

ISOBEL AND I DID JOIN THE CIA.

And then I realized how I was the maker of my own demise.

My instructor with Isobel was a man named Gabriel Monroe. He was my polar opposite. Blonde wheat—colored hair. Icy eyes. Only two years older and what felt like a decade of experience between us.

The way he moved, I knew he was lethal. But the way he looked at Isobel? He absolutely fucking melted.

I didn't even stand a chance the moment I saw her batting her eyes up at him.

Gabriel looked at Isobel like he'd never seen anything more beautiful in his life.

I knew that look.

I had seen it in the mirror every single fucking day I lived with her, since her father saved me, since I woke up to her smiles across the breakfast table. Since we brushed our teeth side by side and linked arms when walking down the street.

She was my world.

And I fucking *knew* Isobel was into him.

She never looked at me like that. Not once in all the years we'd been together, but I didn't...I didn't blame her. I didn't want Isobel to be into me.

Initially I got jealous.

It ate me alive from the inside out. And then one day I had to just fucking realize...he wasn't me.

He wasn't the broken boy I was. He wasn't like me.

Gabriel was twenty—four and he'd been a Navy SEAL. He'd crawled out of nothing to get to where he was.

I knew that much. I knew he was one of the CIA golden boys. He was climbing his way to the top.

He could Isobel everything I couldn't.

And so all I could do was stand in the sidelines and watch her fall in love with him.

I did whatever I could to protect her, while also vetting him for her. It was agonizing.

I loved Isobel. Like I had never loved anything in my life.

More than Mr. Santos.

More than karate and ice skating and activities that kept me from feeling my past, feeling people's hands all over me, feeling anything. She made me feel whole.

But I saw the way Gabriel looked at her, how he treated her, nights without her I spent it with other women.

I couldn't have Isobel.

I couldn't destroy her.

I was still an oil stain. And even if I recognized my darkness inside of Gabriel Monroe? He held a light to him I didn't have. I saw the way he worshipped her. He was pure.

He thought I was her brother.

We were in training together.

We got stationed at Quantico together with Gabriel after he trained Isobel to pass her exam.

Nobody knew they were together. Nobody knew they were a secret. But me.

It burned. It ached. But I wasn't right for her, and I spent my time with every other woman I could but her so she wouldn't know. Sex was weird for me. I didn't like women touching me. But I liked...forgetting.

Control.

Restraint.

Losing myself temporarily.

Isobel realized I was jealous of him. She'd come into my room early on to address it.

"Do you think if he comes to our home, one day I will leave you and forget about you?"

No. Worse. I thought I'd lose her forever if she knew I loved her. Isobel leaned into me.

"It's you and me. Always. Even if I am with Gabriel, I would never forget you. Just because Papi adopted you and brought you into our family, does not make you temporary. A one time thing. You are a Santos. You're one of us. You're my heart. My love. My brother. My protector. Nothing else will replace that.

Even if I end up loving him? I would never forget about you. I wouldn't let him forget you. Understood?"

I did. But I held up my pinky. "Promise?"

"I will never let you go," she whispered. "Doesn't matter what happens. You are my family too."

"Even if he ever becomes yours?"

She just shook her head. "If he's my family—he's your family too then. Remember?"

And the moment she said? I knew she loved him. I knew because she would even *consider* it.

I saw the way Gabriel watched her. I knew exactly how he saw her. You'd be blind not to see it.

I introduced Gabriel to the AI project, Oracle, Isa and I had worked on. I talked to him about the private security company I might've dabbled in starting after the Agency.

Together, we worked on a team of five with Claire Sutton, twenty—five with long blonde hair and these cornflower blue eyes and an older man named Vincent Grant.

The only other person who'd graduate with us working with us was this kid named Jeremy Bradford.

The five of us, including Gabriel—became a team.

One day, Isobel wanted to move in with him. And I knew I was slowly losing her. My love. To her love.

And I had to let her go.

As much as it killed me?

I couldn't keep Isobel mine. She didn't look at me the way she looked at him.

And Gabriel?

He would do anything for her.

I didn't hate Gabriel—but the idea of losing Isobel was worse than losing myself.

She had made me who I was today—my entire identity centered around her.

And if anything happened to her?

I didn't think I'd make it.

MELINA

"BLOW A KISS INTO THE CAMERA!"

I did just that.

The camera flash made me see spots just a little bit as I blinked them away. Trying to focus. Trying to do a good job.

It was really hot in here, and I blinked again trying not to fan myself.

I had listened to my best friend Catalina who had gone to the market and met this lady who gave her a pamphlet.

She was scouting potential models and Catalina who was gorgeous had asked me to come with her.

With her raven hair and hazel eyes, Catalina's features were beautiful and she was taller than me—so she would stand out. But me? I was not like her. I was turning eighteen and everyone said I looked twelve.

I had darker eyes, darker hair than Catalina that was almost blue in the light.

I was short at five feet maybe. But I looked cute to most people. Even Mama said it.

So I asked Mama if I could go to the photoshoot with Catalina.

But I'm turning eighteen, Mama. I can do things now.

Mama hadn't cared. She said no.

We live in a small house about two hours away from Mexico City and Mama had said it was too far and she wanted me to stay close to her.

I was her only baby and she didn't feel comfortable with me out of country. We were simple people, Mama said, we didn't need those big city spotlights on us.

But I always wanted a big city spotlight on me.

Please, Mami. Catalina said it'll be quick.

You are still seventeen and you cannot just go off and do whatever you want to do. Papi is bringing your favorite pomegranates tonight and I think we can have some together. Sound good?

But Mami!

No, carina. No. I said it. Okay? Maybe when you are older.

But Catalina and I had snuck out anyway.

I knew I would be in trouble.

I knew.

But I had to take a chance.

I was the smallest girl there so I didn't think I'd do well. But right now, my chances looked good.

Next to me Catalina blew me a kiss and sipped something that the woman she'd met at the market had given her. A pink drink. Another drink. And another drink.

Catalina was right. I couldn't wait to go back home to Mami and tell her about my day. Maybe she'd let me do this more often.

This was amazing. We were treated like we were models and even in a room full of three dozen other girls my age?

I felt like an adult. Like someone important.

When I was done with my photoshoot, I was offered another round of fizzy pink drinks with cute little umbrellas in them. I had never had alcohol until now.

My head was buzzing with a light sensation but Catalina took another and then another. Giggling and laughing with the other girls who were pleasantly nice to me.

"Melly," she mock—whispered in Spanish. *"This was great!"*

"I know." I said back to her in our native tongue. *"I cannot believe they would even think about me being a model. This is unreal."*

But I still felt guilty. I told Mama, I was going shopping. I told her I would be back before dark, but the guilt twisted in my stomach. I pushed it down because I was eighteen.

A glance outside showed me the late afternoon sun in the air. Mami always said to be home and we were running late.

"Come on," I motioned to her. "It's late, and we need to go home."

"Just another drink," she said grabbing another.

"You had so many."

I had one—maybe half—I was one of the few girls not drinking it. I didn't like how it made me feel and it tasted like nail polish remover.

When Catalina had shown me the glossy pamphlets printed with photos of smiling girls it seemed like a nice opportunity.

But it was getting late and I didn't want to stay here anymore.

I wasn't comfortable and my gut was telling me to go home.

"Catalina," I tugged on her elbow. "We should go home now."

The studio mirrors seemed to close in on me as the room tilted a little.

On the other side of the room? One of the girls passed out.

Maybe from the heat? I didn't know.

The camera man was still taking photos of other girls.

"Catalina." I motioned for us to go.

"Okay, okay," she said getting up and grabbing her things.

The lady who had brought us here looked up from the girl who passed out and instead her head snapped up to me.

Her dark eyes made her look a little scary. I don't know why I didn't think she was scary before the photoshoot.

"Where are you two going?"

Something in me chose to lie to her face. "Taking Catalina to the bathroom," I said in what I hoped was believable. But when I got to the door, I couldn't open it. "Could you open the door? It's locked."

But instead of opening the door the lady frowned and told me to sit back down.

Sit back down.

When she spoke, I felt like I was underwater.

I just needed to go to the bathroom to splash some water on my face. I think I said that, but I was mumbling it.

Another girl passed out in the room and something like dread formed in my stomach.

What was happening right now?

And everything happened fast.

Next to me? Catalina bent over sharply and she gagged.

The photographer stopped clicking photos and the studio lights felt blinding. My heart slammed against my ribs as understanding crashed over me.

The last thing I saw was Catalina's still form in the chair as rough hands grabbed me from behind.

Come home, *munequita.*

Come home.

Just come home.

Lo siento, Mamá. I should have listened.

26

THE FIRST TIME I WOKE UP I WAS IN A SHIPPING CONTAINER.

I felt the metal floor, cold against my skull, and something was hard against my face. It was dark with strips of light and I smelled...something rancid.

Something awful.

Panic like no other filled me. I tried to move and I realized I couldn't move my hands. A noise left me until a hand clamped over my mouth.

Another girl. I recognized her from the photoshoot.

The photoshoot. The modeling. Catalina.

The pink drinks. It all came back to me.

Where was I?

"Don't scream," the other girl said her eyes dark and wide. Haunted. "If they hear you, they'll come back for us."

What?

My entire body hurt.

"Where's Catalina?" My voice was hoarse. Like I swallowed nails.

She shook her head. "I don't know. I woke up here."

Where...what...

Kidnapped. I was kidnapped.

Panic like no other descended into me, fear trapping itself in my stomach as I slowly looked and saw bodies. Some girls awake. Some asleep...

I tried to breathe and I felt my eyes blur. "Catalina..."

I needed to go home. Mama didn't know where I was.

"I need to go home." I said to the girl. "The sun was going down. I told Mama I would be home...by sundown."

I didn't get to finish. A loud noise came from outside.

In another second, the door or something creaked and I blinked rapidly.

"Go to sleep!" The girl told me. "Go."

I closed my eyes laying back down looking through my lashes at the sight of the sun bleeding into the container.

Heavy boots. Men's voices.

"Round 'em up, boys. O'Hara doesn't pay for corpses. Not a single fucking scratch!"

What?

I didn't breathe.

I didn't move. One of the girls began to cry and I heard another start screaming. And another. My eyes flew open feeling nothing but dread and panic.

"Shut up!" One of the voices shouted. Followed by the sounds of someone hitting her. I winced.

"What the fuck did I just say—"

"I don't care what O'Hara wants. If she keeps screaming I'll shoot the bitch and just get a few more..."

Kidnapped.

I'd been kidnapped. And that wasn't the worst part. These men who wore ball caps began picking us up, one by one like sacks of flour. Taking us somewhere.

I saw hands coming for me and I scrambled back or I tried to. I felt hands yanking at my hair and I screamed.

"Shut the fuck up."

Something came at my face and I blacked out with the pain.

3

LIAM

CHAPTER ABOUT HIM AND GABRIEL BONDING.

4

LIAM

I GOT THE CALL BEFORE WORK.

"Mr. Santos," I kept my voice low. I was about to walk out for the day at work.

"Liam…" he sounded weak. In Spanish he told me he was at the hospital.

"What? What happened?"

Brokenly, Mr. Santos explained he had been injured at work and he suffered from a concussion that he was at the hospital.

He didn't wanna worry Isobel so he called me instead.

"Don't tell her, I know you two are working, but I don't want her to see me like this. She's already traumatized from her past."

I knew. He had talked to me a little bit about why Isobel had nightmares sometimes growing up.

Just enough for me to know he had seen some shit.

"You want me to come to you?"

He did. And so I went and told Gabriel. Not Isobel. It cut me open to not tell her.

I flew out the same day as fast as I could not bothering to drive. I couldn't wait anymore. He was in the hospital that night and his weathered smile had me blinking back my emotions.

"Mr. Santos, you had a concussion," I reached out to him. "What happened?"

"I was driving…" he explained how he had almost fallen asleep at the wheel which made my chest tighten.

"You're working too hard," I muttered. "Stop that. I send you money." I always had.

He made a noise with his teeth and waved his hand. "I save it. I cannot take your money, Liam—"

"Stop being stubborn." I didn't understand why he was. "Let me help you. You helped me."

I knew he wasn't feeling good when he laid back in his hospital bed, the white pillows against his tanned skin, and even with the machines around him, something in my gut just didn't feel right.

In my mind Mr. Santos was the greatest thing in the world. The biggest and strongest man I'd ever met. He was a mountain.

And right now? It ached somewhere deep to see him nestled into the hospital bed half of who he used to be.

"I hate that you made me not tell Isa," I told him honestly. "Have you eaten yet?"

His face held an unreadable expression as I said, her name, and his eyes turned to me, and I just knew in the weight of the moment, he wanted to tell me something. Something that wasn't good.

"Liam," he said softly. His eyes so much like his daughter's right now I wanted to snap. "Promise me something."

"Anything." I held his hands, weathered and calloused from years of hard labor. "I'd do anything for you."

He pressed his lips together and I saw his eyes water. In Spanish he asked me flatly.

"Promise me, if anything happens, you will be with her. Take care of her. She's always wanted her dance studio and only you will give her the world. She is your everything. I know it. And my love for you has never been conditional. But I'm asking you if anything happens to me—I want you to marry Isobel."

And just like that my heart fucking shattered as my eyes welled. Pieces of the shattered remains punctured my lungs cutting off my ability to breathe and function.

"Mr. Santos," I whispered feeling my chest ache. Nononono, I can't do this to him. "You don't—"

"Please," he squeezed my hands. "I have never asked. For anything. I'm asking you because I know you love her. I watch how you watch her. I have always suspected you loved her. Only you would love her as much as I do."

I wanted to shake him and tell him about Gabriel.

You haven't met Gabriel Monroe. He's her soul. He is her entire heart.

31

I can't take that away from her.

His eyes implored mine and I closed my eyes feeling them water as I bent my head making the one promise to the man who saved my life. The one promise I couldn't keep.

Thankfully, the fucking doctor walked in after me and filled me in that he was good to go for the night.

"Are you guys sure?" I asked feeling helpless. "Did he get a CT scan?"

"It's not covered by insurance," the doctor explained.

"What the fuck?" I frowned. "That's the dumbest shit in the world." I looked between Mr. Santos who waved it off.

"I'm okay, Liam. I don't need it."

"Mr. Santos—"

"Liam. It's twelve hundred dollars—"

Shit. That was steep. Why was healthcare so expensive? It didn't matter—this was Mr. Santos—no such thing as expensive for him.

"Let me pay for it. I have the money—" I protested, but eventually Mr. Santos shrugged it off saying he wanted to go home and lay down in his bed.

He hated being at the hospital.

"But what if something's wrong?"

"Nothing's wrong." Mr. Santos protested waving off the doctor's. "Just another way for hospitals to take my money."

"My money." I told him but I couldn't force him to take the CT scan.

Fuck. I had anxiety over him.

All the time.

Especially now that he wasn't allowed to work for the next week.

I took the entire week off to stay with him so he'd be solid.

I already was trying to work out a way to bring him to Quantico even temporarily to live with me.

Isa would love it and I didn't mind. She didn't live with me anymore. Maybe Mr. Santos could meet Gabriel and then he'd forget about his promise and mine.

He'd like Gabriel, the two of them would get along.

I spent the evening juggling doctors and taking care of his bills. The next hour flew by and then I took him home.

"I wanna take you with me to Quantico," I told him on the drive back. "I know you don't wanna move but Isa and I are cool with it, so you should come live with us."

He shook his head with a smile. "You are just as stubborn, you won't stop until I do."

"Come on, say yes. Move to Quantico. You don't have to work. You can stay at home. You're injured now and it would mean the world to Isa."

I didn't miss how the two of us pulled out Isobel to leverage whenever we wanted our way.

It was like she was our secret weapon.

I didn't want to him worry ever so I handled everything for him.

"Say yes, it'll make her happy." I teased.

"Okay, okay, but when I go home, I just want some dinner and some TV."

I laughed. "Good, I'll let Isa know." We made it home my grin wide as I took him upstairs, and put him to bed. Isa and I had been gone for a while and he looked thinner than normal.

"I'll get you some soup and crackers and some juice, yeah? I'll be back." I ran around getting him ninety different things and after making sure he was comfortable I told him I'd shower.

"You are not allowed to move," I joked. "Not after that scare. I can't wait to tell Isa you're fine."

He grinned at me. "You worry about nothing, Liam."

"Nothing, my ass. You called me out from work and I'm not suppose to worry?" I made the same noise he did with his teeth and he grinned wider. Isobel had that grin.

After my shower I grabbed a sandwich and some juice figuring I'd go check on Mr. Santos since the TV in his room was running, but when I got there, he was already asleep.

I turned it off and went to go tuck him into his bed like he'd done with me years ago.

"Come on, Mr. Santos. Let me fix you up. You can't sleep like that."

I went to touch him and his skin felt off. He'd been leaning against the headboard so I went to move him and his head dropped forward.

My heart lurched. "Mr. Santos…" A sickening sensation went through me. *"Mr. Santos."*

I shook him and my hands went to his throat. "Mr. Santos?"

He didn't have a pulse.

"Mr. Santos, wake up…" No. No. No. Nononononono.

No.

"Mr—Dad…Dad, wake up."

Nonononono. This can't be happening.

"Dad?" I shook him again, my voice was a croak. *"Dad…Dad wake up! Wake up! Please. Please. Please. No. Dad!"*

33

~

HELL ON EARTH WAS TAKING CARE OF FUNERAL PROCEEDINGS FOR MR. Santos. He'd given me a new life. I sent him off into the next one.

I couldn't stop crying and breaking down.

Alone.

Without her.

She was gonna fucking kill me but he wasn't wrong.

If Isobel knew? She would never leave this place. And all he wanted was for her to live her life. I didn't know what to do anymore.

I didn't have preparation for this. I buried Mr. Santos and packed up his home in that week I was there.

I looked down at his casket feeling my heart shatter.

"I wanted to pack for you to take you to Quantico," I whispered. "Not your funeral. Isa's gonna kill me. And I feel like I killed you. I should've gotten that scan done. I hate how stubborn you are. As much as I love you, I'm really pissed at you right now for once." I snapped feeling my entire heart break. "I love you so much. I do. Thank you for saving my life. I'm sorry I couldn't save yours."

I shattered that night over and over and over again.

And my heart broke even more realizing I couldn't keep any of my promises.

~

AFTER MR. SANTOS'S FUNERAL I FIGURED I WAS A GLUTTON FOR punishment, and so I ended up going back not to our apartment, but to the trailer park that he found me in. To the exact trailer that used to belong to me.

I saw two kids running around in front of it and a woman walking up to it.

"Hey, you know what happened to the old man who lived here?"

She shook her head. "If you're looking for him he died a few years back."

I don't know why it stung. It shouldn't have. It shouldn't have felt like anything.

I drove back to the apartment I had and blew out a breath as I broke into the couch.

Alone.

Again.

～

Isobel lost her mind.

She erupted in a fury I saw coming. From a mile away.

"You...you kept him from me?" She whispered horrified. "This is why?" She was apart from me for a second and then she moved tearing at my shirt and I stood there feeling agony.

She had no idea.

And neither did I.

In Spanish, Isobel went off.

How could you?

What happened? Why did you keep it from me?

You're supposed to be my brother!

I didn't move.

I didn't touch her blinking back my emotions. I let her down too.

I let Mr. Santos down and his daughter.

I held onto her elbows so she wouldn't fall over and Gabriel eventually took her off me.

"You kept this from me! You hid this!" She shouted at Gabriel out of her mind angry and crying. She was sobbing brokenly. Gabriel's face fell.

But it wasn't his fault.

"He didn't want me to tell you," I said it woodenly.

"What?" Her voice came out softer.

"He asked me not to..." I felt the words leave me.

Mr. Santos. In the hospital.

"He asked me to see him. Because you would've dropped your world to stop for him." My eyes finally went to her and Isobel looked at me heartbroken.

I rarely if ever saw her looking like that.

She didn't cry often, but whenever she did, I cried with her.

I swiped at my eyes as she sank back onto the island breaking apart. And when she left the room I felt my horror sinking in.

She hated me.

Lo siento, Papi.

～

I spent the next week drinking.

Something I swore I'd never do. But now I saw why my father did it.

35

"I can't keep my promises." I stayed in our apartment, the old one before Isa moved out to Gabriel's.

She lived with him now and I grateful for it. I didn't need her here setting me off.

Liam, you have to take care of her.

Promise, you'll marry her. She's been yours forever.

I know you love her.

I did love her.

Just not enough to take her away from Gabriel.

"I'm so sorry," I cried. "I'm sorry, I can't do it."

Sometime that week Gabriel came to see me.

I lost all sense of time. I asked for time off and they gave it to me. Even the Agency knew I just buried my fucking father.

I felt him in the room.

Whenever Gabriel walked in everything calmed down.

He was intense as fuck, but pretty chill when it came down to it. Right now, I knew why he was here.

And I didn't know how to look at him.

He did sit down in the room close enough to me for me to know he was concerned. Otherwise he avoided contact with people.

I should've been angry with him.

Because of Gabriel I couldn't keep my promise to Mr. Santos.

I told myself that I should be pissed off at him. But I wasn't. It wasn't his fault. He met Isobel months ago.

It was inevitable. I was the one that convinced her to join the Agency. I knew better. It still hurt to look at Gabriel.

She loved him. She never looked at me like that. I got the feeling she didn't even see me.

"What happened?"

His voice cut through the room. I could smell the alcohol on me right now as stared at the wall.

I was dimly aware of my lips moving.

"He had head trauma," I croaked. "A brain injury from the car crash. She didn't need to see him like that. She's got a softer heart than I do."

She would stay.

Isobel would drop everything to be with him. And he knew.

He fucking knew.

"He figured if she came she'd be devastated. She'd give it all up to be with him. And she would. He didn't want that."

I let the silence fill in the rest.

I figured at some point he would come see me. I knew him. I knew he loved Isobel as much as he did.

Otherwise, he wouldn't be here checking on me. Making sure I didn't off myself.

"I promised her father I'd take care of her."

I did.

But now I needed something else from Gabriel Monroe. I needed him to leave me the fuck alone. I did.

"That's not what I promised him," I continued, my voice low. "I promised Isobel's father, I would marry her."

The silence hung between us as my heart trapped in my chest began to pound so wildly I couldn't breathe around my emotions.

I promised Mr. Santos.

One fucking thing.

He had only ever asked me for one thing—and I couldn't do it. I was cursed. To never love. To never be loved. I couldn't do it. I felt my eyes burning as the confession filled all of the inches and millimeters between us.

"He made me promise I would give her the dance studio she wanted, a life to make her happy, babies, the house, everything. He told me he knew I loved Isobel. He knew all those years I did. He said if I loved her, if I loved him, I would marry her."

I drank more from the bottle I had. Vodka. Gin. I didn't know. It had all blended together at this point.

"I don't want Isobel, I *need* her. She's my sister, my best friend, at times she's my mother," I laughed remembering all the days and nights I spent with her.

She had become my entire world.

I did *need* her.

"She's my *everything*, and then I watched her fall for you, and I knew—*I fucking knew*—it would never be me."

I felt it the moment Gabriel caught on. The moment he knew what I was saying.

I had *never* been her *brother*. Not *once*.

Not a single fucking time.

Not when she crawled into my arms.

Not when I loved her throughout our teenage girls.

Not even now.

Not once.

I would die for Isobel Santos.

37

But not once would I ever be her brother.

I felt the hairs on the backs of my arms rise as I looked over at him lazily. Unable to even stop myself.

There he was, her entire soul sitting across from me. Golden—haired. Pale blue eyes glowing on his tanned skin like a spooky friendly demon sitting in my apartment I used to share with her.

When she was mine. Somewhat.

"Never me." I shook his head feeling the nails digging deeper into my chest. "It was never me."

"You're not her brother."

"*Not even close.*"

I waited for it to sink in. For Gabriel Monroe to realize just what the fucking fuck I was in this house. In this space.

"But I am to *her*."

"*You* loved her," he whispered horror dawning in his eyes. "Did you realize it now after me? Or did you know for years?"

He looked confused now. Poor Gabriel. He didn't get how deep it ran for me. He liked her. I loved her. But I didn't deserve Isobel. Not once.

"I don't understand, why would you give her to me?"

"Because I see the way she looked at you." My eyes held his feeling years and years of memories wash over me. I was still an oil stain. She was perfect. She always had been perfect. The epicenter of my world. I clutched the bottle tighter. "She never looked at me like that."

I admitted it then knowing exactly which direction I was going. I knew from the moment Mr. Santos asked me. I knew exactly what I had to do.

"I see her. I have always seen her, and I thought I could be her brother. I thought I could be who she needed me to be. And then I watched her fall in love with you." I drank from the vodka bottle. "I promised *him* I *would* to his face. And I would die by my word."

I stood then and I felt the energy in the room shift. I did. I always felt him when he moved. Maybe it was the alcohol. Maybe it was something else. Maybe it was the fact that I knew I was going to break Mr. Santos's heart.

Or maybe finally give away mine.

I knew deep down if I went to Isobel and told her everything she would marry me in a heartbeat. But she would never love me. She would watch Gabriel with those eyes and eventually hate me for taking her away from him.

I felt Gabriel move and I held my hands up. He was a trained operative he knew better and who knew—maybe I could just kill him. But Isa…

"Relax Monroe. If I kill you, she'll never forgive me."

I pulled out the box I knew Mr. Santos had. The one he wanted me to give to Isobel and tossed it to Gabriel.

"That is her mother's. Adrianna. He gave it to me. He didn't want to split up their family. But he said he did so that nobody would hurt his girls again. He was afraid if the cartels told their Stateside counterparts they would go after Evie. Or Isobel. So he left and hid and split his family apart. He still loved Adrianna and Evie. Isobel's middle name is her mom's."

My voice shook and wobbled. Like some fucking coward.

"Everything he did was for them. He still loves them."

And I loved her.

I loved her so fucking much it tore through my fucking heart to give anything to Gabriel.

"I'm giving you this, because I want you to know I fucking hate you for making me break my promises. You have always made it hard for me to hate you. But this time—I do. I hate you. I hate William. I hate every-one. But *her*."

Mr. Santos saved my life and condemned me into another spiral.

I did love her. I had always loved her. I couldn't look at Gabriel.

"I can't keep my promise to the man who saved my life. I'm changing my name back to Sullivan. Not just for the Hagen assignment, but losing William made me realize I was *never* a Santos. I'm so fucking pissed at him for what the fuck he did."

"Everything you did—" Gabriel began.

"Has *always* been for her." I finished. "It will *always* be her."

I felt him move. "You're giving me your blessing."

I finally turned to Gabriel Monroe. Wheat—hair. Pale eyes glowing still as he looked at me with wonder in them.

I knew what I had to do.

"I want you to marry her. You have my blessing. Don't fuck it up. *If you do, if you hurt her ever—"*

"I would never hurt her—"

"I will put a bullet in your brain."

I was snapping at the seams of my sanity.

"I promised. *You* are the reason I am breaking that promise. *If anything happens to her, I will kill you. If anything happens to you? I will keep my promise."*

5

MELINA

I TRIED TO BLOCK OUT EVERYTHING I COULD.

I did.

But it was impossible. I felt everything. The metal, the rope burns, the taste of blood in my mouth. My entire face felt swollen.

One of them pointed at us in one corner. "*O'Hara's cut.*"

But my hell was just beginning. We were branded like cattle, the searing of my wrist making me and all the other girls shriek as pain like no other dug into my body. The smell of it made me gag and I wanted to scream even after it was over.

Mama, lo siento.

A boot connected with my face and then my back in sheer agony I laid there. Later one of the girls told me I had been thrown like a sack of flour into the sides of an eighteen wheeler. I wasn't human anymore.

When I woke up, I had a headache the size of my fist growing in my skull and it felt like my head was splitting open. The world was dark and the sensation of fear was back as I began to shake.

Breathing hurt and I felt disoriented like I was seeing everything through a fog. Like I was in trouble but I didn't understand why.

Mama is worried about me.

"They said they're taking us to New York," one the girls whispered. "Better than their Chicago location…"

"How do you know this?" Another girl asked.

The other girl shrugged. "I heard one of the on their phones…"

I couldn't stop shaking. The bone deep chill in my body was there, but I didn't know where Catalina was.

"What's going on?" I whispered. I could barely see anyone.

When we got to New York the back of the truck opened up and the rest of it was a blur. We were quickly taken to a backroom inside of a bigger building. Women were already there and they were dressed up in outfits. Some of them fancier than others.

Glitter and sequins and gowns that swept the floor. But the surroundings were filthy.

"Come, come," a taller woman with platinum blonde hair and high cheekbones came out. "We are going to clean you girls up." She didn't seem the least bit happy about it but I couldn't understand much of what she said in her thick Eastern European accent.

My eyes were stunned by the colors. *What is this?*

"I don't even think half of this pile speaks English, Daniella," one of the guys said.

But some of us did. None of the girls spoke up. These men weren't like the men who brought us here. They didn't bother touching us. Instead, they just instructed the other women to clean us up.

I got my first shower and then I was fitted into a dress.

"What is happening?" I asked one of the girls who worked there.

My wrists still burned as the hot water touched it. The shape taking form now a shamrock.

"This is Teaser's. This club is owned by the O'Hara family—" *The O'Hara's. That's who I belong to?* "And now, we make you pretty. Not too hard. Your picture looked pretty." And then when she took me out to the mirrors and dresses, she pointed to the side of the mirror where I saw the photos of me.

Taken a few...

"How many days has it been?" I whispered to Daniella.

She shrugged. "I do not know when they took you. I got that photo three weeks ago."

Three weeks?

"Don't worry," she said brushing my hair out in my towel while other girls sat around me doing the same. I was shaking and I couldn't focus. All the lights, the movement, everything felt like it was happening with the flutter of wings.

We were carted up and out the door and outside to a floor where a group of men sat. An older man with dark inky hair and deep amber eyes sat at the center talking to them as we were paraded out.

I didn't understand, but deep down I did. We were cattle. And I was being sold. For people to do God knows what with me.

"How much do you want for them?" One of them called out.

Someone else said a number that sounded too big to be real.

And one by one, I saw how the entire line up was pulled apart with girls crying and screaming.

I stayed perfectly still as one of them, the one with deeper amber eyes came around to me. He was in charge. I knew it.

"Cormac, what do you wanna do with this one?" One of the guys called out. I didn't move. I didn't move. Afraid he might do something to me if I did.

"Well, aren't you a tiny little thing," he made a noise with the flick of his wrist and I was carted back. "She'll do fine here."

I learned to stay still. To not do anything as two girls brought me back to the back rooms. Silence was safety now. Anyone making noise was going to get caught. Anyone doing anything was going to struggle.

I couldn't do that.

"Cormac likes you here," Daniella said with her eyes on me, a few of the other girls turned to look at me. "This might be good for you since he is charge." Cormac O'Hara was the reason why I was here?

And another girl said to me. "We should call you Isabella or Bella. Since you're pretty."

I swallowed realizing what was happening. But maybe staying inside of this club wasn't as bad as being around the other girls. Was it?

The next day Cormac called me into his office with Daniella and motioned to a man in a suit. Older, blonde, with features that had once maybe been handsome but now cruelty carved them into something darker. His blue eyes lighter like the ocean were cold as they took me in with a hungry expression.

"He'll take her for a few days." There was ice in Cormac's voice. And that was when I felt panic for the first time. "Charles. She's all yours."

"It's okay, you'll be back," Daniella let me go and I saw the man moving towards me. "Mr. Devereaux is nice man."

No. I don't wanna go. I don't know why I froze or why I followed.

"At least she's more obedient than the others," Cormac said. "She's trainable."

I wanted to scream at the word obedient and trainable but I learned my lessons as the man's grubby hands took me outside.

To his town car in the freezing New York cold still dressed in a thin gown as he pushed me into it. I had never been to the States before. Or even left my town. Now I was here?

"You'll do just fine as long as you don't scream too much," he said casually as he got into the car. He looked entirely too rich and too comfortable as I looked around at the leather seats, the privacy window between us and the drive. Maybe to some it would be a nice car—but to me it was a cage.

"Cormac says you're well behaved. Do you understand anything I'm saying?"

He smirked at me and I felt the urge to throw up.

"No? You don't?" He laughed then looking annoyed. I did understand him but I was in shock. He poured himself a glass of something—alcohol —as he spoke. "All you bitches are only good for one thing anyway."

As he drank I wondered where we were going. And why I would be gone for a few days. I would be back right? To this place he took me from.

I would have to come back right? They said they were expecting me back. Daniella said I would be back.

I needed to go back. I felt panic rising as I kept repeating it.

Mr. Devereaux—that was his name—sat back in his seat eyeing me as his hands went to his pants and I froze a little.

"You understand this, don't you?" I did. He undid his pants never taking his eyes off me. "Get over here."

I didn't want to though. I was terrified.

I didn't want to be around him. He swore a little taking another sip of his drink. And then he surprised me by pouring me a glass. I shook my head but he reached out and grabbed my throat.

And then he poured the contents of it down my mouth when I gasped.

It burned and I gagged the entire time as he laughed a little at my struggling.

"Don't worry, I'll break you in and turn you back to Cormac the best show pony he's had."

He grabbed my hair painfully twisted it back as he threw me to the floor of his car. I scrambled up or I tried to before he threw me down again and he was on top of me in another second. An animal noise left me then as he held me down by my throat and tore at my clothing.

I couldn't stop making noise then as he slapped, punched and beat his fists into me.

I didn't remember anything after that.

❧

I DID COME BACK IN A FEW DAYS WITH DANIELLA CHECKING ME OVER. Putting makeup on my black eyes. My split lip.

"His friends are not so nice," she said conversationally like it was normal for girls to go through this. I felt nothing but numb after the first night with Charles Devereaux. He did have a lot of friends and some in not so good places of life.

I got the feeling they got away with everything they did with how they treated me.

"But I put some makeup on you and you look pretty again and then you can go out and work."

I swallowed feeling the way my lips and throat hurt. Teaser's was a nightclub with burlesque. A fancy word for expensive strippers here. All the girls catered to high end clientele like Charles Devereaux.

"Cormac likes you because he thinks you will bring in money," Daniella applied lipstick to the parts of my mouth not messed up. I wanted to set myself on fire and bleach myself raw from what they'd done to me. "Mr. Devereaux paid good money for you since you were a virgin. This is normal here."

I shook wildly but unlike the other girls I was fond of playing dead. So I did. For months.

If I thought the wilder animals in those houses were dogs? Turns out rich men were much worse.

Especially when men who did not like women—had women like me. I learned men who hated women used them the most. To make up for things they couldn't have.

One night, I had been in a group of four that they said I had to dance for. They could do whatever they wanted if they paid enough to the girls at teasers.

I knew I was in danger when one of them slapped my back with his rings on. And then he did it again and again and a noise left me.

I swallowed with fear as he threw me onto the glass and began ripping my clothes and I waited for the moment he would hurt me—but it never came.

My head turned to the side to see a man standing there holding a gun to the man on top of me.

"Easy, O'Hara," the man on top of me said. "We was just having a good time."

"You can have a good time somewhere."

O'Hara? For a second I thought it was Cormac. But he would never be like this. It wasn't. This man's eyes were brighter. His hair darker and he

44

was younger. He resembled Cormac and I wondered if he was his son. He was close to my age. Although because I didn't know the date or time—I didn't know what had happened.

"Get out," he said without looking away from me. "All of you—"

"We paid for this bitch—"

"Not enough." I don't know what he did but I curled into myself as all of them were escorted out.

He took off his shirt and dropped his gun as he looked down at me with an unreadable expression, and I thought for a moment this man would continue what the previous one started. Instead he dropped it down on me leaving him in his undershirt.

He said something to me I didn't understand and with a flick of his wrist he motioned to the other guy to help me.

They obeyed him.

Cormac's son.

"Aidan, where do you want her?"

"Boss, you want them banned?"

"Back in her room, yes."

Aidan. O'Hara.

He shrugged lightly like he didn't care but I saw him struggling with himself like I disgusted him. I looked down at my hands wondering why Cormac's son saved my life.

Shouldn't he be like his father?

6

LIAM

I FINALLY HAD THE COURAGE TO GO UP TO ISOBEL.

It was at work but otherwise, I didn't see her anymore.

Not since she became Gabriel's world. She lived and breathed him.

Now? We sat in my car and I apologized. "I'm sorry." I felt my heart shattering to tiny little pieces as she looked at her lap like she didn't even recognize me. And that gutted me the most because she had no idea.

She never would know.

I fucking knew Gabriel would never tell her.

"You should not have kept that from me. It doesn't matter what Papi wanted."

"But it does," I said. "It does. Because he knows you just like he knows me."

And he knew I was in love with his daughter. Some part of me ached at that because if Mr. Santos had fucking told me years ago? I would've taken my shot with Isobel. I would've done something about it. I would've *tried*.

Now? What the fuck could I do?

"I'm sorry," I cleared my throat. "I thought he would be okay. I went to go shower thinking he just wanted to rest..." Oh fuck. I was snapping now. I couldn't see properly. I had been holding it back for so long.

"The doctors said it was an epidural hematoma. The short version is... his brain was bleeding. I woke up...he was cold...I called an ambulance."

I was shaking harder now.

I let her down too.

I fucking let everyone down.

I couldn't stop shaking. "I'm sorry." And then she was wrapped around me holding me tighter.

"I'm not angry with you. I'm not." She was crying harder.

Dimly I was aware of saying that I didn't think about the CT scan. I went to shower...I should've been there...I should've...

"But you couldn't stop it—Not your fault."

I didn't hear her at all. At all.

And it was no surprise Gabriel wasted no time in making sure he took what was his when I watched the two of them get married.

I walked her down the aisle, the entire time the fire pit in my chest burning alive.

I was Gabriel's best man. Isobel and Gabriel joked I was her maid of honor and best man.

Which made sense. I saw their matching necklaces I gave to them. Instead of a ring Gabriel proposed with necklaces. His was a geometric key with her name on it. Hers was a necklace he'd gotten to fit her mother's ring inside.

When it was all said and done?

I got to see her happy and I realized as much as I loved Mr. Santos, I loved her more.

I took photos of them when they got married.

"Now come on. Let me take a single photo of the two of you. It's your damn wedding day. Monroe, look at you—shit. I can't call you just Monroe anymore, can I?"

Isobel smiled ear to ear and her canines flashed. "That's Mrs. Monroe to you."

I rolled my eyes playfully ignoring the burning in my chest.

But even as I watched them and played along? I found despite feeling like I betrayed Mr. Santos—I didn't betray the two of them.

I meant what I said—if anything happened to her, because of him? I would kill him.

∼

IT WASN'T LONG AFTER THEY GOT MARRIED, WE GOT THE WORST NEWS WE could get.

Isobel called me upset. Gabriel wasn't known for taking easy assignments in the CIA. And Isobel and Gabriel had never told a soul about

47

their relationship—not just for him, but for her. They were going to keep it a secret and until she was out?

Nobody was supposed to know.

So when Isobel broke the news to me that we were suppose to go hunt down a potential terrorist in New York.

Marcus Hagen.

Dangerous. Deadly. And someone we shouldn't have been fucking around with in the first place. So when Gabriel came home and found me there he didn't even look surprised.

"Amor," Isobel stood on shaky legs and went to him. But as he held her his eyes met mine and I knew he didn't have any good news.

But him breaking the news that his fucking mentor Koller, in the CIA wanted us to swap Claire Sutton for Kourtney fucking Young.

I lost my ever loving mind.

"They can't do that!" I was going crazy in the CIA. "Koller's fucking insane! Sutton for Young? What the fuck! I fucking told you man. I fucking told you. Fuck this place. They don't give a fuck about their people."

I saw the way Gabriel's face fell.

"Gabriel." I would never call him by his first name until now. "Don't do it."

I saw Isobel watching me.

"Don't do it." I shook my head. "I did research on Hagen. I picked up briefings where they dissected him. He's good at what he does. I think he's got a team. We can't do this. We can't go in there without backup."

"What do you want to do?" Gabriel looked at me with wild eyes myself. "You want me to quit? Koller said they would replace me if I did—"

"*I want us to quit!*" I shouted. "*Leave! Leave tonight. Quit. Leave Quantico!*"

"*I can't!*" He shouted back. "I can't leave! I can't leave you two!"

"*You wouldn't! We go with you! The end!*"

"*What?*" Now he looked at me in disbelief. "You want to walk with me?"

Was he insane?

"I have Oracle. We can set up Titan. We can get it all together. Isobel and me—" I motioned to Isobel. And her jaw dropped. "We can do it. We can all leave. Let's go. It's next week."

"You're insane too," Gabriel whispered. "*I can't walk away from all of this. This is my life.*"

"Kourtney Young for Claire Sutton. And you are still wondering if this is your life?" I tapped my temple with two fingers. "You're the only one that's insane here, G."

"Stop it!" Isobel got between us. "Both of you!"

She was shaking, her hands trembling over her stomach.

"We can talk about this," she was trembling as both of us looked down at her. "We don't need to fight about this. It isn't as simple as walking away or staying. You both know it. Both of you sit down. Just because Young is on the team doesn't mean we all die."

She looked at Gabriel. "You need to breathe. Get some air. Breathe. You are still a leader and you are in charge. Even if she does something stupid—the only person who will die is her. Jeremy and I would never let anything happen. And you—"

When she turned to me? I saw something in her eyes I hadn't seen in forever. A steel in them I recognized from when we were kids.

"Stop screaming at him. He does not know everything and this is his entire life, you are asking him to leave all that he knows for the unknown, that decision isn't made in a day."

Isobel didn't look good at all. She was breathing harder and Gabriel reached for her hand. "Baby, sit down."

I realized I must've pushed her. "That's true. I'm not trying to freak you out. I know it's a big choice. If you can handle Young on your team— we can do this. I'll be there. Jeremy is solid. A baker. But solid."

I didn't believe it for a second.

Kourtney Young was a fucking cunt. And she was the type of person who got everyone killed. Isobel leaned into Gabriel shivering.

"It's one assignment," Gabriel said out loud. "I don't want Young anywhere near us."

"But maybe with her father watching it'll make her..." Isobel started. "More...better?"

I shared a look with Gabriel. No. She would still be an absolute fucking cunt.

Gabriel looked at me. "If we do this successfully, you can start Titan without a fucking argument from the world. Everyone would know you. You did it. If we leave now—we get nothing."

"You're saying we either enter a suicide mission or we dip out now and get shit."

He nodded. "If you leave now? It means fuck all if your reputation is blacked out by the Agency. Does that make sense? Nobody will work with Titan Security with cowards."

"So Koller put you in check," I said as I looked at Isobel who just looked a little dazed.

She nodded then slowly. "Gabriel is telling the truth." She looked at me. "Even Oracle cannot stop the Agency from bad mouthing you or Gabriel. The two of you cannot walk away. And even if I did, we would always be known for this. People talk. That will never stop."

I was beyond angry. I was fuming so much I could feel the steam coming off me. "Fuck this."

"Agreed." She whispered. "This world is small. Walking away from critical assignments is bad."

Gabriel chimed in. "It's career suicide. It's a security risk, it shows nobody can trust us, we abandon our duty, we abandon our team. The Agency could flag our clearances and now we got shit to work with. And now we have unofficial black marks that follow us if we choose not to do it."

Isobel watched him warily. "Amor."

"Sorry, baby," Gabriel murmured looking like someone was ripping his heart out. And it probably was. No fucking way he wanted to be a newlywed man going into the unknown with his wife.

Gabriel wasn't wrong. We were damned if we do—damned if we don't.

His eyes met mine full of pale ice and concern. Nobody had eyes like that saw through my soul like he did. He rubbed Isobel's back as he spoke.

"In order for you to start Titan," Gabriel whispered to me. "You need reputation. Professionalism. Credibility. Not this. You can't run. They're counting on it. If you do? It'll destroy your entire life."

"So I'm fucked if I go on this assignment and fucked if I don't."

"Exactly."

"Both of you stop." Isobel stepped in, her voice was calmer than ours. "None of us know what will happen on this assignment. None of us. For all we know? In a few days? We will go. Everything will work out. We'll come back and be good. It'll be okay. We go. We watch each others backs. Gabriel will be fine. Liam you can go start Titan Security. And I will..." her eyes looked at her lap. "I'll be here too. All of us."

Her eyes met Gabriel's. "It'll be okay, amor. We'll be okay."

And I certainly fucking hoped it would.

Even if my gut was churning.

7

MELINA

Cormac O'Hara was a monster.

But Aidan…was not.

"He does not sleep with anyone in here," Daniella mentioned casually.

"Even if we get him to try," Tracey, another girl added.

Lin, an East Asian girl spoke up. "He's saved our asses couple of times, but you know the apple doesn't fall far so we're all taking bets on how long before he goes dark."

I peeked through one of the windows to watch him today. I was tiny enough to slip into the sides of the room and watch him in the alleyway smoking.

He looked like the world was on his shoulders as I peered out at him when I came to the back for water.

I didn't know how long I'd been here. Sometimes the girls got newspapers, but for the most part—we didn't have phones.

We slept on the top floors of Teaser's in cots. And nobody really left the club. This was my entire life.

I didn't feel like the girl I was.

I didn't know how I felt and I numbed myself out. Some of the girls took drugs and they offered it to me, but I didn't like how it made me feel. I watched Aidan through the cracks as a man approached him.

Someone in a ball cap I couldn't see and Aidan looked around to make sure nobody could see him.

I supposed nobody could, but me. I watched him talking to the man and he passed him some files.

Confused, I watched for longer as they talked and Aidan nodded over and over. Finally, the man left and Aidan ran both his hands through his hair. He blew out a breath and if I didn't know any better, his head turned and looked right where I was staring and I ducked. He couldn't see me through the slats. I was too small.

But when I peeked again he was still looking.

I hid from him.

A few days later, I found out why Cormac O'Hara was a monster. A big one. He stormed into the backroom with two of his men. And Aidan. We were in the middle of changing when he came in and everyone froze.

I watched him look around the room. "Which one of you bitches is working with a Fed?"

With what?

"Which fucking one?" He swiped at the counter vanity of one of the girls who yelped. His face was mottled red. *"Which one of you fucking bitches tried to run from me?"*

I didn't know what was happening and I hid halfway behind a mirror as he grabbed up Tracey by her hair and she screamed. "Was it you? Should I break your fucking fingers off so one of you bitches talks?"

Aidan stood stone—faced as he focused on a point on the wall. And somehow his eyes scanning landed on me. Like he saw right through me. I lowered my eyes and focused on the floor as Tracey screamed a little.

"Who the fuck was it!"

Cormac drew his gun out. And I saw Aidan react then paling.

"I don't think it was them," Aidan said low. "Maybe one of them fucked the cop, but I don't think they're smart enough to fuck with you." He motioned around the room contorting his features. "You think these stupid bitches can outsmart you?"

My stomach twisted at the way Aidan spoke. He was just as cruel as his father. I was wrong about him. Just because he had helped me once? I was right—he was disgusted by us. He did think less of us.

He didn't think we were worth any dignity or respect.

I didn't think I was worth anything either anymore.

Cormac's features twisted as he nodded at Aidan. "Fair. Nah. They won't." And then he turned and he held the gun to Tracey's head. "You see or say anything out of the ordinary and you'll be the first one I take out. Don't forget, not a single one of you bitches are worth anything. You're just as replaceable as the next lot."

When he left I stood there as Aidan's eyes roved over mine.

Did he know I watched him? Did he know I saw him…

"What is a Fed?" I whispered to Daniella.

"Federal Agent...like police but for the country. Cormac's business is not on paper—so he gets nervous. This is normal. You will see. He has been nervous since his son has been taking over—he is paranoid..."

"Yeah, and his son's no doubt fucking just as cruel," someone else chipped in.

A federal agent...

"What does this Fed look like?" I asked.

"They come undercover," Daniella explained. As in looking like everyone else, but she thought Cormac was paranoid someone was passing information about Teaser's out to them.

I froze.

No.

Aidan...no, I must've been seeing something. He just insulted us. He wouldn't betray his father...would he?

I ignored the gut feeling I had and kept on with my day. A few nights later I was walking out of the bathroom when I caught Aidan standing outside. One of his eyes were black and his lip split as he looked at me.

"You saw me," he whispered. His amber eyes locked on me. "You know something."

Aidan didn't know me. I forgot he didn't know anything about me.

"No hables ingles..." I whispered shaking my head and not moving.

I did speak English. But he didn't need to know.

Even Cormac thought I rarely spoke and I tried to play dead enough to know to survive even if this place scared me.

His eyes were hard on me. "If you say a fucking word to anyone—" he broke off not finishing his thought.

He looked away his expression tight. I wondered if Aidan O'Hara was like Mr. Devereaux. Cruel and brutal and Aidan was no doubt stronger.

He looked down at my hands which had started shaking and he let me go shaking his head. "Get out."

He made a motion with his hands and I scrambled back practically running out to the floor.

I caught a glimpse of myself in the mirror and I didn't recognize the haunted eyes staring back at me. I didn't know who that girl was. My eyes were black, shadows under them and cheeks hallowed out.

What had happened to me?

I didn't know what day it was. The time. I was just ordered do things with people I didn't know.

And this was my life…was Aidan working with the Feds to take his father down?

If so, was Aidan not like his father at all? It made me wonder if he said the things he did so that his father wouldn't have shot us.

Sometimes I thought about my parents. Sometimes I wondered if they looked for me. Every time I thought about them, my eyes burned and I felt like crying again. I wondered how long they search for me because they certainly didn't find me.

I never should have searched for fame.

For the lights. I never should've left with Catalina that morning. I never should've lied to Mama. Even if I left the phamplet with her she would know where to find me. Or look for me.

I bumped into Aidan a few times after that almsotlike he was paranoid of me. I kept my head down and a few times Aidan stepped in if someone was doing too much.

Other time Aidan wasn't there.

Sometimes those days were the worst.

It almost felt like when he was here, it operated differently because his father trusted him to keep things in order. When his father was here, it was like everyone in the club knew that they could get away with whatever they wanted to.

I felt like a butterfly pinned behind glass.

The men who usually got me didn't want to be gentle. They wanted to degrade me. It was a word I learned from Lin—who was the only East Asian there.

"We remind them of lesser things," she told me one night. "Like maids, like their servants—women they dream of but cannot be with. Some of them hate us for whatever reason. One time this man made me speak in Vietnamese to him only for him to hit me and tell me I had to forget it." She shrugged. "Men are monsters. Who knows why they have the fetish they do?"

The girls here had their own stories. Traumas. Tales of modeling dreams and becoming actresses that turned into this.

I wasn't special. I was one of hundreds of girls who were trafficked. Cormac O'Hara was a big shot. His syndicate was full of drugs, sex, and enough crime to make a normal man lose it.

"You get treated the worst," Lin said softly. "Sorry, kid."

I shrugged. It didn't matter. I was learning to numb it out.

If I thought too hard about anything—it hurt too much to function. I thought about running away sometimes, but I didn't know New York.

That was the point.

They brought girls from unfamiliar environments to this place and transported girls from this environment to places where I came from. The flow of goods was always moving.

I had been turned into less than human.

I was a thing.

"When is Aidan coming back?" I whispered to Lin.

She shrugged. "Sometimes Pops sends him to Chicago. Thats where the O'Hara's are based out of. He's got son's. Treats 'em like shit. You saw his—Aidan's face—before he left? We aren't the only people he shits on. I was downstairs when I saw Cormac laying into him."

I didn't know that.

Was that why Aidan was talking to the Feds?

Because he was just as much a thing as we were?

I didn't know. I just knew I was trapped for another night as Teaser's.

8

LIAM

New York was off putting to say the least.

I was walking around like I was hot shit when I felt like shit.

Nobody like somebody who didn't look like they didn't fit in.

Isa and I had grown up in Connecticut and this was all new for me. But I found I fit right in. I wore all black, looked the part, and I had a day to breathe.

I wasn't happy about this operation doll.

I was pretty fucking pissed at Gabriel for even letting it happen.

It wasn't his fault, even if he ran command, I knew that he was just as much of a bitch as everybody else was.

We were all slaves to the agency. And at the end of the day, didn't really matter what the fuck we thought we were gonna end up having to do it anyway.

I knew I was on edge. I knew I didn't look like myself. Jeremy and Isobel spent more time together. She didn't look good either. Pale, a little off and uneasy. But I blamed it on Kourtney being on this op.

Kourtney—this fucking cunt. I knew all about Kourtney. Way more than Isa knew.

I knew Kourtney because at the gas station when I'd stopped to get snacks for me and Isa before we got to Quantico, Kourtney had been the one a bunch of guys said she was giving blowjobs to whoever paid her enough.

That's how I met her.

I heard a lot of stories about Kourtney Young.

How she made fun of sexual assault victims and spread rumors about them in training.

How she made fun of brown women despite being one herself.

How she catered to anyone who wanted to fuck her. Like it or not—in government work Kourtney Young wasn't an anomaly.

She didn't hide anything though because men catered to women like Kourtney.

Not me.

I did blame myself, though for her, not liking Isa. I had been ice skating privately. Secretly. And she'd been out one morning. I was just getting my legs warmed up and she'd shown up.

I wasn't expecting her to talk to me.

Throw herself at me.

But she did.

I turned her down and she brought up the fact that I was fucking Isobel. Who everyone thought was my sister on paper.

I'd rather fuck Isa any day than an STD ridden cunt like you.

Not my best. But I wasn't about to tolerate it. She hadn't taken well to it—and that was the day. Gabriel had saved her ass. Isa just didn't know it.

I think I put a target on Isa's back. And now Kourtney wouldn't leave her alone.

That night I was restless. I couldn't sleep. Something about this operation is getting under my nerves and it wasn't Kourtney. Maybe. I didn't know. I found myself walking around highly rated. It was supposed to be burlesque and I thought a stripper or two wouldn't really hurt that night.

I could pay for sex if I was desperate.

And so I walked into Teaser's.

The entire place looked a little bit beat—up but with muted colors, loud music, and flashing lights—how could I fucking tell?

I got to the bar and sat down as a platinum blonde served me drinks.

"You want some company tonight?" She asked me in a thick Eastern European accent.

"Sure, why not?" I didn't think twice about it. I thought she was talking about herself.

To my surprise she motioned to the floor and I didn't know if I should follow her lead or go with her. I saw a tiny woman sitting on the perch of one of the couches and if she felt the blonde she turned her head.

I blinked a little. She was cute. Long inky hair, dark eyes—Latina. I knew her a mile away. Not just Latina—*Mexicana*.

Caramel skin. Doe eyes a little innocent and wary. Her features were delicate and youthful, and she was way fucking younger than my twenty —three. But it was her hair, long and thick and dark down to her ass as she stood up and walking over.

I glance back at the blonde bartender who had already moved on passing me my drink just as the little woman appeared those eyes on mine.

I swallowed. Shit. Judging by the way she was dressed? This wasn't just a bar. Not with her clothing. With the lights around her and the way she drifted closer—I wasn't expecting her to be a prostitute.

Shit. I wasn't sleeping with her. Not because she wasn't attractive but because my father's friends still left scars on me. And I didn't pay for sex. Or get paid for it either.

"What's your name?" I asked her. She was tinier compared to everyone here and her eyes held a light to them that everyone's didn't. She didn't look like a dead girl walking.

But she did look sad.

"Isabella," she murmured over the music and my spine stiffened.

No.

I breathed out shakily. "That so?" I eyed her up and down.

Don't do it. Don't you fucking do it.

But I could do it. I could pretend. I could fucking pretend that she was mine even temporarily.

"Isabella," I murmured back. "You wanna do me a favor?"

She nodded, her throat working on me, like she was nervous even if she was closer to me.

"Latina?"

She nodded again although now she looked nervous as her fingers trembled.

"Quiero que me llames 'amor'."

I want you to call me amor.

Her eyes widened as she realized I spoke Spanish too making me grin.

"Amor," she whispered. I closed my eyes a little before opening them as she drifted closer to me. "Pero, su nombre?" *But your name?*

"Liam," I murmured. I definitely wasn't sleeping with her tonight. But it wouldn't hurt for me to pretend she was someone I wanted.

It wouldn't hurt nobody.

"You got somewhere we can be alone, Isabella?"

She nodded and I know I didn't miss her looking nervous and uneasy as she took me to the back of the club, a few of the club goers and guys eyeing us.

Yeah, by some stroke of luck, I definitely wandered into a strip club that pimped out young women.

But I wasn't complaining.

9

MELINA

My heart was pounding out of my chest.

Men his size didn't usually come to Teaser's.

He was bigger, taller, and everyone sized him up as he walked behind me. I couldn't stop shaking at imagining myself being with him because he would break me.

I didn't remember if Aidan was here or not tonight. Because he was the only thing stopping anyone from hurting us.

Liam followed behind me as I led him to one of the back rooms. I shut the door and he sat down in the booth getting comfortable spreading his legs and I thought he wanted me to take care of him.

The moment I sank between his legs though, he reached for me with wide eyes. "Shit, fuck, nonononono, you don't gotta—No, I didn't wanna talk to you out there. I felt like everyone was watching me."

Liam was so strong, I felt it in his fingertips and felt fear sinking into my gut at what he wanted. I didn't understand.

"No, you can just chill, I'm not tryna fuck you."

He looked shocked at the idea and I didn't know what to say. I sat back as he sat there looking a little stunned. Like me. I was processing this man, did not want to use me. Liam was so much bigger than me.

"How tall are you?"

"Six—four. You?"

I chewed my lip. "Not six—four."

His grin was a quick flash, making his eyes twinkle. "I'm not tryna hurt you." And my heart dipped. What was this? Was he…was he playing a game? Because if he was…this was cruel. Liam was confusing.

"Why?" I asked. Unable to stop myself. Everyone hurt me. That's what happened here in this new world.

He frowned then as he motioned around. "I'm not from here. What is this? You turn tricks out here or something?"

What?

His throat worked as he looked around. "I'm not…I'm not trying to fuck you over tonight, I just needed a break from my life." His eyes were green like the forrest, lush, vibrant, and warm as he took me in. "I've been in your shoes before."

At my confusion he smiled. "When I was a kid my father did this shit," he motioned around. "For years I thought it was normal."

Was he saying he had been in similar positions as me? A man as big as Liam? How? It didn't seem possible. As if he could read my thoughts, he smiled. "I wasn't always this big. And when I wasn't I got fucked over a lot."

He blew out a breath. "I didn't realize I was—" he looked around. And then he dropped his voice. "Are there mics here? Cameras?"

I shook my head feeling afraid again and confused. As if he sensed it he shook his head holding his hands out in innocence. "Nah, I'm just checking because I had no idea what this place was. I just got into New York a few days ago with my family. And I just needed a break."

"Why?"

I might as well make conversation if we were sitting here. I didn't know if he was gonna hurt me or not, but he was taking an awful long time if he was.

In the back of my mind I was aware Liam was so big he could break my arms if he tried. But he was just sitting there watching me with a soft look in his eyes.

"I've had a shit year. The woman I fell in love with as a kid just got married. And it wasn't to me. My adopted father died. And I fucked up with him. I don't feel like I'm in a good place and I don't wanna be in New York. I just needed…"

"A break," I whispered. Was he real? Was he true? Was he too good to be true? Men like Liam did not exist here.

Men who came to talk. Nobody came to talk here. Everyone came to try and beat someone's bones in.

My throat worked as I took him in.

"You are here to talk?" I asked him.

He shrugged. "If you want. I'm not fucking you. But I'll pay for your time if you want." He reached into his wallet and pulled out stacks and stacks of hundreds. I blinked at the money in his hand.

He set down a few of the bills under his drink on the table. "It's yours so your boss isn't shit with you. How'd you end up here in the first place?"

I blinked down at the money and then at Liam. He was real. He was... not going to use me.

"You don't want..." I drifted off unsure of what to say as I motioned to my body.

He shook his head looking amused. "No offense, you're like five feet tall. Maybe. I would absolutely break you. And I'm not a fan of hurting women."

As he said it my chest lurched. It actively lurched.

"You are real?"

He smirked. "Yeah. You wanna listen to music or something? Are you allowed to?"

I didn't know. Nobody ever...nobody came back here for music.

He pulled out his headphones and I wondered for a minute if he'd strangle me with them. Some men got off on that. Instead he handed me an ear piece and I slowly put it into my ear.

"You never answered my question," he murmured as he flipped through his phone for songs.

Music.

How long had it been since I heard music?

I shrugged a little as Liam found a song to play, his larger frame next to mine feeling different than other men. I was aware of Liam. "This is my favorite song, well, one of them. But I liked this one as a kid. You like alternative rock?"

"Como?"

His smile was embarrassed. "Right, that's stupid." And I don't know why I smiled with him. "Here, just try it out."

He played a song that sounded like the man was at the ocean with drums and percussion and guitars. I liked it. When it finished Liam looked at me expectantly.

"Bueno."

He smiled a little. "You can tell me if it sucked."

"No, es bueno, pero..." I didn't listen to English music. I told Liam this.

He looked impressed. "You want to listen to something you want?" He passed me his phone. "You just type it into the search." I looked down at the phone in my hand.

At the search bar Liam motioned to, my fingers awkward as I remembered a song Mama played. As I typed I felt Liam's eyes on my brand. The shamrock denoting who I was. What class of person I was.

I quickly hid it and hit play.

"Mami used to play that…"

And as the first note played an emotion unlike any other took hold of me. The first chords took me back to our kitchen in Mexico.

When Mami used to cook and I sat at the table coloring for hours when she did. I felt my eyes well as I ducked my head. The sun filled kitchens, and the crayons against paper, and the simple life—that I snuck away from.

I would never see her again.

I quickly wiped my eyes in case Liam didn't want to see me crying.

"Sorry," he apologized turning the music down. "I didn't mean to make you cry."

I shook my head unsure of what to tell him. He hadn't. I made myself cry. I played something from my old life and as it played Liam's hand came up to my face and I flinched back, the headphone dropping from my ear and he froze.

"Sorry," his eyes widened. "Sorry, I didn't mean to—I know you're scared. I can't imagine what you go through day to day, but I'm not here to fuck you over. I swear." He held out his pinky. "I promise."

What? What did he want me to do?

I moved on instinct linking one of my fingers with his.

My heart was thundering in my ear as he held his phone out to me and the earbud. "Wanna try again?"

I did.

But as I looked down I saw his phone screen.

And I saw the date.

I clicked the calendar instead and Liam didn't snatch it away from me. Instead he looked at me looking at the date.

"This is today?" I asked. Months. Months had passed. "Esto es hoy?"

Months past my birthday. I was eighteen…I blinked back emotions in case Liam didn't want me to cry. I looked down at the date again.

"You don't know what day it is?" Liam's gentle voice shouldn't have hurt so bad but it did.

I shook my head. Or the year. Or the time. There were no real clocks out back. Only people telling us what needed to be done. Strict. Regimented.

My throat worked as I looked at the date hungrily.

Liam was quiet.

"How long have you been here?"

I moved the calendar up to the month I remembered Catalina showing me the brochure. "I'm from Mexico." I pointed to the date. "Here."

His eyes widened. *"You've been here for eight months?"*

Had it been that long? I didn't know.

"How does this place work? Like you don't chose this…"

He didn't know?

Slowly the words formed. "I was…my friend Catalina. She brought me this paper. She said a woman at the market said she was pretty." Slowly, it formed words. Sentences. My story as I told Liam who frowned more and more as I spoke. His massive frame was still as I spoke and I didn't know why I felt comfortable with him.

But I did.

I shouldn't have. He was a man.

I was…this. A thing.

"You were *trafficked…*" His voice dropped and suddenly Liam's enormous body turned to me as he dropped his head. "Who runs this place? What's his name?"

"Cormac…O'Hara. He has a son. Aidan."

Liam nodded. "And you don't…you have family?"

I turned to him suddenly seeing something in his eyes. I told him about Mama and my father. He frowned even more.

"Shit, I didn't know…I mean…I did…but I also didn't. I didn't guess. Fuck. I need to go talk to Gabriel."

Who?

He shook his head at me in disbelief. "Eight fucking months. You…live here. You work here?" And another look entered his eyes. "Your name isn't Isabella?"

I shook my head. "Melina."

His eyes lit up. "Melina suits you way better."

A smile tipped my lips. "Nobody…" It had been forever since someone called me that. My name. "Melina Larissa Mendoza."

That was me.

I was Melina Larissa Mendoza.

"Larissa," Liam whispered a bit of wonder in his green eyes. "That's pretty as fuck. Like Lara. I'd call you Lara in the real world if I knew you."

"Lara," I whispered back. Like it was a secret. He nodded.

"You look like a Lara. And a Melina. But now that you said Larissa? You definitely look like a Lara."

Lara had a pretty ring to it.

He was required for a moment, and he was just looking at me. Not the way men usually looked at me like right before they hurt me but kind of like he saw me as a person. As a girl. As someone worth more than what I was.

Like he saw the girl who ran away to Mexico City to be in a photo-shoot with her friend.

Not...Isabella. The whore.

"I'm sorry," he whispered, his eyes holding mine. "Life is shit. But I try my best to help."

I swallowed. "I don't understand."

"It's cool. G's straight. He'll be solid when he knows."

What?

"What's your name?" I asked again.

"Liam," he smiled at me. "Liam Santos."

Santos?

"Santos?"

Like the Saint.

"I was," he murmured his head back against the headrest. His music playing in one ear. I sat next to him feeling...normal. "Once."

Santos meant Saint.

Saint Liam. I smiled a little then easily.

He didn't want to hurt me.

Liam sat with me for a few hours showing me his favorite bands. I memorized them writing the down on a card and tucking it into my bra. And then he asked me to show him some of my favorite music. I did.

We sat in the back together for a few hours and it felt like the easiest time of my life.

"Why don't you want to sleep with me?" I asked him.

"I do but not like that. Like you're hot. Pretty. Sorry," he admitted looking embarrassed. "But I don't fuck with girls to hurt them or use them." His smile was light. "One day when you're free from here," he motioned. "I can take you out on a date. You ever been on one?"

I was confused. "A date?"

He nodded. "Like I ask you to come to dinner and then maybe a movie —I don't know, I don't date much. But I think that's how it works."

I smiled slowly at him and he mirrored it. "A date."

"A date."

I thought he was teasing and if he was joking, Liam was the cruelest joke life could play on me. What man would want me after this?

His eyes narrowed. "I've been in your position when I was younger. I don't think less of you for choices out of your control."

Something exploded in my chest as he said it and my eyes widened.

"This is not my choice," I whispered.

"I know."

When he left, he passed me a few thousand. I shook my head because I didn't do anything. Liam checked his watch because he said he had an early morning and he was already pushing his time.

"Keep it. Governments got plenty. And Gabriel doesn't mind milking Uncle Sam for cash for us," he murmured. "Something tells me your boss isn't gonna be happy you just listened to music all night. But you can tell them a wild story or some shit."

I liked Liam.

My boss didn't know. I think the girls said Aidan was in house tonight so that meant Cormac was in Chicago and distracted. Everyone breathed when Aidan was around. I told Liam this and part of my chest ached watching him leave. I didn't want him to go.

He watched me carefully as he did. He turned over his shoulder in the room and looked at me.

"Hasta la próxima," he murmured.

Until next time.

Even if some part of me knew like every other man in this place—I would never see Liam again.

Even if some part of me really wanted to see him again.

And I didn't understand what that meant.

Liam was the only man who hadn't hurt me in this new life.

Well, Liam…and Aidan…sometimes.

LIAM

I LEFT LARA AT TEASER'S AND WALKED BACK TO THE HOTEL IN THE COLD AIR of winter.

I knew somewhat of what Lara felt.

I did.

I texted Gabriel about her because I felt for her. I didn't want to leave her. When I left, I saw it in her eyes, she didn't want me to go. My heart ached for that alone.

If I wasn't on an assignment, I would just go back to make sure she was safe, even though I knew she wasn't.

But I had this fucking shit job to do and I told myself that once it was done, Gabriel and I would get her out.

Something about her eyes it made me see a younger version of me. And I don't want her to go through that.

> I just met this girl at Teaser's. It's a burlesque club. On paper. Except…I don't think it's a club, bro.
>
> Her name's Melina Mendoza.
>
> I think somethings wrong here with the club. We can look into it after the op.

Gabriel told me he would.

I gave him all the details Lara gave me and I walked back to my room with a grin on my face. As I walked back to the hotel that we were staying at, I was caught up in my thoughts.

I should've been paying more attention, but it was so late and everything was really quiet so I didn't think anything of it.

My key card beeped me in and the light buzzed green.

The door clicked open and I stepped inside into darkness before I put my key card in and the door closed.

Or at least—I thought it closed. I wasn't expecting it to open and I didn't know who it was.

I wasn't expecting it to be *Kourtney*.

Kourtney Young.

Confused I blinked at what I was seeing. Kourtney. Blood splattered on her clothes. Her hands. But it was the look in her eyes that made me stop.

"What the—" I had a nanosecond to process what the fuck I was seeing.

"Your legs are important to you, huh? *Motherfucker.*"

And then I saw the gun. I saw her aim at me as I stood rapidly trying to duck behind the bed or something. It was complete instinct. I tried to roll, desperate to get behind the bed or move.

I'd always been fast.

I tried.

I did.

But I heard the first shot crack in the air.

One shot rang out after another and I felt a yell leave my throat as I fell. The searing burning pain that blew up inside of me was insidious and dark. I didn't even know where it was hitting me. I just knew that my legs felt like fire.

It came from a place of pure agony as she unloaded her gun into my legs. I screamed.

I couldn't do anything else.

$\sim$

GABRIEL BURST INTO MY ROOM AS I GROANED IN PAIN. THE DOOR CRASHING open again and for a moment I panicked thinking it was Kourtney back to finish the job.

"Liam, what happened?"

The amount of agony I was in was incomprehensible. And my only concern was why he was here. Not with Isobel. We had to find her. He was alive. She might not be.

Isa. I promised Mr. Santos.

I broke his promise.

I broke it.

"Gabriel" I sounded possessed. *"Kourtney...* My leg, I can't feel it. She was here." I was mumbling incoherently. The agony was ripping through my legs and I felt like death would've been easier to tolerate. Death was quicker. And Kourtney was a fan of torture.

She wanted me broken. I didn't know why she was covered in blood and part of me wondered—if she killed Isobel before me.

"Liam. I gotta find her. Let me call for help."

I didn't even understand anything he said.

"I need an ambulance!" I barely heard Gabriel.

"Mr. Santos..." I whispered. "Dad...Dad I'm sorry...I fucked up..."

Liam. Gabriel is here. I heard his voice in my head. Gabriel. Isobel.

It took the effort of every single thing I had, every molecule of energy to grab Gabriel's collar to look at him.

"I can't feel my legs. Find her. I'm scared. Kourtney—find her! Find her!" I groaned. Dad. It hurts so bad right now. *"Gabriel. It hurts so fucking bad right now—"*

"I can't leave you—You're my brother!"

"She's your wife!" I screamed. I was delirious. *"Find her! I promised... Dad...I'm sorry, I promised. I swear—I didn't mean it..."*

I was gone.

"She's my girl too. She's my—I promised him. I promised him." I was sobbing. I was gone. "Go find my girl."

And even as he ran away I fucking prayed to God I lived through this night to tear Kourtney limb from limb for taking this from me.

∼

WHEN I WOKE UP—I WAS IN QUANTICO.

I knew because I knew the hospital.

And I couldn't feel my legs. Claire Sutton was sitting to my right, her eyes rimmed red and her hands clasped as I woke up and she rushed to my side.

"Liam," she brushed my hair back. "It's okay."

I moaned low feeling the pain hit me.

"It's okay, it's okay," her cornflower blue eyes held mine. "I need to call the doctor..."

I passed out. I was in and out and every single time, I couldn't feel my legs. Sometimes Claire iced them. Sometimes, she was there feeding me and crying.

"It's okay," she brushed my hair back. "I'm sorry, Liam."

It took me a few days to come to. The doctor had to explain to me exactly what happened.

I heard it like someone listening to something through a fog.

Multiple gun shot ones. Extensive nerve damage. Major damage to parts of my legs. Joint damaged. Calf muscles shot. And the wheelchair at the other end of the room that gave me a heart attack.

Nobody told me about Gabriel. Isobel. Jeremy.

I looked at Claire who blinked rapidly and wiped her eyes.

"Gabriel...he's still in New York, he's..." she broke off. "Jeremy..." She didn't say a word about Isobel.

She was the only one I cared about.

"I don't know what's happening in New York," she shook her head. "We flew you out to Quantico for emergency surgery. I was assigned here since then."

"Isa..." I whispered.

She shook her messy hair, like she'd been here for days. Her red rimmed eyes blinked again. "I don't know, Li. I'm just here for you."

I laid there feeling the panic crest over me and I had to get put on anxiety meds so I felt nothing for long periods of time.

Claire did everything with me. I barely felt her too horrified by my own helplessness to focus on her.

My day is more together in fragments of morphine dreams and everything felt like I was experiencing it out of body.

And then one day I felt him.

I saw him.

I saw Gabriel. I turned my head to see him standing at the door and the look he gave me?

I knew.

I fucking knew.

I fucking. *Knew.*

He was here alone.

He didn't have to say it. Didn't have to tell me why he was here alone, why he looked like his world had ended.

I closed my eyes and gripped my head, my fingers curling into my heart. I couldn't look at him.

Nobody said a thing.
Nobody had to it.
Isobel was dead.
And so was I.

11

MELINA

A FEW WEEKS AFTER I MET LIAM, A MAN SHOWED UP TO TEASER'S.

Blonde. Wheat hired. Pale blue eyes. He looked like an avenging angel descended from Heaven. And he asked for me.

Daniella motioned him to my section and I didn't know who he was but the moment pale eyes landed on me I realized he might've been the scariest man I'd ever seen.

He held up his phone with a photo of me and Liam.

This is my brother Liam. Do you know him?

He was here to see you? Liam told me you needed my help. Do you need my help?

I can get you out. Get you to Liam. Make you safe.

I can do this. You trusted Liam.

You can trust me. Liam said you are under Cormac O'Hara. Is that the man who did this to you?

It happened quicker than I could comprehend.

One moment Gabriel Monroe asked me for my name and information and the next he left me hunting for Cormac.

Gabriel left me at the top of the stairs clutching a handful of bills.

He didn't take very long. Maybe less than thirty minutes. Maybe more.

I just knew when he came up, there was blood on him.

"Cormac isn't a problem," he muttered. And he motioned for me to come outside.

What was happening?

The next few hours of my life felt like a dream. Because of Liam.

Gabriel gave me his hoodie. It was all black and enormous because he was bigger than Liam.

Gabriel was saying things too fast.

Someone named Vincent. A new name.

He was asking me for a new name.

"Liam…" I whispered. I just wanted Liam.

Where was he?

"Liam isn't here right now, Melina. I need you to pick a name or Vincent will get you one."

What? Why would Vincent get me one?

Liam wasn't here? Where did Liam go?

"When I'm better, you can help me with my Spanish. Where are you from," I said it as I typed it showing her the text.

"Mexico," she blinked up at me. And in that moment as I looked down at her it took everything in me not to cry. My eyes welled a little watching her. "Liam?"

Her eyes watered watching me. "Liam?"

She was like a baby bird. I swore a little moving automatically taking her in my arms without thinking. "¿cómo te llamas?"

What is your name?

She wiped her eyes typing into my phone.

Why do you want me to pick a name?

My hands shook as I typed. "Because this is the first choice you're going to get in your new life. Something tells me you haven't been given many choices." I typed it. I showed it to her wiping my eyes and I motioned to the brand on her wrist. "Choice. You know what that is?"

My fingers shook harder. Liam. Liam gave me a choice. A name.

Lara. *Lara. He called me Lara after my middle name Melina Larissa Mendoza.*

"You wanna be called Lara?" I nodded. "Good shit."

I stared at the photo of Liam on Gabriel's phone. The two of them had a uniform on. Their arms around each other grinning ear to ear. They were friends. Good friends.

But where was he?

I watched the photo of Liam until a woman came and Gabriel motioned for me to go with her. She looked serious faced until she saw me and her eyes softened.

"Hi, I'm Harley," she held her hand out and I gingerly took it.

I looked up at Gabriel who was so tall he blocked out the sun.

"He's a saint," I whispered in Spanish. "Liam's a saint."

He tipped his head. "Harley, call me when she's solid."

The other woman said. "Yes, sir." And motioned for me to go with her to an SUV.

These people they were…going to help me.

And for the first time in forever, I wish I had a phone to take that photo of Liam with me. Because for as long as I was alive I would never forget him,

Liam saved my life. Through Gabriel.

But Gabriel came back for me.

Liam…

I held onto him the entire way to the new place I was going.

12

MELINA

I was convinced Gabriel was sent from an angel. He was a Saint. He had to be. Liam had sent me him.

Gabriel moved mountains to get me everything I needed to become Lara Ford. That was Harley's car. A truck. It sounded American to me.

Everything from Gabriel came through Harley, her red hair gleaming in the sunlight of the new safe house I was in.

She passed me a new passport with my new name—Larissa 'Lara' Ford —after I abandoned Melina Mendoza.

My hands would not stop shaking as I took it from her along with my Social Security card and a drivers license. Everything that I needed in my new world.

"You straight?" Harley asked me pointing to my stuff. "I know you kinda speak English, but I'm afraid my Spanish is shit.

Harley brought clothes and food, she'd point and mime actions, show me how to use the television where I watched the news. The weather. TV shows Harley liked.

"You ever watch Buffy?" She asked me. "She's a badass. I grew up with it." And so Harley and I watched television in between medical examples and doctors.

Through the clinical process I imagined Liam was with me.

I couldn't stop thinking about him and his encouraging smile, and him being the reason why I was free. Why I was here.

I replayed that night in my head every single day I was with Harley.

I imagined his eyes at night, his hands holding me. And for once I wanted to kiss a man. I wanted him the way other men wanted me. I didn't know what happened to Gabriel.

"Gabriel?" I would ask Harley.

She shrugged. "Sorry, lady. Monroe's running around the country but he should be back in a few weeks. Just takes time."

My time with Harley blended together.

She brought me a phone and told me how to use it with patients. She left me alone to heal while she showed me things all around the safe house.

Sometimes I felt like freedom that I didn't really know what to do with and sometimes I just wanted Liam.

Sometimes I had nightmares.

The only thing that I clung to was the card where I wrote down all of the songs, Liam gave me.

I memorized every single band, and I memorized the lyrics, and even if I didn't think I was a fan of alternative rock—I was a fan of Liam.

Every single song I listen to took me back to the moment where he sat next to me, and I could smell his cologne, and I could feel his heat. And how he tapped his fingers.

He just wanted to sit with me and listen to music that night.

And I really wanted to go back in time to experience that.

Gabriel did not say where he was. Just that one day I would see Liam again.

One day.

Some day.

I waited for Liam. Dreamed of him constantly. Hungry for every bit of news I could get.

I wanted to thank Liam for saving my life. For being there for me. Liam had done more for me than I could ever say. His green eyes were in my vision.

I listened to all the music on his playlist for weeks on end while I healed.

Eventually Gabriel did come back but it took him a long time and he wasn't alone. I ran to him. "Liam?"

I felt like a child waiting for him. Waiting for him all the time. Gabriel shook his head looking more tired than ever.

Gabriel was six—five but this man was a few inches shorter, but leaner. Mismatched eyes and the build of a fighter. His eyes—one aqua, one amber—aimed at me and I felt the look in my soul.

He looked like one of the broken dolls at Teaser's, the women around me, and he—looked the same.

"Lara," Gabriel's voice was deep. "This is Killian O'Hara. His father is no longer a problem. But Aidan, you met him at Teaser's he's taken over his father's enterprise—"

For a moment I stiffened wondering if Gabriel was going to turn bad on me now. Or if I was going to be sold again. Or if someone was going to hurt me now that Liam wasn't there.

Terror filled me at that name. The brand on my wrist burning again as it realized another round of pain was coming.

I scrambled back panicking as Harley's eyes widened. "Whoa, easy there lady—"

"No, Lara—" Gabriel's hand reached out like he was approaching a wild animal. "No, Aidan isn't like his father—"

"He's a criminal—"

"Aidan was working with the FBI, to set you guys free, to get Killian out—" Gabriel motioned to the boy next to him who watched me now a little shocked by me. "I promise, he never wanted to hurt anyone, he was trying really hard but he had no power. I gave him connections and information and we took out Cormac. Do you hear me? Cormac O'Hara is dead."

I stopped panicking then as Gabriel explained to me that even if Aidan had worked to take his father out?

He didn't have the ability to take over the family business, and Gabriel didn't want him to become a pawn.

Gabriel spoke his eyes hard. "The Fed's are slow. They take forever to do anything. Putting Cormac in jail is never the solution. So we took care of it."

So Gabriel had killed his father, and had given the brothers back what belonged to them.

"You killed him?" I whispered. Gabriel nodded and I realized he had walked out covered in blood the other day and I knew something had happened. I had been too shaken up, too focused on searching for Liam's eyes.

This was a lot for me to take in as he motioned to Killian.

"I'm training Killian and Kieran, he's the youngest brother and he isn't here right now. But this is Killian. He's old enough to know better and old enough to understand you."

I looked over at Killian O'Hara who looked too lean to be healthy and his eyes held a softer look to them as I realized—he now knew what I was. Or what I had been.

"Neither one of them knew how bad it was." Gabriel looked at me with pale blue eyes. "They were hurt too. Aidan is currently dismantling his father's old empire. Starting new. And he wants the same for you and all the girls he couldn't save. You can go back to your old life, or you can have a new one—the choice is yours."

Gabriel explained that the O'Hara family had resources, connections and things to help me get set up and squared away, but the idea of accepting help from the same blood that abused me left me shaken up.

"You can take your time to think about it," he said. "But Killian is going to work with Harley, under Harley to learn the ropes and help everyone effected by his father."

Killian nodded earnestly like he was trained by Gabriel.

"Start new?" I asked. "Again?"

Gabriel dipped his head. "I'm going to tell you what Harley knows and what Killian is learning—everything from this point on is your choice. Do you hear me?"

My choice.

Gabriel was giving me a choice. To start over. To be better.

"Yes."

~

IT DEFINITELY TOOK ME A WHILE TO ADJUST TO KILLIAN.

I found sometimes he went for training with Gabriel and over the next few months—Killian became bigger, broader, and he reminded me a little of Liam.

But Liam was friendlier.

Gabriel did not mention Liam only that Liam was working on something for himself right now and he couldn't make it.

But Gabriel and Harley took such good care of me with Killian—I knew he wasn't lying to me. Maybe Liam was…doing his own work. Maybe he was helping someone else.

Maybe he was working with Aidan.

My imagination ran wild.

Harley spent her days with me and she asked if I'd ever been to a nail salon.

When I told her I hadn't she took me to one nearby sighing as she sank her toes into the water, her blue eyes lit up.

The ladies at the salon were giggling at how tiny I was compared to Harley who stood at five-ten.

"You ever think about going back to your old life?" Harley asked me causally. "Monroe wants to know if you want."

I shook my head. How could I? I couldn't ever look at Mami again.

The shame filled me as I sat there. I wore Gabriel's hoodie so often that Harley had just gotten me several of them in that size and it swallowed me whole but I loved it.

It was a security blanket.

Harley shot me a sympathetic look. "Guessing your folks don't know or you don't got no folks to go to."

"I don't want to look back," I told her.

Even if it gutted me whole to admit it. I missed Mami so much. Papi was no doubt worried sick. "I have family. A long time ago."

It had been a year of captivity.

A year of unlearning things. Even if I didn't want to admit it?

I wasn't the same Melina I used to be. Even if I wanted to be her. Memories of me and Catalina getting on the bus. Traveling to Mexico City. It came back in flashes.

When the pedicure was gone my hands were shaking too much to stay and Harley took me back to the safe house.

One morning I woke up and heard a familiar song playing from my playlist/Liam's playlist downstairs. In the house.

Excited, I ran downstairs bursting into the kitchen wondering if Liam was here.

It wasn't. Killian stood at the countertop frowning over a broken egg.

"Sorry," he looked over his shoulder cleaning it up. "Got back from training with Gabriel and I was gonna make some food." But it didn't look like he knew what he was doing.

Initially disappointment led me to quiet down.

"What are you doing?" I motioned to his food.

"Trying to make potatoes and eggs," he shrugged looking out of it. Killian was a little prickly as Harley said, but I saw by his arms and legs he was another victim of abuse like me.

I motioned to the music. "You like this song?"

"I like the band, yeah. Gabriel introduced me to them."

Because of Liam.

I saw Liam everywhere. At night he came to me and held me and I cried and told him everything.

I kept a journal in my phone and wrote my letters to him there to keep them saved.

"I can cook." I motioned to the potatoes he was butchering.

He looked almost embarrassed. Killian was taller than me and he ended up just bringing things down from the taller shelves. Becoming my silent assistant.

He did not say anything and I got the feeling Killian hated talking.

Harley came into the kitchen to see what was going on?

I had made hash browns and eggs along with sausage and pancakes. I could cook. As I did, my mind wandered as I cracked more eggs for Harley.

No one rushed me to do anything or pushed me to moving out. I had no skills really. I had just been…a whore.

That was it. And it made my stomach turn to imagine Liam's eyes in my vision.

Saint Liam.

Over breakfast, Killian wolfed down potatoes and eggs and toast like someone was going to take it from him. I knew in little ways he had been abused too. By his father. By the world.

"Where do you want to go today?" Killian sounded uncomfortable with his own voice like he didn't know what to say.

I was turning eighteen at the end of the year. I didn't tell Killian that. I didn't know what I wanted.

"Gabriel, he shut Teaser's down," Killian murmured. "It's gone."

"The entire club?"

He nodded as he motioned to my wrist. "Guessing you're one of the girls who made it out?"

I hid my wrist from him into the hoodie when I had rolled up the sleeves he must've caught it.

"It's all good," he said low looking embarrassed as Harley took us in. She never said anything about what she knew.

"You guys aren't the only people my father shit on."

Killian's throat worked as he showed me his arms where I saw tendrils of scars.

"He liked his knives and his boots. Aidan, me and Kieran went through different things like you."

I glanced over at Harley who drank her juice.

My heart clenched as I realized why Aidan O'Hara might've saved me then. Because he had been imprisoned in a different way.

"Can I…see the club…" I murmured. "Can I see it again?"

"During the day?"

I nodded.

"Sure."

~

KILLIAN TOOK ME BACK DURING THE DAY TO A NOW EMPTY CLUB.

Completely gone. The stage where I had been on display. The back where I had been sold to Charles Devereaux. The seats gone. Now? Without lights or music it just looked like a dump.

"How did you end up here?" Killian asked me quietly as I walked around in his comfortable hoodie.

"A woman came and gave my friend—"

Catalina.

I turned to him. "Do you know what happened to the girls I came here with?" I told Killian everything since it was obvious he was not a bad man, but he was with Gabriel.

He shook his head and swallowed. "I don't know. I gotta talk to Aidan. Ever since Cormac—he's dead by the way. Gabriel—" he made a slicing motion across his throat and my eyes widened. "But Aidan can find anyone. I'll talk to my brother for you."

And so I walked around Teaser's with Killian.

"This place can be beautiful with a makeover," I murmured. "Something else."

I don't know why I didn't want to let it go.

I didn't want to walk away.

Not that being a whore had been my life—but there was something about this place. In a way—Teaser's had saved my life. When Liam came and found me—maybe he could find me here.

"What is burlesque?" I asked Killian who thought about it.

"Fancy strip tease."

My throat worked. "What if you turn it into that?" I motioned around it. "Gabriel is not going to destroy this?"

"Gabriel would set it on fire if he could."

But this place was my identity too.

What if it was possible to make it…better? Different.

I talked to Killian about my idea and he frowned. "I'll talk to Aidan and Gabriel. They'd fund it. And I'd have to see how to make it real. But it's an option." He paused. "If you want to do this, Aidan will speak to you."

81

Aidan.

Who had seen me at my lowest.

I swallowed shaking already and tipped my head. He had multiple opportunities to hurt me—he wouldn't start now.

And nobody mentioned Liam. I didn't ask anyone but Gabriel.

Gabriel sat me down one afternoon when he did come back to me.

"Liam was injured," he told me and I thought the worst. "He's alive. But he's not okay. He won't be able to see you, but I'm here for you. Is that okay?"

I swallowed hard. Gabriel had saved me but...Liam...

"Liam...is...alive?"

"Barely." His eyes were faraway. "But I'm hoping one day he'll come back and find you. One day."

Some day.

Liam.

Saint Liam.

What happened to him?

I asked Gabriel for photos of him. He sent them to me. And I held onto fragments of the saint who took up all the space in my heart.

"One day maybe, Liam will come back..."

Gabriel tipped his head back as he looked at the stage at Teaser's. "If he forgives me," Gabriel's eyes watered full of regret. "I'm sorry, Lara."

I didn't understand. They were friends.

Liam had to forgive him.

"For now, this is yours. Aidan will help. And Killian is your partner. You want it?" He motioned to it. "Some of the girls decided to stay and help you."

He motioned to Liz who stood there eyeing me with wide eyes in a sweatsuit.

To new beginnings.

13

LIAM

Time was relative when you were drugged up and in pain.

I had to *learn* how to *walk* again.

And I never hated anything more than that. I never hated myself so much. There were moments I thought I'd never walk again.

After losing *everything*.

Gabriel never came back. I didn't think he could and I didn't want him to.

The moment I had to sit in my wheelchair—I wanted to die. No more ice skating. No more karate. No more...me.

I needed activity. Otherwise, I'd eat myself alive.

The first time I was in the wheelchair I'd had a breakdown.

I didn't look or interact with anyone.

I couldn't speak to Sutton properly. I didn't know how to. I was angry. To put it lightly.

Each attempt to walk? Was agonizing.

The first eight months I was on nerve painkillers. Most of the time I just practiced walking or I went to sleep.

Sutton had TV shows playing and sometimes she left for work leaving me alone in my own hell. Which was fine with me.

Without Isobel, nothing mattered to me.

Not a single fucking thing.

She was murdered.

Sometimes I have these dreams under medication that I would wake up in my old dorm room, my legs were whole, my heart intact.

And I would across the hallway to her door and she would be there with her sunshine, and she'd asked me what kind of coffee I was craving today just so she could take it from me. And I would tell her about the stupid nightmare I had.

One where Mr. Santos, Gabriel, and none of these people existed in our bubble.

Nobody but me. And her.

And our happiness.

In my dream's she was real.

Not my failures.

Reality always came crushing back whenever I woke up and I realized that Sutton was sleeping in the couch. I had panic attacks. I was hooked up to ninety different machines I lashed out at. I broke down all the time.

"I don't want you!" I'd growl at her. "I don't fucking want you." Sutton would cry and hold me tighter. And I'd snap.

I fucked up, Dad.

Lara.

Isobel.

Mr. Santos.

I failed him the most.

~

GABRIEL MADE IT.

She didn't.

He failed to protect my girl.

And he was gone. Not that I could look at him in the first place. I couldn't look at it. All of my love for her was still there. And now that love was turning into something else. Hatred. For Gabriel.

He killed my Isobel.

If we had never gone on that assignment, and if I had just done what her father had asked me to do, I could have saved her life.

And then it gutted me.

"I could've...saved her..."

I just had to do as he had said. Sutton handed me my bags from the night the EMT's saved me and in it I found Gabriel's geometry key. The one that unlocked Isobel's necklace. The one that I had snapped in my pain. I must've held onto it.

I closed my eyes feeling the agony slice through me at the memory of being his best man.

"I'm sorry, Dad," I whispered. "I fucked up. I gave her away. I'm so sorry."

I begged for forgiveness for weeks.

It was all I thought about. My self hatred ate me alive. Every single time I closed my eyes, I remembered giving Gabriel my blessing. Letting her know that if he ever hurt her, I would kill him. And I would.

I had no doubt Kourtney killed her.

But someone had killed Kourtney. That night. Someone killed Kourtney and Isobel.

I never wanted to see him again.

I never wanted to look at him.

And if he knew?

He never came back.

~

IT TOOK ME YEARS TO PHYSICAL THERAPY TO BE ABLE TO WALK PROPERLY. I'M not because I wasn't trying, but because it was painful having to rebuild your entire body.

Healing was a bitch and a half.

A special place in hell existed for people who lost the use of their limbs properly. That hell was in your head and every single time I tasted blood trying to walk again.

My legs had lost a lot of muscle, and so they were a lot weaker than the rest of my body.

My height made it even more painful to relearn how to walk again and at one point I became almost skeletal in my weight. My six—four frame was the enemy.

In the past I used to be a skater. An athlete.

And now? I was all sharp angles and hollow spaces. Inside and out I felt like someone carved me out. I was alone.

No more Mr. Santos. No more Isa.

Gabriel had left and never came back.

He'd quit the Agency. And he was gone. Vincent had quit. Koller was found murdered. And only Sutton was left. Sutton who went out of her way to be there for me—since I had nothing else in the world left.

I should've been nicer to her. But I for the life of me couldn't summon anything in me anymore.

Walking properly was a joke.

There was nothing proper about the way that my legs were. How weak my knees and my ankles were. Initially every step felt like walking on pins and needles are broken glass.

The doctor's said I was progressing.

I felt like I was existing in a hell of my own making.

Eventually, I was able to leave the hospital and my first night in the apartment that I shared with Isobel—I snapped to pieces.

I finished an entire bottle of whiskey and Sutton found me in the morning, in the bathtub, passed out in my own vomit.

She drove me to my next appointment after cleaning me up and helping me while I snapped at everything. I snapped at everyone. Bitter rage in my veins.

I couldn't walk without crutches or a cane and even then?

My legs were my worst enemy.

My freedom was now my own prison and I knew if I could resurrect Kourtney Young and brutally murder her I thought of all the ways to do it.

Then came the night two years later into my recovery when I needed mostly just my cane—Sutton broke down.

I was four drinks into oblivion, drinking my life away on disability and not eating any of my food. Over the last two years? My body wasted away until I was a skeleton.

Sutton wiped her eyes.

"I'm sorry," she whispered. I don't remember what I said or if we fought. I didn't remember anything anymore.

I just wore the key around my neck.

"For what?"

I could barely talk.

"I told the Director..." Sutton whispered looking at her hands. "I told her...Kourtney went after Isobel..." her throat worked and as she said *her* name—my head snapped up.

Nobody said her name.

Not when I wasn't strong enough to go to her funeral after multiple surgeries. Not when I couldn't stand.

Not when I was a let down.

"Isobel and I were on the phone," Sutton wiped her eyes again. "I told the Director Kourtney attacked her and I got Kourtney kicked off the team. They said she had a mental breakdown because...her father promised her a new car if she did well on the assignment and she wasn't going to get it."

Sutton broke down. "If I kept my mouth shut…everyone…everyone would be alive…I wouldn't…"

Even with the alcohol in me, there was nothing but ice flowing through my veins the kind of cold that burned right into my bones. It singed into my arteries and it stayed there.

For good.

"You need to leave me alone," I managed. "Leave."

Her head snapped up to look at my eyes and whatever she saw there made her look at me like I was the bad guy. And I probably was. I didn't give a shit what she did for me.

Not anymore. Not at all.

Not when she'd been the one responsible for even thinking she would weasel her way into the Director's favor by telling on Kourtney. On the reports?

Kourtney had reacted. I had been interviewed. The footage had been reviewed. No amount of anything could have stopped it.

I saw the entire thing. The only thing missing? Was Isobel. She had been in a blacked out area that let me know—Kourtney and Isobel had died without anyone knowing what had happened.

I couldn't feel anything as Sutton watched me.

"Leave," I repeated. "Or I will fucking kill you."

She did.

14

LIAM

I DRANK AND POPPED MOLLY UNTIL I COULDN'T FEEL ANYTHING AT ALL FOR the next few years.

I lived off disability and being a software engineer.

Turned out my body stopped working but my brain didn't. With my background, I was able to get a remote job and I spent a majority of my time at home getting absolutely fucking lit up.

I made bank.

And then I spent it all.

Drugs were par for the course for me now. I went from nerve pain killers and then to harder stuff.

I did everything I could think of under the sun. Passed out for days wishing death would take me.

Over the years, I became absolutely fucking skeleton and a never—ending cycle of torture.

Getting back into the gym was only after I couldn't get up out of bed some days.

That had been brutal.

So I just did calisthenics at home. Bodyweight was tough, but it was something. I stopped doing physical therapy because I just couldn't take it anymore.

It was funny Gabriel was right about leaving the CIA honorably opened doors I couldn't walk through properly.

Not without my cane that mocked me daily. The constant screaming in my head from my demons was there.

Oracle became my new obsession. Isobel's voice grounding me every step of the way until I realized I was feeding her all my data.

Oracle worked off information. The user would drop all their persona into her and she would become them. Ideally.

Mine?

Stayed Isobel.

It was the only way I heard her voice or when I watched videos of us, some of us at birthdays. Photos of me and Mr. Santos and her.

On the side, I kept doing work designing software and just helping out companies selling my services to the highest bidder because I was good.

The drugs made me even better because I could work longer hours and make more money without a fucking doubt.

I never looked at a mirror anymore, and I didn't even know what I looked like.

In my solitude, I'd find myself thinking about Isobel.

Sitting next to me brushing my hair back and asking me if I ate anything.

Or Mr. Santos moving around the house telling us both to wash our hands. Tell me to go shower. Take care of myself.

I didn't want to.

Everyone left me.

Where was my family?

In dark moments, I grieved.

I did.

It was impossible not to. Did I wish for Gabriel? Sometimes.

Did I know that motherfucker probably didn't know how to talk to me after he killed my sister?

I did.

I was existing in a ghostly world where my family existed and I wasn't the sole survivor of my own hell.

Sometimes I hated myself for Lara the most.

I failed her.

I still remember her hands, her eyes on me. Her hope in them.

And how much I did want to see her again.

But Gabriel was gone. Somewhere—so was Lara.

It took me a year after getting shot to be able to walk properly. It had been four years since that. She might've just been dead. And that was my fault too.

Overtime, my grief compounded with interest.

And all of it morphed into fuel for my anger.

Anger at everyone for leaving me, abandoning me like Mom had, and thinking I could make it without their help.

I needed someone.

Anyone.

Anything.

Somewhere in the space between hungover and passing out—I wondered where Gabriel went. Where he vanished to.

Did he hate me? Did he think about me?

Probably not since Sutton had said he was gone. He had left. I didn't know what happened to him and I couldn't find anything on him anymore. Not even using Oracle.

So he vanished like I vanished.

And when I thought about him?

I thought about her.

I slept in her bed. I drank out of her mug. I existed in my own personal hell where I became obsessed with her. Unable to do shit but be this.

Alone.

Lost.

Afraid.

Dying.

I used to be someone's world.

And I had lost mine. A man who could run, fight, protect the people he loved. A man who hadn't failed so completely at the one thing that mattered.

And somewhere in a grave I couldn't bring my two feet to, William Santos lay disappointed in the son he had chosen.

If I had married her, like he had asked, if I told her the truth, she would be here in my arms. Instead of rotting in the ground she would be here with me. With babies. With her dance studio.

And then one night, I just thought I had enough.

I did.

No amount of apologizing could bring her back.

The night I decided to kill myself I sat in her bed looking at the box of snacks she kept underneath it.

I loaded the Glock with trembling fingers, the weight of it familiar and final. Pressed the cold barrel against my temple as I leaned back against her headboard, surrounded by the ghost of her presence.

I couldn't stop the breakdown that came then.

"Fuck, I'm sorry," I whispered. "I'm so sorry." My hands shook wildly. "I just wanted to love you. I did. I fucked up so bad."

Years of unshed tears finally broke free, wracking my body until I could barely breathe. Through blurred vision, I saw her photos on the walls, her books on the shelves, all the pieces of a life I failed to protect.

The trigger felt like salvation under my finger.

Click.

Nothing.

My heart raced as I tried again.

Click.

The gun had jammed. A perfectly maintained Glock, and it had fucking jammed.

"Fuck!" I screamed at the ceiling, at God, at whoever was listening. *"Neither one of you are going to let me rot, are you?"*

As if in answer, a photo fluttered from Isobel's wall of memories. I recognized it immediately—the day we met, when William Santos brought home a broken boy and gave him a family.

"Isa..." I moved without thinking. "Isa, please tell me that's you."

A chill raced down my spine, raising goosebumps on my arms. If she was haunting me, I'd welcome it. Better her ghost than this emptiness. Better any piece of her than none at all.

That night, when exhaustion finally claimed me, I expected to see her in my dreams. Expecting to see soft caramel eyes and mahogany hair. Expected the woman I'd loved too much, the girl I'd failed to save.

Instead, I saw darker eyes. Haunted eyes. Hair black as night and a face that carried shadows like my own.

Isa?

Not Isa.

Lara.

Why?

Liam?

Lara?

Liam, you are coming back?

I don't know how to find my way back to you.

I can't walk straight.

I'm not a man anymore.

Not anymore.

Why was it *her*?

It took me another two years to leave Connecticut.

Putting my car into storage had been agony. Could I drive? Yeah. I could. But it wasn't the same.

Nothing was the same.

I came with limitations.

I put it away with Isobel's sweater in the backseat, her scrunchie in the cup holder, her little charm still hanging off the dash. Sometimes I swore I smelled her. Except when I did—I kept seeing Lara's eyes in my vision.

And I wondered if I was haunted.

By all the people I let down.

I didn't touch a thing, finally something driving me to leave the apartment we had grown up in. Leave the ghosts behind that I had lurked in forever.

Six years after I lost Isobel—I moved to New York where I could move around better telling myself I would finally face my demons.

I would finally leave Liam Santos behind.

The necklace around my throat burned against my skin with her name on it like a talisman.

All these years later, I never let it go.

And I didn't know how to let her go.

15

MELINA

New York was an enormous city full of possibilities and even though I was not familiar with it, Killian was.

And Killian and I worked to figure out with Aidan how to get the club set up for its main purpose.

To sell sex and bring in money.

But nothing like his father had.

"Move around a little bit," the photographer Killian had hired.

It always surprised me for a man who didn't speak much, Killian was pretty savvy. Standing there with his inky hair and mean looking eyes he frowned whenever the photographer tried to adjust me manually until the man gave up and told me how to move.

The photographer was soft—spoken, but the camera flash still hit me like a nightmare. It was a bad dream I could never outrun.

The white burning against my eyelids echoing memories that I always tried to bury. But I focused on Killian being right there oddly enough on his phone.

At twenty—one now, Killian had gotten even bigger over the years training with Gabriel.

He was working alongside me to learn the ropes of everything he could to become second—in—command of the O'Hara crime syndicate.

Slowly Killian was trying to turn his family name into something not as evil.

Harley had let me stay at the safe house but she wasn't my guard anymore.

"You're doing beautifully," the photographer snapped a few more shots of me in all different variations of lingerie and robes that Killian didn't look at.

I guess I finally modeling now. For Teaser's.

In my own way. Now, they were posters to open up Teaser's and I know it would work out. When the camera stopped flashing, I took off my blue feathered masquerade mask.

Killian stood from where he was and came over to look up everything.

It was odd working with him because in all reality, he should've been the enemy. But over the last few months that I had gotten to know him, I really liked him.

He was two years older than me. But genuinely a sweeter man.

The youngest O'Hara Kieran was chaos.

Absolute chaos and I rarely got to interact with him with Gabriel whipping him into shape.

I rarely saw Aidan who sat in Chicago.

But he wanted to come and see Teaser's sometimes.

Over the last couple of months, my life had completely changed. After spending a few weeks healing from everything that it happened, I needed to move.

I needed to do something with my life.

I couldn't just sit there with no skills.

Maybe it wasn't the career I had dreamed of it in Mexico City, or the future that I once wanted for myself, but sometimes I was real realizing that even if we had to take a detour to our destination—the journey taught us many things along the way.

Once, when I was little, I wanted the spotlight.

I always wanted it.

Killian frowned at some of them. "Can you take thirty more?"

I was exhausted but I nodded.

Killian wanted to do a year's worth of work tonight. In one day. And we could do it.

It meant I just did it one time, and then he used that as advertisement for the entire year just having the photographer adjust it as necessary.

This time, when the camera flashed, I didn't see darkness.

I saw freedom.

∿

I NEVER FORGOT ABOUT LIAM WHEN I STARTED TEASER'S.

The new rebranded one.

I held onto his name like a talisman, tucking him away somewhere deep in my heart where nobody could find him.

Gabriel set up a private security company called Titan Security over the years and he provided us a team mixed with some of the O'Hara's who hadn't been demons—and his own men.

I meet Reed Whittaker, Gabriel's friend.

At six—four Reed towered over me the same way Gabriel did and he wore a complete blacked out jacket as he sat there talking to me about what I needed.

Killian also brought Nathan Wyatt with him, a man who would handle all physical security.

Together, they prioritized everything I wanted. Everything I needed, letting me work on marketing.

Once the place had been renovated, with Killian's help, we got everything set up and I hired dancers and some of the girls from the former Teaser's sworn to secrecy, chose to stay. Choosing to become bartenders or waitresses now and handle the crowd. All of us could.

I took the stage and Liz, out of all people stayed to do the same.

We all promised to never go back and to only look forward.

Liz shook her head in amazement. "I can't believe I'm seeing this."

The place had been decked out in 1920's style glitz and glamour.

I wanted to turn it around completely and I thought it might fit.

"Boss over there looks damn good too."

She motioned to Killian who sat in his dark suit and tie disheveled a little.

Initially, when the girls found out that he was related to Aiden, they have been little bit skeptical, but the more than interact with him and his tattoos *and* his abs, they actually all really liked him.

Nobody told him that—but I thought Killian knew how attractive he was.

I laughed at their expressions as they watched Killian like it was a sport.

He handled the building security systems with Gabriel, every corner with state—of—the—art cameras and panic buttons and access points that would help expedite everything.

Because of their specialties, Gabriel was able to handle security while Aiden influenced permits and licenses.

Aiden was also connected to local law—enforcement, and so he worked with them to ensure that in the future we would operate with legitimacy.

I knew I was building something with shields around it now.

Over the course of the next year, the back rooms became dressing rooms, there was so much lighting in the club.

I didn't know what to do with myself. We put mirrors and lights and decorations and flowers.

The main area had tiered seating for guests and as we made more money, Killian said they would invest it back into the property.

He took over numbers and everything else and unlike Aidan, he didn't make me nervous. Not really.

He did change the entire basement out into an open plan storage area with enough lights and white paint to make me forget the place of horror it used to be.

And so I ended up going on social media and looking up ways to do that for free.

I had all of the girls get social media accounts and set them up using color—coded aesthetics. And then we end up reaching out to influencers all across the social scene.

With multiple accounts, we were able to reach out to more people and we spent an entire month messaging everybody that we could think of.

In the meantime?

I planned out themed nights, arts and cultural spotlights on dances, costumes that I thrifted.

We started catering to bachelorette parties, women only crowds where girls felt safe, and an environment that celebrated sex.

One of the girls suggested I start investing in lingerie and selling costumes and sex toys and I looked at it like I was viewing everything from a distant out of body experience.

When it was finally done and we had people coming for opening night after advertising for months and months?

My former prison.

Turned into my palace.

I smiled at Killian one night after hopping off stage. "We did it."

∽

IT WAS A FEW YEARS AFTER TEASER'S BECAME A COMMON NAME AROUND THE city, I was walking around at night. I was a nocturnal animal according to Killian.

A showgirl.

Someone pretending to be something they are not. Someone who laughed too loud, spoke too much, and carried around tiara's giving them out to girls who didn't know any better about what this place had been.

But I knew. Some of the girls knew. I stopped at the bar to just take a look when I saw a familiar face that stopped me. Stripped my smile from my lips.

I froze in place at a dark—haired woman laughing with a blonde next to her. The blonde was saying something to her and making a face making her laugh harder.

"*Catalina…*" I whispered. It couldn't be her.

Catalina…I was sure was gone.

Aidan wouldn't tell me over the years.

He didn't speak much to me. I got the feeling he couldn't.

Now I realized, he was never disgusted with me. He was disgusted with himself without the world to stop this.

Gabriel had explained that without the right help, Aiden could not have taken anything down.

He was working with the FBI originally years ago, but eventually, Gabriel just gave up on everybody and did it himself.

Gabriel had been a saint.

Like Liam.

But right now, I pushed Liam into a safe place in my heart as I moved to the mirage of Catalina.

I found myself in front of them. "*Hola, chicas.* I'm Lara."

I caught a glint of diamonds on the blonde's wrist as she smiled up at me, and the full force of hazel eyes hit me from the dark—haired woman.

I introduced myself with the name Liam had given me. True and false. Security and a shield.

With my American accent I practiced with Killian. Hiding every ounce of who I really was. What did it matter?

None of this was real. I was pretending with my mask on and nobody could ever guess who I was.

"Alisha," she smiled shaking my hand, her hazel eyes sparkling. "Thank you for inviting me." Her English accent was crisp and light as the blonde next to her smiled. "This is my best friend, Gemma."

"Welcome to Teaser's," I plastered my smile for her while not being able to look away feeling haunted.

Catalina had been taller. But Alisha…she reminded me of the past.

And I found myself looking at her wondering where I went wrong.

The irony of people being impressed with something sexy did not surprise me. I was a model now. And I wasn't even the girl I used to be. I was playing a fantasy.

Only this time I controlled everything.

"What brings you ladies here tonight?"

"You dm'd me," Alisha smiled. "We had a minute and we thought why not?"

Gemma laughed. "She had a minute. I was dragged here and now I'm afraid I am not ever leaving."

I found myself for the first time not going along with it but genuinely pleased when Alisha aimed her smile at me.

"Hang on a sec—" she broke off. "You're Lara. Do you own the club?"

On paper—Killian did.

Out loud?

I did.

Nobody talked about it and Reed and Nathan thought I was the owner.

Nobody knew our secrets.

I smiled wider. "Yes. I am."

PART II | THE GHOST

16

LIAM

"My name's Reed Whittaker, I'm the CEO of Titan Security, and I was wondering if you'd be interested in working for me..."

I replayed it nine times. Now going on ten. I replayed it until I swore I was losing my mind.

Reed. Whittaker.

Gabriel's old friend.

Titan Security. My old dream.

I looked it up. I had to. I didn't even know how he had stayed under the radar so much but then again? I avoided Gabriel's name and never bothered to give a shit and see where he was in life.

Over the years, my hatred for him had grown, festering like a raw open wound.

Just thinking his name was enough for me to feel the burning shame. The memories of getting shot. Isobel's death. His abandonment. Everything.

Everything sank in too deep.

And now, I found the rage rising in me again when I realized what the fuck I was staring at.

"He fucking started the company..." I whispered staring at the screen. My rage was like a volcano swiftly rising to the surface. My emotions clouding over violently at the sensations coursing through me. *"He stole my fucking idea."*

Ugly and familiar sensations twisted in my gut.

If I hated Gabriel before, I absolutely fucking hated him now. It was another bullet to add to the fucking collection that he had left behind.

He got my best friend, he ruined my legs, he ruined my life, and while I was learning how to walk again—he abandoned his family and left me to rot.

To then take all of my fucking dreams and turn them into *his* company?

I wanted to kill him.

I did.

The audacity of offering me a job at the company I designed? At the dream that I wanted. I wanted to open this company, and I wanted to do it to support Isobel's dance studio.

"Does he think after all these years I would ever forgive him?" Why was Reed offering me shit?

As though now he was reaching out to ask me to be a part of his world. After years. Former brothers. Rivals. Partners.

And now? Knowing he had spent the years building himself without me. Without her. Did he move on? Did he get married? That sent me into a fury.

He had taken my entire future and turned it into his just like he stole my life and my woman.

Isobel should have been mine.

Mr. Santos had been right all those years ago—I was the only person in the entire world who would've made sure she was safe.

So I don't know why I listened to Reed's voicemail over and over as though I was dissecting it.

"...thought it might be something good..."

Did Reed know? Was Reed his fucking proxy? Gabriel Monroe had always been a fucking coward.

And even still, I don't know why my hands moved and I don't know why I picked up the phone and I called him back.

"Liam." Reed's voice was strong as he answered. "Thanks for calling me back. I didn't know if this was still your number."

I don't know why I said.

"Yeah, it still is. Although I'm curious how you got it."

Reed laughed low. "I'm just as good as you, but I think you might be a bit better. I take it you got my voicemail."

"I did. And I considered it, I have a few negotiable—"

"I expected nothing less."

I don't know why I said yes to Reed.

I don't know why I said yes to working for the company I had built years go.

I had no idea why I started working with Gabriel.

∾

I MET REED AT TITAN MIDTOWN.

A building two blocks away from where I had been shot. I walked by that now shut down hotel with no name on it all the time.

All the time.

I thought I got off on torturing myself. I must've because when I walked into the sleek building and up the elevator to the top floor where he was—I didn't expect him to be my height and size.

Dark chocolate colored hair curling a little around his ears made him look younger, with pale gray eyes and a solid build.

He smiled holding his hand out. "Hey, thanks for coming. I didn't know you had a cane otherwise I would've just met you somewhere easier—"

"It's all good—"

"I did want you to see your new office if you'd like to work here, but you're always welcome to work from home too. I just send you taskers and we go from there."

Reed was polite, but I could see he was cautious, guarded, and professional. He didn't give anything away if he knew about me and Gabriel. He also never brought him up. The entire time Reed talked about the office. The new space. His job. And he passed me his contact info.

It wasn't until the end of the hour when I had no more questions for him I dared to say it.

"Why did you call me?" I asked him. I had to. I needed to know feeling almost ravenous with the hunger but stone—faced. I'd popped enough anti—anxiety meds to talk to Reed without flipping a desk over. Plus, the more I stood, the more it ached and centered me to the moment.

Reed was quiet as he crossed his arms over his chest, his black bomber jacket on.

"My coworker I think, worked with you? He was Agency. Gabriel Monroe." That was the first time I heard his name in seven years, said out loud. And I thanked fuck I took enough meds before I came out here. Except then Reed said out loud. "I don't know if you remember him, but I

102

know that he doesn't really keep in touch with anybody. I know enough about your last assignment to know that it didn't really go well, and I dug around a bit while your medical issues, I thought this might be a good change of pace for you."

He looked at me and in that moment I paused.

He didn't know.

Reed has no fucking clue.

"My personal hope is that one day you might talk to Gabriel. But I won't force it. He sits in Greenwich. And I sit here, but I'm not going to do anything about you two. I just know that he doesn't really talk about his past and I saw you were the only surviving member of his team." My back stiffened. "I know he feels guilty and I know he's been out of it for years—" Did I feel happy Reed said it? "But I'm hoping having you back on this team, helps him as much as it helps you. I'm sorry for everything, but I hope I can make it easier for you in some ways."

Reed had no fucking clue.

I knew by the way he was talking and the vibe I got off him.

He was…

"You're reaching out because Monroe isn't doing good—"

"No, he's just—" Reed paused checking himself. "I think Gabriel blames himself a lot for things. And I'm hoping you being on the team is something good for both of you. Maybe to fix things, maybe to make up or heal—but he doesn't know you're on the team."

And then I froze.

"What?"

"He doesn't know," Reed repeated. "I haven't told him and I wasn't going to tell him. If he finds out and he wants to reach out to you, he can, but I never told him anything."

What the fuck was happening right now?

Wait a fucking minute.

"You know I was on his team?" I said slowly.

Reed nodded looking innocent. If he was playing with me, he was playing a damn good game.

"Monroe doesn't know I'm being hired by you…"

But if Reed didn't know I was Gabriel's brother—in—law…then…he didn't know about Isobel.

He didn't know he was inviting a wolf in sheep's clothing into his fold.

He didn't know who I was. What I was. What I had been.

And where I wanted to go.

Reed was playing with dynamite under goodness.

That revelation rocked me to my fucking car because I just realized that he had no clue who the hell I was.

He just thought that he was taking in the last surviving member of the team.

Me.

Reed was trying to hire me with good intentions to give me a chance and to maybe "heal" Gabriel?

That didn't make sense to me. What the fuck was he healing? Did Reed not know he was standing on the foundations of my company?

"Gabriel is your employee?"

"Something like that, I run the company."

And suddenly, I was at a crossroads. I could tell Reed absolutely not.

I could see this as a chance to finally fuck Gabriel over from the inside out.

Or I could destroy everything they had.

And then Reed said. "I'm hoping that you can join the team and given your proficiencies, you might want to train Evie—"

I paused as he said that name.

"Evie is Gabriel's little sister and I think she would really like meeting you. I already have a plan to set you up with working with her, and to take over a couple of my jobs as well. I don't know if you know, but we run the club Teaser's now—"

My heart stopped again. What did he just say? *Did he just say Teaser's?*

"And I need a new security person to take over all the things I've been working. You don't have to say anything to Gabriel, and if he asks, I will tell him that you work for me. You guys don't have to interact with each other if you don't want to, and I'll make sure that everybody leaves you alone. I just need someone to get this work done. So if you're willing to, I'd like to give you a chance."

I blinked at Reed in confusion.

Gabriel didn't have a sister.

Isobel did.

Eva...Santos. Evie Monroe? What the fuck was happening right now?

"Teaser's?"

Reed smiled. "Yeah, it's a part of our umbrella. You would be handling a lot of the jobs we have on the East Coast. Just takes it off my plate."

Lara...I forgot about Lara. I forgot about my past. I had been wallowing in my shame so much, all mentions of the old Teaser's was gone...and when I got back to New York? Looking for Lara hadn't even been in my head.

That's because you're an alcoholic and drug addict.

I stayed perfectly still as Reed watched me.

"So what do you say? You want to start?"

"When?"

"Tomorrow. You can meet Evie and the rest of the guys and I can introduce you to the other new guys. Kellan and Garrett are staying at the Manor in Greenwich but I know you have your own place here so I won't ask you to go up."

And because Gabriel...he was right fucking there.

He had taken everything from me. I could always become a titan and take everything from him.

I could take his old company down and ruin everything.

I could do it if I wanted to.

Reed didn't know who he was letting into his home.

His offer was innocent.

He just wanted to help his friend.

He thought I was Gabriel's wounded teammate.

Not his brother—in—law. Not the broken man who was in love with his best friend who became Gabriel's wife. Not the man who failed William Santos. Not the man who failed to keep all of his promises to every single person out there in the world.

And Lara...was she...Reed managed Teaser's? Did that mean...Titan Security had taken over? What was going on?

I needed answers and my brain was swimming.

He was telling me he was helping his friend.

He was trying to create a potential reconciliation without forcing either one of us to talk to each other.

Gabriel had no idea I was even here and he wouldn't know.

According to Reed who had no fucking clue Gabriel had been *married.*

Had been.

Because our everything—she was gone.

Sometimes people didn't recover from loss.

And I wonder if he had never moved on because I had it. But something in my gut twisted as I watched Reed.

Who just had a earnest expression on his face because he genuinely wanted to help.

He was trying to help me and do something good and I was over here thinking about all the ways to use it as a weapon.

"Sounds good."

Evie. Lara. Gabriel…

My past was back in my life in full force.

And I had no fucking clue what to do but I knew when Reed grinned at me—he had no fucking clue what kind of monster he let into his empire.

My empire.

LIAM

I KNEW I WAS MEETING *EVIE MONROE*.

Except...Gabriel didn't have a sister.

I *knew* he didn't have any family.

But I know *who* did. I know who *had*. I should've fucking known that little girl in the photos of the boxes Mr. Santos had under his bed would grow up. He had two daughters. I knew as much.

I was meeting her now.

And she filled up my screen as I took her in. The moment she turned on her camera—I fucking saw *my* shortcake.

I fucking saw her. For a moment I swallowed hard. Thankfully, I kept a glass of whiskey inside of my mug without anyone knowing.

I took a sip of it lifting it to my lips as her caramel eyes and mahogany hair from my nightmares filled the screen.

Isa...Gabriel found her...he found Evie...

It took me a moment to realize, that he had found her.

Wherever Adrianna had been and he had brought Evie Santos to the Greenwich manor where she sat surrounded by her plants.

"Hi, I'm Evie," she said sounding so much like her sister without an accent. They both had a light husky quality to their voices I realized their mother had.

Fuck. She had no clue.

My grin spread my lips as I looked at her feeling pride and joy at the sight of her.

Holy. Shit.

Did she…did Gabriel tell her? Did she know?

She must've been five or six when her parents split. Most kids didn't remember anything. And I wondered if she knew about her older sister or if he told her anything.

"You look really familiar," I murmured. "Do you have any family on the East Coast?"

Did she know about her father? Or her sister?

She shook her head. "Just me and Gabriel."

I felt a little disappointment in my gut, but then I realized, maybe Gabriel never told her about anybody. It would hurt a lot less if she didn't know. But then I wondered what he told her to adopt her.

On paper, she was his sister.

Not really.

On paper—he was dead. By suicide. I saw the faked police reports. I know he was still alive.

Everybody called him by his real name, but on paper, he went by a totally different one.

Raphael Santos. College professor at Astor University Downtown.

It was odd because I had thought that he didn't feel anything, and then I realized his entire identity was paying tribute to Isobel.

He took her name.

Evie though was on paper related to Reed. Since he was…alive.

My eyes narrowed. *"You're Monroe's sister?"*

And she had no clue who I was. I felt a grin tip my lips. This could be fun.

"Do you have a family?" She blinked those doe eyes at me.

"No, I don't have anyone in my life."

"I can be your friend," she volunteered quickly.

And my heart cracked a little.

I blinked back my emotions realizing the girls had a lot in common. Whether she knew it or not.

They were always the first to make friends.

"That so?"

"You can call me Evie."

"Evie?" My lips tipped up. *"Hm.* How old are you, kid?"

She had to be what?

Twenty—two going on thirteen with how little she was. My fingers flew across my keyboard opening up Oracle to test out how good she was. If she was like her sister. Talented. Sharp.

"I just turned twenty—three."

Damn. Close enough.

"That so? All grown up now, huh?"

"Sorta. Grown up enough to know you're fucking with my computer."

Ah. Busted.

"You won't get in, but I appreciate your effort. Reed taught me well."

I was fucking *delighted* by her spark when she shot me that look. *Isa... she's so big now. She's just like you.*

"Are you as good as Reed?"

I didn't think twice as I asked that question.

Evie Santos looked embarrassed. "I was hoping *you* would mentor me."

And just like that my smile dipped. The sensations and memories of me teaching Isobel things late into the night, the two of us ordering pizza, me showing Gabriel Oracle, designing programs for her—it all slammed into me.

Evie didn't know me.

She had no fucking clue what I was. I knew in the way she looked at me.

Not like I had let her down.

But I could lift her up.

And I would.

Anything for my shortcake.

"I would love to teach you everything."

She smiled at me and I returned it taking another sip of my whiskey, feeling it burn through the ache growing in my chest as Evie spoke. "Should I start with everything you need to know first...?"

I nodded and let Evie do her thing. I asked her questions about everything that I could think of.

And then she said. "...well we use Oracle to do everything for that..."

I stopped moving. Oracle.

Before she died, I gave her the second program.

When I designed it, the version that I had had been fully flushed out. If anything happened to it?

I already had a baseline foundational one that all a person needed to do—was to add to it. Emotions. Information. It collected all of the data possible, and then the version of Oracle would become that person.

Evie was telling me she had Oracle.

She had been putting data into it.

"I just can't crack a few of the issues."

It didn't have any issues.

Unless...Gabriel didn't know the password. Which was...kinda wild because it was him.

"How did *you* build it?" I whispered the question to her. "*Everything* is easy to crack with a little persistence."

Or the right word.

The right answer would set it free.

If she input Gabriel's former call sign—it would help her.

But I couldn't tell her that.

Since...I wasn't supposed to know. The more I spoke to the rest of Titan, the more I realized that nobody actually knew who I was. And that meant Gabriel never told anybody anything.

Evie looked a little nervous then. "I *didn't*. Reed gave me the project. He said that Gabriel wanted me to work on it."

"So he took it," I muttered.

"I didn't catch that. Who took what?" Evie said.

"Nothing, I was saying it's good Monroe took you in for the project."

My project. Gabriel had handed Isobel's sister my baby. And she'd built it up to...what? Her version of Oracle. Ours could run by side and because I was a God she would have no clue. I could see most of what she could. What her network was on.

I wiped a hand over my face realizing she had no fucking clue who she was talking to. The creator of the program.

"What did you need?"

And she told me what she thought was the problem. That the data that she was feeding to Oracle wasn't enough. And then I realized Evie had built up her version of Oracle only for the sake of Titan. It was to help operatives and locate people. That was all she was using it for.

Her version worked with everyone's call sign. "Oracle works with your call sign. Who are you?"

"Pluto." I answered without hesitation. She didn't get why I said it and I didn't explain.

And then she said. "Would you like me to set you up on Oracle?"

The smile that tipped my lips I knew was wicked.

Yes.

I would.

I'd love to fucking see what she'd done with my skeletons. See how she thought. What Evie didn't realize is that she had a unique version of Oracle.

Because it was a baseline, by her giving me access to it, I could see exactly how she thought.

Her thought process, the things that she wanted, her innermost feelings, that's what it was designed to absorb.

Because that's how you built it to be free thinking.

"Evie, I would like nothing more," I beamed.

"I think you'd really like it. Oracle has a beautiful voice—"

I know. I knew her voice. She was my heart.

"I bet she does."

Evie went on. "Reed says he could listen to her all day...."

And I listened to her talking with a grin seeing my Isobel in her. Only her sister was a lot like sunshine where Isobel had been like fire. Evie was sweet. Surrounded by ivy and monstera plants she was life.

"Tell you what, why don't I train you on everything Reed doesn't have time for, and in the meantime..." I grinned at her feeling my chest swell as she smiled at me. "I'll make you a better Red Hat."

She looked so adorably confused. "But Reed says I'm the White Hat."

Of course she was. I wondered how protective people were of her. In her chair I could see she was tinier than her sister.

I leaned back. "You think you'll be better than Reed and me by wearing a White Hat?"

I saw Evie squirming as she considered it. Reed had asked me to train her up. Make her better than me.

Not possible. But a good attempt wouldn't hurt. She caught me trying to hack into her system and we both knew—I could if I wanted to, but why would I start off and reveal my hand?

"You don't have to answer now or do *anything*. If you want to think about it, take some time, and let me know what you want."

Say yes. Say yes, and I'll make you better than Isobel ever was. I'll make sure you live.

And in that moment, I felt something else.

A desire. To be different. To be better. Something unfamiliar coasted over me and I wondered if I was drinking too much again.

Evie spoke up. "I don't need to think about it. Should I come down to Midtown to meet you sometimes, or is it easier for you to be home with your legs?"

I sighed as my smile was back. "I'd love to meet you in person, Evie, but I doubt I can. I can teach you over video, share screens, make it easier for you and me. I think you'll have fun being a Red Hat. Plus, consider how surprised Reed will be when you surpass him."

Evie's look of relief was evident and also, some pride in them for taking the plunge. She was nervous. I wouldn't hurt her. Not her. Never her.

"For today, we should look over those taskers Reed had for you."

And back to work. Which brought me to the other reason I took the job.

"Will you walk me through them? I'm interested in what we do for the Teasers club...Who owns the club?"

"Lara Ford." I stopped breathing and moving in one go. *Lara...my...* "Do you know her?"

I composed myself taking a sip of alcohol to drown out my emotions.

"No. Do you have a photo?" Years of being an alcoholic and popping pills had led me to be able to compose myself.

And then, Evie—my pseudo sister—pulled up a photo of the woman I had failed seven years ago.

Raven hair. Doe eyes. And a wide smile on her face, canines flashing into a bright camera. Several shots of her filled my screen. Some on stage. Some dancing. Some of her with friends.

Holy. Fuck. Melina became Lara?

I never was able to go back and rescue her. To stop myself from hurting so bad—I tried to not think about her. My guilt ruled my every breath.

The idea of leaving her there? Gutted me alive.

"This is Lara. She's twenty—five," Evie was saying not realizing I was staring at a photo now on the shared screen of Lara. My Lara. Her name was Melina...she took my nickname?

My chest exploded a little.

"...and she's been running Teasers for a while now..." Evie told me about how she ran the club with the O'Hara's. How Lara had owned it for seven years. The O'Hara's? With Cormac? Aidan? What the fuck happened?

Seven years.

I texted Gabriel...did he...did he go back for her? And then, for the first time in seven years, something different cut through the hatred. If the hatred for Gabriel and me was pitch, black shadows, it was a way of sun—light broke through them.

"...Gabriel is really good friends with her," Evie murmured. "She's just the best...Nate says she's really wonderful, a little insane, but Reed likes her a lot...."

Evie could talk. But I didn't mind. I liked listening to her.

And then Evie showed me she was more perceptive than I gave her credit for.

"She's single. If you're curious."

I mean. I was. But would she...could I...could I meet her again? Face her and apologize and tell her I was sorry...did I let her down? Did I fail her too?

I felt an embarrassed laugh leave me. "No, I can't—" I couldn't face her.

"I'm sorry—" Her eyes widened horrified and I realized...she might've known I was disabled. She might've thought—

"No, you're fine—"

"I didn't know if you—"

"*Evie*—" I laughed realizing she was a lot like her sister. "My legs are fucked, not my dick." I laughed harder. "She's...*something.*"

"Can I ask—" she began nervously.

My eyes met hers. "What happened to me?"

I died, Evie. I'm sorry I got your sister killed.

"I got shot several times when I was on an assignment."

Clinical. Focused. Numbed out.

Evie had no clue. What did it matter? No way Gabriel told her anything. I knew that now.

"I'm sorry, can you...walk?"

I grinned at her shy eyes. "I can do more than walk."

I hadn't been with a woman in forever though. Sutton...and I...that shit had been a hot fucking mess. We tried...but I wasn't attracted to her. No. All I got was my fist. Every so often I did pick up a woman at a bar, but that shit never lasted. It was a one night or one time at best.

Being with women made my skin crawl or my legs hurt and I just wanted to go home and imagine a life where nothing had ever happened to me.

Nothing but her...

My eyes drifted to the computer again and I saw her.

Melina.

Lara.

"She owns the club now..."

And then I felt Evie's eyes on me and I realized I was slipping. "It's easier for me to not do half of the stuff I used to. I'm not in a wheelchair anymore, and I'm grateful I don't have a prosthetic leg, but—Lucky for me, Evie, I still have *everything* I need to be a fully functional man."

I think.

I still had my tongue piercings in.

So I could eat pussy like a motherfucker. Even if my dick revolted at being vulnerable around anyone ever again?

Lara? She was different.

She was the one woman who understood how I felt. Evie's laughter filled my room.

"You're terrible, Liam."

I felt another smile tip my lips. "Part of my charm."

"Have you met Gabriel yet? I think you would be really good friends if you ever get a chance to meet him. Even if you're a flirt."

I stopped breathing again. The shock that filtered through my system took me a second to process. Isa had once said the same. That she thought Monroe and I would be good friends.

"That so?"

When she nodded I couldn't stop the words from leaving my lips as my chest rose and fell with agony laced in bitterness.

"You remind me of an old friend of mine, too," I murmured, "She was a lot like you."

They're so much alike...

"I wasn't aware of a flirt like you having female friends."

So much alike.

I couldn't resist asking. Did she know?

"Are you sure you don't have any family?"

"Just me and Gabriel," she whispered like she was embarrassed. "Do you want to see more photos of Lara?"

I forced myself to let out a sigh as I nodded.

Evie giggled. "I like you, Liam Sullivan."

"Not so bad yourself, shortcake."

It slipped out so easily, I didn't even catch it but she froze.

"Why did you—" she was struggling with her words. "Why did you call me that?"

I stopped moving as my brows furrowed. "I'm sorry, did I overstep? You already called me a man—whore, which is totally true, so I figured shortcake would be—"

"No," she interrupted me. "Why shortcake?"

I tipped my head. From all the data I took in? Evie had no clue about her sister and me.

She didn't know that on paper, I would've been her brother in another life.

So I watched my words as I said it.

"You reminded me of my old friend. I used to call her that. She was

114

short, like you. I can tell because there's no way that chair is that big. Plus, your hands look like they're paws."

I mimicked having paws and she gasped affronted.

"You have a bit of her spark, her fire. I liked it when she gave me push-back. She called me out on my bullshit. I like a challenge—But if you don't feel comfortable with me calling you that, I don't—"

"No, it's okay. I don't mind. I think it must be a common nickname. I'm glad I remind you of your friend."

She had no fucking clue.

"She was my *best friend*," I said. And even now it was agony without her. I thought time would dull it away. It didn't. "Everyone's also super short compared to me, *so...*" I rambled like she did to not draw attention to anything.

Not my agony.

Not my state of numb.

Not my life.

Not my promises. Or being a failure.

And I watched her smiling at me again and I saw flashes of Isobel so much I felt greedy for her. I wanted to talk to Evie all the time but I didn't wanna scare her.

I knew Gabriel didn't know.

Reed had told the truth.

When Evie and I did get off the phone? The sun was going down and I kept Lara's photo up on my screen and then I went down the rabbit hole of her.

Teaser's. How it had been rebranded.

The O'Hara's worked discreetly with Titan now. Aidan O'Hara was Gabriel's business partner and now he had mafia ties?

The old Gabriel I knew—would never have turned morally black. But I didn't know him anymore. I knew that now.

She was now by some fucking stroke of luck—the *owner* of Teaser's.

My heart bottomed out.

And I was seeing her again.

18

LARA

I was supposed to be meeting a new security liaison from Titan that Reed had hired.

I only knew because Nathan had briefly mentioned it before he had gone out on a job to be Gemma's bodyguard.

Despite having more money than anyone I knew, Gemma's life wasn't without struggles and issues.

Some of them coming straight from her family and with Nathan vacating the spot—I knew someone needed to fill in.

I had two hours before I was meeting Alisha in my office to meet the new addition to my team.

And in that time? Some of the new girls, Flor and Gianna had brought in boxes of sex toys for me to hang up on my wall.

I hadn't been with a man since Gabriel rescued me.

I couldn't do it. And every single time I thought about a man—there was only one I wanted—the one who never came back. He was alive. I knew because Gabriel told me he was. He was just...gone.

Lost.

I waited years for Liam to come back and Kieran...the youngest O'Hara kept hanging out at Teaser's and I almost wondered if he wanted to ask me out.

The irony of that never escaped me.

The boys were nothing like their father. Killian over the years had grown up bigger and stronger and now I was sure he had a girlfriend named Nisha he was in love with.

Kieran was still doing his thing and living in his youth.

Aidan had retired to Chicago as his castle while his brother's stayed here. It wasn't as awkward interacting with him. But I remembered the younger Aidan sometimes. The one who had dealt with his own hell.

And Liam?

I didn't know where Liam was. Sometimes I wondered if he had stopped being friends with Gabriel. But why had Gabriel saved me?

I was in my violet themed office, Killian had thought the color appropriate for me. Now, I wandered around hanging up dildos and vibrators that Alisha was utterly tickled by.

Alisha had gotten together with Reed. The two of them had been circling each other for years. Reed had waited patiently before he pounced when Avani went to college.

I turned on the music on my phone and I played one of the songs I knew from my childhood. Liam's playlist was on my phone but it felt too vulnerable to play it now.

Lost in the music, and the mindless task of arranging displays for things that I didn't really care about, I didn't hear the door open.

I shrieked dropping what was in my hand and going to scramble back at the sight of someone in my office. Someone not my girls.

Men didn't just come in here and then I saw his face. Green eyes, darker than I remembered, that face, glasses.

My heart stopped beating. The music kept playing. And all I saw was *him*.

Saint Liam.

He blinked a few times like he couldn't believe I was real and I saw...a cane. He slowly moved to me shutting the door.

"*Melina?*"

It had been years since anyone called me that.

Years.

"*Liam,*" my voice was a whisper as I realized—Liam. Saint Liam. Was back. I didn't think.

I just moved. Rushing to him, into his arms, nearly tackling him, the music stopping when the song ended and I held onto him. "*Liam!*"

His arms steadied me banding around me tighter.

"Oh holy fuck—" he whispered. "Melina..."

"You are back!" I clung to him. "Liam, what happened to you? I waited for you! Gabriel—he saved me, like you said. He—" I broke off pulling back his eyes wide on me. "Liam." My lips spread into a smile. "You're back."

117

Green eyes went wide at my words as he searched my face.

"You're here...you're..."

"Liam." If my chest could explode in that moment it would, I couldn't stop smiling. I couldn't stop taking him in. "Your friend Gabriel, he came for me. He saved me. He told you?"

His brows furrowed as he took me in and his Adam's apple worked in his throat. "You're not...you aren't...I didn't save you."

"Yes you did," I shook my head confused. "Gabriel he came for me." I rambled so rapidly explaining it to him. And his face looked haunted taking me in. "Because of you, Gabriel found me. He saved me. He gave me this place to turn into this. And now you are back. *Gabriel did not tell me you were coming back."* I could implode with excitement. "You are finally here."

But Liam instead of looking happy, he just looked confused.

"You aren't mad at me?"

What?

"Why would I be...mad at you? You saved my life."

"I didn't...I wasn't there..." No. And now he walked with a cane.

"Something happened to you."

He nodded like he was stunned and I didn't know why I just knew I needed to hug him again.

"Liam, it's okay. You helped me. I waited for you, I waited years for you." My eyes blurred as my tears streamed down my face. "I *waited.* Are you okay? Tell me...what happened? Tell me everything. You didn't come back—" I broke off realizing I was rambling half in English, half in Spanish, most of it broken and a weak excuse for words.

Nobody had done for me what Liam had.

When I pulled back wiping my eyes, Liam dipped his head and surprised me. He moved too fast for me, and with desperation when his lips moved over mine.

"I need this."

When his lips sealed over mine my entire body sighed. A fresh wave of tears rose as he kissed me. Over and over.

"Need you."

The click of metal was in my mouth as he did and I realized Liam had a piercing on his tongue.

Brushing into my mouth, the metal sensation sent a shiver through me as I moaned wrapping my arms around his neck as he lifted me up with one arm around me. Somehow I was seated on my desk as he kissed me.

And I let him. I would let Liam do anything to me. I trusted him with my entire soul. This man. Because Liam could have hurt me, he could've taken advantage of me, he could've broken me.

Liam had been the first man to give me a choice and humanity in ways I couldn't have figured I needed.

I moaned into his mouth as he tugged at my dress, my hands reaching for his clothing.

"Melina," he whispered in a broken voice. "You don't hate me."

"No," I shook my head kissing him back, tasting alcohol and something else on his tongue. "I could never."

I would never.

He pressed his forehead to mine catching his breath as I tugged at his shirt. I felt the slight tremor in his body as he kissed me again. *"Melina, I didn't leave you—"*

Nobody calls me by my name.

"I know—"

"I didn't mean to—"

"I know."

I broke off at his legs. "What happened? Nobody told me anything—" but I had never told anyone but Gabriel about Liam. It was like he was our secret.

Nobody knew how close I was to Gabriel.

"Amor," I held his face as he closed his eyes like he was in pain.

"I need to sit, *muneca.*"

I nodded taking him to the chair on the other side. I never even thought of it.

As Liam shakily sat in my large comfy chair he pulled me into his lap almost immediately.

"Liam, are you okay?" I brushed his hair back. "Where were you? Tell me."

But Liam looked so shaken up. "It's good to see you," he looked emotional as he blinked rapidly. "So fucking good to see you. God, you look so fucking beautiful. My girl." He wiped my eyes. My face. With a reverence that told me how much he cared.

I couldn't stop crying.

Liam's hands ran over me, mine over his, and he kept touching me to make sure I was real. Like he was starving for affection. I didn't hesitate to kiss his face. Anywhere I could reach.

Saint Liam.

"Liam, you came back." I smiled wide again unable to stop myself. "You are *back.*" I knew. I knew one day he would come back.

"You own this place," his hands trembled as he took me in. *"I'm so fucking proud of you."*

And just like that I felt my face crumble. I couldn't stop being emotional. Couldn't stop breaking down.

I held onto him so tightly as he kissed me. I didn't know who did it. Who reached for the other person.

His hands moving to my dress hiking it up, my fingers at his pants freeing him. A desperation flowing through me I couldn't explain.

"Liam," I whispered. "Please."

"I know, *muneca*," his hands were on my hips, ripping at the scrap of lace. Seven years of waiting.

I felt him at the entrance of my body and with Liam, none of the fear existed when our eyes locked. His lips parting over mine.

"Make it *real*. I just wanted it to be real."

"I'm real," I held him sinking down, knowing exactly what to do. Or trying to at least.

I winced a little at his size, as he groaned biting his lip.

Liam's fingers reached down and when they found my clit, he rubbed circles as I pressed again.

I felt him rubbing the head of his cock into me and the first inch made me close my eyes. *"Liam."*

He felt enormous and I was struggling, but his other hand tugged my dress down freeing my breasts.

Over the years being fed proper meals and dancing had toned up my body, and changed the shape of it.

Now I had hips and breasts. Ample enough they bounced as I trembled. Liam made a noise of pleasure, dipping his head and taking one of my nipples into his mouth.

I sank lower onto his length feeling the stretch and burn of him, so familiar and so foreign I held on as Liam moved, thrusting up. I couldn't get enough of him, pleasure blossoming in my womb, rising raw and real.

It hurt just enough and until that moment I hadn't realized I had never had sex without feeling pain.

Until now where the pull of his mouth, his fingers working at my clit allowed me to sink lower and lower until I felt like I was being split open in two.

"Liam," I pulled his head up feeling drugged and needing his kisses.

His fingers never stopped moving on my clit and I moaned rocking on his length. Hot and heavy. I didn't ever imagine he could take up this much space. But Liam wasn't a small man and right now, I was struggling.

He swore as he kissed me hungrily. *"Muneca,* fuck, that's so good. It's been forever for me."

"Me too," I whimpered unable to stop my hips from rocking.

Liam groaned low in his throat and I felt it somewhere deep in me. "Don't do that."

I froze. "Am I hurting you?"

He closed his eyes as his lips curled up into a wicked smile. "No, *muneca.* But I'm not a two pump chump and I promised I would never do that to you."

What?

At my confusion, Liam grinned wider kissing me unable to stop. "You feel incredible. I don't wanna lose my mind—"

"But it's okay if you do," I brushed his hair back unsure of what he found funny. This was my first time with a man I liked, and I wanted it, and he was…everything I could've asked for. "Liam?"

"I'm sorry," he closed his eyes again breathing hard. "Don't move, let me—let me just. Fuck. Let me take care of you."

And then he began to *move.*

It was familiar to me, this motion, but Liam made me feel like it was my first time as I clung to him as his hips rose.

I rocked mine and he moaned into my kisses not holding back. His fingers working my clit continued and I felt myself clenching tighter on him.

His breath left him in a hiss as pressed his forehead to mine.

"Muneca," his voice was gruff and like heaven.

"No pude olvidarte, te deseé," I whispered. "I could not forget you. I want you."

The pleasure built in me in a way I didn't recognize. I never felt it for a good reason. Not pain disguised as pleasure, but something more. Pure need. Pure want for him.

For this man. I whimpered as the sensation built.

"That's my girl," he groaned as he rocked up, keeping us so close and I followed his hips.

"Liam."

"Let me have it," he thrust up somewhere sensitive every single time and I sobbed as his fingers increased their pressure on my clit.

His mouth trailed down my neck finding my pulse and sucking on it.

I came apart. The pressure cresting over like a wave and pure ecstasy rushing through me.

The pleasure was endless as Liam groaned into my neck, his body tensing, heat flooding my insides and unlike any other time—it just felt like he belonged in me.

Years of *wanting*, dreaming, needing him. Just Liam.

I held on hiding my screams into his neck as we both shook. My entire body sighed at the feeling of holding Liam. For years, I wanted *him*. Wanted him to love me. Wanted him to make me feel whole again.

I held on tighter until I felt Liam utter a shuddering breath as his lips pressed into my skin. Everywhere he could reach.

Everything he did—no man had ever done for me. Liam had always been and would always hold that space in me.

"Stay with me," I whispered. "Don't leave."

"I'm not going anywhere," he continued to kiss me. "Fuck, I didn't wear anything...are you...are you on something?"

What?

"Hm?"

"I didn't wear a condom," he whispered. "But I'm clean, I swear."

"Oh," I lifted my head up a bit to look into his eyes feeling more intimate now than earlier.

His cheeks were flushed and his glasses adorably askew that I adjusted and then finally gave up, taking them off.

"I'm on the pill."

I couldn't stop my smile at his expression.

And his grin was wide on me, canines flashing, the bit of silver on his tongue making me clench again. "*Muneca*, I missed you."

"Missed you too."

I was never going to move. Even if there was a mess between my legs. A delighted noise left me. "I *knew* one day you'd come back."

"You go by Lara now," he whispered with nothing but softness in his eyes. "I named you that."

We both couldn't stop kissing each other in between everything we said and I smiled so wide it hurt my cheeks. "I *know*."

The Liam in front of me and the Liam he had been felt like two different people and none of it mattered because in my heart I knew—he was mine.

I held him so close to me light laughter left me. I couldn't stop repeating it.

"You came back to me."

He breathed out in an exhale that sounded light as he kissed me again. "I did. I did come back to you. And I'm not going anywhere anymore."

Laughter left me as I all but tackled him.

19

LARA

"LIAM, YOU ARE WORKING NOW AT TITAN?"

I knew I sounded too excited, my accent back and thicker around him, and Liam hadn't stopped smiling or kissing me.

Butterflies were exploding a little in my stomach at the sight of him. Tall, handsome, dark messy hair, and those eyes.

Lush like a forrest after it rained. Liam watched me with them, a sleepy lazy smile as he kissed me again.

When I had his attention, it felt like I had the world, the focus of it too much for my body to contain and I felt like bouncing around with how much energy I had.

He was...*here*. I couldn't stop touching him either, and I didn't know if I should stop. I couldn't let him.

Liam helped me clean up to my embarrassment as he reached for a washcloth and wet wipes. I winced a little holding onto him and he kissed me against infinitely softer every single time.

Despite everything I had ever done—this was always different with Liam. It was like this the first time we met. I felt shy, like a normal girl with a normal man.

He helped adjust my dress, my panties now destroyed, and then his clothes, a white band—tee and dark jeans, before walking back out to my office.

His cane hit the floor and I knew something happened to him I didn't know what to say about it. It felt almost awkward addressing it after what we'd done.

"It smells amazing everywhere," he murmured. "It smells like you. The moment I walked in, I knew that was you."

I felt heat on my cheeks as I realized the first time I had seen him we'd mauled each other.

Now both of us held hands like shy kids and my eyes found his cane again he seemed to lean on less now.

"I know that wasn't your first time. But are you okay?"

Nobody. No man. Had ever asked me if I had ever been okay like this. Not after what we had done.

"Es diferente contigo."

It's different with you.

His smile was soft as he held my face kissing me soundly again and I felt his heat and his length hardening.

Again?

"Sorry," he murmured. "It's been a while, but I'm still a horny mother-fucker around you."

I giggled into his kisses. "You were not like this before."

"No, you didn't sit on my lap, but I said you were hot."

Only he made my chest bubble up with excitement. "Liam, I have people coming in a few."

"How long do we have?"

"An hour..." I drifted off as he kissed down my jawline, down my neck, and lower pushing me back onto my larger violet chair as he sank to his knees dropping his cane to the floor. "*Liam...*"

"Just...let me know if it's too much. I just got you. Let me..." I trailed off as he sank even lower to his knees. "Promise I won't take long."

No, he did not.

But this was my first time for all of this. Being with someone I love. Having that someone go down on me like this.

My fingers threaded through his hair as it tangled with his locks and Liam's tongue, piercing and all touched my clit.

It was electric.

And it went on for what felt like forever.

Hot tongue, heat and that barbell—I shrieked a little covering my mouth as he ate at me practically pulling me onto his face with a hungry growl.

"Fuck," he swore and then he slipped his tongue into me and I shattered my legs closing around his ears as I came and came. Liam didn't hesitate to move—rising up, taking me into his arms and sitting me on the desk spreading my legs.

"Liam, again?"

"Again."

Liam's lips stamped over as he shoved my legs apart and without any panties on, I felt even more raunchy as he laid me out. He was pressing into my soaking wet body. Swallowing my moans. Holding me still as I adjusted to every inch of him.

I held onto him this as he drove deeper and gasped into my mouth.

"Hold onto me tighter, *muneca*."

I did bringing us closer than ever before.

"That's my girl," he crooned. "I can feel you, you're gonna come aren't you?"

"*Yesyesyes.*"

Every slam of his hips shot sparks through my body centering somewhere lower. I threw my head back crying out as he panted into my neck fucking so deep it hurt while at the same time hitting somewhere sweeter.

I came with the bite of pain from feeling him almost splitting me open. A noise left me as Liam dragged his mouth over mine kissing me with a hunger and fervor I felt in my lungs.

A hot heat filled me as Liam came and moaned into my mouth. I loved the noises he made. I loved Liam for how much he *felt*.

Liam was honest, kind and he never held back. Not once.

Not even now as he kissed me moaning into my mouth. "*Muneca*, take me home with you. Keep me there forever."

I laughed low. "Anything for you."

His smile was light as he blinked again.

"Tell me why you're crying, *amor*," I whispered feeling my heart breaking again. "Tell me *everything*." I wanted to fill the spaces between us with kisses and love too, but I wanted answers. I wanted to know why he took so long. Why it felt like he had never felt.

Why he made me feel whole again.

"I will," he kissed me again softer this time. So soft, I almost didn't even feel it. "Eventually. I will. Just let me have this. It's been fucking ages."

"Hmmm, we can do this at my home too," I whispered feeling delighted as I ran my fingers over his cheeks. "*Liam*, we have twenty minutes."

He grinned wide. "I can't have Alisha meeting me like this."

I giggled at the thought.

We both cleaned up in the bathroom before coming back to the office where Liam had marveled at the sex toys, the walls, the awards, the life I had built as it left me.

When I told about Gabriel had found me his face became quiet and unreadable as he looked around at the walls.

Liam turned setting me on my desk and stepping between my legs.

"...and then I made this." I motioned around. "Did you know I was here? Why did you take so long to come back?"

His expression was muted as he motioned to his legs. "Took me a bit longer than I'd liked."

My head tipped back to look at him. Something happened to this man. Awareness for his injuries...his body filled me now.

"Now *you* are the new security person, not Reed."

His smile was light, inky black hair now in disarray as his eyes twinkled. "I am."

I brushed his hair back and both of us seemed to stop from touching each other all over. His lips brushing over mine. I thought I felt starved for something for years—and I realized it was this. His soft affection. His softer lips. He kissed me like we had all the time in the world.

Like he was making sure I was real a little smile playing on his lips. I couldn't stop kissing him.

In a rush of words it flowed out of me and I sat there feeling like being with Liam was the most natural feeling in the world. That is until someone knocked at the door shouting at me.

"Miss Lara!" Her thick, sugary accent rang out. "You got your best friend waitin' on you. *Can I come in?* I've been wanting to talk to you 'bout the damn heater. I swear if that handyman comes back, and tries to sleep with me one more time, I will hit him over the head with a crowbar! I swear that bastard couldn't get laid in a monkey whorehouse with a fistful of bananas."

I winced as Liam's hunter green eyes widened.

"That's Gianna. I have to go. Sounds like Alisha is here."

"I gotta fix me," he grinned and I looked down realizing I was taking his clothes off again. "I didn't know how Deep South she was."

"You have no idea. Some days I have to ask her to repeat herself. This is your *fault*." I motioned to his clothes laughing breathlessly.

I rushed to the door tugging my dress down before Liam could get a hold of me again, he did try and make a playful grab.

And opening it to find my understudy Gianna May, the blonde bombshell staring at me her mouth wide open.

And my best friend—Alisha standing there behind her with a taller gentleman blonde with his red Letterman jacket. Hazel eyes widened and darted behind me to where I knew Liam was fixing his clothes.

After what we'd done. I bit my lip nervous as he walked to me leaning on his cane.

I realized how it might've looked. And Alisha thought I was celibate. I never slept with anyone after Liam. It wasn't that hard.

Men were monsters.

Not all men.

Just enough for me to watch my step.

"Guys, this is Liam," I murmured feeling out of it. "He's the new head of security over Teasers from Titan."

"Liam Sullivan," the blonde next to Alisha who I realized was her bodyguard Kellan looked Liam over curiously.

"Kellan Watts," I forgot how deep his voice was. "Good to finally meet you in real life."

"Liam, this is my best friend Alisha," I motioned to her feeling shy even though he was inside me and he made out with me whenever he got the chance. I felt like he was meeting my world now and it was an adjustment.

"Alisha," Liam nodded to her and stayed on her. He was absorbing her in like he recognized her and I wondered if he knew her from working with Teaser's or he'd done research on her. Reed had done that.

I didn't feel jealous of Alisha, I knew she was in love with Reed but for a moment a wild thought entered my head.

What if Alisha was more his type?

What if Liam found her attractive?

Like Catalina had been prettier than me. For a wild moment even after sleeping with him so many times—I was aware of how I felt.

My own inadequacy. My own past. And what Liam had been through for the last seven years.

"Do you have any family in the States?" Liam was quiet about it as he asked her that.

"I have a younger sister," she replied matter—of—factly, while Kellan watched the interaction glancing between his charge and Liam. I knew Kellan had been assigned by Liam as Alisha's bodyguard—but Alisha hadn't said too much about him.

"Pleasure to meet you, Alisha," Liam's smile was simply polite.

Nothing else and I didn't know why I felt horrible for even thinking Liam could possibly like Alisha. I don't know why I felt that at all.

"I have to head out," Liam murmured. He motioned to Gianna to lead the way. And I felt my smile dropping as he did.

Was he leaving for good?

His voice dropped as he murmured. "I'll text you."

20

LIAM

"So you're the new security guy, huh?"

Gianna May was maybe twenty. Young. But employable.

As far as I knew she worked the floor most nights learning the ropes from Lara.

Blonde, maybe five—eight if not taller, Gianna was a crowd pleaser for a lot of reasons.

Mostly when she did a cowgirl act from what I saw.

Lara's was 'Lady Midnight' and Gianna was the 'Girl Next Door' and the others had themes to their shows.

Was it a little daunting to have made love to a woman I knew—nobody had touched? Yeah.

I felt the pressure to not fuck this up.

To not be a let down for Lara and get the fuck shakes while walking with my cane after multiple orgasms and the taste of her in my throat.

"Where's this handyman?" I asked her instead of answering her question. "You needed help and he was getting handsy?"

"He always tries," she rolled her eyes when talking about him and I felt my irritation flare at that. "But Nate's usually here for this shit, but he's on a job too."

Nathan Wyatt. Reed's former right hand was guarding Gemma Marchand, a former heiress being haunted by her former family.

Gemma's family was a piece of work with cash flow to circumvent her from living her life. It was one of the ninety cases Reed had passed to me.

129

Not gonna lie, all of Reed's work kept me so busy and entertained, I felt myself coming alive in it.

Before I had come to Lara, I had been nervous, my heart racing and needing some alcohol to calm down. But I didn't want to dull the sensations of seeing her and I hadn't taken anything today—not yet.

Not yet.

Right now? I felt the pressure mounting to be the right man for her as I walked out with Gianna.

I saw him immediately leaning against the bar talking to one of the girls like he had all the time in the world. Older guy.

Fifty—something years of arrogance and time had made him think the world catered to him. It didn't. As I approached him I caught the familiar look in his eyes as he took in my cane.

Sort of.

A few years ago, I would catch the dismissive.

Look of people would give me at my limp, and a slight smirk they would give me for a man my size being on a cane.

And because I had seen it too many times to count, nobody knew that I had a blade hidden within the cane. It was a modification I had made years ago, and it was to protect me.

I couldn't always carry a gun and guns weren't always reliable.

I had an aversion to them after my legs.

"That him?"

"Mhm." She did not sound pleased. "Please tell me you're gonna hit him over the head with that cane of yours."

I smirked at Gianna who clearly had a sense of humor.

"I might."

Eventually.

"Are you here about the heater?" Might as well skip the pleasantries.

"Yeah." And then he went back to trying to talk to the red—haired bartender.

Rosa, I think her name was who just shook me a look of curiosity. She didn't know me. Lara hadn't introduced me.

At least I thought that's what her name was.

All the girls here had multiple names and alias's and it was too many for me to keep track of. I caught a few of them milling about cleaning, bustling around the house.

Lara did make them earn their keep.

But right now they were about to find out Nathan and Reed weren't in charge—I was.

I wasn't about to be overlooked.

I tapped my cane twice. "I'm the head of security. I've heard some complaints about you harassing my staff."

That made him pause. Rosa, the bartender looked at me uneasily like she was afraid a little of that. She didn't really interact with him.

"You the head of security?"

He eyed my cane and I saw Rosa look at him with annoyance at the smirk in his expression. Beside me I swore Gianna wanted to growl.

I could feel it.

She'd at least make it in a fight around the place.

"This is a gentleman's establishment, isn't it?" He thought he had height over me because I slouched. Nobody had height over me besides Gabriel.

Once. I pushed his memory aside. Not after what Lara told me about him. I needed to go home and process him finding her.

Listening to my texts. My chest was already brimming with unfamiliar emotions and I could smell Lara's gardenia and roses and white sage on me.

"This is a burlesque club. Owned by Titan. I don't know what you're implying—but this isn't that kind of club." I didn't wait for him to finish. "You're going to fix the heater. And then you're going to leave."

"Or what—"

I didn't even wait to let him finish. I was already annoyed. My head snapped to Gianna who frowned at him. "You wanted a fight—"

I moved faster than he could even blink. I knew I still had it.

Years and years of not walking hadn't dulled any reflex. I had muscle memory working in my favor.

In one fluid motion, I cracked the cane against the back of his knees and his ankle. Rosa stumbled back and Gianna gasped but I was moving. Another to his shoulder and he didn't even see it coming as he went crashing to the ground.

All movement in the club stopped.

I planted my cane into his throat shoving it until he choked.

"This isn't that kind of establishment," I growled. I didn't care if he hurt or if he ached. The memory of a too thin Lara eyeing me like I was her salvation. One I had let down for years was in my head. "Get the fuck out. Gianna. Find a list of maintenance techs within fifteen miles. Rosa, get one of Nate's guys to show this man out. I won't be tolerating a single fucking second of this."

Because Nathan Wyatt shouldn't need to be here. They should've been good without him.

Gianna scampered off to grab her phone, Rosa and one of the guys came up to escort him and two of them came up to me.

I realized the way Reed explained the hierarchy of teams was, I was in charge under him. Leadership had natural flow with one great white shark at the top. *Gabriel.*

Right now, I was in charge of this and any other ventures Reed had.

"I need every single male member of any kind of work order vetted before he steps foot in here. Make sure we're working with a solid company and make sure they understand the rules..." As I rattled off orders both of them stood up straighter and I realized I was working with former military.

I made sure everyone was moving while Lara was with Alisha and when Gianna came back she had a list. "I found four really good ones."

I motioned for her to hand me the list and I found one that was solid.

She looked down. "Call him today." She nodded obediently and everyone else was moving. "Show me the heater. I can see what's wrong with it temporarily."

It was the least I could do with my head spinning in ninety different directions after that.

Teaser's now was stunning. Nothing like the broken down wasteland it had been.

1920's glory with floating umbrellas in the ceiling made to look ethereal. Lush and warm all around even now. I saw different colored wings on the walls and Lara's was the midnight blue going on violet one.

Some of the lingerie was on display and social media props for people to take photos of. Lara centered it around being consumer friendly which was fucking genius. It was her vision.

One that I knew came from my former brother.

And one that I didn't know what to do with anymore.

One thing was for certain—I wasn't about to let Lara down.

~

THE NEXT MORNING I WOKE UP MY HANDS SHOOK WITH THE NEED FOR something.

Something to keep me together.

I really shouldn't have been drinking so much, but home alone? I couldn't stop.

My thoughts were spiraling.

Gabriel had listened to my texts. He'd gotten Lara. He had killed Cormac O'Hara. He went for Lara. Evie…

He had gone back for both of them. Started Titan…why?

Why would he do that?

Gabriel hadn't spoken to me in seven years. He hadn't said one fucking word. Not one. How was I supposed to believe every single thing he had done was for good?

How did I think about him?

When all I felt was hatred for years and years and I laid there processing everything knowing Lara would be here. In my apartment. Looking around at the spare space I realized I had to get rid of my fucking bottles. My meds. Everything.

I moved around tidying up and when she did come over it wasn't empty handed. Lara's inclination was to feed me off the bat and she brought over brunch.

The moment I opened the door after my shower, Lara was in my arms. *"Amor."*

I closed my eyes as I inhaled her scent. Her body pressing into mine, and I saw the takeout bags in hand.

"You brought lunch?" I motioned to it and she beamed up at me from her height. I forgot how tiny Lara was sometimes and it only made me wanna protect her more.

"I did, I thought you might want some?"

Her doe-eyes blinked up at me and I felt my breathing shorten out. And not because I was operating off *nothing*.

Off-nothing.

Fucking nothing but drugs and liqour.

No, I needed a glass of whiskey of any kind and I'd function like a normal man around her.

Otherwise, I was trembling.

My brain too foggy to even process what Gabriel helping Lara out meant.

Instead I lost myself in her kisses. The feel of her real and whole in my arms was one my body was soaking in.

I began spending my days juggling all the tasks Reed gave me, and drowning in her when she wasn't at work.

I began spending my days with her drowning in her. Tearing her into the bed and making love to her like my life depended on it.

Because right now it felt like it did.

133

I took Lara with a fervor that surprised both of us. Sure, I took my meds and my alcohol when she didn't know, but not enough now it would impact me in bed.

No, I wanted to make love to Lara. Wanted to spend every single second with her.

Every single moment I spent without her was a moment I wanted to get back. Like a collection of shiny things, moments with Lara were my favorite, I hoarded memories with her.

I was careening into the sensations I had been deprived of latching onto her with an intensity that should've scared me.

But every single time Lara was in my bed?

It felt like I was in a dream.

In between she told me about Teaser's, her life now, her friends, Alisha, Gemma, Sonya—and so on. And I learned about her. The more she spoke the more I realized how empty I was.

How empty I had been.

How alone I had been.

Without anyone. And then Lara looked at me with those dark doe eyes, her soft hands, her softer kisses as she pressed them into my skin promising me she loved me.

"Te amo, Liam."

She loved me.

Just like that.

Because to Lara, I saved her life.

All those years ago, Gabriel had come to her because I asked him to and he had shown her a photo of me to get her to trust him. Ever since then, she kept my photos.

"This is your playlist," she was fucking adorable and I felt myself getting emotional when she showed me that line up of songs I had loved. "Do you still listen to these bands?"

I didn't listen to anything anymore.

I wanted to scream and tell Lara the Liam she loved? Didn't exist anymore. He died that night. I wanted to tell Lara I was murdered by a maniac and it was kind of my fault Kourtney hated Isobel.

I wanted to tell Lara one night—I had lost everything in one night.

The Liam who 'saved' her didn't do shit but lay there in bed having multiple surgeries while Gabriel had saved her.

But then Lara just kissed me giving me those soft eyes.

When she looked at me my chest filled with this hope. That maybe I could practice again. Be the man she wanted me to be. Be the man I had been,

But I didn't know where he had gone.

I blinked back my emotions as Lara kissed me softer and wiped my eyes. "Amor, Por qué estás llorando?"

Why are you crying?

Was I?

"No," I whispered gruffly. "I don't listen to those bands anymore." I wiped my eyes feeling my emotions overwhelming me.

Her hands brushed my longer hair back now. "*Liam.* You do not have to lie to me."

No, but I didn't deserve unconditional love anymore.

I had fucked up so bad once. I never wanted to let Lara down ever.

"I don't wanna talk about it, Lara. I just want you to kiss me." Forever. And stay that way. I wanted Lara glued to my body at all times, her warmth heating up the block of ice in my chest, her hair fanning out over my arm while she slept. I couldn't leave her alone between work and Teaser's.

One night I went to Teaser's to watch her.

Sometimes she still got on stage and I had no idea how the fuck she learned to do what she did. But I knew she was damn good at it.

I just sat in the back of the house watching her move like she owned the place—Which she kind of did. Not counting Killian fucking O'Hara. I had to meet him still. Aidan O'Hara's younger brother's came by sometimes. Killian, second-in-command, and Kieran the youngest.

I told myself I didn't even want to know how Gabriel got down with the O'Hara's after the death of their father or how he negotiated Lara's freedom.

But I did.

I wanted to know everything even as I watched Lara twirl around her feather boa and bra and panties around another woman.

The thing about Lara was she catered to girls. Tiaras. Feather boas. The entire act was for women. Men were welcome, but all of it was to boost confidence in girls.

All the while Gianna and the other girls moved around interacting with guests.

By the time Lara's finale hit, I was ready to drag her back to come apart on my lap. It was a little strange for me to see my girlfriend on stage. Half—naked. Twirling around in a full size champagne glass looking like she belonged there.

Lara had taken after some famous burlesque stars and gotten herself an enormous champagne glass custom built for herself.

She'd twirl around in it at the end of her act and spray champagne on a few of the VIP guests who signed up for it.

But for me?

I don't know why I had a hard time seeing her. I mean, I definitely appreciated her 'Lady Midnight' show, but some part of me also saw a little tiny Lara. Who called herself Isabella.

Who'd looked at me with soft scared eyes that had seen too much pain.

I didn't know how to reconcile the two or how not to feel like—I needed to pick her up and take her so far away. Somewhere soft and warm where I could just love her. Forever.

Somewhere not here.

Some part of me wanted to run away from here and with her somewhere else.

That night I'd taken her home and fucked her until she cried in my arms with the intensity.

"Fuck," I groaned into her neck. "It'll never stop feeling good with you."

She'd clung to me while I drove deep in her over and over until she'd shivered.

When she passed out in my arms I traced patterns on her skin. The brand still on her wrist a memory of a former life she didn't have.

And my thoughts drifted to Gabriel.

She said he came to her weeks after I saw hr.

Was that why he had stayed in New York?

For her? Or for...something else.

The details of Isobel and Jeremy and my team's death was classified. But it was documented on there that Kourtney Young killed them.

And then someone had shot her.

That was it.

That was all that was documented.

So why had Gabriel stayed there for weeks? What was he doing? Besides taking care of Lara?

I knew enough. Details. Little things. But not enough to formulate enough of a picture on that night. The worst night of my life.

Even as I held Lara in my arms, call it my stubbornness or whatever. I told myself it didn't matter to me what Gabriel had done. He certainly hadn't told me shit.

For the last seven years—he hadn't been a brother to me.
So what the fuck did I even owe him?

21

LARA

LIAM MADE LOVE TO ME LIKE THE WORLD WAS ENDING.

Every single time we saw each other.

He tasted less like alcohol and more like freedom.

And I let him love me like that. Moving in me with a purpose and a wildness to him I expected.

When he went too deep, a pained whimper left my throat as I held him.

"Sorry," his voice was dark but soothing. "Let me."

He adjusted my hips and legs around him as he ground down on my clit turning the pain into sheer pleasure.

"*Liam.*"

"There it is, *muneca*, let me feel you coming."

I felt myself shattering around him and holding onto him for dear life as I came and came in what felt like an endless orgasm. Liam, pulled out of me and I thought he'd finished.

Instead he kissed all the way down my body and the moment his tongue ring shocking against the over—sensitized bud.

His hands, stronger than anything in the world gripped my thighs as he ate at me.

"L—Liam...please...no..."

He rose up a little. "Too much?"

I nodded closing my eyes at the sensations coursing through me. I felt him pause before he sank lower again and then he gentled. Moaning I felt him eating at me like he had all the time in the world.

Coaxing me into another smaller orgasm following the first as his tongue rubbed.

"Oh god," I squirmed in his hold as it hit me. Liam rose up above me as I came, thrusting deep in me with a deep groan as he finished with me.

I held onto him so tight I felt like I was ready to pass out.

"Liam—" I whispered his name feeling a heady sensation washing over me. "I'm tired..." His kisses sank into my skin as I laid there absorbing him as I passed out.

~

I LOVED WHEN HE WAS THERE WHEN I WOKE UP. I DIDN'T ALWAYS NEED TO work.

Most of the time now, the entire operation went on without me. Gianna May was a genius behind the scenes and most people overlooked her because of her accent.

Which let me spend it with Liam.

"I never wanna leave you," he whispered into my skin. We spent the morning cuddling in bed and Liam teased me about me sleeping like a kitten around him. "I've been alone forever."

What?

What about Gabriel? Was he not...

"After your injury," I whispered into his hair as he snuggled me. "Who was there? You were not alone were you?"

He didn't say anything.

My fingers, scratching his back, his hair stopped.

Liam...

He didn't have family. He said his adoptive father had died a few months before he met me. The woman he loved married someone else. And he had met me...that night.

"Nobody cared for you?"

"Someone did, but it didn't work out." His voice changed then and I felt his energy shift and I moved my fingers into his hair rubbing his scalp as he groaned low. "Damn, that's nice. I wish it had been you, but I don't think you would've liked me much."

"What happened to you?"

It left me before I could stop it. He stiffened under me.

"I don't wanna talk about that night," he murmured. And I felt it again.

I swallowed my throat working at the way he sounded. Cold. Shut down. Like someone else.

139

Not my Liam.

"Okay," I rubbed his head. "Do you want kisses?"

Snuggles?

Kisses?

Soft-loving?

Liam was a fan.

Even if he looked vicious with his tattoos and piercings? Liam was the best.

"Sure, why not?"

I felt his smile into my neck as he rose up with his adorable smile in place. I giggled at that look in his eyes.

It was good to have him back.

Even if I knew—that night had changed Liam forever. Maybe I could talk to Gabriel?

I didn't understand why Liam looked the way he did.

He didn't want to talk about anything. But I knew something horrific had happened to him. I knew his hands shook when he thought I wasn't looking.

I knew he made love to me like he was desperate and starved.

Whenever he took me out in the few moments he could, Liam never stopped holding my hand.

He was wrapped around me, asking me ninety different questions, wanting to help me get everything I needed.

He came over to my apartment near Teaser's where he took in the minimal soft white decor at a contrast with my outward image.

"This is you," he motioned to the space with a smile. "Melina."

"Nobody calls me my real name but you," I whispered. "But you can call me whatever you like."

"I'd like to call you mine."

And the way he said it? It was so soft. I almost missed it.

I held him close to me.

"Of course I am yours."

I had been his since he found me.

And I wasn't going anywhere.

"YOU WANT TO GO FOR A WALK?" I MUSED ONE DAY.

Liam had taken me to a shop that sold pastries.

He thought I might like some of the flavors and I did. Now, with a tray

140

of small tiny cakes and bars in front of me—I was stuffed.

And spoiled.

But I thought Liam was making up for lost time.

I saw little prescription bottles everywhere.

They were almost hidden and everything that he did.

I knew he took medication every so often and I knew that sometimes his mood shifted really quickly. Lucky he had to push it all down.

He barely paid attention to movies seemingly lost in his own head and he would get up to grab something to drink.

It was one night when I came to him that I found him slurring his words just enough for me to worry about him.

"*Ven paca, muñeca*," he'd say, pulling me onto his lap as we watched movies I barely paid attention to, too focused on the way his hands shook until they found my skin.

The way he'd bury his face in my hair and breathe like he was drowning, like I was air.

He kissed me like I was salvation.

Deep, desperate kisses that tasted of whiskey and need and something darker—something that reminded me of that night at Teaser's when he'd been trying to forget someone else's name.

But he never went further. Never let his hands wander too far, never let things get too heated.

At first, I thought it was respect—that he saw my past and wanted to be gentle.

But sometimes I'd catch him looking at his trembling hands with disgust, or adjusting his legs with a wince, and I understood.

He was afraid.

I talked to him about Mexico to comfort him and me about my past as much as his. Liam was just as alone as I was.

"You never wanted to go back?" Liam whispered.

"No. There was nothing left for me."

I did want to see Mami. More than anything else in the world. I did. But how would I ever face her?

What did I say?

Lo siento, Mami.

My eyes welled with tears.

"What was your life like? Before..." Liam's voice was so soft. I told him. Liam spoke to me in Spanish for the rest of the night. I was grateful his adoptive family had taught him. And I remembered they had died.

Leaving this little boy alone.

"You're beautiful," he'd whisper, tracing my face with unsteady fingers. "*Mi ángel. Mi salvación.*"

I didn't tell him that sometimes, when he thought I was sleeping, I'd hear him say another name. But I could never make it out.

Didn't mention how he'd stiffen when his phone buzzed with texts from Gabriel. Didn't ask about the wheelchair I glimpsed in his closet once, dusty from disuse. Liam never talked about a single issue he had. No, he just vanished quietly and showed up "better" even when he wasn't.

Instead, I learned his rhythms. Learned that mornings were worst, when the tremors were bad and his legs wouldn't cooperate.

Learned to pretend not to notice when he mixed pills with whatever was in his flask. Learned to love him through it all.

"Are you afraid I will leave you?"

Liam stilled. And when he slowly tipped his head I knew Gabriel had left him. I just knew. They had seemed so close.

Now—Liam didn't say his name.

"Liam," I held his face tighter. "Liam. I will never leave you. Ever." And as I kissed him, he closed his eyes. He didn't open them.

It took long moments for Liam to come back to me.

But even as he kissed me I was worried as he tucked the bottle away into his cabinet where I saw a dozen more.

He came back, swaying a little and rubbing his eyes.

"Bed, *muneca?*"

I didn't recognize this version of Liam.

I didn't know who he was.

But he wasn't entirely the man I knew but then again I wasn't the woman he remembered.

So I accepted it.

22

LARA

I went to see Gabriel at the manor.

It was still nice outside and the Greenwich manor loomed in front of me as I went inside.

The first time I saw where Gabriel lived—I felt out of place and like I didn't belong.

Someone thought I was cleaning staff until Gabriel corrected them. Or Evie's friend.

Now? Gabriel met me in the foyer with a light smile.

"Hey, you look good," he hugged me bending all the way down and light laughter left me as he picked me up.

"Gabriel," I smiled. In the last few years if he couldn't make it he video chatted with me. Checking in on me. Practicing his Spanish and mimicking my words.

I sat with him.

"What happened?"

He shook his head. "I found him bleeding out in his hotel room. On the CCTV footage, the agent shot him."

"What?" One of his own?

Gabriel's jaw clenched as he explained to me that she had been angry at something that happened. Irrationally angry.

She killed his team.

"Liam…his legs are not…"

"He can walk, from what Reed says, but she basically shot him so many times, shattering his knee caps and bones, that even after he recovered and healed—it'll never be the same. I know he has scar tissue that tightens so he needs those worked out. Nerve pain like that is brutal..." Gabriel paused sitting there as he sat there casually.

"So he is not the same Liam..."

Gabriel shook his head. "I fucked up. I should've said something but I felt guilty for leading him into that situation."

I was quiet.

"He was alone."

Gabriel nodded as I wiped my eyes.

All alone.

For seven years.

After losing everything.

Gabriel hung his head.

"I don't know what to say to him. I feel like I took away everything from him."

My throat worked as we sat there.

"You know," Gabriel whispered. "Titan was his idea. I gave the blueprints to Reed who fixed it up in a different image. Modern. Intelligent. Sleeker. Reed has solid taste. He designed everything. We were so young. I wanted to build something Liam would be proud of..."

"And Reed?"

Gabriel's eyes were unreadable. "Spending his days with Alisha."

He said her name dragging it out.

"Have you seen her?" He snuck into Teaser's once or twice and Gemma had almost seen him.

He shook his head.

23

LIAM

"THAT WAS A GOOD MOVIE."

Lara was excited. I was excited for her bouncing along at my side in her little purple get—up. She was cute as fuck. In a tiny miniskirt and sweater and little boots.

Lara's shoe size made me laugh every single time. I put them on for her.

It's like dressing a tiny doll.

I'm your tiny doll.

Yes, you are, muneca.

It was her first date.

Ever.

Her eyes were bright as she bounced next to me.

Dinner and a movie.

I grinned at the idea of something so simple always making her happy.

But my girl loved these kinds of things. I sent her flowers all the time now. Anything purple, anything violet, lilacs, and lush vibrant bouquets she texted me over.

I brought her to a smaller Mexican place where I lived. Lara's eyes lit up. "I have heard of this place but I have not been here yet."

When Lara got excited, she switched to Spanish chattering about the movie and the dinner and I grinned listening to her as she kept pace. Because of my cane I walked slower, but it matched her pace.

And I fucking hated it because I wanted to carry her everywhere. She was so much smaller than me I just wanted to pick her up and take her everywhere.

Even when I slowed down for every one step I took, Lara took two little ones and I wanted to pick her up and hold her in my arms when she laughed.

But I was slower now.

And I fucking hated it.

"I can't believe I've slept with you and have not dated you."

"Not a bad thing," I felt my lips tip up. "I'd still take care of you either way, hm?"

Lara did that thing where she looked like she was going to implode. I laughed bringing her tighter to me.

"Come here, muneca."

She latched herself onto me tighter as we walked into Tony's, an old school Italian restaurant that was highly rated. It wasn't packed at this time so my PTSD wasn't going to freak out.

Over the candles I grinned as we both sat down.

"I feel pressure to be perfect," I murmured honestly.

"Liam," she eyed me with a softer look as she plated my food for me. "You do not have to be—I like you for who you are."

As she said it, something in me unfurled like it was touched by sunlight and even if my demons argued that this girl didn't know about my addictions. My troubles. I didn't care.

I didn't care because Lara…Lara was…everything.

Through her? I realized quickly that if Isobel was my roadmap to love, because she was my mother and sister in one person—Lara was love.

Personified. She glanced my way all night smiling at me over the table and offering me bites of her food.

She fluttered having to stand up she was so small. I forgot sometimes about her height.

"*Muneca*, you keep doing that I'm gonna put you on my lap."

Actually.

That was a great idea. I motioned for her to stand and come to my side of the booth. Floating over, she was now half way on my lap. I motioned to her food. "Better."

"Hmmm," she hummed in happiness as she ate.

And something else unfurled in me as she curled closer. I don't know how long I sat there.

"Mami makes the best pozole," she whispered. "But during Christmas she always made tamales de dulce, like with strawberry…"

"Get it," I murmured into her hair inhaling her scent. It was the sage as the scent inside of Teaser's. "Everything, just get whatever you want." I wasn't hurting for cash.

As she ate she hummed. "I don't usually eat this."

"Why?" I paused as I asked. "Too much of home?"

She nodded. "And you? Your adopted father he makes American food for you?"

I shook my head. Mr. Santos always made food like this so I avoided it too. Whenever I ate it I wanted to cry.

"No, he was Brazilian so we always had a bit of both. His daughter, liked everything under the sun so we always had an assortment of food." And then as I said it I realized what I said.

"His daughter," she murmured, her dark eyes watched me. "You didn't tell me you had a sister."

That's because I didn't have her anymore.

"Neither one of them are in my life."

She quieted turning to her plate. "Sorry."

And then my demons laughed at me.

They cackled at me and I closed my eyes trying to focus on Lara, but I was drifting further down the road. I sipped the drink I'd gotten trying to shut them down. I was on Lara's first date.

I wouldn't fuck it up.

Not with my baggage. She didn't need to know about Mr. Santos and Isobel.

Or anything else.

My demons were chattering louder than anything else in the restaurant right now and I felt her hands on my face.

I heard Mr. Santos and Isobel in my head now. Their ghosts lurking in my skull.

Fucking failure.

Liam, you're a liar.

You killed me.

You did this to her.

You let me down Liam.

Liam.

Liam.

Liam.

"Liam—"

"I'm sorry!" I snapped back into the restaurant to find Lara's eyes wide on me and my jaw dropped when I came to and realized the mostly empty restaurant now was staring at me breathing hard.

Panicking.

In front of Lara.

On her first date.

I closed my eyes. "Fuck," I whispered feeling shame crawl up my face as I turned away. "I'm sorry—I—" I grabbed the drink chugging it down. I couldn't live without it.

Couldn't exist as my hands shook.

Lara's eyes were wide on me. "What happened?"

"Nothing." I said it too quickly. Too much. "I'm sorry. I didn't want to —I didn't want to ruin that—"

"Liam."

Her voice was hard and I felt nothing but shame as I turned back to her.

"You ruined nothing," she held my face and then I felt her lips on mine. Over and over until my body sighed and I calmed down.

"You ruined *nothing*. You cannot ruin this. Every single day with you is a date. Every single moment with you is perfect. It's you."

She kissed me over and over as my eyes watered as she moved onto my lap and stayed there.

"It's you," she whispered.

Lara kissed me quiet.

Over and over until I groaned holding her tight to me.

When she pulled back I felt her fingers brushing my eyes. "It's always going to be you, Liam. You're okay. Everything is okay."

∼

Everything was not okay.

I was still a wreck on the inside. All of me felt like it was falling to pieces unless I was with Lara. And I felt like I glued myself to her more than I should've. Was it right?

Maybe not.

But did I know how to stop?

No. I didn't.

24

LIAM

ONE DAY, BY THE TIME WE MADE IT BACK TO MY APARTMENT, MY SCAR tissue tightened painfully.

It was so excruciating I groaned as I sat feeling the mind—numbing pain setting in and the need for nerve pain killers.

Nothing a little Gaba can't fix.

"Liam?"

"It's okay, *muneca,* I need a bath. That's all."

I popped a few painkillers washing it down with the rum I had on the counter and some soda. I kept going until I felt it silence my thoughts and then did I brace my hands on the counter.

Breathing in and out.

Did it occur to me I had PTSD? No.

Because I didn't go to war. I had one fucked up incident and that wasn't going to define me.

"Liam," Lara's voice was low behind me, as her arms reached for me. "Let me...let me do something for you."

Shit. It was supposed to be her night. I didn't want to make it about me.

"No," I shook my head. "We're still on a date."

Her laughter was low. "Liam, we can be on a date and still do something nice for you."

Her words flitted through places of my heart I didn't know it could touch. Lara instructed me to strip down to my boxers and lay back on my bed and I knew the moment she brought out olive oil and coconut oil where she was going.

"Lara, wait—"

"What is it?" She got all in between my fucked up mangled legs.

"Lara, I'm terrified."

"Why? I've already had you, why would you be afraid?"

"My legs…" I swallowed as she blinked at me curiously like she had no fucking clue what I was talking about. "Lara…"

"Nothing is bad about your legs. I like the way you look."

And then this little woman got to work on me.

"It's okay," she soothed, her tiny frame somehow containing all the gentleness in the world. "I won't hurt you. Let me help."

She repeated it as many times as she could as her fingers, warmer now, reached for my legs. My scars. I closed my eyes groaning a little at the tension. Every part of my body felt strung tight.

I was insanely turned on at the sight of Lara, dark hair over me and lithe body, until she touched one painful spot and I groaned.

"Shhh, it's okay, you're okay."

"Lara—" My voice cracked on her name.

"It's okay," she repeated, her hands already working the oil into knotted muscle. The pain was immediate and intense—like she was touching live wires under my skin. But underneath the agony, I felt something starting to release.

"*Fuck*," I ground out between clenched teeth.

"This is good?" Her voice held no judgment, just genuine concern.

I nodded, sweat breaking out on my forehead. "It's horrific, but don't stop."

Her small hands found every knot, every twisted piece of scar tissue. Places I pretended didn't exist, she touched with reverence instead of revulsion.

I couldn't stop losing it and I felt Lara moving over me and Holding me as I did.

"I know," she whispered. "It's okay, Liam. You are not alone anymore."

My demons told me to push her away, scream at her for giving us sympathy.

Rage.

Scream.

Shove her back.

Stop it!

It's Lara.

150

I would never—
I was struggling.
I was.

And her soft voice was in my ears, drugging me and telling me I was perfect the way I was and she wouldn't change me for the world.

The world.

Lara switched to her native tongue and laid there like my blanket as I trembled and broke down.

25

LIAM

Sex was different with Lara.

Where with everyone else I felt used. Lara's energy soaked into my skin, filling resources and reserves with a high. Something brighter than me.

If I was shadows, Lara was a flame.

If I was king of the underworld, Lara was my light.

Fucking her felt like heaven. Raw. Ramming myself into her body until I fused us together. That was the only purpose I had.

"Liam—slow down," Lara murmured holding me to her. She was sobbing into my neck. "Too much, *amor*."

I pulled out of Lara needing to calm down then as I licked my way hungrily down her body. I was all animal around her, years and years of pent—up frustration coming out as I sank my tongue into her body so I wasn't pushing her past her limits.

I speared her legs apart, throwing her thighs over my shoulders and I fucked into her pussy with my tongue. I could feel her walls clenching around me and I kept going loving the way she trembled and shook.

Her sobs muffled as she whimpered in pleasure.

I ate at Lara with waves of possessiveness washing over me.

Nobody ever is going to touch her like this.

Nobody will ever see her like this.

Her peach tipped nipples shook as she came again around my tongue, her delicate fingers gripping my hair tighter, rocking her hips up. I growled knowing it would make her squeal.

And didn't I fucking love that?

Lara came on my tongue harder and I kept it going until I finally rose up feeling like a hungry demon after taking in every drop of her.

I licked my way up her body burying so deep I groaned. I knew Lara liked my weight on her so I settled in comfortably working my hips like some fuck drunk animal high off his girl.

She was my obsession.

My new addiction.

I fucked into Lara like I needed her to live.

"You like me, *muneca*?"

"I love you, Liam."

Lara's eyes watered just enough for me to feel it somewhere deep in my chest. The icy cold recesses of my body that demanded I make her stop crying.

Seeing Lara anything but smiling did something to me.

I wanted to feel Lara's pulse. To be reminded of her heart racing so that it would be the way it reminded me I was alive. I was still here. Not Liam, the ghost drifting in a faraway world where nobody gave a shit about him.

"Amor?"

"Sorry," I murmured. "I missed you all these years."

"I missed you too," she whispered. "I waited for you. Look at everything I did. I thought you'd be proud—"

"I am so proud of you, baby—"

Lara laughed the sound light and musical.

"God, you did great," I brushed her hair back feeling nothing but warmth. I blinked back emotion. "I'm sorry I couldn't save you."

"But you did," she kissed me over and over again.

Lara and I fell asleep together all the time.

She made me want to stop drinking.

In turn, I made sure to catch her when she fell.

I only felt peace when I was with her. Which made me feel even more ashamed that I even felt that. I didn't feel like I deserved it.

Not after losing my sister. Losing everything I could've ever wanted. And then realizing the only real thing I had ever wanted was Lara Ford.

Killian O'Hara's girlfriend had run screaming from his mob connections.

A nice girl, by all accounts, terrified of what she'd discovered. That she had accidentally fallen in love with the mortal equivalent of a demon prince.

Just another fire to put out in my whiskey—soaked, coke—fueled existence.

I was hunched over my computer, Oracle humming through data streams, tracking Lucy Devereaux's movements.

The attack on Lucas, Evie's boyfriend, had me working overtime.

Reed's intel about the black cards—the same ones from my nightmares, the ones that haunted me since that night—suggested Lucy was being hunted.

By Marcus Hagen. A dead man.

The same Marcus Hagen connected to Isobel's death.

Or was it Kourtney? The details of that night had become twisted in my mind, warped by trauma and time and too many substances trying to numb the pain.

Then I saw her.

My hand froze on the mouse, my breath catching in my throat. A blonde woman in a black coat, entering the hotel. Something about her movement, the way she carried herself...

"Oracle, zoom in on the blonde. Who is that?"

"Unknown variable."

Ice filled my veins. Oracle didn't do "unknown variables."

Oracle knew everything.

"What?"

"Unknown variable."

"Oracle. Is that the same woman from the other night? Mystery blonde."

"Yes, sir. It is indeed."

Everything stopped.

What the—

Was this woman the key to unraveling everything?

Or had she been the one who... who killed...

I couldn't finish the thought. But deeper than the detective's curiosity, beyond the addict's desperation, something else stirred. A recognition so profound it threatened my impending migraine.

That's how Isobel would walk.

26

LARA

THE LAST FEW WEEKS OF OUR LIVES HAD BEEN INSANITY.

Even for me.

Alisha and Avani had been injured by someone stalking her, but it was the weeks that followed Liam seemed to dig himself into a weird hole.

There was something bothering him.

I could tell.

I knew Liam was an alcoholic.

I knew he hid his medications in places I couldn't get to.

I knew he snapped sometimes over everything, like a wounded caged animal, buried under his liquor bottles and pills.

And yet, I loved Liam.

I knew him in his heart. I knew Liam was better.

And then he started vanishing. Liam, the same Liam who leaned on me began vanishing.

Late night again?

Working late, love you muneca

He'd be gone for hours and hours.

Sure, I knew he worked for Titan, but his eyes wouldn't meet my face. And I knew Liam wouldn't cheat.

No. Not my Liam.

Not when he looked ragged when he saw me.

Some nights he'd come to bed and hold me so tight it hurt, like he was afraid I'd disappear.

Other nights he'd move over me like he was on a mission to prove to me that he loved me.

Even if he didn't have to.

And I didn't mind it, but I got the feeling Liam was running from demons that I couldn't save him from sometimes.

But I wanted to.

One night Liam was moving over me, pinning me down and driving into me like a savage. And I was in love. I felt better with him than I had with anyone else.

He was coming home until the Devereaux case.

The few times I asked him he'd change the subject and leave or make an excuse to leave.

The few times I asked about the Devereaux case, he'd change the subject or make an excuse to leave.

I knew what it looked like when someone was preparing to leave.

I'd seen it enough times—the gradual withdrawal, the careful distance, the guilty touches. But this felt different.

This wasn't just Liam pulling away.

This was Liam being pulled by something—or someone else. And I didn't know what was going on with him sometimes.

And I wasn't insecure, but part of me wondered if he had anyone else. Liam had been acting strange, and in my darkest moments, I wondered if there was someone else.

Part of it was the training I had gone through.

But right now? I wished I was just a normal girl.

Not a former prostitute.

The thought would creep in late at night when his side of the bed was cold, when his excuses about work felt paper—thin.

But even as the fear whispered through my mind, I knew better.

Liam wasn't that man.

For all his demons, for all his struggles with alcohol and pills, for all his raw edges—infidelity wasn't in his nature.

He was too honest, too direct in his pain.

And I wanted to be.

I wanted to tell Liam how hurt I was all the time but I was disconnected from those parts of me.

I compartmentalized for my current moments and I held onto that part of me until life forced me to let it go.

When he hurt people, he did it head—on, not in shadows and secrets. And me? That had been my entire life.

How did I even start with feeling worthy of Liam?

27

LIAM

Finding out your sister was alive wasn't an everyday thing.

"Isobel?"

"Liam?"

"Shortcake, you're alive."

She was *alive*. It had been seven years since I'd seen her.

And I thought she was gone.

I couldn't let her go. I couldn't stop hugging her. I couldn't stop crying when I saw her.

Gabriel was looking for Marcus Hagen.

Technically Reed was.

Again?

Marcus Hagen was trying to kill Lucy and Lucas Devereaux for stealing from him?

Lucas Devereaux was a real estate tycoon and he was dating Evie.

My chest expanded when I saw him kiss her in the security footage at the movies. Who would've fucking thought?

No wonder Evie looked off.

What did the Devereaux siblings take?

I didn't use Evie's version of Oracle.

I used mine.

Over the years fine tuning it t find what. Needed and rather than searching for her now, I went back.

I went back to the beginning of the year where I found her in Belize.

"You've been busy Lucy Devereaux."

And I followed Lucy all throughout

Lara was my future, my heart, my truth.

But Isobel... Isobel was my past, my guilt, my penance. And I didn't know how to reconcile the two without destroying everything I'd built.

"You look different now."

Liam had become a part of my life at the Primrose. He filled me in on Lara over dinners and he asked me careful questions about my life.

"You are different too," I murmured over the dinner table. We had come downstairs. Me with my platinum hair. Liam, quieter and reserved as he took me in with his cane.

I had missed his cane.

He thought the woman who shot him wanted to make him suffer longer than death. So she'd shot his legs.

I had known cruelty. So had Talia.

I recognized Liam had sold his car because driving had hurt him. His car that he worked all summer to afford the downpayment on.

He couldn't ice-skate anymore. He couldn't do karate. Nothing.

This Liam spent twenty hours at his desk working and building himself up because disability didn't cover for all his expenses.

I cried a lot over this Liam, the same he cried when he saw my injuries.

"I think we both died in different ways," I spoke over the din of the cutlery against our plates and Liam met my eyes over his wineglass.

He drank a lot more now too. I remember when we were younger Liam wouldn't go near alcohol. Now? He seemed to carry a flask, he drank wine all the time. Even for lunch.

But he seemed steady and stable to me.

Leaning on his cane when he needed to. He was still muscled so I knew it didn't hurt him. But it was painful watching it.

I hadn't spoken to my team in a few days. Not Samara. Not Bexley. I texted them but I didn't know how to look at them.

Not because I was angry with them or because I stopped searching for the necklace. But because after finding out Talia lied to me. For some fucking reason—I didn't even know what to say.

Some part of me shattered.

"You died," he said calmly. "I was awake the entire time." His eyes went darker than hunter green now. "I remember everything."

I did die. I nodded understanding that Talia hadn't been wrong. Losing my memories had been a blessing. I had come back a different person.

Liam noticed it. I wasn't the sister he had.

The girl who shared a room with him growing up. I didn't understand his jokes or tease him.

I kept to myself a lot for seven years and became someone different.

I wasn't going back to that woman. I didn't know if I wanted to.

"It's good you don't remember," he said softer than before, his eyes on mine filled with something unreadable. "It's good you forgot about your pain and started over from scratch. I can't even be mad. I missed you, but I'm glad you're here."

Because Liam had been alive, suffering, and struggling and so had I. My heart had been weaker so I couldn't go to him. I had healed.

Part of me wondered if Talia knew or if his death was the only public information she had.

"I didn't know anything," I filled him in.

Talia hadn't had Oracle then. But she had the power to shut off the grid. I didn't know if she knew. If she assumed. If she chose not to tell me. If she believed if never looking back.

I was angry with Talia for keeping secrets from me.

And I needed to go talk to her but only when I cooled down.

Only when I had drank in enough of Liam to satiate the part of me that had missed him.

"Talia probably had an inkling," he said. "But it sounds like she disobeyed her father directly every single time. It sounds like she kept secrets. You said she was with Andrei DuPont and Malcolm threatened to kill him?"

Liam frowned as I nodded. "That's interesting because as of three years ago, Andrei DuPont doesn't have many photos of him and he keeps to himself. Nobody knows if he's with someone or not. If Natasha killed Malcolm because Talia was pregnant—"

"Talia was keeping secrets from everyone." I finished because it sounded like her. She had chosen to be with Andrei after her father threatened him. "To protect them?"

He shrugged lightly. "She didn't tell her father about the man she loved, I entertained that if her father ordered her to kill someone? And she kept them alive? He would never let her live it down. I don't know. I don't like her very much for keeping you from me." His lips twisted up wryly, his eyes amused on me. "I'm glad you're back in my life."

I smiled over at him. "You are drinking more now."

He nodded with a humorless smile. "I needed it." He changed the subject. "I haven't told Lara about you. But I want to. I want us both to come with you when you go. After I help you that necklace back from Reed."

He had told me he would. He would help me get it back and we would leave together.

As a family still. Even if I wasn't the same woman? I was his family.

"I would love to meet her, I never thought I'd see the day where you fell in love."

As I said it a new emotion entered his eyes as he let out a shuddering breath. "Yeah, me too," his voice was soft and somber. "Me too. Listen, I gotta get going."

Liam did his own IT thing he said. He didn't mind walking away from all of it.

"When will you tell Lara you want to come with me?" I asked him as he stood with his cane. The image of the boy that I used to know, with the man he became was jarring.

He shrugged lightly looking uneasily at me. "I'm figuring it out."

LIAM AND I SPENT ALL OUR TIME TOGETHER.

I felt like I was drinking in moments with him.

It felt really good to be back with him. Memories of us growing up, him always carrying me on his back, protecting me, being family?

It was healing something in me I didn't know I needed.

Sometimes I still saw that boy who my father put into karate, the one whose bruises healed living with us—but his temper flared every so often.

I saw the boy who tried to get me to go ice skating with him all the time or me pulling him to dance classes grudgingly.

He felt familiar and foreign at the same time.

We sat together outside at a cafe he liked he said he brought Lara to sometimes.

"What is it like for you?" I motioned to his legs, his cane. He never talked about it. "Do you still..." I trailed off. Unsure how to approach something like this for him. I knew how it felt, but my legs were fine.

I could move.

"I swim now," he murmured over his coffee. "I don't do anything I used to do." A bittersweet smile touched his lips. "Lara says it's for the best. She says running is overrated anyway."

"Your Lara is good to you?"

He nodded tipping his head forward. "Too good. She's got a sense of humor, she's playful. You'd like her. I met her in my old life and…" he trailed off a host of emotions playing on his face. "And now we're together." He seemed to check himself from saying anything else as he sipped his coffee.

It was awkward now.

I never remembered it being awkward between us.

He was careful with me. But I felt careful with him.

"What's it like in Cape Verde?" He asked softly.

I smiled telling him about the island, the compound, our lives. And how much had changed. As I spoke his eyes softened.

"You like it there."

A statement not a question.

I nodded. "It is warm and nice."

Liam snorted like it was surprising. "Never thought Malcolm Nash's paradise would be something you'd like."

"You know him?" I had never met him.

Liam shook his head. "I heard of him in the past but no, never met the guy." His expression shuttered. "Say, you got any plans today?"

"I never have plans." Not since I came to New York.

I didn't know how to get my necklace back anymore.

"Do you know how to get the necklace back from Reed?"

His expression became unreadable. "Yeah, I'm brainstorming a few things."

He quickly changed the subject. "What do you say I give you a tour around the city?"

That sounded good, but as we both got up, I noted the way Liam leaned heavily on his cane.

"You know," I said softly. "Talia put me through physical therapy—"

"Physical therapy isn't gonna fix me, Isa." His voice was clipped and colder. Firm. His eyes turning dark. "I'm not fixable."

I frowned behind him as he pressed down on his cane.

"I promise I'm good," he said but he grimaced as he stood to his full height.

"Liam, you are not good," I cut in feeling something in my chest ache at his pain. He used to fight and move and live his life. And now?

"Come on." I linked my arm with his. "I'm still hungry. Coffee and croissants is not going to fill me up. Let's go get pizza. I don't want to walk all over the city—it's cold."

He smirked. "Fine, but at the minimum I'm paying."

28

LIAM

ISOBEL WAS *ALIVE*.

She brokenly told me what happened to her.

"You were kidnapped?"

She told me about a secret organization named Talon that came and rescued her. But my Isobel wasn't the same girl I knew.

She'd changed.

She'd dyed her hair after I met her.

Dark hair. Brown eyes. Still the same sister. My hands gripped her face in panic, eyes widening.

My heart was expanding painfully because I couldn't stop.

I couldn't calm down.

I couldn't.

"Isa."

She was real.

She was alive.

∼

SHE DIDN'T REMEMBER HIM.

She didn't know him.

All she knew was me.

And if that wasn't a sign?

I didn't know what was.

I was a monster.

Isobel was alive.

She had been—for the last seven years.

Did Gabriel know?

Did he suspect it?

It didn't matter. I wanted to tell him but I wanted to protect my sister from whatever had happened to her.

And I didn't want her to ever think about someone who got her killed or put her life in danger?

I didn't hate myself as much as I hated Gabriel.

I despised Gabriel with everything I had for saying he would take care of my sister and failing on every level. Every level possible.

And then he put her life in danger and he let her die.

And I'd never forgive him for that.

I didn't know how to speak to him. I didn't want to. And I didn't feel the need to reach out to him or to seek out a bridge to heal whatever fucking wounds he made up he had.

Because as far as I aware Gabriel's life had gotten better and my life had been at a standstill. But I was the one doing everything for Titan while he was searching for his wife.

He was doing everything possible to find her and neglect his team and everyone around him by being an annoying bastard.

And I was the one everyone turned to for help.

I wasn't just bitter.

I was angry.

I was beyond angry. I designed Titan.

I designed everything with my sister.

And I designed the world we existed in. Just me and my sis with the father we no longer had. And I was her brother.

That's all I would be but over time I realized I just wanted her in my life.

And he took that from me time and time again.

And I didn't want to forgive him.

29

LARA

LIAM WASN'T THE SAME LIAM.

Something happened to him during the case he was working. It was strange how off he was. Liam usually was focused, loving, attentive, but he woke up with nightmares.

He woke up yelling. At one point at night, he got up out of bed and I pulled him back down to kiss him. But he was out of it.

What is it?

Something about a necklace?

A necklace?

Someone stole a necklace from Reed and I have to hunt this bitch down.

I just laughed.

I didn't know how to talk to Gabriel about it, but I always went to Gabriel all the time for everything. I never turned to Reed as much.

No, I leaned on Gabriel whenever he'd come over and he checked on me and in turn I taught him Spanish.

I giggled at his accent in private, but in public, he defended me.

I didn't know if he'd be there for Liam.

I didn't know how he'd show up.

I was worried about the route Liam was going and if it was going to get him killed. Or if he wanted something else.

I didn't know how to ask him.

But I knew I loved him and I didn't know how to tell him or if I should because he was on edge about this assignment.

I didn't know but I did know to tell Gabriel. But I couldn't form the words. I didn't know how to say it.

Where did I even begin?

Liam came back :)

Is he good to you?

Yes.

Have you seen him yet?

No, we just had a lot going on

If he's not good to you

Tell me

They were friends...shouldn't they see each other?

It had been years maybe they kept in touch.

And I didn't know how to tell Gabriel I was scared for Liam.

Liam never talked about him and I noticed when I brought up Gabriel he looked uncomfortable.

And I didn't know what to do.

How did I tell Gabriel his best-friend was losing himself?

I didn't know how to form the words.

I was worried I wasn't good enough to Liam. But I was doing my best. Juggling my business. My life. My work.

For a man who didn't even know how to tell me if he was hurting.

And I didn't know how to tell him it hurt me.

LIAM'S APARTMENT FELT WRONG THE MOMENT I WALKED IN.

Too clean.

Too empty.

Like someone had wiped away all traces of life, leaving behind only ghosts.

The rum bottle on the counter stood out like an accusation— empty, abandoned, the only thing he hadn't bothered to hide.

My throat tightened. One bottle a day, sometimes more.

Always chased with those pills he thought I didn't notice.

The ones that made his hands stop shaking, that helped him sleep through the nightmares he wouldn't talk about.

I moved through the space, noting what was missing. His favorite hoodie. The photo of us from our dates from the polaroids.

Small things, important things.

Liam was all of my important things. He was fully love.

Not a love split in half. Into pieces. I had fought for everything in my life.

Everything I had came from sacrifice but no more.

With Liam there was no sacrifice. No suffering. Just love. And Liam made me feel the truth.

I deserved something better.

Something more.

Something kinder.

Something friendlier.

Something softer.

Nothing that I had before.

I had loved until I lost my dignity. The only thing I had ever wanted was to go home.

Lo siento, Mamá. I should have listened.

Come home, munequita.

Muneca, I'm home.

I did make it home.

I made it home to Liam every single day. Every single night.

And Liam was my new home.

And loving Liam is more than enough. I don't need anything else.

Except tonight, something was wrong.

I felt off the moment I walked in. Just like I did the night I lost...I didn't even want to think about it.

Liam was sitting at his desk like always.

And I felt a smile tip my lips as he turned over his shoulder, the arch of his cheeks catching his cheeks letting me know he was stressed. The bags under his eyes.

The way his lips tipped up but it never met his eyes.

"Amor?"

He held out his arm from his desk, his arm muscles and tattoos flexing as I grinned and slid into his lap. Excited. Giddy. I was always looking forward to snuggles with Liam.

"Come with me. Let's leave it all behind."

I laughed lightly. "What are you talking about?"

"You don't think about leaving?"

"New York?"

"Mhm."

"I do." But not like that. "I don't wanna run away from things, Liam. I lost my home once, Liam. I don't want to lose my home again. What's happening?"

He was quiet for a long moment.

"I JUST WANT MY FAMILY BACK."

"I want my family too—"

"You have a life! I never got my life back. I have a chance to have it all back. I have a choice. Nobody gave me a choice. Everybody took everything away from me. And now I finally get her back—"

"Then bring her here!" I shouted. "Bring her to us. Let her join our family. Reed, Gabriel can take care of her—"

And just like that Liam snapped the moment I said it.

"*Gabriel?*" he said his name for the first time out loud and in that moment, my Liam was gone.

The man that I knew?

Had been eliminated.

The light in the room felt snuffed out as ice filled the air. Liam's entire demeanor contorted.

With disgust.

At me.

"*Gabriel fucking Monroe is the reason my entire life is in shambles. Don't you ever fucking say his name around me.*"

"*Liam, I think you've had too much to drink—*"

"I'm fucking *sober*," his voice was lethal and deadly as he watched me. "And I'm sober enough to know you would rather pick Gabriel than me?"

"I love you, Liam—"

He laughed outright. "You love me so much you'd rather have a fucked up life living in your old den where you were bought and sold and Gabriel gave you your own personal hell just like he did to me than to be with me?"

"What are you talking about?"

"I was on his team!" Liam shouted. "*He's the reason I lost my fucking legs!*"

It was like the floor dropped out from under me.

My world didn't tilt. My vision blurred as Liam erupted.

"He stole everything from me. He's the reason why I'm FUCKING DISABLED. DO YOU EVEN UNDERSTAND THAT? WHILE YOU'RE FLYING AROUND IN THE AIR? I CAN'T WALK STRAIGHT. I CAN'T MOVE. I'M LESS OF A MAN THAN HE IS. AND IT'S HIS FAULT."

"Why are you screaming?"

I felt my eyes well. Liam never yelled. Liam never snapped. No. He never did.

But now he was.

Why?

I didn't know what was happening.

"And you are just like them," he snarled at me. "You are just like them. You pick the Titans over me. Because you never fucking liked me. You just held onto me because I was a reminder of the only nice thing you ever had."

What was going on?

And after Liam?

Would I ever have anything nice again?

Was there anything more to my life if I lost love?

Yes.

There always was.

And there always will be.

And it's you.

You are more than enough.

More than enough than a man.

You never needed a man to rescue you.

And if I cannot rescue Liam?

Then go to Killian.

And he'll take care of you.

30

LIAM

THE DOOR SLAMMED OPEN WITH ENOUGH FORCE TO RATTLE MY BOTTLES.

Angry and wheat-haired,

Gabriel filled my doorway—wheat-colored hair, those pale blue eyes I'd grown to hate.

Bigger. Stronger. Everything I used to be. And everything I wasn't.

My legs screamed as I stood, but I wouldn't face him sitting down. Not for this. Not after everything.

"You took my necklace."

Ha. I was waiting for this motherfucker.

"You killed my sister."

He moved first—he always did.

Even with my bad legs, I saw it coming.

Some things you don't forget, even after seven years of drinking yourself numb. He went for my ribs first, fighting dirty.

I wasn't the golden boy he used to know either.

"You did this to me!" I snarled, managing to roll him. My fist connected with his face, a familiar dance from our sparring days. "You killed my family."

"You kept my family from me."

"Still got it, motherfucker," I spat, but the victory was short-lived.

He threw me off like I weighed nothing, my back hitting the coffee table. Glass shattered. Probably more bottles. I was bleeding, but I couldn't feel where.

"You were my brother!" The rage in his voice almost masked the pain. "You kept her from me!"

"You killed her!" But even as I said it, something was wrong. His eyes held a different kind of darkness.

"I didn't kill anyone!"

When he came at me again, I knew I couldn't win. My legs were too weak, my reflexes dulled by years of substance abuse. But I wouldn't give him the satisfaction of an easy victory. Not after he took everything — my sister, my company, my future.

The Gabriel I used to know would have fought clean. This one went straight for my knees.

I would have recognized this stranger in my house if I hadn't been staring at a stranger in my mirror for the past seven years.

My legs gave out the moment he went for my knees.

An animal sound tore from my throat—pain or rage, I couldn't tell anymore. Through the blood in my mouth, I watched him grab a bottle.

The irony wasn't lost on me as he shattered it. My poison becoming his weapon.

The glass bit into my throat. Part of me wanted him to do it.

"Do it," I spat blood at him. "Fucking do it. You always wanted to."

"No." His voice broke. "I wanted you to be family."

Then his eyes went wild.

You knew she was alive. She was alive. She didn't know me. You knew.

I laughed, the sound as broken as I was, pressing my throat harder against his glass. "That was her second chance, you son of a bitch. You know how stupid you have to be to drag her into—"

The glass dug deeper. "Listen to me, you motherfucker. I didn't drag her into anything. She is my wife. She is the mother of my fucking daughter that I lost that night—"

Everything stopped. Daughter? The word hit like another bullet.

"You think you lost your sister?" His voice cracked. "I lost my family. I lost. My. Girls. I lost them both! And you stayed the victim. I saved Evie. I buried Adrianna. I saved everyone. You stayed the victim."

My mind reeled. Evie. Adrianna. A daughter I never knew about. While I'd been drowning myself in whiskey, thinking I was the only one who'd lost everything...

"I lost my world," he continued, his voice raw. "Over and over and over. I reached out to you. I looked for you. I asked Claire Sutton where you went. She said you left her and you turned into your fucking parents!"

The truth of it carved deeper than his glass. I had become my father — drunk, violent, destroying everything I touched. While Gabriel had saved what was left of our family.

"All this time, I thought I had fucked up," he said, disgust dripping from every word. "She wasn't just your family. She was the only good thing about you. You're a scumbag, Liam Sullivan."

He threw the glass aside, my blood staining his hands. Standing over me, he didn't look like my brother anymore. He looked like everything I could have been if I'd chosen differently.

"You're a piece of shit. And you deserve everything that's coming for you. I will never forgive you for keeping my injured wife from me. I will never forget it." His final words hit like a death sentence. "And neither will you."

As Gabriel stood over me, memories crashed through the alcohol haze.

Teaching him to ice skate—his legs shaking like a newborn colt, both of us laughing until we couldn't breathe. Isobel catching us trying to sneak out of training, her hands on her hips pretending to be mad but fighting back a smile.

Late nights in the dorm, introducing him to bands he'd never heard of, watching his face light up at the first notes of songs that would become our anthems.

Flashes of what we'd been. Brothers. Family. The three of us against the world.

Now he looked down at me with those pale eyes, and I saw no trace of that golden boy who'd once followed me around like a shadow.

No trace of the man who'd trusted me with his heart, his future, his everything. I'd taken that trust and shattered it like the bottles littering my floor.

"Neither will you," he said again, softer this time.

But there was something worse than hatred in his voice now—disappointment.

Like he'd finally accepted that the brother he knew had died that night with Isobel.

He was right.

I watched him turn away, my blood on his hands, leaving me alive. It was a crueler punishment than death—forcing me to live with the knowledge that while I'd drowned myself in guilt and whiskey, he'd saved what was left of our family.

Protected Evie.

Built something from the ashes of what we'd lost.

The door closed behind him with a finality that felt like a coffin lid shutting.

~

I LAY IN THE WRECKAGE OF MY APARTMENT, IN THE WRECKAGE OF MY LIFE, counting bottles I couldn't see through swollen eyes.

Devastation wasn't a strong enough word.

Neither was demented.

Seven years of hatred had led to this—my brother's blood on my hands, Lara's tears in my ears, and the truth about Isabel's daughter burning holes in my gut.

Everything hurt. Everything ached.

But the physical pain was nothing compared to the realization that I'd done this to myself. I'd chosen this.

Chosen to drown in grief while Gabriel saved what was left of our family. Chosen to push away the one person who saw me as a saint rather than the demon I'd become.

Lara wanted you. You fucked that up too.

The thought broke something loose in my chest. Hot tears slid down my face, mixing with blood I couldn't bother to wipe away.

Part of me wished Gabriel had finished it.

Death would have been kinder than this understanding—that I'd become everything I used to hate. My father. A drunk.

A man who destroyed everything he touched.

When the door opened again, I didn't move.

Maybe someone would rob me, put me out of my misery. Instead, soft footsteps approached. I would've been on edge.

"Liam?"

I must be hallucinating. Why would Sonya come? Unless... the O'Haras sent her. Unless Lara still cared enough to...

"Liam," Sonya's hands were surprisingly strong on my face, grounding me. "Liam, say something."

I couldn't. Seven years of pain tried to claw its way out of my throat.

"Vera, wait..." Sonya didn't hesitate to wrap her arms around me as I shattered. The sound that left me wasn't human —

"It's okay," she held onto me tighter as I snapped in half.

173

"I fucked up."

"It's okay, you didn't—"

"I did—"

"You did not fuck up," Sonya held onto me tighter as I shattered for what felt like an eternity of fucking up. "I'll take care of you. I'm not losing you or letting you go. Not anymore."

31

LARA

I<small>T WAS MY FIRST TIME LEAVING</small> N<small>EW</small> Y<small>ORK</small>.

I never packed up my apartment in the city.

I left it in all of its jewel-toned glory. I missed the texture of my pillow, the comfort of my blanket, and the ease I moved around my room. I missed it all the moment Killian whisked me away to Chicago with Kieran O'Hara.

When I left for Chicago with Kieran?

I couldn't stop breaking down. Every single moment with Liam felt like a lie and it broke me even more.

He had never loved me.

Not like he loved her.

Never like her.

Sonya checked in with me all the time. Asking me if I was good, sending me takeout and sweet treats.

Sonya checked in regularly, her texts arriving like clockwork.

She never mentioned Liam directly, but I could feel her concern. Killian, with Nisha pregnant at home, became my constant lifeline — sending me photos of nursery preparations, keeping me tethered to the family I'd chosen rather than the love I'd lost.

The irony wasn't lost on me—finding shelter with the O'Haras again. But they were nothing like their father.

Aidan ran the Chicago operation with a quiet strength, while Kieran was learning to take his place in the family business. T

hey gave me space to breathe, to process, to understand that waiting

175

seven years for a saint had been my choice—and now choosing to heal was also mine.

In turn, Aidan introduced me to Rachel, a Titan operative who worked in Chicago.

A bubbly ginger who was an IT professional at Titan, Rachel was fun to be around and I had a few Titan's to guard me as well as a few O'Hara's.

I thought I was adjusting, healing, until the mornings started bringing waves of nausea.

Exhaustion crept in, bone-deep and unfamiliar.

I blamed it on stress, on heartbreak, on the stomach flu that had been going around.

Rachel didn't buy it.

"Enough," she said one morning, finding me hunched over the toilet. "We're going to the hospital."

I sat in the sterile exam room, Rachel's hand in mine, as the doctor delivered the news that would reshape my entire world.

The last few months made so much sense now realizing what I suspected but didn't want to admit out loud.

"You're pregnant."

PART III | THE SAINT

THREE YEARS LATER

32

LIAM

"You did a good job today," Sonya's praise was soft on me.

For some reason today, her eyes were warmer and filled with something I didn't see often.

Sadness.

"Everything good at home with you and…" I motioned in a way she knew.

"Yes," she said quickly ducking her head in her green skirt. Her dark hair had grown out and now she had bangs. Motherhood had made her gain a little more weight that settled around her hips and thighs.

Overall, Sonya looked warm.

Over the last few years, I didn't need my cane anymore.

Sonya had trained me with patient instruction to lean into the burning in my legs without drugs or alcohol. Now? The old nerve pain was muscle fatigue and I was strong.

Stronger than ever.

"Aidan and I…" she drifted off. "We are going to a friend's daughter birthday."

Because they had lives. I still didn't know why she looked like that. Three years of Sonya and I knew when to listen.

"Is everything good with her daughter?"

"Her father…he is not in the picture."

I paused watching Sonya's slower movements.

"Sometimes I think every little girl, she needs someone like Aidan. He always picks up Selin and Kiraz when he's working out and he puts them on his back," she smiled at me with sadness in her eyes.

"He sounds dope."

"He is," Sonya smiled warmly at me. "He teaches them how to speak when I cannot. He feeds them and I come home to find all four of them asleep next to each other. Alexei will hold Selin and Aidan holds Kiraz and the movies are playing on silent."

I imagined Sonya's idyllic little life.

"Sounds sweet. Never thought Aidan O'Hara would be a stay at home Dad."

Her smile was warm when I said his name.

"Sometimes I think my friend's daughter deserves her father too, but it's not my place to judge her choices," Sonya said it carefully, her eyes on me now.

"You judge her?"

"No," Sonya ducked her head with a smile. "I understand her choices. As painful as they are. I do. But I also think it's time for them to talk about their daughter. Because I don't like seeing her baby alone."

"Why isn't the father in her life?"

"He made some mistakes," Sonya looked at me with a look in her eyes that spoke to me directly. "He messed up. I don't think my friend thinks he has changed, but I always think it's worth giving a chance."

I swallowed around that. "How bad could he be?"

"Not bad at all." Her smile was light. "I know them both. And I know their daughter could use her father too."

I knew Sonya had heart. Too much of it to the point where people had taken advantage of her for years.

"Whatever it is, I think if you talk to your friend about it? Maybe she'll listen."

"Maybe," she murmured slipping into her boots.

Sonya knew best.

She had saved me, opened up a lot of her home to me, and fixed me up. She was Mr. Santos in another life for me. Only this time was different—I wasn't alone. Not with her.

She was one of the few reasons I wasn't alone the last three years.

The other spaces were filled with me and Nisha sometimes doing things for her blog 'Slice of Life.'

Killian bought Nisha Butterscotch's, the cafe Nisha had loved and turned it into 'Slice of Life' for her—she'd become pretty fucking popular.

181

There were several pop—up shops across the city and Nisha needed help.

I didn't need to work. Not really. I earned enough and had enough to make it by.

The first year of Sonya in my life was hell.

I had to relearn a lot of bad habits. Sonya had me stay with her and Aidan and Alexei.

Out of all the people I saw coming?

They were not the ones I expected to stay with.

Alexei was like their kid or something because he was glued to my side as my sobriety companion.

He took me everywhere and shadowed me and together we trained. He was familiar in every single thing Sonya did so when Sonya was pregnant and she couldn't make it anymore.

Alexei and I trained together.

And it was there I learned all about him.

A former human trafficking victim picked up by Aidan. Now treated like his son.

Sonya had adopted me too. Aidan might've not been happy, but I could tell he wasn't going to disagree with Sonya. She ran her house and even if he wasn't happy about it—Alexei didn't care. He went with whatever Sonya wanted.

So I was welcome.

I had moved out after a few months of sobering up and I went back to my old apartment haunted with memories of her.

Everywhere. Little trinkets. Little signs of life.

The first few weeks without Lara had been hell. The words trapped in my throat to apologize. To find her. To see her. But I was detoxing off drugs and by the time I healed and went by her apartment?

Someone else answered the door and said the previous tenant had moved out. When I used Oracle to find her?

She was gone.

My Lara. The closest I got of her was a still at the airport of her boarding a plane with a familiar O'Hara at her side. And she'd snuggled into his chest.

And I broke.

Lara. Left. New York.

With Kieran.

There was no fucking doubt Kieran was the head of the O'Hara syndicate.

Which meant Lara was his? *His* girlfriend? My chest burned at the thought of her seeking comfort in Kieran.

No, Lara saw him as nothing more than a brother. But then again, Lara had loved me once.

Once.

I finally moved out of my apartment after a year. It was nauseating.

Moving over and over again but Sonya insisted I move into Laurel Apartments which wasn't too far from some museums on the West Side and really good restaurants.

Plus, she owned them so I didn't have to worry about rent. The Laurel Apartments. It was one of the oldest apartment houses in New York City, owned by a member of the Kennedy—Devereaux family and now Sonya.

The real estate was impressive. Palatial apartments in a vibrant neighborhood with seven different halls.

Each named after some type of wood theme. I had a five thousand square foot apartment now, with five bathrooms and bedrooms for some reason at about fifteen million.

Sonya was comfortable.

Because that was the cheaper end of the apartments here. It was like living inside of a palace.

This was by far the nicest thing I had ever experienced, with a cleaning service, housekeeper, one lady who prepped my meals and kept the fridge and house stocked with groceries—and Sonya dropping by all the time to see me.

Sometimes with Alexei.

Sometimes not.

And all together? In a new life? Sober? With a new outlook?

I should've moved on.

I could've moved on.

But I couldn't.

Somewhere deep down? I knew life had moved on without me. Now? I ached for pieces of my family. My old life. Isobel and Gabriel.

Even Reed and his wife now, Alisha.

I only knew because of a singular story Alisha had posted with two rings and a caption that had said 'Yes' causing the internet to break.

And then followed the whole day where Alisha's suitors had waited outside Titan Midtown for Reed with Titan operatives getting rid of them as they threw things at Reed for marrying her.

Some of them begging for money.

Some of them screaming at him losing their minds.

Guys were weird.

That had been…an experience to see on the news.

Out of all things.

But that was all I knew about Titan.

I knew Lucas and Evie had their baby girl Belle, and she would be maybe three by now? Killian had Kiara and then Marissa. Aidan had Selin and Kiraz.

Sometimes I did check up on folks like a weird stalker, but Titan had a new tech person and that shit was locked pretty tight now.

I hadn't heard from Isobel in years but this time, it didn't hurt as much as the first time.

The only one that ached was Lara.

And my mistakes.

I hated myself every single day.

33

LARA

"Mama!"

"Carina," I murmured wiping my daughter's face. Luna's dark curls were escaping her birthday bow, bright green eyes blinking at me with apparent joy. *"Que linda, mi amor."*

So pretty, my love.

Her eyes were Liam's. One-hundred percent his and full of mischief and joy when she smiled at me.

"Did you have some Aunty Nisha's gnocchi?"

"Mama, boo."

Killian grinned from where he stood in the kitchens surrounded by little girls all holding out their bowls.

In the three years since I left New York, Killian was a dad to two little girls who loved him.

They loved coloring his tattoos, riding on his shoulders, and they loved his story time sessions he gave out willingly.

I never thought I'd see him become a great father.

But he was.

"Daddy, please—"

Kiara's raven hair fell into her bright amber eyes as she pouted up at him. He never said no to her.

"One at a time," he laughed harder his face turning redder as he looked up at me. "They're like cats."

His white t-shirt stretched across his tattoos and muscles as he bent to straighten Marissa who might as well have started in on the tablecloth.

"No, Mari. No biting."

She pouted at him as he slipped a bite of gnocchi into her mouth and she was all good.

I laughed as my daughter Luna ran over to her cousins, dark curls tumbling. She'd been born with a full head of hair and it had surprised me. But she was a lot smaller than her cousins.

Aidan's twins, Selin and Kiraz forgot about their pasta as they ran to Kieran.

The twins matching brunette locks waved as they giggled when he lifted them up into his arms the moment he'd stepped in behind me.

"Ladies, ladies, not all at once, Unca Kieran has plenty of presents for you."

Sonya had insisted on giving them Turkish names and the girls resembled their Mama which Aidan had no complaints on.

"You guys get so big every single time I see you!"

Kieran kissed both of their temples, both of their amber eyes sparkling in delight.

I only knew how to tell them apart because Sonya always put Kiraz in a blush pink color courtesy of Nisha's girls and Selin in green.

I watched Luna run up to Killian and he picked her up easily having passed food to his daughters. "Unca."

"Yeah, I gotcha, sweet pea." He cuddled her to him passing her some gnocchi.

Kiara and Marissa were absolutely content in their chairs munching on gnocchi.

Kiara, the picture of her mother munching politely. Meanwhile, at one —years old, Marissa scaled the table and nobody said a word as she ravenously shoved gnocchi in her mouth.

Killian grinned down at her while Luna tucked herself into his chest.

"I'm beginning to classify the gnocchi as a food group," Killian sighed playfully. "Nisha did this. She created this."

Kieran laughed with me.

Years ago, Nisha had this lemon ricotta gnocchi when she'd been pregnant which she swore was the only thing she could really keep down.

Her daughters had loved it so much she made jars of the sauce to put on all her pasta.

She'd even branded and marketed her sauce and now made so much freaking money from it—Killian was proud.

But now? All of the girls in the house demanded lemon ricotta gnocchi like their lives depended on it.

As parents we swore to keep Nisha's recipe a secret or the girls would throw a revolt without it.

"You hungry, Luna?" Killian asked her as she shyly ate and ducked her head. She loved the gnocchi. "Come on, sweet pea. Let's sit and eat."

My chest clenched as Luna *Sullivan* tucked her head into Killian's chest as he took her to get more gnocchi.

The entire place smelled good as I walked up to Marissa who had finished up her teething phase painfully so. I rubbed her hair back and aqua eyes bat up at me.

"Lala."

"Yes, it's me Lala."

"Silly, no," Kiara giggled. "It's Aunty Lara."

Luna's birthday party was today.

She was turning three.

Nisha had wanted to do something sweet for all the girls all the time. So all birthdays took place at Nisha's.

Plenty of cake, food, and Wally the Whale cartoons later? All the girls would pass out in our arms.

Kieran brought over Aidan's twins giggling like wild monkeys in his arms. "Where's Alexei?"

"Nisha's out grabbing some ingredients she wanted, and Alexei and Aidan went to get Sonya." His eyes met Kieran's. "She's at ballet."

Sonya took ballet classes all the time over the last few years. Especially after having the girls. Both of her daughters took ballet and Killian thought Kiara might love it, but his daughter liked cooking with Nisha more.

The smell of gnocchi now made my stomach growl. I was starving after the flight. Killian sat with Luna in his arms and her own bowl he fed her as Kieran wrestled the twins in his arms.

"Daddy!" Marissa called him and he snapped his head to her on the table. "Boo."

She pursed her lips and Kiara's eyes went wide and she did the same like the girls could share their father.

"You gotta finish your food first, mini—luv." He dipped his head kissing her hair as she pouted up at him from the table she'd sat on.

All the girls did this now because of Killian's kids.

I think they'd watched Nisha do it too many times and now Kiara did it too.

Killian grinned kissing the top of her head and then her sisters. "I gotta get Aunt Lara some food, girls."

"No, stay, I can do it. I have free hands." He'd taken Luna.

Kieran grinned easily at us. "He's turned into a stay at home, dad!"

"You're lucky the girls are listening otherwise I would say not nice things to you!" Killian scowled at his brother.

Kieran's eyes twinkled with amusement. "Ladies, mind if I help myself to some of your snacks?"

He motioned to Kiara for her gnocchi and I laughed as all the girls hoarded it.

"It's a thing," I laughed. "You know better than to tease them."

"I blame Nisha for their addictions," Kieran shrugged holding Kiraz in his lap. "Kiraz, is Unca Kieran wrong?"

I laughed harder as Kiraz nodded and Kieran looked mock wounded. Selin laughed with me and then all the girls were giggling.

"The mighty O'Hara's felled by an army of toddler girls," I laughed. But Luna blinked up at me then and she handed me her little plastic fork.

"Mami."

"No, carina. That's all yours. Mami has plenty." Another habit she learned from her cousins. Kieran passed Selin and Kiraz some bowls and then he sat them down.

Kieran grinned down at all of them. "It's a little eerie to see them like this. They're all so adorable."

Luna glanced at him then curiously.

"But not you my princess, you have my whole heart," Kieran amended. Luna shyly ducked her body into mine and I laughed at him.

"Little bites!" Kiara yelled.

Killian smiled at her softly. "Little bites, everyone."

Kieran grinned at his brother in domestic bliss even if I saw the tension in his smile.

As the day progressed *everyone* showed up.

Sonya and Aidan brought so many balloons the girls lost their minds with Alexei as the dutiful big brother.

Nisha baked a cake shaped like a moon. And the number three. Sonya brought Luna enough dolls to make the girls lose it again.

The giggling and squealing was so welcome Killian grinned holding Kiara who leapt in excitement on his lap.

Marissa climbed onto Aidan's lap while the twins stood on either side of Luna and their mother excited for my daughter.

She had sisters.

A family. Even if she didn't have a father—I told myself her relationships were enough.

Sonya brought out a little tiara for Luna and I almost burst into tears at this family.

It was idyllic. Nisha and Sonya worked hard to make sure the O'Hara's lives were softer. Filled with lush flowers, and cookies, and homemade pasta. Love.

My daughter had everything and she looked overwhelmed as Kieran grinned down at her.

Everyone in the room besides the kids knew—Luna was Liam's. It was evident in her smile. Her eyes. The way she held herself quietly from everyone. Sometimes she sat there quietly and I wondered if my daughter knew. No. I was being crazy.

She didn't know.

The girls didn't know where Luna came from.

We all made up stories for them.

Like I had a story once. Another life. Another wish.

Once.

Sometimes I found family was forged in a different promise. One of a better life when you were lost and afraid and heartbroken.

By the end of the evening I was exhausted.

Aidan had sat on the couch with all the girls crawling into his massive arms. His twins and Kiara curled into him comfortably with an ease that told me they had done this before, Kiara settling on top of his enormous chest.

He wrapped a blanket around all three of them on him and settled in watching TV.

Kieran had corralled Marissa from jumping off the couch in a death defying stunt, and kept her tucked into his arms cuddling her for the entire night. She eventually relented when he showed her his tattoos.

"Boccoli," she murmured over and over at his clover and he gave up trying to teach her it was not broccoli.

Aidan had a great time laughing about it quietly.

"Did she just call the family crest broccoli?" Aidan murmured.

Kieran rolled his eyes covering Marissa's briefly to give his brother the finger.

Now Luna blinked up at me and then slowly shyly walked over to Kieran who sat on the floor looking like a lazy tiger felled by Marissa. Her blue tulle dress covered his arm.

He smiled at Luna who crawled into his other side and I passed them a blanket so he could wrap the girls up.

"They're going to be asleep in no time," he whispered.

189

"They haven't brushed their teeths yet," I reminded him.

He groaned a little. "Damn."

"But you look adorable surrounded by all this tulle and pink," I motioned to his arms. Marissa, in her blue and Luna in her purple.

"I'm exhausted," he murmured back, amber eyes darker now. "I need a nap too."

I chuckled turning on the heated blanket for them knowing all the girls loved it. "Get some sleep with them, I'll be back."

I was exhausted.

I found Nisha and Sonya in the kitchen with Killian who was doing the dishes.

Nisha was eating some pasta while Sonya drank a mojito.

"I need a mojito," I motioned to her. And without saying a word she handed me hers and grabbed another one from the fridge. "Are those pre—made?"

"I thought ahead," Nisha winked. "Besides, I don't have to pump for a few days and it's great."

I laughed at her relief and Killian smirking.

"The girls are tired too, this was great," I murmured to her feeling shy around her all of a sudden.

Her smile was wide. "It was our pleasure, we miss seeing you guys and the girls love when Luna comes over. Come over more often."

Sonya smiled at me but her eyes were a little tired. She looked down at her drink. Her husband was a softie for the girls.

"I had never seen Aidan like that," I told her softly aware Killian was loading the dishwasher and grabbing a roll of bread and butter.

He was bringing it over to Nisha and setting it down for her before going back for more clean—up.

Killian took the duty of house husband seriously.

"He's good," Sonya murmured with warmth in her eyes. "He is good with the girls."

So was Killian who was rummaging around the fridge and bringing Nisha assortments of things like an emperor penguin.

"Baby," she murmured with amusement in her eyes. "Come sit with the girls."

He obeyed dutifully kissing her again and Sonya smiled at him. And for a moment I got to pretend all was well.

Everything was right in the world.

Kieran was with my daughter.

Everything was perfect.

Sonya smiled at me again and her eyes were contemplative on me. "Come over sometimes, we miss you too."

I smiled. "I will, I wanna try and come to the city a little more often. Luna likes her cousins too much for me to stay away."

Sonya's smile lit up the kitchen. "Kiraz likes to play with her and I think Selin likes Kieran."

I laughed. "Everyone likes Kieran."

I never did get to call Mama. But for now I had these girls and sometimes I pretended this was my new family.

And that I didn't miss Liam.

Or wish he knew his daughter just turned three.

34

LIAM

I NEVER WALKED BY TEASER'S ANYMORE. BUT A WEEK LATER I WAS THERE.

I rarely did, but for some reason I had been thinking about her lately. More and more than ever.

Maybe I was a glutton for punishment.

Or I missed her enough to find myself there wandering down the street today.

Sonya had been doing physical therapy with me in barre class with her for three years now.

Aidan who had moved in with her to her Upper East Side townhouse lived there as a stay at home dad with his twin girls.

He fucking loved his life.

And Sonya ran her household. She had final say in *everything*.

Including me. So now I had mandatory dates with her and sometimes Nisha brought Kiara along.

It was the closest I got to kids.

Somewhere along the way I'd lost touch with everyone. Everyone I had in my old life including Lara. When I lost her? Isobel? Gabriel— everyone. Reed wouldn't say a word to me he was so fucking livid.

Because if I had said I had found Isobel? It would've saved them all months and months of stress and heartache.

Only today as I went to cross the street I felt something hit my cane and umbrella. No, someone stumbled into me. Which rarely happened. And it was someone tiny.

At first I thought it was an animal. Because she was pretty fucking tiny

192

in a little fur coat. With a tiny little fluffy beanie on her head with a bow. A little purple bow.

A pair of big green eyes blinked up at me.

She has my eyes.

Well, my eyes before they went dark. The light in them extinguished.

"Well, hello there," I slowly bent down to greet her shy self. "Oh, short-cake. Where's your family?" I looked around and I didn't see a single person rushing to her. And she'd just walked on up to me?

I didn't even know how old she was. "Do you have a mommy? Where's mommy?"

"Mami." Her adorable little pink lips pursed at me. "Mami, boo."

I didn't understand what that meant.

"Are you lost, shortcake?" I looked around wondering why the fuck nobody was stopping for her.

She grabbed my cane tighter, clutching it with her little fists like a toy. "Mami, boo."

She sounded panicked now. "Oh shit, I mean—shoot. I gotta find your Mom. You're lost, aren't you?"

I looked at Teaser's. No way she came from there, but hey, they could call the cops and go get her Mom right?

Or I could call the cops and hand the cop over.

"Mami, boo." She kept repeating it holding onto my cane. Those big eyes starting watering. *"Boo."*

I didn't know what *boo* was.

But it was clear I needed to find out.

"All right, tell ya what, *munequita*," she was so fucking tiny I had to call her my little doll. "I'm gonna pick you up and take you somewhere warm where I know a bunch of nice ladies can help you until your Mami comes."

"Mami." Those larger green eyes were gonna stare into my soul at this rate.

"I know," I slowly reached around wrapping my arms around her feeling nothing when I picked her up. "You're so light, kiddo…Do you eat food? How old are you?"

Her lower lip wobbled. *"Mami, boo."*

Gotcha. Probably two or three but I didn't know kids. I just knew this one only had two words in her vocabulary.

I adjusted her little fur coat. "Damn, you are so adorable little Miss, you know that? Let's go find your Mom and get you somewhere warm."

She was an adorable little thing in purple tulle and a little bow on her head slightly askew now. Inky black hair long to her elbows and her little dress aside, she looked adorable.

Bright green eyes bat at me like tiny headlights.

"Now is about the time I would ask you where your Mom is, but unfortunately you have a limited vocabulary, so I'm going to on a limb here and say you don't know your Mami's name."

But she was Latina. I could tell based off her skin color and features. She called her *Mami*.

"Mami, boo."

I sighed. Yup. We weren't going anywhere.

She pouted up at me and gave me those eyes. "Papa."

I bit back a laugh. "No, I'm not your Papa. But I can help you find Mami." She had come out from the same block as Teasers and I was about to walk into the establishment that I had sworn never to go back to.

Not after I broke her.

"Mami." The tiny girl in my arms gurgled. My heart ached a little as I lifted my cane up into my hands so I didn't click on the floors. The moment we walked inside it was warm and the girl in my arms began doing a dance. A little wiggle.

I grinned down at her. *Adorable.*

"Yeah, it's warm, huh. Cold as hell outside."

"Mami!"

I winced. "Okay, noted. You got a set of lungs. Let me go and find someone to help you."

And me? I held her as I walked inside Teasers.

"Hey, can someone help me? I found her outside."

I didn't recognize the bartender behind the bar but she looked at me, and her eyes widened on the girl in my arms.

"Holy fucking shit balls, Luna!" The bartender ran at her. And I took it, it was her kid. *"Luna, baby where did you run off to? You scared your Mama!"*

As the bartender came to get her I pulled back. "Hang on, who the hell are you? Where's her mother?"

The bartender looked almost embarrassed. "Sorry, did you find her? Her Mom is in the building—"

"Great, you can go get her," I finished. No more fucking questions or grabbing a baby out of my arms. "I won't be handing her to anyone without ID. Or without proof. I'm not just turning in babies to strangers."

Not after being sexually abused as a child. Not after the things people had done to me.

And the little girl in my arms had been wandering the street, she could've been hit by a car, or worse.

My stomach turned at the idea of her being kidnapped. I looked down at her in my arms.

"Your Mami and Papi are coming, okay?"

"Papi." She held my face then as she said the word.

My chest twisted at that word.

"No, kiddo. I'm not your dad. But I'll get Mami for you." I turned back to the bartender. "Go get her mother. I don't care who she was. And she better bring fucking ID."

I didn't care about cursing around—

"You said her name was what? Luna?" I looked at the girl in my arms. "*Luna?*"

Her green eyes widened and she bounced. "Boo!"

Luna.

The bartender scrambled to get her mother.

"Boo!" She chirped.

"I promise we'll find her." She looked ready to cry though.

I cuddled her close even though she was a total strangers kid.

"It's all good, shortcake. She's gonna be right here. I promise. I got her. I do. You found me at a good time too. What if some awful idiot had picked you up, huh? You can't just go running into the street. Life's tough, kid. You can't do that. Okay?"

If she knew I was being stern, she pouted at me and sniffled.

"Oh no, don't cry. I'm sure you and your perfect little nose couldn't do any wrong. But I think you worried your Mami sick. And she's coming, I know it."

I brushed her dark curls back. It was the same color as my hair. I grinned. "Look, you look more like me than I do."

She watched me with soft eyes like mine and a strange sensation filled me.

"I gotcha," I cuddled her tight to me as she whimpered. "You know you have my eyes too. They used to be mine." As I said it her lower lip wobbled. "Oh no, baby don't cry." I wrinkled my nose. "Don't cry. Mami will be here soon."

"Mami."

I know. She only knew one word.

"I know. You want Mami. And boo."

"*Boo.*"

And that one.

195

"What is boo?" I shook my head. "Is that code for milk?" She had to be what? Two?

She pursed her lips at me. "*Boo.*"

"Ah, I can't kiss you, shortcake, but wait—I think I hear someone coming."

She put her hands on my face then, her fists tiny as she rubbed it. "Papi."

I didn't get to correct her. Not when I heard the click of heels.

I was ready to give her mother a piece of my fucking mind.

Losing her kid in the middle of New York goddamn City? What the fuck was wrong with this woman?

"Luna?"

I stilled recognizing the shoes, the outfit, the hair. Shorter. She'd cut it off to her ears. And she looked completely tiny in her sweater and jeans.

I stopped breathing and my world tilted on its axis as I looked into the eyes of the one woman who could disarm her.

Lara. *Melina.*

My girl.

My former girl.

Here.

Except what the fuck was Lara doing here?

"Luna?" She looked at the bartender who pointed to me.

And then her head swung over to me.

Holding a little girl.

Named Luna.

Who Lara was looking for.

It was like a car accident in slow motion.

Her eyes didn't even see me. Dark wide—eyes landed on—No. Not Lara. Lara didn't have kids. Not...No.

Panicked and worried all she saw was...her...*daughter.*

The wind was knocked out of me. When it hit—it didn't hit. It slammed. Like a tsunami.

I thought she was in Chicago.

Her eyes widened as she saw me standing there holding...I looked at the girl in my arms who lost it.

"Mami!"

"Oh, *carina.*" And just like that Lara took her...fucking daughter out of my arms and into her body. *¡Dios mío! Pensé que estabas jugando en mi oficina. ¿Cuándo te escapaste?*

I thought you were playing in my office. When did you run away?

196

She didn't look at me. She didn't see the confusion in my eyes. The hurt coursing through me.

Lara had a *baby*. A little girl. Right there. Who weighed next to nothing.

No fucking way.

And then the most horrifying thing of all.

When I picked the little girl up outside...Luna had my eyes.

She had Lara's hair. My hair.

The ink curls.

My heart stopped for a moment watching mother and daughter hugging and crying.

Lara kissing her as Luna...*Luna...*

She was my sun.

I was the moon.

Luna...

I couldn't breathe needing a second.

And then Lara turned to look at me. "Thank yo—" her lips froze in an O as she stilled watching me.

My throat worked as it dried out. Everything in me *stopped*.

"She—" I couldn't fucking move.

"*Liam.*"

A million and one questions ran through my brain.

A million and one. And only one formed right then.

I pointed at the girl in her arms. The tiny girl. With my eyes. With her hair. Who was maybe two.

Give or take—if I did the math—three.

She had to be three.

Three.

Years.

Old.

"*Why does she have my eyes?*"

35

LARA

HE HAD ALWAYS BEEN LETHAL AND SHARP.

Time never dulled his beauty.

No, the universe was cruel like that.

They made sure Liam Santos/ Sullivan was the prettiest man they'd made with an edge. Even now? He was thirty—two?

And when I was standing there holding Luna who was crying into my arms, I got a good look at him.

Sin and salvation. And completely not mine.

Those eyes of his hunter green and irresistible were hungry on Luna's face. "Why does she have my eyes?"

Right now, eyes darker than my daughters—our daughters—searched mine. And then he looked at Luna.

All around me every single bit of life stopped and I felt Liam drawing near her as I tucked her crying face into my neck.

"She doesn't," my voice barely went above a murmur holding Luna to me. I was trying not to tremble. Not to shake because Luna picked up on everything for some reason. "They are not your eyes."

His throat worked. "Yes, they are. She's three. She has to be."

Horror dawned in Liam's eyes as he looked down at her.

How did he find her? Who let him in?

How did he—

"I found her," he croaked. "Wandering the streets. She found me." He whispered the last part as his mouth opened in a horrified gasp. *"She found me."*

198

Liam was standing in front of me after three years.

Three years of pain.

Suffering.

Postpartum.

And now this? I curled her into my neck.

She was usually shy around strangers and I couldn't stop crying when I knew she'd run off.

I looked down at Luna, her tiny fingers playing in my hair as she sniffled. "Mami."

"I know, *carina*."

"Fuck," he whispered his lip wobbling. "Fuck. *Lara*."

He *knew*. All this time. I hid it so well.

And now, my daughter had walked outside quietly right into her freaking father. The odds of that luck were uncanny.

And they happened.

Of course they happened.

The same stroke of luck I had—she had. She was Liam's.

Of course she'd find him in this lifetime.

"Lara," his voice broke as his face crumbled. "She's mine."

No.

And just like that I remembered my labor, I remembered what it felt like to be up all night with her crying into my chest.

I remembered how alone I felt and if it wasn't for Sonya and Kieran and the team over in Chicago, I didn't think I'd make it.

Did I ever imagine assassins babysitting my daughter? No.

But they were trustworthy.

"She's my daughter," I held her tight to me and she made a small noise. "She is not yours."

"Lara," Liam's voice was haunted. Panicked. "Don't lie to me, *muneca*."

And just like that all the memories of the past slammed into me. Something had happened to me since I became a mother.

It was something I saw in Alisha, and then later Gemma who had daughters now too—This wave of protectiveness that existed inside of me for my baby.

"She is not your daughter," I growled. His eyes widened on me, haunted and so lost. "She was never yours. I am not yours. Do not call me that. Get out of my business. You're trespassing and you're not welcome here."

"*Lara*—"

"No!" I held Luna so tight to me she whimpered. "No, you don't get to come in here. You lied to me! I trusted you! And you lied to me."

This was not *how* I saw it going down.

And thankfully nobody but the new bartender was around to hear this.

"You left me," my voice broke. "You left me."

You left us.

Liam's face fell. "*Muneca…*"

"No," I growled again the old endearment like kindling to a fire. "You don't get to say a word. *Nothing.* You get nothing. You chose *her.* Not me. Not us. You chose someone else."

And he would every single time.

"*She is Kieran's daughter.*"

More than Liam's.

Kieran had been there every step of the way for my pregnancy. Short of being there when I had her, Sonya had been there with Nisha for that. Not Liam. Never Liam.

Liam had never been mine.

He'd always belonged to Isobel.

Not me.

And my heart broke as I held my baby.

"Mami," her soft words let me focus on her not Liam. "Boo."

She pursed her lips. Even if she wasn't Kieran's, we considered all the O'Hara girls, Aidan's and Killian's her cousins. And Kiara O'Hara had taught my daughter about boo's. Her secret weapon.

"You want boo?"

I kissed her lips and nose. "There."

I worried she picked up my emotions. She caught on to my feelings and right now, I was distraught and Liam wasn't healthy for me and my body and my baby.

"I need to go. Thank you for finding her."

But Liam's eyes were haunted on her. "She isn't Kieran's."

My heart dropped.

His throat worked as he said it and he slowly shook his head.

"I know my eyes when I see them, and she's mine. She knows me. She found me. Why didn't you say so?"

"If you have to ask that question? You've learned nothing. I can't do this with you anymore," I held her to me. "If you do not leave I will call security. As far as I am aware—Reed will hurt you. And I don't care anymore."

I turned to not say anything to him. To the father of my baby girl and I quickly walked through the long halls of Teaser's. The same I had laughed with him through.

"Wait—" I felt him moving but I thought Liam was still slower. I wiped my eyes as much as it broke my heart to. And then I felt his arm around me. "Wait, wait, wait—Please."

"Let me go," I whirled with her to me.

Luna made a noise of discomfort and both of us froze.

Liam's eyes were horrified. "I'm sorry, *munequita*. I don't wanna freak you out."

My heart stopped for a second time at his nickname for her.

"Liam, stay away from me," I his her face a little. "Stay away from us."

"Not until you tell me," his eyes bore into mine in the hallway. "She's mine. I know she is."

He dipped his head lower and I forgot how tall he was.

His eyes took me in then with a frown and her.

Immediately my daughter—his daughter—reached for him. Pursing her lips and breaking my heart in the same moment.

She was never friendly with strangers. It took her forever for Kieran to hold her without crying. "*Boo.*"

Liam's face fell. "What does that mean? Does that mean she wants kisses? Is that boo?"

"No, *carina*." I held her to me shaking my head. "No."

Not him. Never him. I still remembered the things he had done. How his mistakes, his self—esteem had cost us our happiness—my happiness. Never again would he hurt her like that.

I turned to Liam then the words coming from somewhere so deep in me I knew in that moment I didn't care about anything but protecting my little one.

"I will never let you break her the way you broke me. The way you broke my family up. I will never let you near her. Luna is not your daughter. She never will be. *And you will never hurt her.*"

I took her clutching her to my chest as I turned away practically running out as fast as I could as Luna watched her father.

I didn't need to turn to know his expression was broken.

I JUST WENT TO MY APARTMENT AND PACKED MY THINGS.

We were supposed to leave for Chicago. It was a quick pit stop to Teaser's I hadn't needed to take. But I had.

My mistake.

Luna was quiet in the car, her lower lip wobbling the entire ride home.

She cried a little in the airplane ride but a bottle of warm milk and some biscuits Aunty Nisha made for the girls with cream inside made it better.

"*Galletita*." Cookies.

"*Galletita, carina.*"

When she got to Chicago I could tell she was exhausted. And Kieran lifted her into his arms the moment he saw her.

The last three years had changed him. Just like me.

The Kieran O'Hara of three years ago wasn't as dark as this version of him. His hair was cropped, eyes harder and darker than before.

His jaw clenched until he saw me. Then he softened. Luna was immediately tucked into his coat as we walked to the town car that waited for us.

"Girls," he murmured as he took Lara into his big arms, hugging her to his chest.

His eyes flickered over me. "What happened?"

I texted him on the way home.

He didn't judge me but he looked upset. "She was on the street?"

Right now, Luna was half—asleep in his chest. When she had been a baby the only way she'd stop crying is if he let her hide there.

"She ran into him on the street?" His brows rose.

"I didn't know she wasn't in the kitchen, she took off and he bumped into her—" I already felt guilty enough but Kieran was quick.

"I'm not judging you, she's tiny and fast—I just think it's a stroke of fucking luck that he found her. You've got one hell of timing, kiddo."

He passed her some snacks in the car and she picked apple sauce. Some water. He made her sip some water as he spoke to me and handed her another Wally the Whale stuffed animal, while he pressed his lips to her hair.

"*Juice.*"

"Apple sauce, sweet pea."

She did get some words wrong all the time but we all knew what she meant.

Luna didn't speak much for her age. Unlike Killian who talked to Kiara all the time allowing for her to have more sentences than anyone else,

I told him about Liam asking if she was his.

"I told him no," I shook my head emphatically. "I can't do this."

Kieran went quiet. "You want me to—" he made a slicing motion.

"No," I frowned. "Why do you always do that now?"

He shrugged as the car drove through the streets. "Beats talking to the motherf—" his eyes darted down to Luna who glanced up at him with wide eyes.

Kieran leaned back, rubbing his face.

Three years had changed him too. He wasn't the impulsive youngest O'Hara brother anymore. Running the family had aged him, but in good ways. Made him solid. Dependable.

"What did he say?"

"He knew." My voice cracked. "The moment he saw me, he knew. She has his eyes, Kieran. His exact eyes."

He was quiet for a long moment, and I knew he was thinking of all the times Luna had looked up at him with those green eyes.

"Do you still love him?"

In three years, Kieran had never asked. Had never pushed. Had just been there, holding me through morning sickness, painting Luna's nursery, learning to put her hair into a pony—tail.

We'd never been lovers. But I knew Kieran, wanted a wife and a family —I was the closest thing to one.

I didn't say a word as I watched the streets go by us.

He nodded like he'd expected this. "That's why you never let me in... You love him. Even now."

I always would. As ashamed as I was to admit it. Liam had always held a piece of me.

The first man to show me humanity. But then he'd broken me too.

Maybe I didn't have to hold onto him forever though.

"I don't love him," I murmured looking at my hands and then Luna. "Not anymore."

He tipped his head looking down at Luna who he'd put into the car seat. "Sauce, sweet pea. More sauce?"

Luna nodded eating quietly watching us.

"She liked him," I murmured careful to not say his name. I swore Luna understood everything.

"She looks a lot like him," Kieran said softly handing her some more apple sauce in the package. Amber eyes watched me. "He knows about her. He might come after her."

I frowned. "Li—He would never hurt her."

"I'm not saying he will, I'm saying…" he paused. "Sonya's been taking care of him the last few years." I felt that hit me then. "Sonya's worried about Luna and you. She thinks Liam

HE STOOD, STRAIGHTENING HIS SUIT JACKET—THE ACTION OF A MAN preparing for battle. "Let's keep it that way. For now."

The knock came again, more insistent.

"Stay here," Kieran said, but his eyes were on the stairs leading to Luna's room. "I'll handle this."

As he moved to the door, I saw him transform. Not the gentle father who read bedtime stories. Not the man who'd held me through labor and midnight feedings.

This was Kieran O'Hara, head of the family. The man who'd built an empire while raising my daughter. The man who'd give his life to protect what was his.

And Luna was his. Had been since the moment he'd first held her and promised to be whatever she needed.

The door opened, and I heard Liam's voice—harder than I remembered, colder.

"We need to talk."

Two fathers. One daughter. And me, caught between past and present, between what could have been and what was.

Something was about to break.

I just prayed it wouldn't be Luna's heart.

3 6

LIAM

My rage was a living demon.

A living fuming demon pulsing with every inch of my heartbeat as I stood in front of Killian's door.

My hands shook this time not from withdrawal or weakness, but the fury I felt inside of my body making me lose it. I was going to explode.

He kept my daughter from me.

He was the closest to Lara. He would know.

I didn't even remember taking, the cab right here or taking the elevator upstairs, I just knew that I needed the answers. And Killian O'Hara had them.

There was only *one* person who would know about *my* daughter. And he just so happened to owe me.

I found my feet in front of his door, banging on his apartment, feeling the storm brewing inside of me.

He knew.

He had to have known. He was Lara's business partner and he knew everything in the city. This was his domain.

My hands shook with the need to grab him as I heard nothing and then the click of the door.

But when it swung open he wasn't alone. My rage sputtered to a halt that felt so abrupt it was like hitting a visible wall.

Killian did open the door. Only he wasn't alone.

There was a baby girl in his arms, in a bright blue dress made up fluff and she was gnawing on something in her mouth.

A plastic chew toy looking thing she was gnawing. Little sniffles left her as she whimpered like she'd been crying.

His lips pressed into her temple as he looked at me for the first time in years.

"While you were playing with your daughter, you kept mine from me," I growled feeling frustration boiling under my skin. *"You judged me for keeping secrets and you had your own. Was that a fuck you to me? Did you get your kicks out it?"*

Killian's initial lightness faded in an instant. His dark menace taking over as the girl shifted in his arms wide eyes watching me now.

He tucked her head into his neck as she sniffled again letting out a low moan. "You watch your mouth around my kids. Marissa is teething and she hasn't slept all night. Sonya said you were better—"

"I am better! I would be better had I known I had a daughter!"

Something dark and dangerous flickered in those eyes as his hands stayed gentle on the back of a softly crying Marissa's head. "Come closer, mini—luv."

Marissa burrowed closer to him and he shook his arm out. I didn't even see the blanket tucked into his side as he wrapped it around her and bundling her up to him.

"It's okay, daddy's gotcha...Liam, come inside and go sit in the living room with Kiara. I can't put Marissa down."

I followed him into the massive penthouse, child—proofed and lived—in with all the toys, the stuffed animals, the pink—the candles every few feet. The entire place smelled like a home.

He led me into the living room where another little girl lay playing on her stomach as she made a happy noise when Killian walked in. Dark curls, amber eyes glanced up at Killian.

I didn't even know he had two kids, let alone daughters.

"Kiara, this is Uncle Liam. Daddy and Uncle Liam are going to have a talk, okay?"

"Daddy," she held up her whale stuffed animal. "Wally wants puffs."

"Daddy can get Wally puffs," he smiled down at her and he motioned for me to sit while he opened one of the ottomans and pulled out some cracker—like things in different shapes. "I can't spoil your appetite for dinner, little—luv."

The moment the bag crinkled, Marissa poked her head up out of the blanket burrito she was in and she looked down at the puffs licking her lips.

Killian chuckled a little handing Kiara a tiny bag and then grabbing another one for himself.

He threw one at me and I caught it deftly sitting on his couch.

"Wally the Whale yogurt puffs?" I murmured reading the label.

"The girls—all of the girls—are obsessed with Wally. Lucy's pregnant and we went to her baby shower, she introduced Kiara to him. And since then Kiara won't talk about anything else."

Killian opened the bag and gently fed Marissa inside her burrito blanket. "There you go, little bites, yeah? You can take little bites for daddy."

Where the fuck is my rage?

Disarmed by a three—year old currently eating whale shaped crackers in her playpen watching me with the same eyes her father had. And his other one being fed while alternating with her ice pack.

After seeing him after three years? I was livid. But Kiara, paused eating her food as she looked at me curiously. "*Daddy.*"

She pointed at me. "Man."

I was.

I was a *daddy*. To one tiny little girl.

"Uncle Liam," Killian murmured looking at me. "I have velcro—kids. I can't walk away from them without them crying and I'm not putting her down so you're going to have to rain—check our fight. No cursing. No yelling. If you make Marissa, I will K—I—L—L you in your sleep. Painfully."

I couldn't be happy for him. "You kept me from mine. Is she a velcro—kid? I don't know what she is."

Not when I knew what *he'd* done to me.

"I messed up, I know I did," I felt beyond frustrated. "But did you have to hide my daughter from me? She's *three*. She missed out—I missed out. Did you get your kicks and giggles out of that? Making me look like a fool and keeping her from me?"

"You were an alcoholic," Killian said giving Marissa another puffed cracker. "On drugs. You didn't even like her—"

"*I loved Lara!*" I hissed. "I fu—"

I cast a nervous glance at Kiara who was blinking up at me innocently while putting another puff in her mouth.

She chewed adorably, those amber eyes eerily bright like her uncle's and like she was warning me to watch myself around her daddy.

The quiet crunching the only noise as Killian looked down at her with his mismatched eyes warming.

A little smile played on his lips as she looked at him.

"Daddy," she smiled holding out a puff.

His smile grew as she watched him. Marissa whimpered and he soothed her passing her another puff.

"I *fudging* loved Lara—"

"Not as much as Isobel—"

"Isobel was my first love, of course I loved her. But I loved Lara more. I chose Lara. Every single time—"

"When? When you told her she was a W—H—O—R—E. And she should've been doing other things than running a fudging *empire?"*

His eyes went dark and predatory and for a moment I realized how well Killian O'Hara, juggled two little girls.

One of them who was watching me quietly.

"You tried to convince her to run away?" Killian hissed passing his youngest another puff. His entire demeanor hardened and I saw Kiara look at him with wide eyes as he softened. "I don't like my girls seeing me like this. So I'm going to say this once. *She's not your daughter. You donated DNA. You are not her father."*

He might as well have slapped me in the face in front of his daughters.

"I *donated* my DNA?"

"You aren't a father figure. In the slightest. You're a former alcoholic who turns to *drugs* to *cope*. I know your life was shit. So was mine. But even I stopped drinking when I *knew* Nisha was pregnant with Kiara. *Hang on—"* he broke off to adjust Marissa in his arms and nestled the cookie packet between his chest and her little hands gripping it now. "Come here, little luv."

As Killian spoke he reached out to Kiara who stood shakily from her playpen.

Her lower lip wobbled. "Daddy."

"I know. Daddy wants to hold you too. Yeah, you need hugs and cookies?"

"Cookies."

"I know, little luv."

He waited until she gripped his tattooed arm and he lifted her easily with one arm from the playpen into his lap.

"Grrr." He playfully teased her and she burst into giggles.

My entire chest tightened painfully.

Marissa made a noise as he adjusted them both, wrapping the blanket around Kiara now so he had them both on his chest.

Something about watching him was undoing something in me.

His eyes flashed with fire as they met mine the moment both of the girls started eating again. They looked so small in his arms compared to six—three of pure muscle he was.

"You threatened Gabriel after he built a world for you! *Isobel* after she told you she didn't remember him, and *Lara. Everything you claimed to have loved—for your own selfish needs. You think I would consider you a father? Let alone a family man? Look at how you treated your family.*" Killian hissed, pulling the blanket over his girls.

And then I realized in this position they couldn't see his face.

They couldn't see him transform into a monster. That's why he hid both of them, his hands coming up to cover their eyes a little.

His expression vicious.

That *burned*.

Hearing it like that? It was brutal. Agonizing. Painful. It ripped through me.

The rage that I felt was red hot, and it licked at my skin, I wanted to tear into him in that moment. And just as I open my mouth someone cut me off.

"*You never gave me a chance to know she was pregnant.*"

"Because you were dangerous to her and Luna! You were a drug addict. You couldn't control yourself. You think I would ever let you make Lara feel like garbage because you can't handle ten hours or plus of labor? Because you don't know how to handle Luna crying all night?"

"I can handle my daughter—"

"No, you *can't*," Killian barred his teeth, his voice dropping so low as he held both of his girls. His hands were tattooed and protective over their heads. "You can't protect your girls. You never could. You walked away from your family. You kept Gabriel from his—"

"I made a mistake!" I shot back.

"That cost people *everything*."

A whimper came from inside the blanket and he looked down at Marissa who was cooing up at him.

"Ohhh, mini—luv. It's okay, it's okay," he burrowed his head into the blanket laying on kisses on both of them. Snapping back from a fire breathing dragon into Dad—mode at the tiniest sound from her.

And my chest tightened watching the girls snuggle up to him.

That was supposed to be me.

"Daddy," Kiara held his face her mouth turning down. She pursed her lips up at him. "Boo."

Boo.

"Daddy's sorry, I know, was I scaring you two? I didn't mean to, no,

Daddy was upset with Uncle Liam. Not you two. No, daddy would never be upset with his little angels."

Kiara smiled shyly as he said it and she pursed her lips again at him. "Boo."

"I got boo's for you, little luv."

My chest clenched as I realized Luna did the same thing.

Killian kissed her cheeks and then her forehead. The same thing Lara did. Her nose. She giggled, sighing happily, and going back to eating her crackers as Marissa reached for him.

"Boo?"

"I got boo's for you too, sugarplum. I was saving the best of my boo's for last." His voice softened as a smile lit his face up on her. "My sweet brave girl, you got two whole teeth now. I'm so proud of you. Yes, you're my mini—luv, aren't you?"

Boo's were kisses...

Luna wanted them from me.

Boos.

He takes care of Luna. My daughter learned this from him.

Marissa giggled in his arms and he grinned looking up with a sigh.

The Killian I knew years ago wouldn't be caught dead like this.

Now, these two had him wrapped around their fingers.

"You're pissing me off," Killian growled switching gears as he snuggled them back again. "And you're scaring my kids. This is another reason why I can't let you in to see Luna. I heard you chased after Lara scaring Luna once—" My stomach turned at that. "You can't be around kids. You can't control yourself."

"You met Luna," Killian looked at me with hard eyes cuddling both of them again. "She's healthy now. But Lara lived with the fear for months that because you were on drugs and alcohol Luna would face complications."

The truth hit me like another bullet: While I'd been destroying myself, Killian had been teaching my daughter how to be loved.

His lips pressed to Marissa as he watched me. "My daughters are my world. Their Mom is living her life because I'm willing to be there for them. I would do anything for Nisha. I would never have done her dirty—"

"But you did," I said it feeling my jaw clench. "You did. And I helped you when you did. I helped you when she had Kiara. I never once judged you for your stupidity in keeping a darker secret from Nisha."

He stopped then.

"You think you're better than me. When you did the same thing. You think it hurts more because it's Gabriel? It ripped pieces of my soul out," I whispered fiercely. "Just like it did for you when you lost her. When she ran away from you because she knew she was marrying a monster."

Killian's eyes were predatory then.

Even holding his girls I saw hints of the man he was and a wild smirk, wicked and cruel lit my lips.

"You dared to keep my daughter away from me for three freaking years. When you came and ran to me and asked me for help with Nisha. To break in and enter into Sonya's home, to find her pregnant and miserable with you—"

"That's enough—"

"It's never enough," I raised my head tipping my head back aware, if he thought he was a monster, I had been raised by some. I knew how to shift into one. "You kept my flesh and blood from me. Should I take one of yours? Does that make us even?"

He paled holding his girls then.

I smirked again. "You asked me for help despite being so morally black, your wife ran from you terrified you were going to get her killed for being second—in—command of the fucking mafia. Do your little girls know the same hands that tuck them into bed, I watched those hands gut men alive? Who was the man who followed Nisha home in his cab? Didn't you flay him alive?"

His jaw clenched as I said it.

"Do your girls know daddy is a murderer?" I pointed at myself. "Because I healed. I sobered up with Sonya. I stopped taking pain killers and I faced my fears. I did everything I could to fix myself. All you did was tell Nisha the truth. And remind me again, she didn't even take you back, did she? Her adoptive father kidnapped her. And then suddenly Nisha realized, she needed a bigger demon in her life than her parents. And so she picked you. Does Nisha know you're a serial killer? Do your girls know?"

I was livid. And controlled now more than ever feeling it coursing through me. "I am a monster. I always have been. At least I know it and I don't pretend to be any better than my worth. I did make a mistake. I did keep secrets from Gabriel to protect the woman who raised me who saved my life."

I knew what I had done.

I paid for it daily.

"But you should've told me after she had Luna. You should've given me a *chance*. You out of everyone, when I helped you. When I put your family together!" The last bit came out as a growl and Killian looked down at Marissa checking on her and Kiara before looking at me. "My daughter doesn't know my name. She doesn't know my face. She called me Papa the other day and I shattered."

His eyes widened.

"She knows me, I know she does. Even if you kept her from me, she would always look at me and see her soul staring back. Do you understand me?" I was done. "I'm going to Chicago. I'm going to find my daughter. And I'm going to win her mother back."

The decision was coursing through me already.

"You might not care about me after I saved your ass. But I care about me. I care about me. And my girls. My family. I'm leaving for Chicago. Warn your brother that I will absolutely rip him apart if he keeps my future wife and my daughter from me."

I stood up as he looked up at me.

Luna grew up around them. She comes here.

She spends time with them.

He knows my daughter.

Killian didn't move as he looked at me with a hard expression.

"I wasn't stupid enough to think that you hadn't learned your lesson bouncing between Gabriel's *wife* and Lara. Not telling you about your daughter was not punishment, *it was trying to keep her safe from an unstable father.*"

I stopped breathing then.

An unstable father.

"*This was never about Luna.* Lara left because you *broke her.* You met her *seven years ago,* when she was at her lowest, you *knew* and *you still led her on.* You made her think that she was not enough for you. *You think some kid is gonna fix what you can't give? You are not capable of loving someone. Because loving someone means choosing them. Not yourself.*"

And just like every single time, Killian met me head to head.

"*You spent three years lurking around the city, never once apologizing to Isobel—*"

"*Isobel won't speak to me and neither will Gabriel—*"

"Because you kept her from him!" Killian raised his voice a little holding the girls. "*And then you think because you ran into Luna you deserve her?*"

"*She's my daughter—*"

"No, she isn't." Killian lost it. *"They were never yours! You don't break the girls you love! I would never—"*

"You lied to Nisha once—"

"You lied to Isobel about her still breathing husband. Who she is legally still married to. You thought you'd lie to her and him and think they would never know! Isobel was in a zombie state for years without him."

"So you took my daughter—"

"You fundamentally misunderstand what love and family is. You see your daughter as something you are entitled to. You have no capacity to put someone else's needs before your own. You put your own needs before Gabriel's wife, before Lara, and you will *eventually* put your own needs before your daughter. *You are not entitled to anything. Everything you have is a privilege you did not deserve. Even I knew that!"*

In his arms Marissa started wailing.

"Oh, my baby. I'm sorry, Daddy's sorry..." he looked distraught his entire face falling and I felt for him then. He made soft nosies as she cried out in pain. "Daddy's sorry, I am. No, no, no, don't cry. Kiara, give your sister Wally for a second. I know, baby."

As Kiara handed it over I saw how Killian's cheeks flushed a little watching Marissa who cried out. A little wail left her as her face contorted in pain watching him. His lips twisted down.

"I know, it's bad, it's only a few days, I promise." He pressed kisses into her face as she cried. Kiara tucked herself closer to him grabbing his shirt and snuggling into him.

Killian kissed Marissa's hair over and over. "I'm sorry. I need to replace your ice. It's just water now, isn't it? That wasn't good of Daddy, let me go get you some more."

Even if I was angry with him, I realized Marissa was crying because of her teeth. And she probably needed ice.

"Where is it?" I said woodenly. "Where's her ice pack?"

He looked up at me stunned that I would even ask which burned me deeper than I cared to admit. "In the freezer. They're molds, Nisha made."

I tipped my head walking into his kitchen finding it across the living room and going into his freezer where an enormous amount of milk bags were.

I found the iced molds and took out one shaped like a popsicle and then found another normal popsicle figuring it might be good for Kiara.

I grabbed another pack of wet wipes from the kitchen and walked back to help him clean up his daughters.

My own anger took a backseat as I walked back easily to his daughters and found he'd dropped the blanket and Kiara was quietly snuggled up petting Marissa with him.

His little one was sniffling and crying looking at him.

Killian's entire face was turned down on her. "I know, Uncle Liam went to get it—there he is. Liam, just hand it to her, she knows what to do."

I did trading it out for her warmer one, it was like a jelly substance that was filled inside of something else.

Marissa took it from me and shoved it into her mouth.

"There you go," Killian pressed his lips to her face over and over. "Better, hm?"

She sniffled and nodded, hiccuping a little from crying. And for once I saw how exhausted he looked sitting back with Kiara and her.

If Marissa hadn't slept all night neither had he. This was fatherhood. Kiara licked her lips at the second pop I gave her.

"Here you go," I handed it to her and she looked all shy and warm now on me. She took it and ate as Killian looked grateful.

"Nisha will be back in an hour," he murmured. "But Marissa isn't getting any sleep at all. Lucky for us, we mastered this with Kiara, and now she's doing better." He smiled down at both of them but I saw the worry in his eyes for his youngest.

"I have no vendetta against you. But you have consistently shown that you don't know how to love without *breaking* the people you love. This is about protecting instead of starting another cycle of trauma and you turning into an alcoholic because she's up late at night for months teething. Or because you were exhausted by how many fucking rules there are to pregnancy—*Whenever* your life gets tough? You run. *All you do is run.*"

His eyes met mine. "What happens when Luna wakes up every night like Marissa does, because she's in pain and she's teething or Nisha wakes up because the baby is kicking all night or Kiara has a nightmare—I don't quit because it's not easy. *I want to get my girls through it.* Instead of hating Gabriel you could've let Isobel know the truth. You could've loved Lara."

"I love Lara," I argued back standing there looking down at him. "I love her with my entire heart—"

"Then why did you break it?"

I stilled.

"If Luna did not exist? Would you still love Lara?" His eyes met mine. "Kiara and Marissa are my entire soul. They are every bit of me as they

214

are their mother. But I don't love Nisha because of them. I loved their mother first. I loved her. I stood by her. Yes, I lied. But I loved Nisha so much I never wanted to lose her. Every second she was out of my life, I died a little."

He looked down at his daughter before glancing at me with nothing but emotion in his eyes.

"These two are an extension of my love. Not the reason for it. You cannot want Lara. Because. Of. Luna. You have to want her. Period."

I didn't know why I was processing that.

"If Lara never had Luna, you would've kept on running. It's been three years, Liam. This isn't about Luna. Or her. This is about your ego. You think us keeping Luna from you is about you? You were never in the picture. *This is about us not repeating cycles but breaking them. You think we would let you go near Luna with your baggage.* You fundamentally misunderstand what love and family mean. You see Luna as something you're entitled to, *but you have shown no capacity to put anyone's needs before your own.* You betrayed Gabriel's wife, broke your girlfriend, and I kept Luna from you because I knew eventually you would destroy your daughter too. Lara and her daughter are my family. I will protect them with everything I have. Like Luna is my own flesh and blood."

As he spoke, Killian ripped my soul to pieces right there. His words echoed in my head.

Eventually, you would destroy your daughter...

That hurt so fucking bad.

"Sonya said regardless of Isobel's father, she knew you lacked a support system. You were alone during the worst moments of your life. Gabriel did mess up. Is that what you want to know? He should've reached out to you. He should've told you the moment you came to Titan. Reed will argue otherwise, but that's his best friend—I can objectively look at the situation and see that you did not mess up alone."

As he said it?

The room under me tilted, and I didn't even know what to do with that moment.

Validation was...something Sonya gave me for years now.

"Sonya is the reason why you have what you do," his jaw was tight. "And we all agreed with her."

That made me stop.

"Gabriel shouldn't have let you go and not said a word. Learning to walk is not easy. I know, because I'm watching my girls grow and it's painful for them to navigate those emotions. It's painful for me to watch

Marissa suffer." He motioned to the little one now blissed out in his arms with her ice pop.

"I talked to Gabriel. I explained to him, if he had reached out first, you would've known him. You would've told him. You thought he was the bad guy, he thought you were. Misconceptions are a bitch."

And it had led to consequences across the board for everyone.

"You should've told Isobel Gabriel was alive," he looked at me then. "But Sonya said if anything happened to me or Kieran, Aidan would do anything possible to ensure it never happened again."

He nodded at me then like I understood what he was saying.

"It wasn't right, but it didn't mean you were wrong. Sonya doesn't know Gabriel or Isobel. She's coming from the perspective of somebody who was isolated for nine years. And she knows what you went through. And she knows what it can do to people. And she felt for you so she stepped in."

"Aidan didn't like me—"

"Aidan doesn't like anybody, but we all knew we couldn't tell you about Luna. At least, not until you grew up. Because to repeat that cycle with Luna—that is where Aidan drew the line. They're a team. They talk. Sonya saved your life. But Aidan will keep Lara and her daughter safe. I think you are worth saving. I do think you need people to care. And I think isolation can drive someone to madness."

He paused holding them and I was surprised they were so calm now. Kiara looked like she was falling asleep to him talking.

Because he makes her feel safe.

"We don't abandon people, and I'm not saying you were abandoned, but—"

"I was."

We went quiet. I was abandoned. Again. And again. And again.

I ached everywhere and my eyes burned with the sensations of being left behind all the time. Losing my legs. Losing my life. Losing my Isobel. Losing Lara. It was all loss.

"Luna is the first time, I felt something more than loss in a decade." I felt hope. Just like I felt with Lara.

She made me feel things Isobel never had.

I did love Isobel, she was my...roadmap to love.

Lara was my compass. My north. All of me had been for her.

And now...our daughter.

"I know," he looked at me then with softer eyes. "I know what you went through. I met Nisha because I kept getting hurt and when I didn't

216

have her? I turned into you. Kieran was you three years ago even with us. So I know."

I guessed the O'Hara's had similar traumas.

But Killian validating my emotions was not what I had been expecting.

Because the truth was, he wasn't wrong. I had been an alcoholic, and I did rely on prescription meds to get me through the day. If I was better now, three years ago, I would've been the worst person in the world to become a dad.

The pain lurched through me. My inner monsters had always been too authoritative for me to not obey them to every whim and desire they had.

The insidious sensations of my father's influence in my life crept up as Killian took me in. His gaze softened on me like he knew my thoughts.

"You are not the only person who struggles with their demons. All of us have them. But Kieran asked me why I never fought Nisha. I never ran from her. And the answer to me was simple—why would I hurt the one person in the world, who was going to give me every single thing I could ever ask for and nothing in return but me?"

One aqua and one amber eye watched me.

"Isobel wasn't yours. You weren't gonna marry her—and I know what you told her father. Listen to me, he didn't know about Gabriel. He didn't know. You didn't know what to do. You were twenty—three years old. You were a kid. You're a decade older now. If you went back in time and you met that kid who said yes to Mr. Santos, what would you tell him?"

"That he should tell him about Gabriel—"

"And—"

"And that he can't do it because he doesn't love Isobel the same way."

As soon as I said it, something in my heart latched open and my eyes widened.

"I don't love Isobel the way I love Lara."

"I know." He was quiet. Marissa's fist curled into Killian's shirt and he looked down at her. "What is it, sugarplum? Still hurting?"

She nodded, her chin wobbling.

"I know," he whispered. "Kiara—" he broke off realizing Kiara had fallen asleep popsicle in hand. I nabbed a pair of wet wipes and went to clean her up and lay her down.

Easily, I took her sleeping form into my arms barely weighing anything and oh so fragile like my daughter and laid her on the couch tucking her in while Killian soothed Marissa sniffling.

"Daddy," she whimpered.

Killian sounded distraught. "I know, baby. I know." He held her closer as her face contorted. "It's worse at night," he explained as he motioned for me to follow him while he stood wrapping the blanket around her again.

His lips pressed into her cheeks as he walked down the hall leaving Kiara fast asleep now.

"I'm not going to stop you from going to Chicago," he kept his voice down. "But if you so much as make Luna or Lara cry—Kieran won't let you go this time. He's determined to protect them—"

"Are they together?"

Killian turned to me then his expression hard. "I don't know what Kieran does anymore—"

So yes.

Some part of me twisted at that sensation of her being with him. No. Lara wouldn't. Not my Lara.

But she said Luna was his.

Why would she say that.

"But Kieran is protective of her. He was there for Lara. He helped raise Luna. She's his daughter in his eyes. Not yours." Killian cuddled Marissa close to him kissing her over and over again looking distraught as he rocked her little body in his arms.

She sniffled reaching for him and he kissed her some more leaning over to inhale her scent.

"I know, baby. I know…" he was soothing her for a bit and I just stood there processing what he said.

Kieran considered Luna his daughter.

Not mine. He wasn't going to make it easy.

Too bad I was determined to be a part of her more than he was.

I didn't care if he had three years with her, I wanted the rest of her life. And if he was with Lara—I would respect that. But I wanted a slice of my daughter's life.

"I'm not an unstable dad."

"Not anymore," he murmured over Marissa's hair. "But you were once. And we knew that. We kept you because we didn't want you to hurt Luna. If you go to Chicago. *When.* You go to Chicago, just understand you have to go with Lara in mind—Luna will come naturally. You didn't fall in love with Luna. You fell for her mother. You have to respect that too." His eyes met mine head on then as he straightened. "I need to get some medicine in her. She can't stay up two nights in a row crying like this. It's gonna hurt her more than me."

He motioned to Marissa in his arms.

"She's my entire world. The other half is sleeping in the living room." Marissa made another softer noise of discomfort.

"Daddy."

"I know, baby." He rocked her again as he said to me. "I won't stop you from what you need. But I will draw a line if you hurt Lara. You won't be welcome there—"

"I know—"

"But I'll talk to Kieran for you when Nisha's back. We'll talk to him. He won't be happy."

"I don't care—"

"See that's the thing," Killian said. "You have to care. You're her father now. You have to care about everything in her life. You can't do what you did before. Change starts every step of the way. Not just when it's convenient for you. Kieran raised her. To Luna—Kieran is her father."

My stomach twisted as he said it and Killian was too busy soothing a crying Marissa now who was whimpering more.

"I know, I know, it hurt's Daddy as much as it hurts you, mini—luv."

He looked up at me again.

"Kieran will do anything for her. And you're about to walk into Chicago, which he runs, to take her?" Killian shook his head as Marissa began crying again. "You need a better approach. You need a plan. And you need to get your life together before you do."

37

LARA

I was a little emotional today.

I always had been over Liam.

But today felt a little different. My heart felt heavier somehow. Every single time I looked at Liam?

He always broke my heart because I just pictured a little version of Liam alone in the world. Alone and seeking love and my heart broke for him every single time.

Did I know now Isobel had been his map? I did.

It didn't hurt any less but I knew he had once loved me and *liked* her. Isobel. The woman who had been his mother, his sister, his first love, his only obsession.

No wonder he never spoke about her.

She was the reason he had walked into Teaser's years ago.

She was still the reason he was walking by. His roadmap to everything he wanted in this world was through her. Not me.

Never me.

It had *always* been her. And I had never stood a chance.

My phone rang and it jarred me out of feeding Luna her some bits of sausage and pancakes.

I passed her sippy cup with warm milk in it.

"That's good, hm?"

"Bueno."

I smiled at her speaking a little more. Keeping one eye on her, I answered the call from Sonya.

"Hey."

"Hello, beautiful," Sonya's voice was lilted with a light Turkish accent.

"What is that in the background?"

Sonya laughed lightly. "Aidan was doing how you say—"

"Push-ups," came the male voice in the background followed by the sound of little girls giggling. I grinned watching Luna who was now eyeing me as she stuffed her face with avocado.

"*Carina*, little bites," I reminded her gently.

Luna and Marissa both ate like this at this stage even if Marissa was younger she liked food. Killian joked around she was turning out to be more of a chef like her Mami.

"Aidan was doing push-ups," Sonya explained. "And the girls thought it would be fun to climb him. Now he is still doing push—ups, but the girls are sitting on him—" Sonya laughed. "Aidan, they are falling..."

"Nah, I got 'em, princess." Aidan's voice was clear and I heard him kissing her before moving on. "Come on, girls. Daddy needs a protein shake."

"That is not real food—"

"I know, baby, I got snacks for them too."

I laughed at their domestic life.

I hadn't pictured Sonya to like Aidan who was pretty rough and tumble. But it worked. It fit. He balanced her the way Nisha balanced Killian's darkness.

"We wanted to know how you were doing," Sonya murmured. "I know you are with Luna and Kieran, but I found out about Liam meeting you."

The O'Hara's worked faster than anything I had ever seen.

Sonya and I were acquaintances in the past. Girlfriends who got together and sometimes drank together. I think Aidan forgot that I knew Sonya when he mentioned she was staying with him.

So my secret at being related to the O'Hara's in a way had come out when I'd visited and Sonya had seen me.

Now? She was just a big sister who was Aidan's wife.

Kieran's source of wisdom where Nisha was his comfort.

The O'Hara ladies filled in the gaps the men couldn't.

And in turn they became like family.

Even as I felt out of place with Luna, I took care of them and in turn they took care of me.

38

LIAM

DARK HALLS AND LIGHT MIRRORS, POLISHED WOOD CAUGHT THE AFTERNOON light as I stepped into the ballet studio.

I was meeting Sonya Amin, Alisha's Turkish friend who carried herself with grace and elegance.

The softer lights, bars and practice mats and Sonya was at the center stretching. She traded in her put—together look for yoga pants and an oversized comfortable sweater.

I wore my sweats and a hoodie.

I began going to barre classes with Sonya and we ended up talking.

Aidan had passed me to his wife because she was the only one who could tolerate me.

"Aidan and I promised ourselves we wouldn't let Selin or Kiraz go through anything like that. To be better than our parents. If you want your daughter in your life, you have to be better."

Listening to her made me realize how fucked up I really was. Every person around me had survived their own hell, but they'd chosen to break the cycle.

Killian wasn't wrong.

He hadn't had much choice in his life. But several times in mine, I'd been granted better options and run from them.

"I could've held onto Gabriel," I murmured, the admission echoing in the empty studio. "Instead of hating him."

But I didn't hate Gabriel.

I just didn't understand where the fuck he'd been coming from and we didn't know how to talk to each other because of—our differences. Worries about losing the woman we loved. And lacking communication in general with everyone since neither one of us had a dad.

She nodded, her reflection in the mirrors making her words feel like they came from everywhere at once.

"But you cannot hate yourself, Liam. You did what you thought was best at the time. It does not matter if you think it's a mistake right now. Right now, this version of you has information the past did not—we cannot judge ourselves by new information. If you had this knowledge ten years ago, that you would have a baby with the woman you loved, you would be better. Maybe. Maybe not."

My throat worked as the truth of it hit me.

I'd made myself the victim in my story for so long, I'd stopped being someone else's hero.

Lara's hero.

"Even when I was out of it, I remembered Lara."

The words scraped raw against my throat, echoing in the empty studio.

"I thought about her a lot. I don't know why I didn't reach out to her."

"You were scared."

I turned to find Sonya watching me with those knowing eyes.

"Scared to feel ashamed of your legs," she motioned to my scarred limbs—the ones Lara had once kissed with such tenderness, telling me she loved all of me.

"Maybe even afraid of the unknown. I was. I stayed in an abusive marriage for nine years because I was afraid, and even after I divorced him he tried to kill me."

The weight of what she was offering—this piece of her past— settled between us.

"I have a daughter," I whispered, the words still strange on my tongue.

"She is very sweet. She does not talk much, but she comes over sometimes to play with the girls."

Something hungry and desperate clawed at my chest.

"When's her birthday? What does she like? What does she do when she's around you?"

Sonya's voice was gentle as she told me about my daughter, each detail both gift and knife to the chest slicing into my arteries when I realized how much I had missed out on.

"When she was a baby I went to see her often because, you know, Lara was alone sometimes. Then Kieran got her Rachel as a babysitter..."

She laughed lightly, but all I felt was pain imagining Lara struggling alone with our baby.

"Rachel is a Titan in Chicago. Kieran said he only wanted someone with a gun to protect Luna in case something happened. But Rachel is just as big as Lara so it's funny to see them all together."

She must have seen something break in my expression because her smile faded.

"She has your name, Luna. Her name is Sullivan."

I knew. I saw her birth certificate.

And I knew why Killian reamed me out.

She didn't deserve an alcoholic dad with his issues. She deserved a man who would choose her every single time. Who would love her without holding back or worry he would leave her.

The more I lived in my trauma the more I was turning into my parents.

And the ones I didn't want to be.

"I need to go to Chicago," I told Sonya.

She nodded. "Aidan says you may say that. Killian talked to him."

Her darker green eyes watched me. "Lara and your daughter they like it there. It's good for them. That is their home. If you go, you are going because you want to be there, not for you—for them."

"Aidan doesn't...he doesn't care if I go after them?"

She shook her head. "He thinks you need a chance. He thinks you have never been given one—"

"Mr. Santos—"

"That's not the same. You were too young. I do not think that after losing Gabriel and Isobel, you had support. A system of people to hold you together. Now you do. But if you hurt Lara or your daughter? I do not think Aidan will be okay with that."

No. I knew he'd killed Michael, Sonya's ex—husband brutally on the top of Titan Midtown's tower.

Everyone knew about it.

∾

EVERYONE HAD SOMEONE BUT ME.

And all I did want was someone. I wanted someone to hug me all the time. Like Lara had.

224

Someone who ran to me with happiness because I was her happiness. Someone who stayed.

Like Lara had.

I had made a lot of mistakes in my life.

But it wasn't without saying that I also didn't understand that it didn't help having a father who abused me to communicate and friends who taught me that everything came with the price tag.

Mr. Santos might have saved me, but even then I kept running.

All of the things that I wanted to do for good I ended up fucking myself over. And the one good thing I did, was her.

Lara.

And then she'd gone and had the best thing I could've had given myself—unconditional love in the form of someone too tiny to know who I was.

I didn't know why I felt this obsession to get to my daughter.

I just wanted to be around her all the time. There was something about the way she looked at me like she recognized who I was.

What I was.

And loved me anyway.

Killian's daughter's didn't know he murdered people and tortured them. All they saw was the man heating up their pasta and blowing kisses onto their face.

I had been clean for years. I hadn't touched alcohol. The first couple of weeks, if not days of intensive therapy were tough.

The moment I saw Luna again, I realize why the last three years had built me up into who I was.

I couldn't be a fucking coward around my daughter.

Watching Killian cracked my chest open. Marissa and Kiara watching him like he was their entire world—and he was.

That's why he picked them over himself every single time.

Luna was three feet of pure sunshine in that purple tulle dress she wore, her little feet walking in that crowd of people until I scooped her up. The memory of her small hand in mine. Her eyes on me curiously but not scared.

She knew. She knew I was hers.

Standing outside Kieran's door in Chicago, my heart thundering against my ribs, I knew this was it.

My last chance to prove I could be more than my past, more than my failures. More than the scared boy who learned to run before he learned to stand and fight.

"I wanted to win my girl back," I whispered to the night air. "Both of them."

I was done with running.

It was time to come home.

39

LIAM

I had been brainstorming starting my own private investigations firm.

For the last few years I had done research and I looked into it.

All of it. Figuring it out until I had all the components I needed to start hiring eventually.

With Luna in my life I needed more income no doubt. And because of that alone—I was looking to starting it.

I was hiring a few people from all around the world I had built connections with.

And I didn't have to interview them, I had an office space scouted it in an industrial part of Chicago.

It was an upscale penthouse worth about fifty-million dollars.

I bought it the moment I came to Chicago hellbent on getting my girl back.

And my daughter.

And right now my phone went off with a text from a new hire setting up everything for me.

One was a warehouse we owned where we kept equipment and everything we needed.

And the second was a building.

Gideon Walsh.

What do you want me to do about the rafters?

It isn't. But it's old and when it rains in Chicago which it
does often—I'm worried about storage

At the same time one of the other guys over the lofts contacted me asking me if I wanted him to hire a decorator now.

There was a lot to do.

Levi Montague was a POC with his older brother Micah handling all of this. And I didn't work too much with Titan's anymore.

Better for my mental health.

I was debating between Urban Investigations or *Incognito*.

I didn't want to go down there I wanted to go stop by a flower shop, and a few boutiques that Lara would like.

And while I was out I got a few things for her. My daughter. In the hopes I'd see her again.

I stopped by the Chicago Lofts. The warehouse.

But my third stop was with Kieran who was with Titan Chicago.

Cade Rodriguez was the head of Titan Chicago under Reed Whittaker who I hadn't spoken to in forever.

But Kieran was having a meeting while I was waiting outside his office.

There was a team in there working a case for Kieran who was in charge of the O'Hara's who were phasing out from being Irish mafia to just strictly Titans.

Titan Chicago.

I didn't want to be Titan anymore and I had to talk to him since he protected Lara.

"What did you want with Lara?"

Kieran wasted no time now.

In the last three years he'd changed. He'd gone from a laid-back slacker who didn't take anything seriously to studious brother-in-law who wanted to do everything for everybody.

And now he was taking care of my…girlfriend?

I didn't know what to call her anymore or right now.

I told myself when I did, I'd make it up to her. Planning all the ways I could.

Except I didn't know what the fuck to do when I saw Lara.

I just knew that I fucked up enough once to never fuck up again.

228

40

LARA

"He is somehow staying one block away from us."

Kieran was trying to maintain his composure and keep his annoyance in check, but it was impossible to do so with Luna on his lap.

My daughter was coloring in his tattoos with her giant markers that he got her.

Kieran sat perfectly, still that she hummed along while she worked.

I grinned over at the two of them when I'd spotted them as I'd come from the kitchen.

Now, perched on my side of the other couch in the enormous space, I ate lunch while Kieran sat there holding his e-reader in one hand and Luna coloring him in the other.

On his other side was his companion, a massive orange presence that felt like more of an oversized pillow and not a cat.

Cheddar was the rescue had Kieran had been given years ago. And he was *obese*.

Kieran was the only O'Hara that I knew not allergic to him, and Luna had fallen in love with him.

Now, the giant fur ball migrated between the space heater he loved and the kitchen where Luna knew how to sneak him tuna.

"Did she give him a treat again?" I asked biting back laughter.

Kieran shot a devious smile over. "Where do you think I found these two?"

Luna looked up at us like she knew he'd caught her red—handed in the cupboards. Kieran's smile was warm on her as she colored.

"Unca Kieran."

Kieran looked down at Luna where she was coloring, and where she was focused on the new tattoo he'd gotten on his sleeve. Her tiny fingers moved over his chest now.

"Unca...look."

"I see that, sweet pea. You're doing such a good job," he murmured at her artwork. "That's a nice color you picked. Green."

"Green." She giggled as she said it and Kieran's entire face shifted. "Broccoli."

He fought a smile and lost. "Close. Clover. Can you say clover?"

"Clova..."

She tried. For a moment.

"Broccoli."

I pressed my lips together to not laugh and that laugh twisted somewhere when I saw what Luna was coloring. A few years ago I had seen a shamrock on Killian's arm.

The same shape and markings of the brand on my wrist.

All three of the O'Hara's had that brand tattooed on them. Not because someone had given it to them, but as a reminder of what they would never do to anyone ever again.

I knew the girls loved coloring their father's in. A trait Luna had gotten thinking Kieran was her coloring book and not her Uncle.

She didn't know what it meant.

But I did.

I always knew and maybe that contributed to my own shame that I internalized over my background.

But I always felt guilty for being a former prostitute, a former dancer, and sometimes I wondered if Luna would be better without me. If she could pretend Killian or Aidan was her father.

And those thoughts made me feel ashamed of myself even more.

I didn't know what to do about my emotions.

I just knew they existed with me every single day.

"Are you okay?" Kieran's eyes were on me worried. "You don't look okay."

I blinked back my emotions and nodded. "Fine."

His smile was humorless. "I know when you're lying to me."

Luna looked up at him again and pointed at his clover.

"Yes, sweet pea. Broccoli."

"Broccoli." She went back to coloring her broccoli in.

I didn't say a word. If I took Luna back? I'd leave Kieran alone here. And he couldn't be alone either.

We were like two survivors of a shipwreck clinging to it together with Luna between us.

I couldn't abandon him.

But it ached inside of me.

"Tell me why Titan wants to talk to you about a painting."

He sighed now looking annoyed at the subject.

"Lucy Devereaux went and told Sonya a couple of years ago thankfully, that everything in Hyacinth Manor, the shelter Sonya runs, is worth millions. There's a painting in Hyacinth Manor. It's the second half of a set of two..."

Kieran explained that Sonya had a painting that was one half of two.

The second one had been lost in time.

Nobody knew who had it and nobody had found it ever.

The first one belonged rightfully to Sonya and she had put it somewhere safe.

"What is it?" I shook my head.

"The lore behind the painting is that it's a map. If you flip both of them over? It leads somewhere. Someone out there has the second half or the rumor is, the second half has turned up."

I blinked. "You're serious. There's a treasure map inside a painting."

"Treasure." Luna piped in.

"Yes, sweet pea. Treasure and gold." Kieran explained dryly that the Titans had heard a rumor the second painting had appeared. "Somewhere out in Hong Kong, and it's in Chicago right now. One of the Titans—Rachel—traced it back to here. It's in the city."

"The second half."

Kieran tipped his head, his eyes sharp. "And we made sure when Sonya dropped off the original painting, nobody knew where it was. Save for Sonya and the company she hid it inside, Nash Group. Specifically Natasha Nash. You don't know of her—"

"No."

"Nash Group has the painting. They are also tracking the second one and a bunch of operatives known as Talon, Sonya owns them are being sent to Chicago. Nash Group wants their hands on the second painting—"

"For the map?"

Kieran shook his head. "They're collectors. They want the painting for the sake of having it. Natasha Nash likes a complete set. Talon works inside of Titan so they're just doing her bidding."

"And the person who has the second painting?"

His eyes narrowed on me as his lips tipped up.

"There's a jewel thief in town Lucy Devereaux is familiar with. Vivianne Valentine. Vivianne Valentine is a huge catch and so besides Titan Chicago, Talon, and Nash Group—" Kieran broke off with a wild laugh as he looked at the ceiling for help. "The FBI is in town too."

I clapped my hands over my mouth as I set my sandwich down. "Stop talking."

I couldn't hold back the hysterical laughter that threatened as Kieran burst into laughter. "What is my life?"

Neither one of us knew what to do but laugh then.

"You're telling me four different organizations are in town, lookin for Vivianne Valentine?" I wiped my eyes.

"And Vivianne Valentine herself has to be in disguise. Honestly, sometimes I wish Sullivan wasn't such a dipshi—shoot. Sorry, sweet pea. Because I'd just ask him to use his version of Oracle, find Vivianne Valentine, get the second painting and be done with it. Technically Titan and Talon are all the same team. They work together. But the Fed's want Vivianne Valentine and they've wanted her for a long time."

Kieran explained how Lucy Devereaux didn't work with Vivianne Valentine because she was messy. "Lucy says if people think she's trouble—"

"I didn't even know Lucy Devereaux was a jewel thief until right now—"

"Former jewel thief. She reformed once she met Adam. But Lucy says Vivianne Valentine's trouble. Younger. Bolder. Maybe twenty-one. Maybe. Lucy thinks she's hunting for the second painting."

"But Sonya has the second—" I broke off at Kieran's knowing gaze. "Vivianne Valentine thinks the second painting is in Chicago."

"Because Sonya was staying here." He pointed to the manor. "Three years ago. Vivianne Valentine doesn't know about Sonya and Aidan. Not many people do. Aidan never goes out with her in society and so Vivianne Valentine thinks—"

"Dios," I whispered. "Vivianne Valentine thinks you have the painting."

"She's in for a rude surprise when she realizes it isn't here. She can try and break in all she wants. Which is why I have Josh and Nadine coming over today."

Kieran explained tight in Chicago was fully expecting Vivianne Valentine to break into the mansion.

And if that was the case, Kieran had a duplicate painting, set up purposely in his room.

"But if she breaks in—Vivianne Valentine might hurt you," I was against it.

"No," Kieran smirked. "She wants the map. I'm going to give her a fake and Titan Chicago wants to catch her before the Feds do."

"You think Vivianne Valentine is going to break into your bedroom?"

He grinned. "I know she is. And when she does, I'll be ready."

Amber eyes met mine. "So…what do we do about your problem since you know mine?"

I puffed out a breath grabbing my lunch my appetite now ruined.

"I'll go talk to him."

"I'll take care of Luna."

"Broccoli!" Luna chirped.

"Clover, sweet pea. Try clover."

"Broccoli."

~

I DID GO SEE LIAM.

Alone.

His townhouse was five houses down from Kieran's which was a quick walk for me and when I knocked, my heart thundered louder than it ever had.

My ribcage felt like if I didn't hold my hand to my chest at any moment it would explode.

Luna and Kieran were going to spend the afternoon together and Kieran let me handle Liam now.

Since Liam wasn't listening to his warnings—I didn't want Liam here, but that didn't mean I wanted him dead.

As Liam opened the door, I craned my neck up. Liam filled the doorway in black seats and a hoodie that did nothing to hide his leaner form, broad shoulders, chiseled body.

Inky hair falling across his forehead like he'd just gotten up out of bed. His eyes a deeper green as he took me in surprised.

"Hi," I said feeling nervous as I bit my lip. "Can I come in?"

"Yeah, it's cold outside, come on in." He held the door open for me and then I got a load of the place.

I had passed by this house so many times on the street.

And I always imagined it just looked so beautiful on the outside. Like a little white castle. All of the house houses on this particular street were absolutely beautiful. But this one was gorgeous to me.

I didn't know it had been for sale.

A stunning white and cream and lilac home with gorgeous antique features all around it, the hydrangeas adding pops of color, the large plants.

"Your home is beautiful," I turned to take in Liam who I found watching me.

His lips tipped up a little. Liam's energy in this space seemed more at peace.

"Do you have a second?"

"Yeah, for you. Of course." He motioned to the living room a light laugh leaving him at my breathless gaze on the house.

The entire place smelled so familiar to me I couldn't place it.

I moved over to one of the massive couches, sinking into it and Liam's eyes twinkling at my feet dangling from the couch.

He ducked his head and sat on the opposite couch facing me, a coffee table between us.

I knew in New York, Sonya had given him a place to stay to recoup at the Laurel.

It had upset to me to know the O'Hara's had been protecting me without me even knowing how much.

But Liam had sobered up under Sonya. He did classes with her and now moved around without his cane. Without alcohol. Without meds.

Without me.

How was he doing?

"You live here now?" My throat worked as I asked that question, his expression calm and collected. Unreadable.

Liam looked present now in a way he hadn't before.

"I do."

"Why did you move to Chicago?" I said it. "It wasn't for Luna. It wasn't for me—"

"It was for you." He said it so quietly I almost didn't hear him.

"Because of Luna—"

"No, because you're here."

I swallowed around the sensations in my throat. "Three years later?"

He paused and looked at the coffee table.

"I spent the last three years dreaming of you, thinking about you, every step I took was with you—"

"I don't believe you—" I didn't know where it came from but it came out. "I don't believe you at all."

He nodded. "Even still, it was always with you in my mind. I never forgot about you. I would never have left you for anyone. I wanted you to go—"

"To run away—"

"With you. Never without you," he continued on. "You were always mine."

"No," I felt something happening to me. Something was crawling over my skin. It felt like the invisible spiders I felt for so long back. I didn't know how to calm down and my temper flared. "You came here for her. If it wasn't for Luna—"

"I loved you before Luna." It was said with the force of a sharp knife, smooth and cutting into my skin. "I have always loved you."

"You loved Isobel."

I swallowed as I said it and I saw the shift in him immediately.

He leaned back into his couch and sighed lightly.

He looked at the electric fireplace crackling. I saw the lean lines of his throat work and his tattoos creeping up his neck.

"I loved Isobel," he repeated softer this time. "Did I ever tell you how I met her?"

"No."

I didn't want to hear it.

But his lips tilted up as he told me his story. I didn't know his clothes had smelled bad or been ripped.

I didn't know she fed him snacks. I didn't know her father took him home like that or defended him and saved his life.

Liam spoke softly with a smile on his face about his adopted family.

"Mr. Santos did the whole nine-yards. Sent me to school. Everything. And Isa...became my mother. My sister. My entire world." Liam smiled leaning back comfortably. "I did love her. I always would love her. I accepted that fact that some part of me learned love through her. But when we were Agency, Isa met Gabriel."

Liam told me their story. Quietly.

He told me how Gabriel fell in love with her on sight. But he worked his way to her heart. Earned her love.

Something Liam could never do.

Isobel only had eyes for Gabriel and because she'd never looked at Liam like that he relegated himself to being her best friend.

Not her brother.

"And then…she died."

Or they thought she had. Killian had sat me down and explained Isobel was alive. She had been.

But she had no recollection of her life and Liam had.

Reed had told me enough for me to know it was absolute madness in the Titan world for a short time when Isobel's team had been hunting Gabriels' when Lucy Devereaux and Reed had stolen Isobel's necklace.

And it woke her up.

Liam nodded as I commented on it. He filled me in on everything. From start to finish and how he found Isobel, because of Lucy Devereaux.

He had been hunting for her.

And found her at the Primrose Hotel—owned by Sonya—and Liam had gotten her and Adam together several times to know they were a couple.

"And then…I saw her…I'd know her a mile away. The first time I saw her, I kissed her."

I stopped breathing as he said the words.

My hands went to my stomach slowly remembering what it felt like to be pregnant and to not have him.

To have Luna the first few nights the hardest nights ever.

To remember feeling like a failure because I didn't know how to be a good Mami to her.

What?

"I was so desperate for connection from the one woman who gave it to me. I remember breaking off the moment I did and saying your name. Just yours. It was in my head over and over again. *Muneca.*"

How did I even feel right then? Like he'd ripped my heart out several times.

Should I feel comfort he had thought of me?

The me I was used to be before my body changed, my hips grew in, my breasts were off and enormously uncomfortable, and the shadows under my eyes became prominent.

The dancer.

The teaser.

My body never returned back to what it was after motherhood.

It might never. And I had to learn to live with this new figure.

"I said your name," he closed his eyes, pain etched into his features. "I didn't even want to kiss her. All I wanted was you. But a part of me had to make her real to me."

I felt my eyes water as the hormones made everything sharper. Three years should've made it easier for me to cope. But it hadn't.

Liam reopened every single surgical incision I had and then some. I had cried a lot because of him. Because of my birth.

"You kissed her..." I croaked feeling not just inadequate. I had always felt inadequate. Not good enough. Now? It didn't matter I had his baby. It didn't matter at all.

He dipped his head and he took a shuddering breath. "But it wasn't you. It was never you. And I did it to feel close to her again."

I covered my mouth horror and understanding warring in me. "Is that why you kept your distance from me?"

"I felt guilty. I dreamed and slept next to you and part of me wondered...I wondered if I could just have her as my family and you as my wife."

As he said it my stomach clenched violently, my insides twisting and turning.

"What?"

Dark green eyes met mine. "I wanted to marry you, but still have Isobel in my life—" At my frown he continued in a rush. "Not with her. But she is my family. I do love her. But not the way I love you."

I shook my head unable to process what he was saying. Or how he said it.

He kissed Isobel. I couldn't even think straight after that. Or at all. I needed air. All I could think about was how perfect she was to be Gabriel's wife. To be loved by Liam. Everyone liked her. She was a God among people. And I was this...I was this...thing.

I hated myself.

"I can't—" I was breathing harder feeling all of my inadequacies leap to the surface. "I can't do this." I leapt up off the couch.

Part of me had always loved Liam. And always would.

"Wait—" his eyes widened alarmed.

But I was up and running out the living room door unable to stand being in his company. Liam...he kissed her. How was I supposed to move on?

"Lara!" He was right behind me and I was right at the door. And then the next thing I knew I was being picked up, arms made of iron wrapping around my waist.

"Waitwaitwaitwait, *muneca*—"

"Don't call me that!"

"I'm sorry. I'm sorry, I swear I thought of you—I did—"

"Not when you kissed her! Get out of Chicago! Get out!" I cried out.

It didn't matter how much I struggled. Not once. Because Liam was still bigger than me and he held fast his lips against my temple whispering his apologies. "I'm sorry."

And I didn't think Liam would hurt me. Not as much as he already had. I could feel my eyes watering as he held me. His lips working down my cheek. To my jaw. Lower. I whimpered as I closed my eyes.

"I missed you, *muneca...*" he whispered. "I missed this so much, you're all I think about. You filling my home and my soul with your laughter. You in every street corner telling me the best parts of life. I thought about you for years. And then..." he took a shuddering breath. "My daughter finds me on the streets of the city out of the millions of people she finds me. I know why you didn't tell me. I was a shit father. A shit boyfriend. A shit everything."

I felt the tears streaming down my eyes now as he held me and I realized I was up off the ground as his lips found my pulse.

"There it is. This is the one thing that kept me going," he murmured into my neck. "You are the only thing I think about. The only thing I wanted. More than Isobel. More than anything. When you look at me, my soul finds peace. And when you're around me—Isobel didn't matter."

I stopped tensing in his arms as I absorbed the impact of his words.

"Isobel stopped mattering the day I saw you in your office and you ran to me. And you hugged me. And I kissed you then." His breath heated on my neck. It made a shiver run down my spine as he wrapped both arms around me now.

His breath left him in a ragged shudder. "I think about you all the time. Just you. Not her."

"You were willing to live everything for her."

"I wanted to go to an island and live off the coast of it with you and our ninety kids," he chuckled without humor against my pulse as I closed my eyes again. "I wanted Isobel to be happy with seeing you as my wife. It was never about her. It was always about me being too much of a fucking coward to face myself and the truth."

My chest rose up and down as I took in air by the lungful.

This was what terrified me the most about Liam. How my body had always felt safe around this man. This man who had shown me humility when nobody else had. His heart pounding behind mine.

"You came back for Luna," I repeated. "Not me. You saw her and you wanted her. But you can't have her. I won't let you."

He was quiet.

"That's fine," he whispered. My heart sputtered as he said it. "I don't want Luna for her. I want Luna for her mom too. It's a packaged deal. If I would've known you were pregnant when you were in New York I would've dropped the entire world for you. I wouldn't have cared about anyone—"

"*I will not let her be hurt. Ever.*" She was my entire heart.

He paused. "I know."

He didn't say a word as he breathed onto that sensitive spot on my neck. "Put me down."

Slowly, Liam did until I stood in front of him.

Everyone had abandoned him.

All because of one promise.

William Santos's promise. Liam had done everything he had done for a father figure who had essentially tormented him for years to come. His love for Isobel wasn't his love for me. And I didn't truly believe he was here for Luna.

No.

I didn't.

"I'm sorry."

"Me too."

I felt him moving, around me Liam sank to his knees slowly in front of me with a grace I didn't expect. The last time I'd seen him I'd been crying and screaming.

He tipped his head back, inky hair, deep green eyes.

"I'm so sorry, I didn't mean to run. I've been running my whole life, muneca. From my father, from love, from you. Luna—Luna was the first time I saw something more than that." His entire expression broke. "I'm sorry, baby. When I saw her, I just saw every single fuck up I ever made. Every single thing I threw away."

I felt my vision blur as I wiped my eyes.

"I have never seen myself as deserving of anything as good as her. But she isn't here without you. I came to Chicago for you. To win you back, to keep you with me by my side. I know Kieran loves Luna. He will always be her father to her. I'm not trying to be Luna's father. I am trying to be a part of her life."

I blinked surprised as I wiped my eyes more.

He pressed his forehead into my chest, the words muffled.

"I want to come home to you every single day again. I don't expect your forgiveness or anything. I just ask you give me one chance. Just one.

Let me show you. You don't even have to bring her. Let me be there for you."

And you know what? That was everything I wanted to hear. Every thing.

What Liam said? I wanted for three years. But time had changed me. Time had made me a different woman.

Time taught me, sometimes the scariest thing isn't when someone fails us, but when they show potential to be everything we hoped.

But I couldn't say yes.

"No," I shook my head wiping my eyes and seeing his face fall. "No. I waited for you. For seven years. I waited. And you came back and you broke me." His entire expression looked pained. "You broke my heart and then you left for her. You lied to me. You kept secrets from me when all I wanted to do was love you. And the reason you are here now is because I have built a life with you. I have created a world without you. And here you are now—trying to be a part of a life you are not welcome in."

Liam looked like I'd shot him.

I didn't stop though.

"I know you're going to hurt Luna. And I will do everything in my power to never let that happen. I'm sorry about your past. But we all have things we are not proud of. I didn't let my past tell me how to treat you. I loved you—"

"I love you."

I didn't know what to do and I walked around him and reached for his door unable to stop myself.

I walked out more terrified than ever now leaving Liam's broken expression and wiping my eyes frantically.

Because while I had expected Liam to break my heart.

I hadn't expected Liam to say all the right things.

41

LARA

I RUSHED BACK HOME TO KIERAN WHO WAS LAYING ON THE COUCHES IN THE living room with Luna asleep with Cheddar, in her arms purring like a sewing machine.

"The two of them are out," he motioned to the cat and my daughter who were about the same height at this point. "You good?"

I wasn't. We stepped out into the hallway to keep an eye on her and the words left me in a rush. His amber eyes widened.

"*He kissed Isobel?*" Kieran's eyes went wide. "*That son of a—*"

"*And then he says he said my name when kissing her.*"

Kieran broke off and looked down at me. A noise like "huh?" left him. I explained it to Kieran who frowned then and looked almost curious.

"When he kissed Isobel, he said your name?"

"Yes."

"And he stopped kissing her and told her about you?"

"*Yes.*"

He frowned deeper. "That doesn't sound very scummy."

"What?"

"Think bout it, he's in love with this girl for twenty—nine years. He meets you. He sees you and dates you and treats you right—Isobel comes back and sure, he kisses her but that's like a 'I'm so happy your alive kiss' not a 'Let me cheat on my girlfriend kiss' you know?"

"What?" I was so confused. "Kissing is kissing, Kieran."

"No, it isn't. I made out with Gianna all the time. My dick felt nothing for her."

241

I blinked as he said it.

"I just did it because it was empty for me and a replacement for something else." He looked at me. "I'm a guy, Lara. I have issues. I can kiss one girl and think about another."

"That's disgusting."

He smirked. "Yeah, but at least I know it. Liam sounds like he didn't. He might've been relieved to see Isobel but his only thought was about you." He frowned deeper, his eyes raking over me. "You've never kissed one man and thought about anyone else?" He raised a brow and I flushed.

The weeks Liam had been gone after he left Teaser's I just imagined every man I met was him.

I didn't say that to Kieran though.

"But he kissed her while he was with me."

"True," Kieran tipped his head back. "Pretty shitty of him. But Liam's always been…somewhere in the middle of good and evil. Between cheater and faithful man. In the past at least. Between Titan and Talon. Between his family and the world. Sounds like he's been caught in the middle every single time. Shit sucks." He rubbed the back of his neck looking almost embarrassed. "I would know."

I frowned up at him. "You think there's a difference in how he kissed Isobel versus me?"

Kieran's eyes went a little dark as he took a step forward. "Stay still, Lara," his voice was dark as he dipped his head faster than I could stop him and his mouth sealed over mine.

I froze as he did. It was intense. But it was quick, hungry, and so fast I didn't even feel it. It was impersonal. He pulled back.

"That is how I kissed you in relief to know you're okay."

I blinked a little dazed as he did it again. "That is how I kiss my girl-friend," he murmured.

Kieran all over me was something else as he held my face with his hands eating at my mouth in a way that left little to the imagination.

And then he did it again, only this time he stamped his mouth over mine hungrily hauling me up into his arms. This time his tongue thrust into my mouth as he lifted me into his arms.

A noise left me at the sensation, unfamiliar and not—not Liam—and not mine. I held onto his shoulders as he growled into me.

He pulled back with a gasp. "That is how I kiss the woman I want to fuck. Feel the difference?"

I nodded dumbly.

"There's a difference. Between you and someone else. Between you and Isobel. Between what Liam wants and what he says he doesn't."

He straightened and set me down, his cheeks flushed, something unreadable in those amber eyes.

"Good," he smirked. "Give him a chance, Lara. He did fuck up. But he's also an idiot like me. A lonely idiot. He moved to be around you. You don't have to introduce Luna to him. But maybe just see if his word holds up?" Kieran shrugged a little like he hadn't just made out with me. "Who's it gonna hurt?"

I licked my lips as he grinned down at me.

"Wanna make out again?"

"Ugh, you're an animal." He chuckled as I heard a whimper from the living room. "And that's Luna."

"I'll go to her, can you go make her some milk?"

"On it."

42

LIAM

"She doesn't want anything to do with me," I told Killian.

He was on the phone with me.

Marissa and Kiara were with their mother and cuddling watching a movie tonight together while Killian got a breather with me.

"Keep trying," Killian sounded annoyed with me. "Get her those white chocolate strawberries, she likes."

"How do you know this?"

"Because Nisha makes them whenever the girls come over, and she loves them." He sounded like he was taking clothes out of the washer and dryer. "Damn, where do her socks always go? I feel like this dryer eats Marissa's socks and shoes."

I just imagined him doing laundry now with all his daughter's baby clothes.

"Do you wash her dresses too?"

"No, I get those sent to the dry cleaner's only. Kiara loves her dresses."

"I was joking."

"I know, I wasn't." He snorted. "Welcome to fatherhood."

I covered my eyes. "How do I win her back? I'm here, I moved in, the house is comfortable, everything is stocked. I have more milk in my fridge than a normal man should be allowed to have."

"I thought Lara just pumped, why didn't you ask her for milk?"

I felt my cheeks heating.

"Because unlike you, I look like a psychopath asking my former girl-friend for pounds of breast milk." Even as I said it my cheeks heated.

"Right," he sounded like he honestly forgot because I was sure him asking Nisha for anything or any part of her body wasn't weird to her. "I mean, if Lara's still got postpartum you might wanna just start there."

"What?" I stopped rubbing my eyes. "What do you mean?"

Killian paused on the other end like he hit the buttons of the washer. "If Lara has postpartum. You know? After she had Luna, I would've thought Kieran told you, but she has postpartum depression. Comes with the territory of rapid changes, hormone fluctuations, and just having to adjust to a kid in general."

He continued like I wasn't going on my computer in my study and signing in to research as much as I could.

I put Killian on speaker while I searched it up.

"I took Nisha out after she had Kiara. She wasn't doing too good after a few months. So we had Aidan and Sonya babysit Kiara for two weeks and I took Nisha away somewhere warmer..."

"I can't ask Lara that," I muttered looking up everything I could through Oracle.

"Pregnancy is stressful," Killian murmured. "It took Nisha plenty of time, and lots of help. Evie was the same. I know Lucas was the one who recommended we hire a nanny. I think Kieran tried that for Lara but Lara couldn't stay away from Luna. She didn't want that help."

He continued like I wasn't processing all this. "Nisha and I talked about having Marissa before we had her, because we both thought Kiara having a sibling was important. Evie's daughter at least has cousins, but Lucas swore he'd never see Evie go through that again."

As he said it my stomach twisted a little. Evie's daughter. Cousins. Isobel. Isobel had kids now with Gabriel.

Lara hadn't gotten that help. "She didn't want help?"

"No, Lara wanted to be close to Luna. They slept in the same bed and Kieran said they were inseparable. I think Lara's afraid somethings going to take Luna from her."

"Because of her past?" Because she'd been kidnapped?

"Maybe, or just because she's been through a lot. It's normal. When Nisha had Kiara, she couldn't stand being apart from her. But now with Marissa it's like Nisha feels like she can breathe. Lara doesn't have that. She has support—Lara's afraid of a lot of things."

Because of my fucked up ass.

"I fucked up."

"Yeah." At least Killian didn't mince words.

"What do I do?" How did I help my family?

"It might be worth taking her away from Luna. She can always call a babysitter. Kieran has a nanny who watches out for her. But definitely getting her a second away and getting her to calm down. Nisha had support, but Lara chose to stay in Chicago."

I didn't understand why.

Wait.

I did.

"Because of me."

Killian was quiet and then I heard something else in the background. "Baby?"

"Luv, sorry, I'm on the phone with Liam."

"Oh, how's he doing? Hi, Liam." Nisha sounded tired. "The girls went to sleep, help me bring them to bed?"

"Yes, luv." Killian was an obedient house husband. "I gotta go. Just look up all the things you can do, there's options."

I knew, I was already looking at one potential one.

~

I SENT HER FLOWERS EVERY SINGLE DAY. CHOCOLATES. CANDIES. SNACKS. Takeout.

Finally a text popped up on my phone a week later.

> Stop sending chocolate chip pancakes.
>
> You're spoiling Luna.
>
> She thinks the pancake fairy keeps sending them to us and I can't explain to her what happens when they stop

I paused. The number didn't announce itself but it didn't have to.

I felt a smile creep up on my face.

> You can tell Luna, the pancake fairy is here to stay.
>
> Not going anywhere.
>
> What do you want?
>
> A chance
>
> Just one

246

And I still send pancakes no matter what your answer is.

I waited patiently for her answer.
And then some.
I saw the bubbles.

Fine. When and where?

My place. Whenever you can. 8pm. Come alone.

Tonight?

If you want. It's on your terms.

Tonight.

I'll come walk you over.

It's five houses down. I'll live.

Small victories. I smiled leaning back against the couch. I already had a plan.

I DROPPED THE BATH BOMB INTO THE TUB JUST AS THE DOORBELL RANG.
   "Coming."
   Maybe it was wishful thinking but I didn't know if she ran baths for herself or if Kieran ran them for her. The thought of the latter happening made my blood boil. I didn't want Kieran anywhere near a naked Lara.
   I didn't think they were together thought.
   Not after what happened. Lara appeared at the door dressed in her in her winter coat and comfy clothes. I didn't tell her to bring a change of clothes because I didn't want her to think I was down to fuck.
   I was.
   But not...like this.
   Not so early.
   As she stepped inside my mind lost it when she took her coat off. Three years of motherhood had changed her body to a point where I didn't recognize her the first time I'd seen her.
   I didn't think Lara was a stranger to how much her body had changed. Wider hips. Curving more. Her body completely transforming and then

247

there was her lush breasts now. Fuller. Bigger for her frame, and I knew if I ever was lucky enough to see Lara without a stitch of clothing on? I would worship this woman's fucking body.

Jeez. She was so fucking beautiful. And I was so fucking glad I made the effort. Candles. Hot towels. Snacks. Those white chocolate covered strawberries.

"You wanted me here tonight?" She looked up at me with wariness that I wanted to get rid of immediately. I hated that she watched me like that.

I nodded. "I have something for you. It's upstairs though."

I was nervous. Getting her naked might be playing dirty, but I had it all planned I did.

She followed behind me as I led the way to the master bedroom's bathroom. I did want Lara somewhere comfortable and close. I didn't feel comfortable letting her into the other rooms. Not right now.

I felt the anticipation and trepidation coursing through me as I led Lara into the bathroom and heard her tiny little gasp.

"Surprise." I smiled turning over my shoulder. "It's all yours. For tonight at least."

I quickly explained seeing her stunned eyes.

"I thought you could use a bath to relax. I did some research and new moms are always stressed and I didn't know the last time you took a night for yourself. So I wanted to give you a night. To relax. Comfort you. No strings."

I motioned nervously to the bathtub as Lara looked at me a little stunned.

"You did all this?"

I nodded feeling anxious. "Do you...like it? Can you stay? I got you some books Nisha recommended and I thought you'd hang out while I make dinner downstairs."

One night of not being a mom. Just her. The Lara I did remember.

She blinked like I was a three headed alien speaking a different language.

"You're going to make dinner and..." she motioned to the tub. "I just sit there?"

"Yeah." Both of us stood there silently. And when I turned to the tub I saw the bath bomb had melted. "Might be a bit colder now, but I can add more epsom salt and run the hot water a bit more. I got you some extra towels and—"

"Stop."

248

I froze adjusting the towels and turning to her.

"Something wrong?" I swallowed watching her blink rapidly.

"No, just…" she motioned to everything. "It's just a lot…"

"It's all good," I murmured. "It's all…I don't mind. And it's not a problem for me. You can relax for a bit and head home. I promise. If you don't want dinner, I'll just leave it alone."

Lara's throat worked. "Dinner?"

"Yeah, I thought I'd make some pasta—" Why did this feel so big now? It was just dinner. "If you want."

It took Lara a minute to gather herself as she looked around. "I haven't had a bath in years like this, I just take quick showers."

I wanted to smile reassuringly but I was pretty sure my smile was pained.

My fault.

That was my fault.

This was all my fault.

I blinked back my emotions. "Sorry." I motioned to the bath. "It's all yours, like I said. I'll be downstairs prepping food if you need me."

43

LARA

A BATH.

With bath bombs.

Scented candles.

White chocolate covered strawberries.

A virgin Pina colada.

I was in Heaven.

My toes wiggled in the water as I sank in, the purple swirls moving around from the bath bomb.

True to his word Liam left me alone and I sighed leaning back wanting to cry. I couldn't remember the last time I felt this good.

Quick showers with Luna there making sure she had eyes on her mommy.

Kieran running in and out giving her milk. I swore after I gave birth I couldn't even stand on my own without Vivianne helping me.

Sonya had sent her to Chicago and Kieran had found a nanny but neither one of them could comfort Luna.

Finally Cheddar who seemed to be all knowing began snuggling with her.

Now?

Luna was asleep with Kieran and Cheddar. The three of them watching movies.

All was quiet with the Titan's tonight for once and Kieran had beefed up security around the house discreetly. They just sat downstairs in the base level which was just as cozy.

It was a tiny bit unnerving but I could always run over to Luna if she needed me.

I laid back my mind fighting to stay calm in the hot bath water. Thoughts were erupting in my head like steam.

The candles, the eucalyptus,

I didn't know how long I laid there but when Liam knocked again he poked his head in. "Hey, good if I come in?"

I nodded feeling shy as I pulled the curtain a tiny bit.

This bathtub was so pretty just like the rest of the house.

I could see the blurry outline of him.

"I brought you dinner." I could smell it.

"Is that pesto?"

"Mhm, Killian said you loved it when you were pregnant."

"I used to have Kieran get it from this Italian place—"

He set it down on tray that went across the tub and his breath releasing shakily. "Let me know if you need something else." And then he passed me another virgin Pina colada and left. Just like that. Nothing else.

The warm bite of pesto and the hot bath and the cool coconut—I died a little. I sighed leaning back into the bath.

I couldn't remember the last time I did this.

"I could *totally* get used to this."

I WAS PADDING AROUND LIAM'S BEDROOM WHEN I REALIZED I DIDN'T HAVE any clothes.

You could always take his hoodies.

No, but that felt too personal. But I didn't want to put on my old clothes. Not right now.

I wrapped the towel around me as I dared to walk into Liam's closet and grab a hoodie off the rack. His wardrobe was entirely black and mine had always been sequins and colors.

Shadows and sunshine. Liam would always call me his sun. And so I named Luna after him being the moon.

Right now, I felt almost guilty for enjoying the bath. That guilt of taking that time for myself. And then the feelings of shame that sank in were one I couldn't quite explain as I took one of his hoodies. One I was learning to accept might just be a normal part of motherhood for me.

I wanted to have the bath with Luna. Wanted her to experience things with me. I felt like if she didn't?

I was failing.

I dropped the towel over his chair and his desk as I went to put the hoodie on.

Just as I grabbed it I heard his voice.

"*Muneca?*" I heard the door opening and I yelped a little as Liam's eyes went wide as I covered myself. "Sorry," he whispered. "It's been thirty minutes, I thought you were done changing."

I quickly turned around breathing a little harder.

"Sorry, I knocked, I don't think you heard me."

Had he? I didn't know how much time had passed.

Did he see how ugly I was now?

Did he know?

Did he...I couldn't breathe.

"Are you turned around?"

"Yes. I'm sorry," he repeated. "I didn't know—"

"It's okay." It wasn't. I couldn't stop shaking.

"Lara..." Liam's voice was a whisper.

I turned to look at him with his back to me now holding up a shirt. "I didn't know what you had, so I thought I'd bring you something clean."

I swallowed around my emotions and the unfamiliar sensations blossoming after three years. When Kieran kissed me—I felt nothing. But a few seconds in Liam's presence, in his room, in his home, and I was drowning in all the sensations from years ago.

"I found a hoodie."

Liam didn't say a word but I saw how tense he was. Just standing there. "You look...fucking beautiful..."

I felt my thighs clenching together the moment he said it and my hands over my body tighten.

"It's dark in here," I murmured. "You don't know that."

"Oh, but I do." Liam's voice was dark as sin. "I've seen you in clothes. Now I've seen you without with that body? I can die in peace."

A startled laugh burst forward out of my mouth. Only Liam said things like this.

I went to grab my towel again instead of the hoodie to wrap it around myself. I didn't know what to say. Not anymore.

Liam slowly turned to look at me tossing the shirt to the bed.

I don't know why I felt the arousal after three years when I thought it was dormant. It flared up bright hot, my nipples pebbling the moment his eyes raked over me. Open admiration in his expression. Eyes dark with lust and want.

252

"I don't look like how I used to," I whispered clutching the towel tighter. He tipped his head in understand.

"You look better," he murmured taking a step forward and then another. "You look so beautiful, *muneca*."

I took a step back and another hitting his wall as Liam stalked towards me and bent his head to me his lips brushing my cheek, his hands gripping my hips tighter.

My body was more present and aware than it had ever been. Every nerve ending sparking alive.

"You look fucking edible."

I shivered as his lips grazed my ear, and then lower finding that sensitive spot. "*Liam*."

His lips moved over that spot sealing his mouth over it. I moaned a little, my knees going weak, and a shiver skating down my spine. My nipples pebbled harder and I could feel the arousal building.

I didn't think this was why he brought me here, but I also hadn't planned ahead for a bath. I didn't know what to do.

Was this okay?

Was it too much? Was it too soon?

Liam had just come back into my life after three years and my body acted like no time had passed at all. Like I didn't have Luna and like I was still the same girl who let him sleep with me after the first time I saw him.

And that should've scared me, even if he had never scared me.

"Lara," he breathed. "You're so soft...you smell like flowers...all the time...fuck, you're so beautiful..." his breath coasted over my skin and I felt my hands dropping to grip his shoulders letting the towel drop.

A shaky exhale left him as he gripped my hips tighter as his mouth trailed lower. Pressing kisses into my skin. Down the center of my chest where my breasts rose and fell.

I didn't even stop him the moment he flicked his tongue over my nipple. It was electric. I didn't expect to be so sensitive. A noise left me as he opened his mouth and sucked over it hungrily then.

The rush of moisture, the heat I felt, the arousal built and rapidly.

After three years of doing nothing but being a mom? I felt like a woman for the first time and Liam sucked harder as I cried out, threading my fingers through his hair, feeling my pussy clenching on nothing for him.

Just for him.

"*Amor*."

He growled as it slipped out of me and he sucked harder his hands coming up to hold me in place, massaging the other while he sucked. I moaned spreading my legs and leaning back as he sank to his knees in front of me.

"Fuck," he swore. "You taste even better."

I felt my knees buckle as he wrapped his arms around me then, latching onto my body holding fast. From that noise he made alone, I wanted to come. I needed it.

I hadn't done anything remotely sexual in years. With sharing a bed with Luna sometimes I couldn't even give myself release.

And now? All of the sexual tension in me that had built felt like it was exploding out of me. For Liam. With him.

I was going to die as he tugged and suckled and then moved onto the other one. A whimper left me as I felt my body trembling in his hold.

"I could do this all fucking night," he groaned. "Fuck, these are beautiful."

"Liam," I moaned. Relief mingled with desire as he all but picked me up never letting go and I felt my back hit the bed as Liam trailed his tongue down my stomach and lower.

A noise left me in protest. But he was too fast. His tongue moved over my clit and I almost came off the bed as I looked down.

Lying there, I saw Liam sinking to the floor, his arms banding over my thighs as he growled against my clit.

The wet sensations of his tongue were insane against my body. Liam ate at me like a man starved and having already built up from when he was at my nipples, the moment he sank his tongue into me—I exploded. I couldn't stop it.

The intensity of my orgasm surprised me as ragged cry left me. Liam was groaning as I came latching onto me harder, his fingers moving up to toy with my nipples as he did.

He kept licking and tasting me like he had all the time in the world. Bringing me down from my orgasm with slow and long strokes of his tongue before ramping up again. And I just laid there taking it.

I didn't even know how long it went on for or how Liam kept going.

I just knew I was trembling wildly into his mouth a second time, this orgasm cresting over me in a rush as Liam sucked on my clit this time.

Nobody did this like Liam. I gasped and moaned and cried out as I held onto him. "*Liam.*"

Thighs shaking. Hips rocking. Liam kept that rhythm again and increased his tongue as I felt his fingers pressing into the entrance of my body. Normally I would've panicked.

Nothing had come near me and then the slow slide of his fingers, his groan against my clit. Liam pumped them in and out slowly, angling them in a way that drove me insane as he grazed his teeth against my swollen clit.

"Liam...please...Liam—I can't—"

I didn't think I'd beg him. Or sound this ragged but the moment he slid his fingers deep into me, and sucked on my clit hard—I fell apart again.

This time it ripped from me long and slow and it felt like Liam was taking every single pull into himself. My cheeks heated, my fingers fisted his hair as I came and came and came.

"Liam..." his name came out of me in a low aching moan, tears flowing from my eyes. "Liam..."

"I'm not finished," he growled over my pussy. "Not even fucking close, *muneca*." Liam's fingers were buried deep and I felt myself clenching down on them.

"What are you doing?" I whispered unable to see clearly, shaking so hard I could barely breathe. My chest rose and fell as he pressed kisses to my lower abdomen, all over my inner thighs.

"Isn't it obvious?" He whispered. "Apologizing."

"Liam—"

He rubbed a spot deep and sweet in me and a ragged moan left me as my body lit up from the inside out. I thought I'd tap out and that would be enough, but Liam kept going.

Until I was shaking so hard, I was scrambling to get away.

My hips bucking up into his tongue with a squeal. He let go panting, breathing on my inner thigh. Shivering uncontrollably, I felt Liam's mouth move to my abdomen pressing kisses there. Over and over. All over it.

Over my stretch marks. Over the soft bits I didn't know what to feel about.

"I'm sorry." Liam's voice was muffled and gruff. "I'm so sorry, baby. To both of you."

And suddenly I realized it felt too intense to even process what he'd done. I covered my eyes with an arm feeling like mush as he continued to kiss my body, dropping his frame over mine slowly as he licked up a path to my neck and settled over me while I sniffled.

Wiped my eyes.

Held onto him.

I buried my face in his neck not realizing how emotional a little oral made me. A lot of oral apparently made me cry.

I squirmed in his arms feeling my body tremble and shake as I cried into his neck.

"I'm sorry," he repeated. "I couldn't stop myself. That was three years of me wanting some. I only stopped because I didn't think you could take anymore."

No, I couldn't.

Even now I felt the violent aftershocks as I trembled.

"The last time my body shook this bad was after labor," I whispered. "She was small, but it was painful. I thought I'd have to have an emergency c—section." The words left me then in a confession.

Liam was quite buried into my neck as I said it.

"Sonya was there though for me. A few weeks after Nisha had Kiara. She was experienced enough to help me. She helped rotate me and worked with me for hours to get Luna out. I felt like if Luna could she would've stayed in me."

A light laugh left me at those moments.

"I was terrified. If it wasn't for Sonya—I don't know what I would've done."

I was calming down as I wiped my eyes remembering how horrifying it was and how Sonya had stepped in and told me—conventional ways to have babies were overrated and painful. Sonya had turned me onto my knees and Luna had pushed out so easily—Sonya had caught her.

Sonya was her godmother, Kieran was her god—father.

I admitted it openly to Liam who listened his weight feeling comforting and safe like it always had.

"It was rough," he whispered.

I nodded. "But I've never heard a woman say it was the easiest thing she'd ever done so there's that."

My joke fell flat as Liam nodded.

"I should've been there."

"You were going through a lot."

"No," he shook his head gently his lips moving over my pulse again. "No, not as much as you. I should've helped. I should've held you."

But that didn't happen. I felt my breath leave me in a shudder.

"Her birthday was a few weeks ago," I whispered wiping my eyes. "She's three. She's very impressionable. She mimics everything you do and say and she likes comfortable settings. Wally the Whale. Her blanket. Cheddar, Kieran's pet cat."

I felt him holding his breath.

"Thank you for the bath tonight."

I felt him nod.

"Will you come back sometime?" He whispered. "Anytime. For another? I can make you dinner, take care of you—give you a break."

I felt him scrambling as though I was leaving him.

I wasn't.

I just needed time and multiple orgasms were nice—I just needed time to let Luna back into his life.

"I can come back, but it can't be all the time. It's late and Luna likes my snuggles too before bed."

As I said her name he let out a shuddering breath.

"Luna..."

"Luna Sullivan is her full name," I whispered feeling myself getting emotional. "If you wanted to know."

He lifted his head and I saw him blinking back emotion.

"You named her after me? After all this time?"

I shook my head wiping my head more. I couldn't stop being emotional.

"I named her after the part of you I was proud of. The parts you weren't."

That had been the truth.

"I didn't hate you Liam, I just didn't love you anymore," I let out another shaky breath as he nodded. "It's going to take me time to let you into her life."

"I know," Liam's throat worked his eyes pleading with mine. "I know. And I don't care if it takes year or however long you wait. As long as you're in my life. I came back for you. I fell in love with you. I want to be a part of her life too, but Luna isn't my sole motivation."

And time would tell if he meant it.

44

LARA

I did go back and see him after sneaking into the house.

Well, Liam walked me back to the front steps, kissing me softly as he did. I rushed into the house feeling the warmth on my cheeks like I just got home from a first date.

Technically Liam had always been my first date.

I found Kieran asleep but Luna awake in his arms playing with his shirt and licking her lips when she saw me.

"Hola, mi amor," I kissed her cheeks feeling warmer by the second as Cheddar and Kieran lay fast asleep while I lifted her into my arms.

I snuggled Luna tighter that night and fell asleep with her next to me in bed after dinner and brushing our teeth.

The next morning I woke up to another delivery of flowers, pancakes, and a giant Wally the Whale stuffed animal for Luna.

Luna was delighted and Kieran blinked at the assortment of cupcakes and treats that arrived in our home.

"He's doing this with pancakes?" Kieran raised a brow down at Luna who was loving her strawberry shortcake ones. I sat munching on chocolate chip.

I laughed at Kieran's expression. "He sent more." I motioned to the countertops filled with pancakes.

Cheddar was meowing at Kieran from the floor.

"No, you're on a diet," he eyed the cat. "Luna snuck in another can last night to you after I fed you. You're supposed to be in a deficit. So we can cut together."

I laughed as Cheddar flopped to the floor.

"Kitty!" Luna giggled trying to throw a pancake piece on the floor.

"No, Luna. Don't throw your pancakes at Cheddar," I stopped her. "Here's a flower, carina."

Luna took it distracted by the pretty violet's. "Mami, boo."

I kissed her while Kieran grumbled about Liam buying us over.

"If he thinks he can come into my life and steal my fake wife and daughter he's got another thing coming," Kieran said while grabbing a wrapped stack of chocolate chip pancakes, butter, and syrup.

"I doubt he's trying to steal us away from you."

Kieran grumbled as Luna tried to sneak food to Cheddar.

"Luna," I held out my hands and she released her grip on her pancake. "This is for you. Cheddar cannot have any." I turned to Kieran. "I'm going to—"

"Date him." Kieran raised a brow sitting down to eat pancakes while Cheddar yowled from the kitchen floor.

"No," I corrected him setting the pancake down. "I'm going to simply see him every so often—"

"For a date." Kieran smirked. He was trying to get to me and it was working. "You think you're ever gonna introduce her to him?"

"He's already met her."

"You know what I meant."

I puffed out a breath as Luna's lower lip wobbled and she shot big green eyes at Kieran who stopped eating.

"Oh, sweet pea. Don't give me that face. I can't have a diabetic Cheddar. You already fed him all the tuna in the cupboards."

I bit back a laugh as Kieran looked devastated at her pout.

"Oh, she's good," he looked worried at me. "You think she knows I'm the one who hid the tuna from her too?"

I giggled unable to stop myself at their antics.

Luna eyed him and I watched the staring contest as I said. "I'm seeing him again."

Kieran frowned at Luna playfully while eating his food looking adorable. "Sweet pea, you're going to be spoiled if I say yes. Of course, you would see him again. It's Liam. When do you think you'll introduce him to her?"

I watched Luna pout more. "Boo. Kitty."

"Kitty get's plenty of boo's," Kieran said to her pointing to her strawberry pancake. "That looks good. Can Unca Kieran get some?"

"I don't know," I murmured watching Luna try and feed Kieran her pancake bite as he put some chocolate chip ones on her plate. I laughed as she missed, Kieran deftly catching it in his hand as he set a chocolate chip pancake down on her plate. "But I want to get to know this Liam before I introduce them."

We finished up breakfast and I passed Luna some milk as she kept looking at Cheddar. Kieran needed him to move around more so I would take both of them to the park. After the park, we came back for bath time and story time and then she passed out in my arms after chasing Cheddar around the house as best as she could.

I did go and see Liam. Every single night.

The moment the door opened, he kissed me again and brought me inside. Every night he set up a date with me and he didn't sexually make a move on me again. I was kind of waiting for it, but instead he set up pedicure dates, spa dates, and movie nights for me to unwind.

Kieran was home with Luna who fell asleep with Cheddar now and it felt a little good to be living my life. The guilt of it passed.

It took me a few days of realizing when talking to Liam about the last few years that I already knew I wanted them to meet.

"How long do you plan on staying?"

He paused as he grabbed a pair of socks. "As long as you'll have me."

"What do you do now?"

"Nothing, I'm retired."

"You have all this time?" I was curious.

He tipped his head. "Aidan made me realize being a stay at home dad is pretty sweet."

My heart flipped at that and I looked down at my bowl of popcorn.

"Do you want to meet her? We go to the park in the afternoon with Cheddar…" I trailed off feeling silly.

I felt the shift instantly.

I knew Liam was trying to win me over. It was working.

But maybe I needed to see them together. He hadn't seen her or held her since New York.

"I'd love that."

45

LARA

When the doorbell rang the next morning Luna squealed in joy, Cheddar yowled, and it was just me rushing to let Liam in.

His deep green eyes watched me with a little smile on his face as I heard another yowl, Luna squealing, and I gasped running after Cheddar. "Liam, close the door!"

I rushed after Cheddar picking him up as Luna giggled running after us as I caught him. "Bad kitty!"

"Bad kitty!" Luna giggled and I burst into laughter at her half—dressed self.

"Carina, your pants, what happened to them?" I put Cheddar down as I heard the door shut and Liam appeared and I went to help Luna while Cheddar took off again. "Liam, stop him!"

Luna seemed to realize someone else was here as she looked at Liam now trying to catch and wrestle Cheddar.

"I'm so sorry, it's not usually complete chaos around here," I helped Luna fix her pants. "Do you need to change your pull—ups? Let me see, Mami can change you before we go, carina."

"Lara, he's like the size of a pillow." Liam held a yowling Cheddar a foot away from him and the contrast of his scowl to Cheddars shouldn't have made me laugh as I fixed Luna.

But it did.

I laughed even more when Liam frowned at it. "Please tell me this does not go on a walk with us."

"Unfortunately," I muttered checking Luna's pull ups and pants to

261

make sure she didn't need to go to the bathroom. "He needs to lose weight. We take him everywhere."

"Kitty!" Luna cried. Liam's eyes finally met hers and they focused in on her with a laser like intensity. They went wide for a moment and I watched him taking her in from where he stood holding Cheddar who flopped over to play dead.

I fixed her clothes as she giggled and pointed to Cheddar. "Kitty!"

"Kitty is in big trouble right now, *carina*."

Liam set Cheddar down without ever looking away from her. And I paused in everything I was doing.

"Oh damn, I forgot how tiny she was."

He sank to one knee to make himself level with her and even then he was bigger.

Luna smiled up shyly at him from where we were. She smiled at me and then him like she wanted me to know he was here.

"Luna," I murmured brushing her curls back. "Remember Liam? You met him in New York? Recuerdas a Liam? ¿Lo conociste en Nueva York?"

She looked at me a little confused and then Liam.

"He's going to the park with us today, do you want to say hi to Liam?"

I motioned waving my hand as Liam looked at her like she was his salvation. His sunshine. Everything.

I saw now how badly he wanted to meet her written on his face. The desperation. The want.

"Hola," he held out his hand, enormous compared to hers, the tattoos on his knuckles flexing a little and Luna latched onto that.

She pointed at them excited. And I grinned.

"She colors Kieran's tattoos sometimes, I think she's excited to meet you now."

Luna walked to Liam slowly while I covered my mouth with my hand.

Luna watched him as he stayed still like he was being approached and he didn't want to frighten her.

"Hola," he smiled reassuringly but I saw him breaking a little.

I saw all the emotion in his eyes. He kept his hand extended and I waited with my breath in my heart for Luna to take it.

She giggled a little as she approached him and the moment she took it I saw Liam's eyes close.

Slowly, I watched her approach the circle of his arms and when she got close enough, Liam lifted her up into them. Luna made a delighted noise gripping his face.

"*Boo.*"

"Hi," he whispered brushing her hair back. "It's so good to finally meet you again."

"Boo."

His eyes searched mine. "What do I do?"

"Kiss her forehead," I croaked. "Or her nose. Wherever, boo means—"

"She wants kisses."

"Yes. And you can kiss her." Because he was her father.

Luna was comfortable with Liam. From the beginning I saw it.

Liam leaned down and pressed his lips to her forehead and I saw the way his lip wobbled a little. He was shaking too and I closed the distance coming closer in case he needed to set her down.

For a long moment he stayed there and didn't say a word.

His lips on her forehead. Luna's eyes closing like she loved the longest boo in the world and when Liam finally pulled back his eyes were red and he was blinking rapidly.

I wiped my eyes as I watched Liam tuck her closer into his chest like he wanted to keep her there forever.

"What does she need?" His voice was hoarse and rough as he looked at me worried. "It's cold outside, does she need...does she need a coat? a scarf? This isn't all she's wearing right?"

Luna was distracted by his tattoos as he asked me ninety questions about her winter outfit.

I was going to respond until Cheddar began yowling again and hacking. I gasped *horrified*.

"Bad kitty," I went after him. "We talked about you and your hairballs."

"Kitty!" Luna squealed.

"What do I do for you, *munequita*, do you have a jacket?" Liam adjusted her in his arms as she giggled. "Do you have gloves? Do you get cold easily like Mami?"

And the day was just getting started.

46

LIAM

"*MUÑECA, SHE'S SOMETHING ELSE.*"

I watched Luna run up the stairs of the slide again as best as she could to come back down. I thought my heart was going to explode.

That was the only reason for the sensations coursing through me. My chest was going to implode.

Lara smiled at her, her dark eyes twinkling with delight.

"She's good," she laughed as Luna's little legs carried her up. Her little bow askew again.

"She's strong too, look at how she grabs the rails, Lara. Look at her little legs…Oh, she's so cute. Look at her hat…there you go…come to daddy."

I was so *proud.*

I was a little bitch getting emotional every five fucking seconds watching my daughter running, playing, walking around independently.

"Come on, *muñequita,* I'm right here."

I kneeled against grateful for my legs being stronger as she giggled the entire way down the slide. I grinned holding her.

Lara came to the park with her in the mornings or afternoons depending on how warm the sun was.

I couldn't let her go as she met me at the bottom of the slide.

"Again!"

"I gotcha," I led her to the stairs and she climbed up excited with her little body. At the top she went to come down. I was *never* getting bored of this. "I wanna bring her to the park often."

"I bring her every single day."

"She's amazing," I watched my daughter giggling and running around again.

"Again, again," she squealed.

"I gotcha, shortcake. We'll go again."

Lara had me hold her when we went to the park as she took Cheddar on his leash.

"He doesn't get a carrier anymore," she explained holding him to the side as he played dead. She gently rocked him. "When he gets nervous he pees on everything. Come on, I know you are not dead."

I blinked down at the enormous thing that qualified as a cheese puff instead of a cat.

Luna was tickled by him as she came down the slide and ran to him. And then Cheddar woke up from his fake death and engaged.

"There's her accomplice," I muttered.

"He's soft on her because she steals food for him," Lara explained brushing Luna's curls back. "Wait until they have to take a bath, it's chaos."

"I want to be there for that," I volunteered feeling like my heart was going to explode out of my chest. Me. Liam *Sullivan*.

The piece of shit from nothing. From nowhere. And now her.

Luna.

My flesh and blood. My entire heart. Dragging a poor kitty's face up to kiss it.

Lara made a soft noise. "*Carina*, no. He has emotions. You cannot pull him. Remember he is alive."

She made a noise with her teeth that both of them seemed to understand. Luna pouted as Lara showed her how to engage with Cheddar without hauling his face.

And I marveled.

My heart was gonna explode.

That was the only way to describe how I felt.

Watching her who had raised this beautiful little girl—my two girls—interacting with each other. Lara smoothing her cap and fussing over her little mittens.

"*Galletita*." Cookie.

"You want your cookies? Liam, will you get the bag from the stroller? It has her snacks and milk in it."

I was on it. Rushing to the stroller two feet away to hunt for the damn cookies. Nisha apparently made the girls these cream filled cookies that were basically just baby friendly smaller macarons. She would bag them up by the dozens for Lara or mail them to her.

Luna didn't say much for a child.

Killian's girl said full sentences but I took it her parents had conversations. They spoke. They interacted.

Besides Kieran who might've not been home, did she have any interactions? My chest clenched at realizing I needed to talk to my daughter. Killian always talked to his girls.

I went back to Luna and got on one knee in front of her to hand her the bag.

"No, Liam," Lara's voice was sharper. "Only one. Just hand her one."

"You want a *galletita*?" I murmured handing her one. "*Quieres una galleta?*"

Luna dipped her head and reached for it and I held it back a little. It was early but I wanted to test it out.

"Can you say cookie?" I murmured low for her knowing Lara was listening. "Cookie."

She reached again and I felt bad but I realized in that moment why I couldn't just give her the cookie.

"Luna," I held her tiny hand wrapped around one of my fingers as she looked nervously at it. "Cookie." I held it up.

"Cook—" she broke off.

"One more time. Otra vez? Luna wants…"

Luna licked her lips, her eyes on the cookie and she looked confused. Of course she did. Nobody corrected her.

"Cookie."

"Cookie," she tried again. "Luna…Galletita."

Close enough. We'd give her that.

"Si, *munequita*."

As she took it happily breathing out I pressed kisses to her forehead, her hat and she drew closer.

Slowly. I'd get her to talk more slowly.

I looked over at Lara watching me with a proud expression.

"She doesn't speak much like her cousins."

"Because of her…like her development?"

"No," Lara shook her head. "She's shy. When she's with her cousin's, she's fine. But when she's alone she only says a word or two."

I nodded looking down at her polishing off her cookie.

"I'm going to practice with her more often."

Halfway through her cookie she looked up at me and pursed her lips. "Boo."

I kissed my daughter on the nose handing her another one she squealed over as Lara passed me some milk.

"It's cold, Liam, let's get her home after her second cookie."

"Cookie!"

"Such a good girl for daddy," I murmured holding her to me as Lara groaned over Cheddar who was sniffing his way into my bag of cookies.

"No, you already ate..." she grumbled. "I don't know what his old family was like, but I don't think he was taken care of."

"Explains why they named him Cheddar. Kieran never changed it?"

"No, he says his identity is important to him, even if he's named after cheese."

"Cheese!" Luna mumbled eating her cookie.

Toddlers were messy eaters I was learning wiping her face and hands with a wet wipe.

"Does Luna like cheese?" I asked Lara. I wanted to know everything about her.

"She does, she likes everything," Lara said easily.

"Daddy can buy you all the cheese," I murmured to my daughter who pointed at Cheddar too distracted to notice I was losing it.

∾

I WANTED EVERYTHING. WALKS. PICNICS. BREAKFAST. LUNCH. EVERY SINGLE thing.

Bath time was a wreck. I didn't even know I could get this wet bathing someone else.

"You're incredible, muneca," I said passing Lara a mug of tea after we put Cheddar and Luna to bed.

I had never doubted it was hard being a mother. But now?

I was convinced Lara was superhuman.

Getting Cheddar into his bath and Luna into hers was an adventure.

Cheddar yowling the songs of his people.

Lara had called it night time opera without Kieran in the house.

"Whoa, Cheddar—" I got cut off with Luna wailing.

"No, carina. Mami needs your ears..." Lara frowned washing behind her ears. "She's sensitive there, she doesn't like the sensation of water there..."

267

Lara was amazing. Lara knew every single thing in the world.

"Let me try," I murmured taking the washcloth with one hand on Cheddar. I bent my head over being taller than my girls, and kissed Luna's nose. "There you go, that's not so bad, is it?"

And then Cheddar got a little creative and squirmed knocking over a bottle of soap. Lara gasped and caught it before it hit Luna.

I had a minor heart attack and Luna began wailing when water got in her ears.

Bath time. Was. Hard. Hauling them both out and drying them off was a project.

Luna, I realized, was a little eel out of the water and I had to wrangle her giggling body out into the bedroom where she was rolling away.

"Nononono, come back."

"Kitty!"

"I know, baby. Daddy's gonna get you dry and bundled up."

Lara laughed wrestling Cheddar as I said it and I would've laughed with her until I realized Lara did this on her *own*.

Now?

Sitting on the soft velvet couch like I survived war, Lara laughed at me. I felt a grin split my lips my eyes drifting to a nearby bookshelf with a mix of Luna's board books and what looked like Kieran's books.

"You do that every day?" I sighed.

"Kieran bathes him sometimes but in the shower which is easier for him." She smiled at me sipping her tea. "But yes."

I shook my head in amazement. "I need to give you an award."

Lara's laughter was light and musical. "Or foot rubs. Or head rubs."

"I can do that," I was eager to please reaching for her as she laughed. We had both dried off with Lara's blow dryer and thankfully, I felt remotely better knowing Luna was fast asleep.

"Kieran's at Titan?" I asked her pulling her into my lap now.

"Mhm." I loved how easily she melted into my arms, a testament I guessed to how tired she was as I adjusted her now, fitting her into my lap. Inky black hair thrown over my arm, Lara's long lashes fanned over my high cheekbones as she laid against my chest. Fuck. That felt fucking perfect.

We just put our daughter to bed curled into her violet comforter and Wally the Whale plushie.

The cat was asleep with her at her back snuggling her now.

My wi—Lara was in my arms. I was cozy.

Shit. Why didn't I ever marry Lara?

I had to pause myself there for a second. Because I was just starting this with Lara again, but honestly? It felt like I never left.

How did I get here? I felt my fingers brush over her scalp as I tugged gently and rubbed. A soft moan left Lara.

"God, you have no idea sometimes what my days are like," she murmured.

"Tell me about 'em."

And so Lara did. I listened to her as she murmured about her nights and days and I rubbed her scalp pressing kisses to it.

It ached I hadn't been there.

Not once had I shown up for my girls.

That was going to change now.

At some point I grabbed a white plush throw and threw it over us as Lara dozed on me. Shifting us both, I laid on the couch with her, both of us dozing in the lamp light.

"We should...sleep near Luna..." she murmured slowly. "Sometimes she has nightmares..."

"Okay," I was so sleepy I couldn't even stand properly, but something in me forced myself to pull Lara into my arms and take her up the stairs with me until we were in her room.

I had a second to take in the lush lilac tones that matched my home before I fell into bed with Lara. Exhausted, I tore my shirt off and crawled in with her not able to process anything else.

Lara turned on the baby walkie talkie thing and I was out like a light with her in my arms.

∼

FOR THE NEXT FEW WEEKS I DID EVERYTHING A DAD WOULD DO. I GOT yogurt puffs Luna loved, obsessing over every detail.

"Which ones?" I asked Lara on the phone. "There's so many. Does she like chocolate?"

"She likes strawberry."

"*Muneca*, there's nine strawberry flavored ones."

I heard Lara's laughter making me grin.

"Get the ones with Wally on them."

"Fuck, I forgot about the whale." I found the box and grabbed several of them before moving onto her favorite apple sauce brands.

My days turned into weeks of navigating fatherhood now. And the way I began helping Lara made me re—evaluate everything I thought about Mr. Santos.

I began helping Lara with everything she needed. Holding Luna and Cheddar tighter to me every breath I got with them while Lara cleaned them both up.

The obese cat was an O'Hara after all and had to be pampered like one. Lara warned me to never give Luna access to the food cabinet.

"She has a bad habit of feeding him after he's eaten his meals, I know she loves him, but he's much healthier now than he was before." She eyed Cheddar watching us with a lazy look on his face. Lara pointed her finger at him. "*I see you, Quesito.*"

I grinned at her nickname. "Little cheese is ironic."

"Don't fat shame him," Lara whispered her accent coming out. "He has feelings too. Just because we know he's obese doesn't mean he needs a reminder. I think he thinks he's Luna's size."

And Luna, my adorable girl would color in my tattoos in her purple tulle dress and bow askew still.

She loved the ones on my chest and I let her climb on me to get to those while Cheddar mad biscuits on me. With me lying shirtless on the couch and Luna coloring me in, and Cheddar purring like a sewing machine—I made a sight for Lara to burst into laughter.

Once Kieran walked in on me while on the phone, rolled his eyes in amusement and left.

Over time I got into Lara's routine. I came over before Lara woke up, she never stayed at my place but I understood Kieran's home was home for Luna.

Lara didn't want to uproot and I was still earning it.

But day by day, I got Lara in bed. Luna wrangled into her new dresses. I began spoiling both of my girls. Luna got new dresses and clothes and Lara got comfortable pajamas, nighties, sweaters.

One night she walked into the room in a white silk slip and I all but died a little watching her get into bed. My heart pounded wildly as my dick responded.

"Muneca...is that new?"

She smiled a little looking unsure of herself as she did a twirl making her tits jiggle.

I bit the inside of my cheek to keep from losing my mind. My dick already was hardening and lengthening with a mind of its own.

"You got it for me."

And I hated that she doubted for one second she was beautiful. Not when she looked like a goddess emerging out of the night.

"You look edible right now," I murmured hearing how rough my voice was as she crawled into bed looking almost shy.

"It's so soft and comfortable."

I was patient and I waited until she was fully in before pouncing. Grabbing her around her waist and loving her little gasp.

I didn't even hesitate to roll her, pin her under me, and make out with her. The moment my lips stamped on hers my body sighed calming down while the arousal in me tamped out every other rational thought.

Get naked.

Get inside Lara.

Get inside your girl.

I made out with her hungrily, my hands all over her, cupping her breasts, mouth traveling lower—and then the cry of a baby monitor jarred both of us out of it.

My head snapped up at the whimper.

"Oh shit, that's my shortcake—" I broke off rolling off Lara with practice. "I'll go."

Daddy's coming.

I didn't even wait leaving a bemused Lara in bed while I rushed over all traces of lust gone as I found my adorable little girl crying in her bed.

"What happened, mi amor? Que past?" I had her in my arms a moment later as her whimpering stopped.

She wiped her eyes in my arms now and I saw Cheddar was missing and her little heating blanket was clearly gone. "Where'd he go? Are you upset you woke up and your friend was gone?"

She nodded. "Chedda."

"Yeah, let me go see where he is." Hopefully not sneaking in more food or something. I didn't like the big fur ball in bed with Luna but my daughter slept like a rock. I rocked her in my arms grabbing her Wally the Whale toy and slowly rocking her in my arms rubbing her back.

When I turned around I saw Lara at the door holding Cheddar. "I caught someone in the kitchen."

"And he's playing dead again," I muttered. I gave him a stern look as Luna's sleepy form reached for him.

"Lay her down, I'll put him in with her."

It took a long time for Luna to get to sleep and even with her grip on the cat, she stroked him soothing herself to bed.

By the time Luna was asleep, Lara was dozing in the day bed and I carried her back to the bedroom that was becoming ours.

"Foiled by a cat," I whispered to her as she laughed lightly still in her white nightie.

"Tomorrow?"

"Tomorrow." I kissed her crawling in with her feeling better about being a part of her life while always acknowledging—I did miss out on all these nights.

And I was determined to never miss out on a single one ever again.

4 7

LIAM

"I NEED YOUR HELP."

Kieran was in the room I was hanging out in, Luna coloring my pecs with her markers and giggling when Cheddar came back with his ball.

The cat did in fact grow on me.

I swore he understood everything I said. I just threw his toys across the room and he played fetch.

"With?" I threw the ball gently back and off he went.

Luna turned to Kieran who smiled down at her despite his stress. I respected Kieran not standing in my way.

I was envisioning he would but either his work, or his first conversation, or knowing he had two brother's who would keep me in check— Kieran left me to my girls.

Now, he sat across from me and explained his situation.

I slowly sat up adjusting Luna to my shoulder so she could continue coloring there.

"You have a jewel thief who wants to steal a half of a painting you don't have. Sonya has the other one?"

He tipped his head forward. "Sonya gave the other one to the Nash family. And Teo has another one. I just found out."

"I forgot Sonya knows Talia and Natasha."

"Distantly."

But he didn't know what the girl wanted?

The Nash sisters were a tiny bit infamous. Just enough. For one thing,

Talia Nash was the one who saved Isobel and kept her a fucking secret for years without explaining why.

I still didn't know to this day why Talia did what she did. But that empire they had was insanity.

It was conjoined with the DuPont conglomerate, Durand.

Combined? Both of them formed an empire spanning continents. And they had one son between them—Drew DuPont who stood to inherit every single thing.

It was an insane amount of power but I still didn't know how I felt about Talia let alone Natasha. Nobody knew anything about her.

"So the Nash sisters have the first original."

"Correct."

"The second one is with Teo now."

"We think Vivianne Valentine has a duplicate of the second one she intends to sell," Kieran explained. "We think she has it and she's searching to complete her "set."

"Except it isn't a set—"

"No, it's not even remotely real and she has no idea. I got intel about some guy named Jonathan Green or "Greenie" for short and he's pretending to be a Fed. Trying to get info from us about...us."

"Us?"

That made me pause. "Us?"

Kieran didn't look phased. "Aidan said there were hounds sent after him all the time. Valentine's another hound after us with a crew?"

Internally I swore, externally I stayed composed.

"What do you need?" I knew I owed the O'Hara's all the time.

"Your version of Oracle." Kieran muttered. "It's the only one we know of to find anything extensively."

Because my version was built off me.

Evie's version had limitations because she wasn't experienced and Isobel's was limited to what information she had.

I knew everything.

The keeper of keys was me. I threw the ball back as Cheddar went scampering into Kieran's legs and nestled in between his feet.

"You want me to find Vivianne Valentine?"

"Yes."

"And you want her captured?"

"Yes."

"Are my girls in danger?"

Kieran paused. "I don't know."

I blew out a breath as Luna looked at me, those eyes seeing everything. "Do I have to take them to my home?"

"Probably. Eventually. I'll talk to Lara when I get more info from you."

"Which is?" I eyed him aware of something new in me building. I needed to get the girls out now. "I'm taking them home with me tonight. I don't care about your info."

"Vivianne Valentine is in Chicago. She hasn't made a move—"

I sat up then, ready to murder him, tucking Luna into my chest. She made a small noise. "Sorry, shortcake. Let me help you."

I sat her up propped with pillows as I gave her back her marker.

"Mistake." She pointed at the mark I accidentally made when I moved her. "No."

She didn't want that. I licked my thumb and wiped the mistake off until it was good.

"There you go, shortcake."

"Dank you."

I grinned at her words as she crawled into my lap again and continued coloring.

Kieran was watching us interact with a softer look in his eyes. "You're good with her."

"Focus, my girls are in danger because of some painting and thief you wanna catch—You couldn't ask Lucy Devereaux to contact her?"

"Not if I want Adam pissed, Lucy is out of commission."

"Since when?"

"Since she was pregnant with twins. She's like halfway along and ready to murder everyone."

I blinked a little stunned. "Lucy and Adam got *married*?"

Kieran tipped his head looking bored. "Finally. He said he'd do it once he finished his residency so he had the time. You can find Vivianne Valentine. And we can get rid of this whole problem."

"And what are you gonna do with Vivianne Valentine when I find her?"

I needed a week. Max. Maybe two.

Lara and my baby would be safe in my home.

But Lara wouldn't be happy.

I hugged Luna to me as she drew hearts all over. "Boooo."

My lips pressed to her head.

"I don't know," Kieran murmured his eyes narrowed. "But that's on me and Titan Chicago. If you find her—"

"I'll help you find Vivianne Valentine but I want a part of this. I'm not about to let my family be in any kind of danger."

"Deal."

"Deal," Luna squealed giggling. "Deal."

I grinned. "Are you hungry, *munequita*? It's been forever since your last meal, hm?" I think it had been three hours but I was sure in toddler time it qualified for a snack. "I need to get her some food, you good?"

He was watching us with an odd expression.

I couldn't quite place it as Luna giggled when I flipped her this way and that.

"*Boo*."

"Did you ever..." I asked him curiously. "With Lara?" I wouldn't blame him if he did.

"No," he shook his head looking tired again. "I don't love her. I do however have always wanted to see her happy. I proposed to her several times over the years."

My blood ran cold.

"And she said no, because I knew she was in love with you. Luna's last name is your name. And she would never ever stop loving you. Even if she had married me."

His amber eyes harder now met mine. "It would never be me."

And for a moment...I felt for Kieran. I ached for him.

Because those had been my exact words to Gabriel.

"You fell for everyone you met," I murmured.

He tipped his head with a hard smile. "That I did."

"That's why you let me have her?"

Because he saw more in common with me. Turns out, I had a lot in common with the O'Hara's more than the Titans.

It would never have been me with Isobel. It wasn't right.

Because Lara was never Kieran's. She was my Lara.

I named her. I was her saint. She was my savior.

Luna was our love personified. Nothing would ever take that away. And nothing in this world would make Lara his.

Nothing.

Just like no matter what I had done? Isobel and Gabriel were meant to be. From day one. The moment she was in his eyes—just like Lara was mine.

And now I had to tell her and Luna they'd be living with me temporarily.

~

LARA HADN'T BEEN HAPPY BUT SHE TOOK THE NEWS BETTER THAN I thought she would. My guess was living in the world of the O'Hara's—she had to.

They packed up their stuff and Luna thought she was visiting my place. She didn't call me Daddy or Papi or anything, but she called me her Boo. Specifically if she yelled Boo it was me.

And so I helped Lara pack while she got Luna together and I took them to my place where Lara settled in with all Luna's things. I went back and forth a few times.

Lara seemed anxious and I was surprised she didn't want to sleep in the guest room.

"Why?" She shrugged lightly. "We always sleep together."

I agreed.

That night Luna woke up several times, after I put her to bed. I didn't know if she was uncomfortable or what, but I held her for the third time feeling exhausted.

I picked up a board book from the library and passed Luna some warm milk.

"...little owl went to sleep..."

Luna yawned in my arms.

"*Galletita.*" My chest rumbled with laughter I fought as she smiled up at me.

"I gotta get you saying full sentences, shortcake."

More like a mini-cake.

But I ended up carting her into my arms and taking her downstairs to make her something since she was hungry. Watching me eat?

Luna ate more food in general.

At three she could pretty much eat everything, but I'd seen Killian cutting things up for his girls so it would be easier.

I put something together for her into a little plate.

She stayed in my arms while I did it one—handed. "You want some avocado? I know it's late, baby. Daddy's sorry you had to move out of your home, but I hope you'll have a new home with me."

I held up the avocado and she hid in my neck.

I laughed. "No, got it. But it's good for you. Just a little maybe."

Turns out cutting an avocado one handed was a fucking feat. But somehow I did it to her delight.

She liked watching me do things and I saw why Kieran said she was struggling.

If I tried to set Luna down she cried. So I just held onto her.

"Look, daddy likes avocado," I took a bite of it with some salt.

Her mouth open and closed watching me. "Yum."

I exaggerated my moans and to my delight she reached for my mouth, closing her little fist around my lips.

"You want some? Quieres un poco?"

I knew Lara spoke in Spanish with her.

She nodded. "Aboo…"

"Avocado."

"Abocadoo."

"Close enough, here have a bite. Open for me…little bites…"

Now I realized why Killian was hyper focused on Marissa. Because if he looked away long enough she'd just shove the entire avocado into her little mouth.

"No, little bites, shortcake…little bites…Daddy's gonna have some too. Because now Daddy is starving."

Luna smiled at me like her sneaky plan to get me midnight snacks worked. I grinned down at her passing her avocados while I threw together leftovers. Lara was asleep. All was well.

Passing her more avocado and some mangos. I tried to introduce her to tajin. The tangy little seasoning salt Lara fucking devoured whenever she got into it.

I dipped some mango into it when Luna noticed me eating it. She licked her lips at it and I grinned.

"Quieres?" I held it out to her. *You want?*

She licked her lips again and grabbed it and tried it and it was like watching a baby have a revelation.

"That's good, huh? Your Mami loves that late at night when she wants a snack. She probably had some when she had you in her belly."

Luna made an excited noise as I handed her the plate and she went back for more.

I was overjoyed at how much more she was eating. And then I passed her some hot milk.

"See, Papi's place isn't so bad, is it?"

This was just tone step in the right direction, I hummed as I put the food back in the fridge. I was gonna be groggy tomorrow since neither Lara or I were nocturnal anymore unless it was for Luna.

"P—papi."

My head snapped to her as she said it, my heart pounding like a wild bird out of my chest at the word.

"Papi…" She held out those grabby hands when she wanted something.

Green eyes like mine were on me the curls messy around her head in her little purple onesie. "Papi…"

She was waiting for me to respond and I had stopped breathing.

"Si," I cleared my throat not wanting to break down in front of my daughter. Not right now. Maybe in a closet in the back of the pantry.

"Quiero más." She pointed to the tajin. "Mango."

"You want more?" I felt a smile tip my lips. "Yeah, Papi can go get you more mango."

I was up and moving for her, my lips brushing over her hair ready to give her whatever she wanted from me.

4 8

LARA

I POUNDED DEEP INTO LARA LOVING HER LITTLE WHIMPERS AND SCREAMS.

She was incredible. Sensitized beyond belief from arousal and previous orgasms.

I felt like every few thrusts she'd come and it would be like a little mini orgasm. She was coming again.

And I had a fucking blast.

My eyes rolled back feeling it.

She was going to lose her voice. It was going to hurt to walk. She was going to be sore. And I would make it better.

Take care of her. Run her a bath. Massage her hair.

Watch her squirm until she begged me to lick that pussy better.

Fuck. I pounded deep through it relishing the fluttering around my cock but aware that I kept going for her.

I wanted to come the moment Isobel said she didn't have birth control. I was lose it. But I held back. And now?

Inside of her? It took everything to not come but I knew I wanted to see her come apart. Over and over.

She was great without toys.

With toys. She was fucking explode. Tied up and and vibed within an inch. So sensitive. She came so fast.

As she calmed down an animal noise followed and I just knew.

"That's it, let go, baby, let it go, I got you."

Only I go to witness a side of her that most men only ever dreamed of.

I STOPPED AS I HEARD GIGGLES.

"Yes, you're gonna be a good girl and clean up?"

More giggles and I heard the sounds of Liam...the smattering of kisses. More laughter from the room joined to mine for her.

She never slept in there. But it sounded like she was in the bath with all the splashing. I heard squealing laughter as Liam laughed with her.

"You want more soap?"

Her giggles came through muted.

"Here's your Wally, don't forget Wally needs his ears cleaned...and so do you..."

"Wally..."

"Yes, shortcake. Wally also needs his tail cleaned. Do you have a tail too?"

Her giggles made me smile.

"No?" His light laughter came through and I laid back closing my eyes feeling my heart warm listening to the sounds of the two of them having fun. "I think we outgrew tails thousands of years ago. Hopefully."

"Tails."

"Yeah, that's a new word for you, huh?"

"Tails."

I blew out a breath to calm my heart down realizing I had nothing to be afraid of.

She was safe. She was fine.

Liam was here giving her a bath.

Moments later, I heard the sound of rinsing and Liam laughed. "You're having a great time, huh? Splashing daddy all over the place."

"Papi, boo!"

"I know, shortcake. Kisses are coming. I gotta dry you off first and make sure we get Mami food..."

As he spoke my heart sputtered. She called him daddy now?

I slowly rose up to find Liam urging Luna. "Shh, Mami's asleep. We have to be spies. We have to be secretive. Can you whisper for daddy?"

"Si." She whispered. I grinned at the two of them slinking by me and to my surprise Liam was shirtless in his briefs looking just as soaked as Luna wrapped in an enormous towel.

She looked adorably askew her hair all on one side as he snuck on by and when he saw me smiling his face broke out into a grin.

"Busted, sorry…she was splashing me and we didn't mean to wake you up—"

I shook my head. "It's okay. Are you two clean?"

"Nah, she is." He grinned as she giggled in his arms. "We got caught, shortcake. Mami's awake."

My daughter giggled and cuddled into his arms.

"Let me go put her down to bed and then I gotta shower since short-cake here *ruined my clothes*," he said the last part dramatically gasping, and Luna did the same and they both burst into laughter.

My heart could not take it anymore. I was going to explode seeing them interact as he carried her into her room.

"Gotta moisturize you, and then gotta get your pull—ups, and then your hair creams…for your curls…"

I was exploding. That was it.

I laid back in bed realizing for the first time in a long time I didn't really have to think or worry about anything. I just laid there listening to her laughter.

Her giggles.

Liam talking to her through her routine.

And the sound of my family existing.

I washed up and went to find Liam tucking in Luna into her bed.

"Yeah, this is for big girls, hm? Big girls go to bed here. So cozy. You're gonna sleep so well tonight with the heated blanket hm? Daddy turned it on a lower setting, okay?"

Luna stared at him like he was the moon.

And right now, in his briefs and nothing else with his hair messy and his grin—he looked irresistible.

I crossed my arms over my chest feeling my nipples tighten as he brushed her hair back and turned the lights down on her little moon light.

"You gonna be a big girl, tonight?" He whispered. "Daddy's right there with Mami. Okay?"

She nodded adorably, her little fist curled around his thumb.

"I'm right here too." Liam bent down and pressed his lips against her temples and then her chest. "I'm always with you."

"Papi."

"Si?"

"Besito?"

He grinned and kissed her and she snuggled into him. "Bedtime, Luna."

I watched him tuck her in as he turned off the light and she closed her eyes. Liam stood to his full height rising off her bed and seeing me he paused.

"Hey," he murmured. "Good?"

I nodded unable to even speak at how attractive he looked. All of this.

Every time I saw him with her, my heart pounded, and my entire body responded to him.

I walked out with Liam as he closed the door to her room and I saw him flick on her night light before we left so she wasn't in the dark.

"She never sleeps in there."

"I know," he murmured. "And maybe she won't fully tonight, but we can start training her to slowly go to bed, and then slowly get comfortable."

~

"RACHEL'S WATCHING LUNA," I WHISPERED.

"*Muneca*," he murmured. "Let me hold you."

I didn't even protest as he lifted me up easily into his arms. I would never forget how protected Liam made me feel despite his size. His strength was safety not danger. It was never dangerous. And despite being smaller than everyone, it didn't make me feel vulnerable.

I was in his arms a second later feeling tremors and shaking. It had been years since this and his lips brushed over mine.

"Let me...let me..."

Liam spread my legs sinking down between them and finding my clit. His tongue ring was gone but his tongue darted out and flicked it. I muffled my moans with my pillow.

He kept going and when he finally rose back up I was losing it.

"Liam," I whispered. "It's been forever."

"Me too," he stamped his lips over mine as he pressed into me and like every other time I had to adjust.

"Liam," I whispered.

"I know," his eyes met mine as he sank in and both of our mouths gasped into each other. "Forever."

He didn't look away. And I didn't want him to as he worked in me. It

283

took forever and by the time he was fully in me I was shaking. Trembling. Losing it.

Liam kissed me then as he rocked into me and I moaned louder.

He paused and broke off looking around. "We're gonna wake her up."

I blinked up at him dazed. "Do you want to stop?"

"No," he whispered. "Never. But I need to…" he looked around again. "Fuck my life."

He groaned as he picked me up into his arms. "Hold onto me, *muneca.*"

I did as he slowly rolled us over to his back. I squealed as Liam stood with me on him. Gasping and hiding my moans as he walked us over to the freaking closet.

"Fuck, I knew this was huge."

I was going to come.

Little noises left me. "Liam—"

"I know, I can feel you." He sank to his knees and drove into me then. "Doors closed. It's quieter in here."

Oh, thank God.

I moaned and lost it as he drove deeper, finding my pulse at my neck and I came the moment he bit down.

"Oh God…" I screamed as he fucked into me. *"Liam."*

"That's my fucking girl."

My eyes rolled back when he hit somewhere sweet as I came and a wild noise left me as he groaned. Heat filled me as he came and I held him tighter to me.

LIAM

One evening, we stayed too late and Luna fell asleep on me. I didn't move at all too cozy in Liam's couches as I laid there watching television.

Somewhere I woke up, with a blanket over me.

Panic filled me for a nanosecond when I realized Luna was gone and I looked around slowly, the first thing my eyes landed on was Liam sitting against the couch, his laptop on his legs and Luna sitting in between them.

"What's the matter, *carina?*"

Luna yawned in my arms and snuggled.

"I downloaded all the episodes so you can watch it whenever you want," he murmured low.

"Nice," she nodded looking serious. "Wally's nice."

"Wally is nice, he's purple. Can you say Wally is purple?"

"Purple," Luna whispered. "It's secret."

Liam grinned lightly. "Only cuz Mami is asleep. You wanna say that word for me?"

"Purple..."

"Mhm, purple?"

"Purple secret."

Liam's grin was quick. "Close," he handed her a cheese puff, she wasn't supposed to have. "Wally is a purple whale."

My daughter's eyes landed on the cheese puff with wonder.

"Wally...is a..."

"Purple." Liam was patient.

"Purple whale."

He smiled at her and handed her the cheese puff. "This is our secret. Mami won't know. I know you're not supposed to, but I think you've been so good, you can have a cheese puff."

I bit back a laugh as he took one for himself.

They both were sharing a bag and eating cheese puffs while watching Wally the Whale go to school.

And my daughter took it with a smile as she wiggled her little toes and watched Wally the Whale with Liam.

I felt my chest clenching tighter and tighter as I watched them. Liam coaching her through sentences with Wally as his guide.

If he said, he asked her to repeat it and eventually, stopped giving her cheese puffs. Opting for a juice box instead.

My daughter was having a good time.

"...Daddy and Mami...go home..."

"Yeah, Wally's going home with his daddy and mommy."

"Go home..." she looked up at him. "You home."

Liam paused. And I saw him struggling with himself as she looked up at him in wonder.

I stopped breathing as she said it. She didn't talk like her cousins did. Not when she spent a lot of her time alone or with Rachel.

His voice was hoarse. "You wanna practice that, *muñequita*?"

"Papi. Home."

I saw Liam take her in blinking a few times and he pressed his lips to her temples.

"Yeah, papi's home." He murmured brushing her hair back. "I'm not going anywhere, baby."

"Papi, home."

His throat worked as he held her.

"Papi," she squeezed his hand. "Juice?"

He shook his head. "Try again?"

My daughter looked like she was struggling.

Liam helped her out. "I want juice."

"I want...juice."

He smiled and handed it to her as he held her. "One more episode of Wally?"

She smiled up at him. "Purple."

He grinned. "Yeah, he is purple..."

"Home."

"He is going home, can you say it for Papi?"

"Papi."

"Fair enough," he laughed low. "Cheese puff?"

Luna took it without question.

~

LUNA IN MY ARMS WIDE AWAKE AND PLAYING WITH MY HAIR.

"Mami," she murmured. "Liam bring me this." She was cuddling a stuffed whale in between us.

When I found them both on the couch, Lara deep in sleep, Luna's bright eyes had met mine immediately.

She was so alert, so aware—watching everything like she was memorizing it. Like mother, like daughter.

I couldn't help but grin as I carefully extracted her from Lara's arms, my movements gentle so I wouldn't wake her.

"I want..." she started, her voice soft but sure.

"Juice?" I prompted, fighting to keep my voice steady.

"Juice."

My throat tightened as I helped her through it.

"There you go, doll," I whispered. "Better? I gotta get you some real food. You want some food? Hungry?"

She pursed her lips up at me.

And my chest sputtered.

I watched her do it to Lara so many times.

I moved my lips over her face to her cheeks, her nose, her forehead and by the time I got there, my hands shook wildly in hers.

"Daddy."

"Yeah?"

"Hungry."

"I'm hungry," I murmured closing my eyes.

"I'm...hungry."

"Good girl," I brushed my lips over her temples unable to stop. "Let's go to the kitchen, I got you some dinosaur chicken tenders, because it's universal kids love it."

"Dino..."

I laughed low holding her close. "Don't worry, muñequita, you don't gotta say everything in one day. Let's take Wally with us, hm?"

I held my laptop in one hand and her in the other, grateful for all the barre classes from Sonya because I easily rose with her.

I padded to the kitchen hoping Lara would smell food and come find us.

Once there, I placed her in her high chair setting the laptop down far enough for her to watch Wally while I grabbed some items. Cheese.

Dinosaur nuggets. I needed her to eat some veggies so Nisha suggested mixing it into pasta sauces. But Nisha's kids ate everything, I just knew Luna was a little pickier.

So I did that and made pasta for her setting a plate down with her and me.

"Your *mami* would hate me eating like a child but it's good," I shrugged. Luna glanced up at me with all quiet patience as I sat down with her and watching Wally the Whale.

Over lunch I realized why Killian was attentive to Kiara and Marissa. Toddlers were fast. Lightening hands on her.

Any moment the sippy cup would go down or the nuggets. I cut them into tiny pieces like Killian had and she happily munched on hers. Eventually reaching for mine.

"It's good, huh?" I asked her.

"It's good," she murmured back up at me and my chest did that funny thing again where it clenched tighter. "Daddy, broom."

What was broom? I wasn't prepared for broom.

I looked around. She wasn't asking me for cleaning supplies. She held her arms out. "Broom."

I swallowed nervously. "Sweetheart, I'm trying—"

"Broom," she whimpered.

Shit. I needed Lara.

As if by some fucking miracle I heard. "Broom is bathroom, she's potty trained." Lara was rubbing her eyes and walking over to Luna who looked worried at me. "She probably has to go. Come on, *carina*. Let's go to the bathroom."

I followed them out wanting to know everything about my daughter. And how to make sure I didn't bother Lara for every little thing.

I wouldn't be inept.

Lara was patient and kind with her, and I watched her wash her hands on the little stool we had and clean up.

"She's so smart," I murmured watching the two of them. I'd never get over how much smaller Luna was.

Her entire hand gripped my thumb on the walk back to the kitchen.

She couldn't climb things the way her cousins could. And her clothes looked so much tinier.

Kiara by comparison was taller than Luna and her cheeks fuller and rounder like Nisha's.

~

MY DAUGHTER PURSED HER LIPS AT ME AND DEMANDED I GIVE HER KISSES. I'd seen Lara do it a million times as I cuddled her.

"Boo."

I didn't know why she called kisses boo's. But she did. I let her press her lips to my nose. And she giggled as she did it.

She was smaller than her cousins. Technically, Lara called all of the O'Hara girls her cousins. Kiara and Aidan's twins were the same height but my daughter was tiny for three.

I passed her another chocolate milk. "That's good, huh?"

"Mmmm." She was on it and I laughed holding her and the tablet.

"You want some Wally the Whale?"

"Mmm." She drank her juice and watched her whale tv show as I sat there with her feeling contentment fill me.

Did I imagine having a little girl would calm me down?

No. But I knew once my family cut me off completely?

If Nisha hadn't taken empathy on me? I would be fucked.

Nisha was nice to me. She had been the one pleading with Killian to help me.

She held things the way I did, mimicking everything I did.

She liked spending time with me and the moment she ran into my home she was in her perch on my side of the couch.

And over time I started falling in love with the idea of just being just a dad to my Luna.

And nothing else.

Just a normal man.

With a normal wife and a normal life.

LARA

I DIDN'T FEEL VERY GOOD.

I just felt off.

The last time I felt like I had been in labor and I didn't know why I instinctively let Luna sleep in my bed tonight.

Liam's house while warm with all the nightlights felt spooky tonight.

Which it never did.

Something was off. Liam told me to close the curtains of the house completely, lock the doors and gates, and Josh was downstairs in the dark on his phone.

It was a little spooky.

When I couldn't sleep, I locked Luna's door and checked the closet like I was trying to find ghosts inside.

I closed the curtains and made sure everything was good leaving Luna and going downstairs in my robe to the kitchen.

Josh was in the living room so the kitchen was empty.

I paused when I saw the glass of water there.

Did I leave that before bed? Or did Josh have some?

Josh was meticulous and being around Liam had made me more paranoid than usual all around.

"Josh?" I whispered padding out into the living room where I saw him passed out on the couch. "Josh, are you asleep?"

I went to touch him, his platinum blonde hair glowing in the moonlight and I felt a little more than spooky.

"Josh..." I nudged him and his head lolled back and I gasped. "Josh!"

I shook him harder.

Oh God…I felt for a pulse. He was alive.

But then what happened? To him?

Luna.

I tore off upstairs. Or I would've. When I turned around there was someone standing in the doorway. And a wild shriek was trapped on my lips at the masked figure. In all black.

For a second I thought it was a Titan.

I froze. Neither one of us moved.

My heart stopped beating. Completely.

And fear like nothing else filled me.

"Vivianne Valentine…"

She tipped her head to the side. "Don't scream."

It came out muffled as she took out something that glinted in the moonlight. A gun.

My heart stopped for another second. And another.

Luna was upstairs. My daughter—*Liam.*

"Why are you here?" I whispered. Like anyone could hear us.

"I heard you have something of mine." The gun cocked. "Where is it?"

"You're looking for the painting."

"I am."

I realized it was Vivianne Valentine underneath the mask but I couldn't compute the mask and her under it. The fear skated down my spine.

"I don't have it."

"Yes, you fucking do—"

"It's in the O'Hara manor."

"It's a fake," she growled. "A damn good one too."

My heart began pounding out of my chest.

"I'm not Sonya. I don't have the painting—"

"Stop lying!" She cried out. "I know you know where it is. Is it in this house?" She cocked the gun again. "Where is the fucking painting!"

I swallowed. "I don't know." My voice was a croak. It was somewhere inside a Nash Group vault. "I don't know. Please…let me go…my daughter is upstairs…"

And she might be having a nightmare.

Behind Vivianne Valentine I saw a shadow and it freaked me out even more and I couldn't stop the noise from leaving me as Vivianne Valentine turned slightly, and a woman leapt out from the darkness tackling her.

The gun went off and I heard a groan as someone rushed at me. A scream erupted as green eyes met my vision.

"*Melina.*"

Liam was all over me his hands on me as I shook wildly. "*Liam.*"

He was apologizing, running his hands over my body as I shook and trembled.

"She's shot," Nadine growled. "I need to call a medic. *Is that Josh?*"

"He—he's alive," I whispered trembling as Liam quickly checked Josh's pulse.

I had never seen Nadine so angry, her dark eyes narrowed into slits as she raised her gun at Vivianne Valentine.

"*Stupid bitch,*" Nadine held down a bleeding Vivianne Valentine from what I could. "Stop crying, it's a flesh wound at best. You tried to kill *my* partner."

And then something else happened as I looked at the them.

"*Luna.*"

I was moving without even feeling it as I ran around everyone to my daughter.

My heart was pounding as I felt Liam's footsteps right behind me.

The moment I opened the door, my daughter was laying there fast asleep with Wally and Cheddar around her.

Somehow the cat had found his way into her bed again.

I breathed out a sigh as she didn't stir when I was panicking and I felt Liam's arms around me.

"It's okay," he whispered. "She's all good. I figured it out. I knew she was coming here. I'm sorry."

I sank into his arms feeling my heart racing.

With my whole heart. I always had. Liam had admitted to his sexual abuse at the hands of his father's friends. At just a little older than Luna.

Luna.

My baby.

The idea of a man touching her sent me into a rage. Let alone someone touching Liam. In exchange for food. For clean clothes?

Liam had learned from a young age this was love.

It wasn't. Isobel had represented love for a lonely boy. I saw the way he talked about her. Like Isobel and Mr. Santos had been angels.

But in reality?

They were both just decent people in a cruel world.

The only person I understood I was upset with was Mr. Santos but his promise to Liam had come from a place of not knowing Gabriel.

I believed if he had known about Gabriel, he wouldn't have sent Liam into a spiral.

But Liam...

He had been through hell and back. His legs. His addictions. His suffering. Right now holding Luna, I cried at his wonder as he kissed her.

Something pure.

Something good.

Something whole.

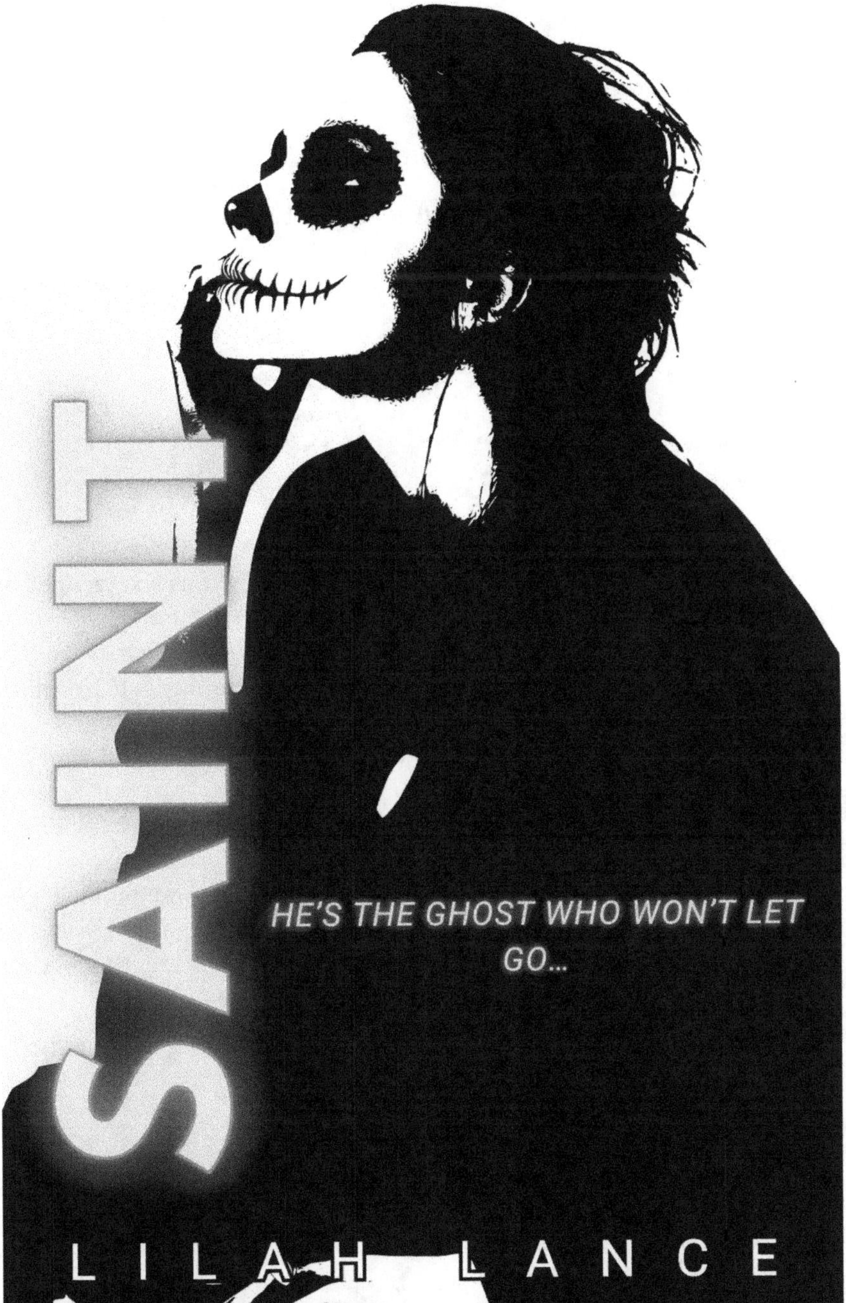
SAINT
HE'S THE GHOST WHO WON'T LET GO...
LILAH LANCE

ONE YEAR LATER

LARA

I TOOK US ON A BREAK TO MEET ISOBEL.

Isobel's mahogany hair glittered under the sunlight as she grinned at Liam rushing to us.

"Hola, it's good to finally see you." She hugged me first. To my surprise and Liam grinned holding Luna who blinked at Isobel in surprise.

"Oh, she looks just like you," she looked at Luna and then Liam, her entire face softening.

Behind her, Gabriel walked up with Thierry and Isobel wasn't kidding about him being a bigger kid.

He was calm with a full head of wheat colored hair and big blue eyes and it was no question who his father was.

"Hey," he grinned at us easily holding Thierry. "Thierry, this is your family. Meet Uncle Liam."

I saw how emotional Liam got the moment he saw him and Gabriel focused in on Luna as Isobel went to hold her.

"Ayeeeeee," she squealed holding her giggling.

Luna got all shy reaching for Liam again and he laughed.

"Sorry, she doesn't like letting go."

"Hey!" A little voice came from behind them.

Little feet ran up to us and another girl Luna's age ran to Gabriel latching onto his leg.

"Unca Gabriel."

"Honey!" A man's voice came from behind her. "Don't run off!"

And then I froze in fear. The man walking at breakneck speed chasing after his...daughter?

Which meant...this was Lucas Devereaux.

The world tilted sideways the moment I saw him.

Those eyes—Devereaux eyes—ice blue and haunting, carved from the same genetic code that had once looked down at me in that dark room at Teaser's.

My body recognized the threat before my mind could process it, every muscle tensing, every instinct screaming to run.

Lucas Devereaux. Charles's son.

Bile rose in my throat as memories crashed over me like waves— hands that hurt, eyes that watched, pain that never seemed to end.

The same face, a generation younger, smiling at Gabriel like he belonged here. Like he wasn't carrying his father's legacy in his bones.

I clutched Luna closer, my arms trembling. My baby.

My innocent child.

The thought of her anywhere near a Devereaux made my chest constrict until I couldn't breathe.

She sensed my fear, her tiny body going still against mine, her eyes wide as she watched Lucas with an instinctive wariness that broke my heart.

"I need some air."

Liam moved instantly, positioning himself between us and Lucas like a shield. Did he know?

Could he see the ghosts dancing behind my eyes? Lucas's smile faltered as he looked at me, confusion replacing warmth.

"Hey Liam, you two are here—"

But I was already backing away, each step carrying me further from those familiar eyes, that familiar face.

Isobel frowned at Gabriel, the tension in the room suddenly thick enough to choke on. They didn't know.

How could they? I'd never told Gabriel about those nights, about Charles, about the way a Devereaux had been my first taste of hell.

Luna's fingers curled into my shirt, anchoring me to the present even as the past threatened to drag me under.

"Mami?" she whispered, and the word was both salvation and terror. Because now I had something to protect.

Someone to keep safe from the demons of my past.

I saw the moment understanding dawned in Lucas's eyes— saw him recognize my fear for what it was.

His face drained of color, and somehow that was worse. Because now he knew. Now everyone would know.

The shame of it burned hotter than the fear.

Did he know?

Did he know his father abused me? Raped me? Hurt me?

Did he know what his father was? I was paralyzed standing there staring at him and he paled.

"Lara?" He murmured. "Everything good?"

No. It wasn't. Liam's green eyes filled my vision then.

"Hey, hey, it's ok. Isa, give us a second."

He said something in Spanish over his shoulder I didn't catch as he moved me away.

With Luna in my arms and she squirmed. Liam pulled her into his arms kissing her cheeks as he soothed me.

"What's the matter? Do you know Lucas?"

I shook my head. I didn't know him.

Not him.

Just him with another face.

"I knew his father," I whispered. "He worked with Cormac...he was a customer."

"Shit. I didn't think—" he broke off swearing. "Shit shit shit. *Muneca*... Lucas isn't...he's not..."

Liam shook his head blowing out a breath. "Damn, how am I supposed to go about this?"

I knew Lucas wasn't his father. I did know this.

But I didn't know how to interact with him.

"He's Evie's husband," Liam explained. "He's fantastic, but I know it's hard for you right now, we can go to the sunroom, or somewhere else you don't have to interact with Lucas."

"No," I shook my head. "That would make it weird." Even now I felt weird but I knew I couldn't calm down around him. "I want to meet your family."

Because Isobel and Evie were his little sisters really. Now at least. I wanted to meet his family. He met mine all the time.

Lucas's presence was like looking at a ghost—every feature, every angle of his face an echo of Charles that made my skin crawl.

"*Muneca*, you don't have to do this. I know how much it bothers you."

His gaze dropped to our daughter, who had gone quiet and still— our little emotional barometer.

"It bothers her too."

"No," I wiped at tears I hadn't realized were falling. My voice strengthened with each word. "I can do this. I can."

I met Liam's eyes, finding strength in the way he looked at me— like I was something unbreakable, even when I felt like shattering. "Please."

As the day wore on Isobel and Evie became a buffer for me. Sister's I didn't know I needed.

"Reed removed all the tech stuff," Evie murmured with a sad wistful smile. "Now, it's a sunroom."

It was beautiful.

The three of us sat and I felt oddly comfortable.

As the sun painted the sky in soft oranges, Lucas came to collect Evie, his movements deliberately measured around me—like someone trying not to startle a wild animal.

Watching him with his daughter cracked something open in my chest —this man, carrying the face that haunted my nightmares, cradling his child with such tender reverence.

People weren't their pasts. I'd proven that with Teaser's, hadn't I?

"Her shoes are falling," I heard myself say, reaching forward before I could think better of it.

"Thank you," he murmured, embarrassment coloring his voice. "Look, I don't know what—"

"No, it's okay." The words came easier than I expected, soft but steady. "It's okay. I promise."

"Was it because of something I said?"

"No," Heat crept into my cheeks as Evie said her goodbyes to Isobel in the background. "No, I knew...your family...some people in them."

"Ah." His face flushed, understanding darkening his features. "I'm definitely not affiliated with them unless you count Lucy."

Lucy—his baby sister, the art curator who'd married Reed's brother Adam.

The black sheep who'd chosen her own path.

Just like Lucas had.

Just like I had.

We were not the sum of our mistakes and our parents.

No, we were better for constantly overcoming and constantly relearning our wrongs to make them right for our kids.

Our kids wouldn't ever go through what we had and I know the people who abused us hoped that they would—and Liam and I did everything possible to ensure we didn't have to ever endure that. Or our daughter.

In that moment, I saw what we really shared—not the darkness of the past, but the light we'd chosen instead. We'd both built something beautiful.

And we would always strive to build something beautiful.

Luna's dark eyes bat up at me.

"Mami, you made it home."

And I felt my eyes well.

"I did make it home," I whispered wiping my eyes. "I did make it home."

When are you coming home?

By sundown.

Now?

I made it home after all these years.

After all this time.

I finally made it.

ABOUT THE AUTHOR

Lilah Lance writes romance for all the girls who dream of being seen, being *accepted*, and being loved for *who they are*.

For more info check out http://lilahlance.com to contact Lilah.

www.ingramcontent.com/pod-product-compliance
Lightning Source LLC
Chambersburg PA
CBHW061938170626

46813CB00006B/2450

9 7 8 1 9 6 8 5 3 3 1 5 1